THE WEEKENDER

DEDICATION:

THE WEEKENDER is dedicated to my beloved husband Roddy, without whose help, my life or this book would not have been possible. All my love, now and forever.

Diane.

EPIGRAPH:

'The power of love should never be underestimated,
it is the one thing that you will never forget'

The Author.

BY DIANE McDOWELL

THE WEEKENDER

*

THE COLONIAL CLUB

*

THE ASHINGFORD SERIES - BOOKS 1 - 7

AMELIA'S LEGACY – BOOK 1

THE DAY OF THE BUTTERFLIES – BOOK 2

THY WILL BE DONE – BOOK 3

MOONLIGHT ON THE LAKE – BOOK 4

DREAMS OF TRUTH – BOOK 5

THE PATH TO MATURITY – BOOK 6

THE DAY OF RECKONING – BOOK 7

*

NAMES IN THE MIST - BOOKS 1 & 2

NAMES IN THE MIST – BOOK 1

CRADLE IN THE VALLEY – BOOK 2

*

MA'S BAIRNS - BOOKS 1 & 2

DRUMMOND - BOOK 1

MACAULAY - BOOK 2

CHAPTER ONE:

I was under attack... branches were whipping my face, while down below mud was playing havoc with my favourite jeans and trainers. Raising a hand to feel the damage, I found blood on my fingers. "Damn," I shouted, " does nobody care about this wretched excuse for a path?" You fool... this was his creation and back then he had chosen to share it only with me... it could have been thirty years since anyone had passed this way. "Thirty... no... it could not have been that long, surely not!" Stopping in my tracks I did a quick calculation... it was twenty-eight.

I plonked myself down on the ground to lick my wounds, and as I did so I allowed our shared past to flush over me.

My first thought was that our houses must have stood within four hundred yards of each other on the outskirts of *Cloverley*. I compared our solidly built and modern holiday house with his home, a wreck of a single-decker bus surrounded by crude extensions. It was sparsely furnished... or at least that was how I imagined it back then. I had been told not to take one step along the track that led to it and this warning from my folks made my interest in it soar. I would have swapped it for ours... or I would have back then, when everything seemed so different through my young eyes.

My quest at this moment in time was to reacquaint myself with our special spot; to convince myself that it actually existed. If it did, it would lie upstream in the nursery where it was born... in the place where tiny waterfalls cascaded into the river's welcoming bosom. I closed my eyes and smiled, until I remembered my immediate problem... namely fighting this damned excuse for a path.

I did not spring to my feet but pulled myself up cagily. The crooked finger of middle-age was definitely beckoning.

He would already have celebrated his fortieth, and my day of reckoning would follow in six months time... that was unless I came up with a cunning plan to throw it off my scent. I smiled at this thought, and moved forward with renewed determination. I had come this far, so was bloody well not going to give up now!

Ahead of me through the mists of time, I sensed him showing me the way. His familiar mop of hair bobbing freely on the nape of his neck... with that unique fragrance of his floating on the breeze. He had become my hero from that first moment we met.

CHAPTER TWO:

"What's your name?" he asked, his voice ringing out like a steadily chiming bell. I smiled but didn't answer. His words sounded so full of confidence, it scared me to hear them delivered by one so young. "Can't you speak?"

I half turned, smiled, and then skipped away along my garden path and through the open front door of our Weekender. If he'd said anything else, then it was taken by the breeze... but our meeting had left me feeling strangely excited, as if something extra special had happened.

My mother was with me the next time our paths crossed. We needed groceries delivered from the village store, and there he was, standing outside the shop like a fixture, with his left foot resting on the sill of the shop window. He nodded and smiled, as we entered Mr Sugar's mini emporium. "Is there a boy stood outside, Mrs Pearson?" asked Mr Sugar, the greengrocer.

"Did you see anyone, Dawn?" she asked, looking at me. I nodded. "Yes, I believe there is a boy, Mr Sugar... our Dawn's good at noticing such things, not like her old mother," she answered.

"Mrs Pearson, I'm sure that's not true. Your eyes look as though they would take in all sorts of information," he replied, raising his bushy eyebrows. "He's the lad who'll deliver your order; his name's Joe Doubleday. You realise I'd love to bring it myself, but Friday's the busiest day of the year for this overworked village provider."

This prompted them to chuckle, which I thought odd, as there had been nothing funny in what either had said.

"Not to worry, Joe Doubleday's the most reliable of the local urchins, Mrs Pearson. He's always on hand when needed. The other businesses find him useful too, not just me," droned Alexander Sugar.

"I trust your judgement completely on such matters," replied Madge Pearson.

I looked up at my mother. She appeared to enjoy talking to Mr Sugar, as her face bore an unfamiliar radiance, and her bottom lip occasionally curled in a most strange pout. They laughed a proper laugh this time, and I found both him and the sound of his laughter somewhat creepy. I tugged at Mum's jacket to let her know it was time to leave, but she paid no attention, preferring to continue with their inane conversation.

I gave up, wandered over to the open door, and upon looking outside, found him still there, standing like a statue. "Boo!" he said, suddenly springing to life.

"You gave me fright, that wasn't very nice," I replied.

"So, you can speak," he remarked, "I was beginning to think you were just a big dolly."

"A big dolly? What a stupid thing to say," I answered.

He stood grinning at me, whereas at that very moment, I wanted to show my annoyance. However, I became confused, and it must have shown.

"What's your name?" he asked politely, his grin fading as he spoke these words. "I'm Joe... Joe Doubleday."

"I liked the face you had a moment ago," I replied, then instantly wondered why in heaven's name had I come out with such a silly childish remark?

"I like your face all of the time. I think you're very pretty," he countered.

"Really?" I replied. "Do you really mean that?"

"Of course I meant it. What a strange girl you are," he said. "I don't make a habit of telling girls they're pretty if they're not."

"It's just that nobody's ever called me pretty before... apart from my family," I replied.

11

"Well, I have, so will you now tell me your name?" he asked once more.

"Dawn, my name's Dawn Pearson," I replied, glancing down at my scuffed shoes.

"I already knew that was your name," he said, his grin reinstated.

"Then why did you ask, if you already knew?" I asked, again somewhat confused.

"I was just being polite," he replied, "no offence meant."

No offence? My friends and I didn't use such grown-up words, and I was uncomfortable hearing them from a mere boy. I turned on my heel and left him standing outside, whilst I marched back into Mr Sugar's shop, found myself a seat, and waited patiently until Mum was ready to leave.

When we eventually did, Joe Doubleday was nowhere to be seen.

CHAPTER THREE:

I reached our special spot and to my amazement nothing appeared to have changed... the hillocks were still smothered with dandelions and daisies, and our little waterfall continued to pour its sparkling waters into the dark pool below.

The river too appeared to pursue its familiar course with unerring urgency, divided and separated by the large stones that had once offered us so much fun.

With my trainers discarded, I dipped my bare feet into the icy stream... no holy water could ever have given me such a spiritual uplift.

CHAPTER FOUR:

Joe duly arrived at our Weekender with the groceries on Friday morning as arranged. Mum opened the front door and sent him around to the side door with his wheelbarrow. "I'll bring them in for you," he offered.

"That contraption isn't coming into my kitchen, so you'll have to lift them in carefully yourself," she replied.

I was in the hall, and on hearing their voices, came into the kitchen. "Hello," I said, with a smile in Joe's direction.

"Hi," he replied, giving me a wink.

"Just get the groceries inside, will you please," sniped Mum, "and be as quick as you can." She then glared at me, and I giggled. I could see Joe found my giggling amusing, as he carried in the groceries and laid them on

our outsized kitchen table. He tried to conceal his amusement from Mum by keeping his back to her, then all of a sudden let out a dreadful sounding snort, as he failed to contain the laughter anymore within his now vibrating body.

"This rudeness has gone far enough. What's wrong with you, Dawn? Stand outside until you've composed yourself," she instructed.

"Sorry, Mum," I replied, giggling even more. I left the door slightly ajar, so I could overhear whatever was said.

"Sorry, from me too, Mrs Pearson," added Joe. "Mr Sugar won't use me for deliveries, if he learns I've been rude."

I crept to the door to sneak a peek... Mum was staring at him with her mouth screwed up, while he looked at her with puppy dog eyes. I observed this from my now excellent viewpoint, and she did what I knew she would... she relented. She was not a hard woman, and hated to get people into trouble unnecessarily. "Young man, Mr Sugar won't hear any bad reports about you from me. However, if you take my advice, you'll avoid my daughter, as she can be a little minx can our Dawn."

I could see Joe didn't quite understand the word minx, but he smiled and thanked her, as he lifted the last of our groceries onto the table.

"Here, take this," she said, as she gave him a handful of loose change from her purse. "None of this was your fault."

"Thank you very much, Mrs Pearson, and sorry once more for... well, everything," he replied.

Mum then closed the side door behind him and called my name, "Dawn, in you come and help me put these things away... and pop the kettle on, there's a dear."

In I came with a cheeky grin, and pecked her on the cheek. She smiled whilst shaking her head. I opened the side door, looked out, but he was gone from sight. "Can I take a few breathes of fresh air first, Mum?" I asked. "I'll go open the front door so you don't catch a draught."

I didn't wait for her answer, and when outside I spotted him walking backwards along our path pulling his wheelbarrow behind him, which made his progress painfully slow. I waved, and he dropped the wheelbarrow to wave back, whilst blowing kisses into the wind. I responded with a similar gesture, then watched as he then turned around and set off at speed.

"Tea or coffee, Mum?" I asked, as soon as I returned to the kitchen.

She shook her head at me once more, but also smiled, "Tea please, dear, but let's put these groceries away first."

CHAPTER FIVE:

I slipped off my jacket and placed it on the ground. Up until that point, the clouds had cast a gloomy shadow over my reminiscing, but suddenly the sun decided to switch on its rays.

Lying back on my elbows, I allowed the soft grassy bank to absorb the weight of my body, whilst I closed my eyes and let my mind recall the time when I first met Joe's three little sisters, and when I also received my first proposal.

CHAPTER SIX:

Mr Sugar arrived at our house around eight that Friday evening. Alexander's busiest day of the year was now over, and his shop door firmly fastened. The Summer Fair was due to start tomorrow, and today the village had been invaded by visitors. Everyone had been eager to stock up with local produce from Mr Sugar's shelves, including bottles from his large liquor larder. I was surprised to see him standing at our front door, holding two outsized bottles of what looked like… wine? "Your mother's expecting me," he said, looking down at me, his chest heaving with the laboured breathing that was his trademark.

"Have you been running to get here, Mr Sugar?" I asked, with a grin.

He did not answer, but took two steps past me into the house.

"Oh, there you are Alexander... good. Mr Sugar's kindly brought around the local wine that silly Mummy forgot to order," she blustered, without giving me a second glance. She realised that I would have pulled a face and begun inwardly giggling by now, and obviously didn't want to be caught joining in on the act. "Dawn, go out to play for an hour or so with Val, there's plenty light left in the day... but don't stray too far."

"Thanks, Mum. What time's Daddy due here tomorrow?" I asked.

She didn't answer, but cleared her throat, and turned her attention to Alexander. "Let's take ourselves into the parlour. These bottles look very heavy, and I guess you've had a grinder of a day? In you come and rest your legs. If you can spare me a little of your precious time, that'll make my evening delightful," gushed Mum.

What could be delightful about sitting in our parlour with the panting 'Sugar-man' for company? Sometimes my mother gave me great cause for concern. However, tonight I didn't dwell on it, but made a rush for the door, and was soon skipping merrily along the lane. I was on my way to visit my best friend Valerie, when my eyes strayed towards the Doubleday's converted bus, from where three little girls were running towards me, waving frantically.

"Are you Dawn?" one of them called out.

"Yes," I replied. "How do you know my name?"

"We heard our Joe telling Mummy about you," replied the tallest one.

19

"He said you were special, and that he was going to marry you," chirped in the smallest girl.

"That means you'll be our big sister," added the middle one, "I'm Mandy Doubleday, Melanie's my big sister, and Nicolette is our baby." Mandy then reached out and took my right hand, whilst little Nicolette reached for my left.

"Let's go and watch them set up the last of the stalls," suggested Melanie.

I decided straight away to give Valerie a miss, as this would be far more interesting. There was a glow hanging over this trio of pretty little girls... they looked fun... and they were!

Nine o'clock came and went, and it must have been around half past, when I heard a familiar voice. The sisters turned and rushed to him, whilst he looked over their heads and smiled at me. I could see how much they loved him, and how much he loved them. "Time for bed my little girlies, or you'll be too sleepy to enjoy the main event tomorrow. You too, Miss Dawn," he said, looking at me.

I did not answer... I already felt guilty, knowing I should have been home some time ago. The girlies ran on ahead, while we walked behind. He took my left hand in his right and I didn't pull away.

"What's this about you marrying me?" I asked, without looking at him directly.

"It'll not be for a while, but I shall... one day," he replied, with a wink.

For once words did not come spouting forth from my mouth, "I haven't said yes, and I've only just met you," I said, slowly.

"You haven't said no neither, and you know me well enough. Remember, you're promised Dawn... don't ever forget that," he replied.

We parted where their track met the lane, and I had to let go of his hand. Holding it had felt good, and not at all strange.

"Night, girls, night, Joe," I called, as I skipped homeward.

"Night, Dawn," replied the girlies.

"Good night, my Dawn," called out Joe, with a wave of his hand and a kiss blown into the twilight that was fast approaching.

CHAPTER SEVEN:

The sun disappeared behind a dark cloud and the temperature dropped sharply. Rain was imminent... and the birds who always knew when a storm was brewing, were noisily telling me that it was now time to leave.

We hadn't owned our Weekender for almost twenty-eight years, so I hurried back to Mrs Grimes' Bed and Breakfast. Thank goodness the owner's name had not put me off, for it was spotlessly clean, thoroughly modernised, and I could really not have wished for better.

"I could do us a spot of lunch for old times' sake," suggested Josephine Grimes, "you being from the old days... the good old days, may I add!"

"That would be lovely, Josephine, but not too much as I'm not very hungry at the moment," I replied.

"You will be," she said, "but first tidy yourself up. I'll give you a shout when it's ready. You look as if you've been in a fight, and may I add also a roll in the mud judging by the state of you!"

She waited eager to hear my response. I smiled and nodded… which I definitely thought was enough of an explanation… as what's private is private.

I showered to rid myself of the mud and blood, changed my clothes, and then sat back in the comfy armchair by the window to await her call.

CHAPTER EIGHT:

Mr Sugar's car was still parked at the front of the building when I arrived home that evening. I slipped quietly into the kitchen by the side door, made myself a mug of cocoa, and then plonked myself at the kitchen table with my current library book. I liked reading about girls of my own age, especially if they were at boarding school, lived in some exotic place, or had an enquiring mind!

I heard footsteps coming along the corridor. "Ah, good... you are home. You should've come and told me you were back," said Mum, as she entered the kitchen.

"Have you just remembered about me?" I asked, glancing up from my book.

She looked at me as a naughty child would, and nothing else was said.

"Has he not got a home of his own to go to?" I added.

"Now, now, Dawn, Alexander has problems you wouldn't even begin to understand," she replied.

Try me, I thought, I'd soon straighten him out. "Will Mrs Sugar not wonder where he is?" I ventured.

"Mrs Sugar isn't being very nice to him at present, Dawn. She's been keeping herself to herself," she replied.

If I was married to Mr Sugar, I would do the same, I thought. Why Mum was entertaining him was a mystery? "Can't you ask him to go home, Mum? I'd like there to be just the two of us for a while before bedtime. Daddy will be here tomorrow... what time did you say he'll arrive?" I asked.

"I didn't, but around eight I imagine," she replied. "He's going to leave home very early so as not to miss any of the Fair." I was pleased. She hadn't asked what time I'd come home, with whom I'd been, or any other awkward questions. "Come and say hello," she added.

She left the kitchen and I followed her into the parlour... he was lolled out on our sofa. I glanced around the room, taking in everything that was important, in the way my Junior Detective library books described. On the table, I spotted two large wine glasses containing liquid dregs. The bottle stood beside them... two-thirds of one of the outsized bottles Mr Sugar had brought with him, had been consumed.

"I thought you would've kept the wine you forgot to order, for Daddy and yourself?" I announced.

They both looked at me; Mr Sugar with amazement, and Mum with a frown. "Dawn, you can be so rude at times," she scolded.

"The girl's just telling it as she sees it," slurred Mr Sugar. "She's a bright girl Madge, takes after her mother."

"But she doesn't get her rudeness from me, Alexander," Mum replied.

"Well, I don't get it from Daddy... he is never rude to anyone," I stated, in his defence.

"Madge, thanks for... a delightful evening. It's made such a difference having someone who takes an interest... you've made an old man very, very happy, as they say," added Sugar.

"How old are you, Mr Sugar? I didn't realise you were an old——," I asked.

"Off you go, Alexander... Dawn, stop asking dear Alexander questions, and let him get on his way," interrupted Mum.

He was now on his feet, and when I noticed how he wobbled and stretched out his hand to support himself, I came to a conclusion. "Do you think he'll be able to drive himself home," I asked Mum, "he looks rather... tipsy?"

"Ignore her, Alexander, she's just a child. What does she know about us adults?" she replied.

26

Huh, what indeed, I thought!

CHAPTER NINE:

"Dawn, it's ready," called out a distant voice. I returned back to the present feeling a little confused, and it took a moment for my mind to settle. Here or there? Here… I'm here, and that's Josephine calling me for lunch.

I rose, splashed cold water onto my face, quickly dried myself and then headed downstairs. She had indeed heeded my words and not made anything heavy. A salad, with fresh bread and fruit had been laid out on the table, and as I helped myself to a cup of coffee, she made herself comfortable on the chair opposite.

Throughout lunch, she twittered on about this and that, telling me tales of folks whom I had no knowledge, or had forgotten, and she was a shade surprised when I suddenly interrupted her mid-flow with a question——

"Josephine, do you remember the Doubleday family?" I asked.

"Argh! Who could forget them?" she replied.

At that moment I must have sounded as blunt as when I was a child; seemingly adulthood had not completely robbed me of my youthful forwardness. "Why would one not forget the Doubleday family?" I spluttered. I felt awkward, even guilty, to be asking such a question.

"Oh, probably because of what happened," she casually replied.

"What?... What happened? I've never heard of anything," I said, my curiosity now aroused eliminating any lingering traces of guilt.

Josephine looked at me, while she thought over the past timescale of events. "You're right; it was after your time. I'm surprised it didn't filter through to you... through the grapevine, so to speak, or something similar," she replied. "Of course, they split up, didn't they... your folks, I mean?"

"Yes...," I slowly replied, now beginning to wish I hadn't come, or at least had found somewhere else to stay where nobody knew me.

"Sad business when a couple split; you could've knocked me over with the proverbial feather as they say, when I heard about your mum and dad," announced Josephine. "You never know with folks though... what exactly's going on... inside their heads, I mean."

I sat bubbling angrily inside, but outwardly numb. I had no way of stopping her; my tongue was letting me down big time today.

"And Alexander Sugar of all people… your mum must have had a real sweet tooth," she added, with a stifled titter. She realised I wasn't amused by her remark. "Oh well, you have to laugh over such things… although it looks as if you don't agree with me Dawn? No need to get all shirty though, it's not as if it happened yesterday."

"Excuse me," I said, "and thanks for lunch." I didn't wait to hear her reply, as I left for the safety of my room. I didn't wish to share air with this woman any longer.

Once back in my temporary sanctuary, I sat back in the comfy armchair, closed my eyes, and tried to shut out the world.

CHAPTER TEN:

When I came downstairs the following morning, Dad had just arrived, and I noticed that all bottles, glasses, and evidence from the previous evening had been removed. Furthermore, the table had been wiped clean of fingerprints, and the cushions on the sofa well plumped.

Mum must have risen early to tidy, as all had been left untouched when she'd gone to bed. Old man Sugar's visit hadn't felt right to me last night, and the memory remained as sour this morning. Never mind, Dad was now here, so life could perhaps get back to normal?

We ate breakfast together, while he told us of the business deals he'd dealt with over the previous week. He glowed with pride as he told us every detail of his new business, which I found so cute. Mum was attentive but rather quiet, not that Dad noticed. I checked him out carefully, as I listened... he was the genuine article and his enthusiasm rang true. Why did this matter to me? It mattered because I'm the sleuth of the family, I'm the one who digested things that they didn't, and my library books had given me a good grounding in judgement and how to detect the trail of evidence.

On my bedroom wall, hung a plaque with my incentives. I'd saved up months of my pocket money for it, and it looked very professional...

'NEVER ACCEPT A SITUATION AT FACE VALUE'

'KEEP ALERT AT ALL TIMES'

'THE CLUES ARE THERE TO BE DISCOVERED'

I also had a badge that showed me to be a paid-up Member of the Junior Sleuth League, from whom I received quarterly newsletters. None of my friends were into sleuthing, but I found it utterly fascinating, so I didn't care!

Dad thought it all very amusing, but was nevertheless supportive. Mum however, told him that she worried about some of my more odd interests, and I knew exactly to which interests she was referring! To her, it was not proper for a girl of my age to have an interest in such peculiar things, and I got the distinct impression she'd rather I dressed like her, to attract members of the opposite sex. "You've now turned eleven, Dawn," she would say to me more and more often. The significance of the age eleven escaped me, as to me eleven only meant ten plus one?

"Let's get going, it's a lovely day. It's going to be warm and balmy," said Dad, once he'd finished breakfast. "You're quiet this morning, Madge?"

"Oh, I've been busy... busy getting the house ready for you coming," she replied, sheepishly.

He didn't notice, but I did. More like hung over, I thought, remembering the evidence from last night.

"Let's all walk into the village, before it gets that overcrowded way," he suggested.

"I'm ready," I said excitedly, pushing my chair back. And I was; it was a new sensation for me, I felt pretty and hoped it showed. My hair had a shine I hadn't noticed before, and my eyes sparkled.

We waited for Mum, who was taking her time doing we knew not what. "Don't mention about us having to wait for her, Dawn," whispered Dad, who knew what to expect from me.

"Okay, I won't... but only because it's you who's asked," I replied.

"Come here, sweetie, and let me give you a hug; you're looking extra beautiful today, there's something different about you," he continued, looking at me somewhat perplexed.

Whilst we continued to wait, I went and sat on an outside bench, where I sang happily, while Dad took the opportunity to assess what work needed done in the garden.

When she eventually arrived we set off, without a word from me. Dad smiled. Mum's spirits had lifted, and they walked with their arms linked, while I skipped alongside.

I could see the track to Joe's house appear on our right and felt a strange sensation come over me. As we walked a little further, I spotted a group of people coming along the track from Joe's house walking towards the lane… it was them!

The little girlies ran ahead to greet us, with Joe trailing behind. "Hi, we're going to the Fair. Is that where you're going, Dawn?" asked Melanie.

Mum and Dad looked surprised, "Do you know these girls, Dawn?" asked Mum.

I nodded.

"Good morning, Mrs Pearson," said Joe.

She peered at him.

"It's Joe Doubleday, Mrs Pearson… remember, I delivered your supplies to the house from Mr Sugar," he added.

"Oh, yes… of course I remember. I didn't recognise you all dressed up smart," she replied.

This remark annoyed me, and also Dad, by the look on his face… or was it because Joe had uttered the 'Sugar' word?

We all moved off together along the lane, and little Nicolette slipped her hand into my mum's, much to her surprise. "My brother's going to marry Dawn, so that will make you my second mummy," she suddenly announced, smiling up at her.

"Well, there's no answer to that one," replied Dad, "what's your name little girl?"

"I'm Nicolette, and my sisters are Mandy and Melanie," she answered, with a smile.

I could see their charms melt him before my very eyes... these little girlies were gorgeous.

"By the way, I'm Joe, Mr Pearson——," began Joe, introducing himself.

"He's our big brother... he's great, is our Joe," interrupted Nicolette.

"I can well believe that," answered Dad, as he looked at him with fresh interest, "So you deliver for Mr Sugar, do you?"

"Only when he needs me. I'm always on the lookout to earn some cash, no matter how small. Can I take this opportunity to thank you for the tip you gave me Mrs P... it counted up to a goodly amount," Joe replied.

Dad looked over, wondering just how much she'd given him? "You're welcome, it was just a handful of loose change I had in my purse," said Mum.

"It was a lot to me, Mrs P. I'm grateful for anything," he replied.

Joe had been winking at me at intervals throughout this conversation, and I wanted to laugh, but ran on ahead with Mandy and Melanie so as not to let my amusement show.

"We've to call in for Valerie," Mum reminded us.

I could have conveniently forgotten all about that, but I suppose that wasn't a very nice thought. She was okay was Valerie, albeit in small doses.

Mum rang the doorbell at Valerie's folk's cottage, and waited on the doorstep, accompanied by Nicolette. I hung back with the rest of our group, not wanting to encourage Valerie, if she was having second thoughts.

Jean Brown, Valerie's mum, opened the door and looked down at Nicolette standing hand-in-hand with my mum, "Hello there, and what's your name little lady?" she asked, stooping to look at Nicolette directly.

"My name's Nicolette, and my big brother Joe's going to marry Dawn, so this is my second mummy," she beamed.

"My, that's lovely, Nicolette... are you by any chance going to the Fair?" asked Jean Brown, although she already knew where we were bound.

"Yes, I'm going with my second mummy and daddy," she replied.

The two women looked at each other, "Valerie love, Mrs Pearson's here for you," called out Mrs Brown. "We weren't sure if you were calling in for Valerie, as Dawn didn't come around last night, and you know how young girls can be when their hormones come into play?"

"Of course we were coming for Valerie, they've been friends for years, and we always take her," replied Madge. "I haven't noticed any hormones!"

Valerie arrived, pecked her mum on the cheek, waved goodbye, and joined our merry band.

"Hi, Valerie," I ventured.

"Dawn, apologise to Valerie for not calling in for her last night. You can tell me why later," scolded Madge.

"Sorry, Val," I said, with a smile and a quick hug. I didn't really mind apologising, as I liked her... well, most of the time. I could see Joe was amused at me having to apologise, and pulled faces as he tried to make me laugh.

Mandy and Melanie came over to meet Val, and began to skip, hop, and jump in front of her, until she joined in with them. She looked at home with the little girlies. Childish as ever, I thought.

Joe noticed me shaking my head in Val's direction and winked at me. He'd got up close by chatting with Dad. I listened, a little embarrassed, as Dad quizzed him on old man Sugar. "Does Mr Sugar pay you much for your help?" he asked.

"No, he's——," began Joe.

"Miserly tight, I bet," interrupted Dad.

"S'pose so, they're all tight, these business folks," replied Joe.

"You should ask him for more money," I suggested, which prompted them to look at me, in the way that men sometimes do. "Why not?" I continued, as I did have a point to make.

"Leave Joe to handle Mr Sugar and his likes, Dawn," replied Dad. "Sorry Joe, I shouldn't have asked; your money's your private business."

"It's okay, Mr Pearson. Give me a few years, and I won't need to depend on the likes of Mr Sugar," he replied, allowing his arm to brush against mine.

Suddenly, we could hear the sound of the rides and the beating throb of the Carnival music. Squeals and shrieks floated our way on the breeze, but above everything, we caught the unique aroma of the Fair.

With heartbeats now racing in increasing anticipation, we hastened our steps… and when we arrived at the 'Welcome to the Fair' sign, the noise was overpowering. Judging by the numbers already there, we weren't early.

CHAPTER ELEVEN:

The Cloverley Village Fair, on the village green, spread out in front of us with not a blade of grass in sight. On one side, the fairground rose majestically, with its magical rides and stalls all bright and brassy, whilst on the other, the farmer's tents stood cheek by jowl with the trestle tables hosted by the ladies of the Church. Produce and home baking covered their stalls, and the contrast between the serene, delicately decorated cakes and preserves with the noisy prize heifers and livestock, seemed strange bedfellows. Adjacent were smaller stalls with tables, laden with even more cakes, sweets, old books, comics, cheap watches, antiques, tools, toys and even clothes and shoes... the list seemingly endless.

Madam Zelda, who was really Mrs Gwen Sutherland, was present... I had sussed her out last year. I also noticed Tom Franklin, who ran the Lotto every year, already had his seats filled with his regulars.

We came to a sudden halt. "Mr Pearson and I are going to look around the stalls first. Does anyone want to come with us?" asked Mum, looking down at Nicolette, whose little hand was most unlikely to free itself from hers any time soon.

"Nicolette, do you want to come with us or with Joe and the girls?" asked Dad, bending down and smiling at her. She looked up at Mum, and smiled with her eyes, giving an I'm-coming-with-you, kind of answer. Mum smiled back, and appeared pleased with the little one's decision. It made me happy to see her and Dad working as a team for once. Things had not been good between them for a while.

"The rest of you meet us for lunch at twelve o'clock in the café, and don't be late," instructed Dad. "Dawn, here's some money to pay for rides for you all, but don't spend it all in half-an-hour, because that's your lot."

I waved Dad's notes in the air to show Joe, and he waved his to me.

"Put that in your pocket, Dawn. If you lose it, your day will be spoilt," cautioned Dad.

"I won't Dad, I promise," I replied.

"Look after Nicolette, Mrs P... she's only little," added Joe.

"Of course I will," she replied. She momentarily looked angry with Joe for saying such a thing to her, but instantly thought better of it and smiled. "What a good big brother you have, Nicolette, thinking about you all of the time," she continued, "and you needn't worry Joe, I'll not let go of her."

After Mum and Dad had gone on their way, with Nicolette now taking each of their hands, we huddled together to work out how many rides we could afford. The idea being, that we'd try to spin them out until lunchtime.

"Have you any money with you, Val?" I asked.

"Yes, Mum gave me a little for the rides," she replied.

"We're going to put ours together and divide it between us," said Joe.

Val looked at him with a, why-should-I-share-mine-with-you-and-your-sisters look?

"Val," I said, "do you want to come with us this morning or not? That's what we're asking?"

"I don't want to go around the Fair on my own," she replied.

"Well, you won't have to if you share. How much do you have?" I asked. She pulled out her money and showed me. "You'll not get far on that… two rides at most. What do you think, Joe?" I asked.

"What's it got to do with him?" Val remarked.

41

"Dawn's with me... we're on a date," Joe replied, with a grin.

"Yes, we're on a date," I agreed, also with a grin. He then put his arm around my shoulder and I tingled, whilst Val looked at us in disbelief.

"If we put our money together, we'll have enough for four rides each," suggested Joe. "My little sisters' rides are cheaper, because they only go on the little ones, and with Nicolette not being here, it gives us a bigger share."

"See Val, you'll be getting a bargain," I added. She still looked unsure. "Well, suit yourself, but we're off now."

"Come on girls," called Joe, to his little sisters, who'd begun to play one of their pretend games. As we moved off, Joe let his arm slip slowly from my shoulder and took my hand. I was in heaven... I was... in love.

"Wait, I'm coming with you," called out Val, as she ran after us.

She looked at me with disgust when she saw my hand in his, and then ran on to join up with Mandy and Melanie.

First, we went to the 'Merry-go-Round' which was the girls' favourite. Joe settled them and then we stood and waved each time they came around to the spot where we were. Next, we headed for the 'Waltzers' to give us bigger kids a treat, and I could tell that Val wasn't too happy. "I don't want to go around with him," she whispered to me. "Why have you brought him? I like it when it's just us."

42

"Val, I love him," I replied.

"Don't be so stupid, you're making a fool of yourself. My dad says that the Doubleday folks are no better than 'Tinks'. He wouldn't want me anywhere near them, especially him," she whispered. "Give me back my money... I can see Silvia, so I'll go around with her."

Silvia, Val's elder sister, was a trouble making pain in the butt, to put it mildly, and I knew I was heading for a big fall from everyone's grace, but I didn't care. I looked out Val's money and gave it back to her.

"Joe, I've given Val back her money," I said. "She's decided to go around the Fair with her sister."

"Fine with me," he replied, winking in my direction.

"And with me," I muttered, in agreement.

Val then ran over to Silvia and I could see her immediately telling her of our situation. Silvia displayed her furrowed brow expression I'd seen many times. Her face contorted as she looked over in my direction. I ignored her frosty gaze and looked away, relieved that I didn't have to put up with such a sister.

We quickly realised we could only go on the rides that also catered for the little ones. Joe and I wanted to try the 'Waltzers', so we placed Mandy and Melanie in the middle of our car, whilst Joe and I sat on each side of them. "I hope this isn't too much for them. The nice guy hasn't charged for them," whispered Joe. "Hold tight everyone, we're about to move——"

It was too much for Mandy at first; she screamed and screamed, but with Joe's arm tight around her, she soon settled. "Let's go on again," she gushed, clapping her hands, once it had stopped.

"Later, pumpkin," replied Joe. "Melanie, how did you like the ride?"

"Good, but I'd like to go to one of the stalls where you can win a prize. I'd like a teddy or a dolly," she answered.

"Good idea, Mel... does everyone agree?" asked Joe, looking my way.

"Fine... let's see what you can win for me," I replied.

"And for us, Joe," cooed the girls, as they jumped up and down with excitement.

"No pressure on me then," he replied, laughing.

He took my hand as we pushed our way through the crowds. There were a number of people I didn't know, but there were also a good few that I did. The news that Dawn Pearson was holding Joe Doubleday's hand would soon filter back to Mum and Dad, long before lunchtime.

We spent our money as fairly as we could, before heading to the tent, which doubled as the Cloverley Café. Already sitting at one of the tables with Nicolette wedged between were Mum and Dad. The little one looked happy, and so were we as we walked into the café still proudly holding hands. Neither of my folks appeared to notice or if they did, they kept it well hidden.

"Spot on time," said Dad. "We expected you to be late."

"Why should we be late, you told us twelve?" I replied, with a beaming smile.

Dad then went to order buttered bread and a large bowl of chips, all to be washed down with ice cold fizzy drinks. Nicolette must have already had an ice cream, as the evidence was plain to see sprawled around her little mouth.

"Had a good time folks?" asked Dad.

We really didn't need to answer, as our faces still glowed with excitement, "Yes, it's been great Mr P," replied Joe.

"Yes, it's been great, Dad," I agreed, as we began to giggle.

"Wait a moment, where's Valerie?" asked Dad, looking around for her.

"She went to join her big sister, you know the one with the grumpy face," I replied.

"No falling out I hope?" asked Mum.

"No, Mum, no falling out," I answered. "She said she didn't want to go around with us as she was bored, so when she spotted Silvia, she ran off to join her. She'll be fine; she now has her big sister for company."

Mum frowned at me.

"Look at what we've got," said Melanie to Mum, "Joe won them for us and he also won a necklace for Dawn."

The girls each held up a gaily coloured rag doll. Melanie's - a baby doll dressed in baby clothes, whilst Mandy's - a grown up doll, was dressed in a starched pink dress.

"These are lovely, girls. I can see Joe's been good to you. Let me see your necklace, Dawn?" said Mum. I was wearing it, so I pulled it from inside my top to show her. She raised her eyebrows, "Nice... it doesn't look too cheap either," she added.

Her words rattled angrily inside my head. What a thing to say in front of Joe!

"The man wasn't pleased with Joe, and he told us to move along," revealed Mandy.

"He didn't say it quite as politely, though," replied Joe, laughing, who then produced from behind his back, a cute cuddly teddy bear for Nicolette. She squeezed out from between my folks to be beside him. "Wait a moment, Nicolette. Let's not touch the nice teddy with your sticky hands," cautioned Joe, as he took a paper napkin from the table, wet it with water from a jug, then bent forward to wipe the traces of ice cream from around her lips and hands, before drying them with another.. She put her arms around his neck, and when he stood up, he swung her around while she held on tight as she cuddled into him.

46

Surely, Mum and Dad couldn't help but see that Joe wasn't like most boys of his age. His love for his little sisters was as clear as the blue sky above?

After we'd finished eating, we headed off in the direction of the entertainment once more. There were singers, bands, dancing troupes, even a magician, along with various kids' shows.

During the entertainment, we stayed together as a group. Mum and Dad hadn't said anything, so during the rest of the afternoon, Joe continued to either take my hand or place his arm around my shoulder.

However, later that afternoon, a cloud appeared on the horizon in the large form of Mrs Sugar... there was an ugly exchange between her and Mum, and the words spoken were not the kind anyone would wish to hear, and most certainly not in public. Needless to say, Dad was not well pleased!

Their mood changed, and the walk home seemed much longer than when we'd set out this morning. Towards the end, Joe carried Nicolette, whose tired little legs had had enough. Before he turned onto his track, he whispered to me that he'd meet me tomorrow at ten, "I'll wait at the trees beside your house."

"I'll be there," I whispered back.

It was like a volcano erupting when we arrived back at our Weekender. Mum and Dad screamed at each other and the word 'sugar' turned from something which was ordinarily sweet, into that which was most definitely sour.

47

They then suddenly turned on me, and told me that I was not to meet or go anywhere near that Joe Doubleday ever again!

"Why? You liked him and his little sisters, I could tell you did," I protested. "Look at how you were with Nicolette for goodness sake, taking her with you and holding her hands, both of you!"

"We didn't say we didn't like them, but that was for today only," replied Mum.

"Do you understand what your mum's telling you, Dawn? Keep away from the Doubleday family, especially him," instructed Dad.

"But that's not fair," I cried, "you and Mum have fallen out, and you're taking it out on me."

"It's got nothing to do with us falling out, Dawn. It's just not going to go any further," said Dad. "We're cutting it out now, it's a non-starter."

"What are you saying, Dad? I don't understand? Have I embarrassed you by holding his hand?" I asked.

"Yes," screamed Mum. "My goodness Dawn, the little one was on about you and Joe getting married and all that rubbish. That's not what we want to hear about our eleven year old daughter."

"And certainly not when it concerns a Doubleday," added Dad, for good measure.

Mum then stomped from the room, and banging and clanging noises were heard coming from the kitchen. "You'd better see to Mum before she hurts herself," I said. "You know how she can be."

He was about to say something back to me, but thought better of it, and left to go to her, after giving me the dirtiest of dirty looks. "Don't you go near that boy again, Dawn. I mean it, keep... well... clear."

CHAPTER TWELVE:

I heard a knocking noise and opened my eyes… where am I? Then it all came rolling back. I was slouched in the comfy chair beside the bedroom window in Mrs Grimes's B&B. I heard a woman's voice. "It's me, Dawn dear. I'm sorry if I upset you earlier, but I sometimes forget to whom I'm talking. You must appreciate I get all kinds here. Will you let me make it up to you… for old times sake?" said a contrite Josephine Grimes, " I've bought us cakes… come and have a cup of tea with me, please?"

I didn't answer at once, as my plan had been to keep out of her way until I left sharpish tomorrow morning.

"Dawn, are you all right?" she called.

Her voice sounded panicky and remorseful, so I reluctantly relented. "I'll be down in five, Josephine," I said softly, but loud enough for her to hear.

"Thank you, Dawn," she replied.

When I arrived downstairs, I saw that she had indeed been out to buy cakes. What's more, I also noticed she'd bought meringues, my all-time favourites.

"I hope I didn't disturb you, dear?" she said.

The change in the woman was remarkable. She was now pussy-footing around me, which was strange, but I decided to milk the experience and give her a chance to redeem herself.

"Dawn, take a seat and let me pour you a cuppa. I'm sorry there's not more of a variety of cakes, but as the day goes on the choice gets less and less," she continued.

"Meringues are my favourite," I replied. "I'm surprised you managed to get any at all, as you can never buy them at home this late in the day."

She poured my tea and looked at me with a serious expression written on her face. "Dawn, Doubleday was a rogue. Not the wife though, who was always polite enough on the few occasions we met. She appeared tied to that ramshackle place of theirs. He probably bullied her and didn't let her mix, that sort of thing. The kids were—," explained Josephine.

"Great," I offered, without further expansion.

She nodded. "Doubleday got himself into bother in the village... stealing, fighting, and the likes, and a group of the menfolk decided to take the law into their own hands. It wouldn't have been long after the time when your mum and dad..." she paused, and looked at me full of sympathy, "... well, they were intent on going out there to force him to leave, but overnight Doubleday and family had taken off."

"Was it their own land?" I asked.

"Yes, Doubleday inherited it from his father, who from all accounts, was a hard working, well-liked normal sort of man. His son must have been a throw-back, a real rotten apple," she replied. "He'd left for the city when he was young, but when his old man died returned to claim his inheritance. There was a small farmhouse on the land, but that idiot of a man decided not to use it, and instead brought a converted bus to live in, along with a wife and three children... the youngest girl arrived a little later. The villagers always frowned on him and his lifestyle... in fact, nobody liked or trusted him."

We sat licking the cream from the centre of our meringues. Josephine had cream smudged over her lips, which had spread onto her face. It reminded me of Nicolette all these years ago... and when I remembered how Joe had dealt with the little girl, teardrops formed in my eyes. I lifted a napkin to give to Josephine, and then one for myself.

"Are you all right, dear?" she asked.

"Yes, I'm fine," I sniffled, "it's the cream... it brought back memories."

"I'll not ask, as that sounds somewhat personal," stated Josephine.

"It was to do with the day of my family's last *Cloverley Fair*… just before my world tumbled down around me," I answered.

"I'm so sorry to cause you pain dear," said Josephine, "I remember that year. That was when you and young Joe Doubleday held hands for all to see. It was the talk of the Mother's Union and the meetings of the Institute. A few thought it sweet, but most couldn't understand your parents allowing it… mind you, I myself didn't get involved, live and let live, I always say."

My God, it seemed as if it had only happened yesterday, the way she was recalling the details. All the fuss over two young people who liked each other and had held hands in public. I could've stood up at one of their damn meetings and told them many a tale about what youngsters got up to out of sight and in hidden dark places around this village. That would've stopped them needing to put curlers in their hair each night!

"One night the local menfolk took it upon themselves to burn the place down," Josephine continued.

"They what?" I exclaimed, thinking this was beyond belief, "Whatever for?"

"To stop them from coming back," she replied.

"But that was… the children's home," I protested.

"People don't often think straight when they're angry, Dawn," she replied. "But when they arrived at the place the menfolk found that Doubleday had already done the deed!". She then went quiet, and I finished my meringue on autopilot.

Suddenly she was off again, "But... he came back," she exclaimed.

"Who came back?" I asked.

"The young Doubleday boy... he came back to the village about eleven or twelve years later. He looked prosperous... nice clothes, nice car... you know what I mean," replied Josephine. "He rented a house and business premises."

"Really! I exclaimed. "How did the village folk take to him?"

"Well, to be honest they were wary at first, but with him being a builder, and a damned good one at that, he started helping folks out with small jobs at first, and his business gradually blossomed. A few years later, he built a lovely house on his land," she replied, "on the very spot where they'd lived all those years ago in those makeshift buildings."

"So, is he accepted now?" I enquired.

"Oh yes, a pillar of the community in fact... married with four children, a boy and three girls," revealed Josephine.

"That's the same as his folks' family," I remarked.

"Yes, you're right... I'd never thought of that before," she agreed.

I excused myself at this point, telling her I'd someone to meet, and once back in the sanctity of my room, tried to think of what to do next? Having told her I'd to meet someone, I decided I'd better go out for a while.

Dressed reasonable smartly, I went out to my car, reversed out of the drive, and pointed its front in the direction of our old Weekender. The streets were quiet, for which I was grateful, as my concentration was wavering. I decided to try and find somewhere quiet where I could park unobtrusively while I tried to sort out the thoughts spinning around in my head. However, despite my best intentions, the car continued to pull me in the direction of the old place, and I soon left the cluster of stone built cottages and houses for a world of fields and trees.

Ahead of me, through the trees, I spotted an unfamiliar house. Its white exterior sparkled in the bright sunlight. It was a large bungalow, that sat at ease within its plot. I didn't stop to stare, but continued along the track to our Weekender.

Luckily, there didn't appear to be anyone at home when I arrived, although it did look occupied. It was no longer the tidy house we'd visited at weekends or during holidays and high days. Instead it now had kiddies bikes propped up against its garage wall, along with an assortment of other play things. There was also washing billowing on a line around the back, in fact, it was an altogether different house to the one I'd left, and never returned to all these years ago.

I felt awkward and turned my car to make my escape, only to find another speeding towards me. It pulled up alongside, and I noticed the driver's window was open. "Can I help you, this track's a dead end... it only leads to my house?" said a youngish woman.

I found myself taking in her details, including the contents of her car, which included two children. I guess once a sleuth always a sleuth, "We owned this house many years ago, when we used it as our Weekender," I replied.

"Oh, how lovely," she said, and then turned to her kids, "this lady used to own our house——"

"No, not me... my folks," I interrupted hastily.

She then turned back to her children, "... a long, long time ago," she stated, which made it sound as if it was some sort of a fairy tale, and perhaps that's what it was, a fairy tale fast disappearing into the mist... lost in time... a place not unlike Brigadoon?

"Would you care to come in for a cup of something?" she asked.

Caught off guard, I struggled with my answer... should I or shouldn't I? "Yes... that would be very nice," I decided.

When she opened the front door to the house, the place was unrecognisable... apart from the kitchen which remained in the same place as of old.

"Can we go and play with Brian and Shirley?" her kids asked, jumping up and down excitedly.

"Of course, and take this letter. Tell them it was mixed in with our mail," she replied, handing them an envelope. "I hope it's not the important letter Joe's been waiting for." She then turned back to me, "Before you all disappear, say hello to Mrs...?"

"Brennan," I answered, "Dawn Brennan."

"These two are my Charlie and Charlene, and I'm Brenda... Brenda Warner," she said. "Have you any children, Dawn?"

"Yes," I replied, "I've three... a boy Sean, who's seventeen, a girl Lorraine, who's sixteen and my baby Angela, who's eleven, well nearly twelve. They've all gone to visit their gran and grandad over in Ireland this week with my husband. I had business to attend to on Monday and Tuesday, so had to give it a miss. We visit them lots, so it's not as if it's the end of the world."

I must've been going on, as I could sense the kids itching to get out to play, so I stopped speaking sharpish and smiled at them. At last, they were able to gallop out into the fresh air, with Charlene grasping the letter tightly.

Once they'd left, Brenda put on the kettle, whilst I sat in a state of numbness, and once more switched on my autopilot. I didn't stay long, just long enough to be polite. As I said my goodbyes, I noticed the children were playing on a piece of land I would have to pass on my way back to the main road. Charlie and Charlene now had two playmates, a boy and a girl of a similar age.

I waved to Brenda, climbed into my car and drove off. On seeing me, all four children began to run towards the side of the track. "Please, just let me pass," I muttered, but they kept coming until I had no choice but to stop. I rolled down my window and smiled at Charlene, "Is everything all right?" I asked.

"Yes, we just wanted you to meet our friends, Mrs Brennan," replied Charlie.

"Oh, how nice," I said, "let me see if I can remember their names. You must be Shirley, and you must be Brian… am I correct?"

They both nodded somewhat surprised that I knew their names. "Nice car, Mrs Brennan," remarked Brian, "my dad has one just like it. It's also the same dark blue colour." He then looked in at my dashboard, in a similar way a grown-up would, "Yours is an earlier model than his, but it's still very nice."

"How can you tell which model it is?" I asked.

"Oh, lots of little things have been tweaked," he replied, without elaborating further.

"Tweaked?" I asked. "You're very knowledgeable Brian, can I ask how old you are?"

"He's twelve," replied his sister. "Come on Brian, you're wasting time looking at the lady's car."

I looked at his sister and then at Brian, who smiled back at me, "I've to be somewhere too," I said, waving as I drove off with my mind stuck in overdrive.

*

Josephine caught me as soon as I arrived back at the B&B, and asked if I'd eaten? When I shook my head, she invited me to join her for a snack later, that was if I wished. I nodded and muttered "Perhaps," before making yet another run for the sanctuary of my room.

After turning up the heating, I plonked myself in the armchair by the window. My hands rubbed against the fast warming radiator, as I tried to rid myself of a strange internal shivering. My mind was churning with what had just happened. I'd recognised the boy from his looks and mannerisms as being his son... and the girl... well, she looked strangely familiar too?

I picked up my phone, settled back in the armchair and pressed my most familiar number. "Good you're there. I'm missing you and the kids... I'm in *Cloverley*... in the local B&B," I said.

"Whatever for?" asked James.

"I got my business tied up sooner than expected, and felt lost in the house with you guys away, so I set off for a short visit here. I thought I'd come and see what, if anything had changed over the years. It's just one of those crazy things people sometimes do. The past was luring me, and as you know, I haven't been back since they were divorced."

"Are you enjoying your visit?" he asked.

"Well, no… not exactly enjoying… this place is packed full of ghosts and memories," I answered.

"But, is the place nice enough to stay," asked James, "I mean the B&B?"

"Oh yes, the owner… Mrs Grimes… she remembered me, so is giving me special treatment," I answered.

"Mrs Grimes? That name wouldn't exactly inspire me," he laughed.

"No, really it's fine… she lets me call her Josephine… for old times sake," I replied, also laughing. Thank goodness for James, I thought. The man always makes me feel okay… normal.

"So, are you heading home tomorrow?" he asked.

"Yes, one day's been long enough here. I need to get back to reality. Love you darling," I replied. "You lot will no doubt be enjoying the forty shades?"

"You know me so well, I always enjoy going back to my roots, but I'm missing you, and I'm not coming back here again without you," he said.

"And I'm not going to let you go without me either," I replied. "Love to your folks and our kids. I do hope they're behaving themselves?"

"They've been great. I'll go now, as that's tea ready, and you know how Mum is if you don't come through immediately," laughed James, once more.

"I do, and bye love," I said.

As I laid down my phone, I wished I was anywhere on Earth but here, and especially that I was over there with the people I loved. I would have left tonight but it was now dark and driving in the night was a no-no for me, so early tomorrow morning would have to do.

I decided to take a hot shower to heat myself up, and afterwards slipped between the sheets. Josephine would have to eat her sandwiches by herself.

CHAPTER THIRTEEN:

At ten o'clock, Joe was waiting for me under the trees. What a struggle I had to get out of the house to meet him.

"We're leaving for home as soon as we're packed, Dawn, so if you go outside, don't dare go far," instructed Mum, "in fact, don't leave the garden."

That will be right, they wouldn't dare go without me? I thought.

Joe passed me a paper bag as we ran through the long grasses towards the woods. I slowed slightly, peeped inside, to find freshly baked buns and biscuits... "A picnic?" I asked, panting hard.

He nodded.

"Joe, when can we stop running?" I asked.

"Once we reach the trees," he replied.

After a few minutes, we slowed down and walked hand-in-hand through the woods. Joe led the way through the denser undergrowth where no path existed, until we came upon the river. I was stunned! In front of us was a waterfall, whose cascading waters drowned out every other sound. Further along the bank, the noise gradually subsided until only the soothing sounds of the waters surging over smooth flat stones remained. We found a large flatish rock on the bank which we used as a seat.

"Joe, in all the years my family has come here at weekends and holidays, I've never seen this part of the river, or the waterfall before," I said, smiling at him. "You've been here before though, I can tell."

"This is my special place, and you're the only one I've ever brought here," he replied.

"Joe, I've something important to tell you… we're leaving… today. They're probably out looking for me already," I confessed. "Mum told me not to leave the garden, and I can imagine them calling out for me."

We laughed, and he squeezed my hand. "So why are you here and not there?" he asked.

"That's a silly question," I answered.

"I'm meant to be helping my dad this morning, so he'll no doubt be raging when he gets hold of me," disclosed Joe.

"So why are you here then, and not there?" I asked.

We laughed again, and it was abundantly clear at this moment in time, we just didn't care!

"Let's look and see what's in the bag?" I suggested.

"Dawn, I already know what's in the bag, I packed it this morning and there's not much. But we could at least pretend it's a feast?" he replied.

I opened the bag, "It is a feast to me," I said, "because meals are often missed in my house, as things are ropey between the two of them."

"How do you mean... ropey?" he asked.

"Well, not good... not good at all. In fact I think something's going on between my mum and that man Sugar," I answered.

"Mr Sugar!" he exclaimed. "Surely not with that old tight-fisted guy?"

"Yes, I'm afraid so... I don't understand it either. He gives me the creeps big time," I replied.

We both laughed again, and I put my head on his shoulder. He then moved his arm, so that it rested comfortably... we were as one. Nothing was said for a few minutes as we each gazed at the flowing waters. I loved it here, and I loved being with Joe.

"What do you think's going on between your mum and old man Sugar?" he suddenly asked.

"I think she likes him more than she does my dad," I replied. "They don't tell me much though, I have to look for clues, so it's just as well I'm a sleuth... and a Member of the Junior Sleuth League."

"What in heaven's name is a sleuth?" he asked, looking at me.

"Well, it's like being a detective," I replied.

"A detective? I knew you were special and the girl for me, but a detective, that's awesome! You're so different from other girls. I like that, and Dawn, you're by far the prettiest," he said. "I wish you could stay on here. Is there any way your family could settle and live here all the time?"

"Joe, I don't think we'll be coming back, not even for weekends or holidays anymore, let alone to live," I replied, sadly.

His face told it all. I lifted the bag of food, to soften the moment for him. We munched the buns he'd brought, and then worked our way through the biscuits, as he slowly digested what I'd said.

"If I'd known we were going to have a picnic, I'd have brought something to drink," I said, trying to lighten the mood.

"Look here!" he exclaimed suddenly, as he rose and rummaged amongst the tall grasses. He next produced a tin cup from inside a gap in the rocks, washed it out in the river, and then ran upstream to fill it from the edge of the waterfall. *"Here you are. This is the water of life, take a sip, Dawn."*

I took the cup from him, slowly raised it to my lips and… sipped. "Oh," I exclaimed. "I didn't expect it to be so icy cold. Boy, it doesn't half refresh though." I took another sip, and then passed the cup back to him, and he drained the remainder in one gulp.

"Plenty more where that came from, m'lady," he said, with a grin.

"Do you mean it when you call me your lady?" I asked. "Nicolette told my mum and dad, she overheard you tell your mum that you were going to marry me."

"Dawn, I always say what I mean. Yes, I'm going to marry you one day… when I'm successful, and not wearing my old man's label," he replied. "Dawn, you can't begin to imagine what it's like having him for a dad… he spoils most things for us."

I felt so sorry, I lifted my head from his shoulder, and kissed him softly on the cheek. He kissed me tenderly on the lips… Joe and I had crossed the border, a line where life and relationships change. We held each other tight and felt smug satisfaction at having become grown-ups.

The next moment, with socks and shoes removed, we were back as children, paddling in the shallow pools between the stones, and splashing each other with icy droplets. Our laughter took on a new hue of happiness, until we saw that the sun had risen high in the sky. Reality suddenly hit me, and I could see from his eyes, it had struck him too.

"Joe, we'd better hurry back," I said reluctantly.

"I know, Dawn. I hope you think this was worth the pain that's coming," he replied.

"Yes," I said, "I'll remember this day, forever... will you?"

"You know I will," he answered, "always."

We walked back hand-in-hand, stopping on the way to exchange kisses. We held hands right up until the very last minute, when I was met by an outraged Mum and Dad.

"Get away from here you mangy dog," Dad shouted at Joe.

"He doesn't mean it, Joe," I called after him.

"Love you, Dawn," he called back, as he headed towards a house and homecoming which would forever remain a mystery to me.

"You Madam, get in the car right now! We've been ready for hours. What a thing to do Dawn," yelled Mum.

"I need to go into the house to change, I'm damp... in lots of places," I protested.

"I'll give you damp in lots of places! Just get in the back of the car right now, the house is all locked up," she snapped.

"And there's no way we're going to open it up for someone who's behaved like you! I can't find the words to tell you just how disappointed we are in you," shouted Dad.

I reluctantly climbed into the back of the car, and we left our Weekender for the very last time. As we passed the road end, I could see the girlies running and playing in the distance... "Nicolette's just fallen," I shouted, as I turned to take another look out of the rear window.

"What's with your obsession with the Doubledays? Keep your eyes to the front," Mum ordered, turning her head to look at me. "I don't want to hear another word from you."

Dad gave me a fright by thumping his hands on the steering wheel, and shouting out an array of colourful words. At least they were acting as a couple, sharing their joint annoyance at me.

After that, I didn't say another word until we eventually arrived home. I sat silently in my dampness, my eyes closed, reliving that morning, and afraid that my precious memory would somehow fade or get lost with the passage of time.

There had been no breaks for coffee, food or for any other needs, on our weary journey home, and when Mum finally unlocked the front door, I pushed past and ran to my room where I threw myself onto my bed in tears.

I could have caught pneumonia? The very thought haunted me... and my damp clothes would be the cause. I had always been told to change out of damp clothes

immediately, but they had made me sit for hours in my...
dampness. This would most certainly be the death of their
only daughter... yes, pneumonia would be the end of me!

CHAPTER FOURTEEN:

I could have caught pneumonia... I heard the distant tinkling sound of a bell ringing somewhere, opened my eyes and thankfully remembered where I was. I'd been dreaming... thank God. I was in bed in Mrs Grimes's B&B in *Cloverley*.

I gave James a quick call... "James, I'm so looking forward to seeing you and the kids. I'm definitely coming with you the next time you go to Ireland," I gushed.

"Have you not enjoyed your time in *Cloverley*, has the place been spoiled," he asked, "sometimes it's not good to go back, as it can spoil precious memories?"

"That's true, and it can also be somewhat disconcerting," I replied.

"You'll recover once you're home, and see your handsome husband and beautiful children. We'll be back tomorrow," said James. "Do you fancy meeting us at the airport?"

"I'll be there," I readily agreed.

After speaking to James, I made my way downstairs for breakfast with a sunny disposition, and having not eaten recently the smell wafting upstairs was most enticing.

"Morning, Dawn," said Josephine, "sleep well?"

"The bed was very comfortable, but I experienced a strange dream," I replied.

"Oh, anything of interest?" she asked, her busybody eyes lighting up.

"No, Josephine, and the content is fading fast," I answered. She looked somewhat disappointed, which made me light up inside with a hidden smile.

I then looked around wondering where to sit. Josephine had four tables, three of which were already occupied. Not spoilt for choice, I nodded to the people at the other tables, helped myself from the buffet style spread, and then got stuck in, as the kids would say.

Josephine arrived at my table with a cup of coffee in her hands, plonked herself on to the chair opposite, and looked me over before she spoke, "Don't suppose I'll see you again for a while," she began, "you could always bring hubby and family for a short break and show them your old Weekender?"

"I could," I replied, "but probably won't. My husband's folks stay over in Ireland, so we try to visit every chance we get."

"Nice!" she exclaimed.

"Josephine, can I ask exactly when did the Doubleday family leave here?" I asked.

She sat and bit her bottom lip, as she carefully pondered my question. "I suppose, it would be about six months after your family left for good. Where they went to, I've no idea," she replied. "I once asked Joe, but didn't get an answer, you know what he's like, always polite with it, though."

"I see… thanks for that. I must get off now; everything's been great, so I'll settle up with you and then hit the road," I answered.

"Before you go, can you tell me how your folks are? Is she still with Alexander Sugar?" enquired Josephine.

"Yes, I've old man Sugar as a step-daddy," I replied. "Mum's happy enough with him, so what can one do?"

"And what about your dad?" she asked.

"Ah, he remarried years ago, and I now have two half-brothers, which is rather nice," I answered. "I like my step-mum Barbara very much, and we get on really well."

"Nice," Josephine replied, as she filed the information in readiness for her next opportunity to gossip. I then paid my bill and we parted company.

As I placed my travel bag into the boot of my car, I became somewhat confused... had my visit served any purpose, and had it settled the thing that had hovered in the depths of my mind for so long? Hmm, I suppose it had, I concluded, as I climbed behind the wheel of my car, and left Mrs Grimes's B&B to drive through *Cloverley*... with my mind still churning.

When James and I married, I'd felt a little guilty about Joe. I know it was stupid to bother, but I'd secretly hoped he'd moved on... in the same way as I had. Whilst here, I'd learned he had married and had children of his own. There was no doubt that young Brian was his son, and I suddenly wondered if Joe had introduced his family to our special place by the river? Judging by the condition of the path, probably not.

As I drove through *Cloverley*, I tried to concentrate, but familiar buildings kept grabbing my attention like insistent ghosts. I approached Sugar's old shop and was startled to read the name hanging above the door, **'The Doubleday Building Company'**. I then remembered him telling me that he would come back here one day, but only when successful.

So that made sense, particularly when I remembered his family owned that piece of land. He must have inherited it from his old man... fancy having Joe's name on my step-dad's old shop... the very thought made me smile.

Suddenly, I noticed someone I recognised and stopped instinctively, "Excuse me," I began, as I wound down my window.

"Yes, can I help you?" replied the woman, as she peered at me. "Do I know you? It's not... Dawn is it?"

"Yes, it's me... Dawn Pearson, now Dawn Brennan. How are you, Mrs Brown?" I asked.

"Fine, Dawn. I'm a grandmother now," she replied.

"That's lovely, Mrs Brown," I said.

"Call me Jean. We're both women of the world now," she replied. "If you can spare half-an-hour, come and have a cuppa with me, and tell me all about yourself?"

Did I want to spend half-an-hour with Jean Brown? She was surely worth thirty minutes of my time... I'd spent many a day playing at her house with her daughter Valerie, and she'd always been so nice to me. "Oh, go on then, of course I can spare you half-an-hour, Mrs Brown... I mean Jean. I'm also keen to catch up with your news," I replied.

After Jean unlocked her front door, I found myself standing in a hallway I hadn't stood in for nigh on thirty years. As we passed the lounge on our way to the kitchen, I was surprised by its transformation. The furniture was modern and colourful abstract pictures adorned the walls. A lovely fireplace made its presence felt, which definitely wasn't there previously. On entering the kitchen, I found it wasn't too dissimilar from my own streamlined kitchen at home, "Jean, this kitchen appears so much larger than I remember," I remarked.

"It is... we had a small galley kitchen in your day," she replied, as she led me through into a large bright sun room which had a tiled roof and panoramic views across the garden.

"Jean, I can hardly recognise this as being the same house I used to visit," I said with genuine surprise.

"It's all thanks to our local builder," she replied. "He came to do bits and bobs at first, and then we got talking. He showed Harry and me what was possible with the kitchen and the rest of the house. Harry liked what he saw and told me that if I wanted to modernise and extend, we could. We'd money in the bank, so why not use it?"

"Well, all I can say is that the house looks gorgeous," I said. "Did you get this new room built at the same time?"

"No, that came much later. In fact, it's only been up around four years," she replied, "Harry died a few years ago and left me comfortable as far as money's concerned. My thoughtful son-in-law knew I'd always fancied a room to enjoy my garden from, and put on hold his own business to build this for me. The work kept me occupied, which greatly helped in my time of sorrow. I only wish Harry had been able to share the pleasure I've had from sitting and reading in this magical room."

We went back into the kitchen, and I sat at the table while she brewed the tea. She brought the teapot over, joined me at the table, and poured two cups. "Where does the time go, Dawn? I remember you as a little girl as if it was yesterday. You and Val, playing around my feet, and then, when older, the two of you disappearing upstairs to her room for hours and hours," she said.

"I suppose we did," I replied, tentatively, "how is Val… and Silvia?"

"Val's fine… she's now married with four children," she replied, "and Silvia's married too, but as yet doesn't have a family. I wish I could help her in some way, but… how about you Dawn?"

"I've three of my own… two girls and a boy. I can't imagine Val being a mother of four," I answered, somewhat surprised.

"She probably can't imagine you being a mother of three either," she laughed.

We sat companionably for a short time, each lost in our own thoughts. How did I arrive here of all places after all these years? A short time ago, I was glad to be on my way out of *Cloverley*, yet found myself sitting in the bosom of Jean Brown's house.

At that moment, she looked over and smiled, "Sorry, Dawn, my mind disappeared into thoughts of Silvia. She's forty-two now, and this whole baby thing's affecting her badly. It seems to be either famine or feast in this family of mine. With Val, it was the most natural thing, where one child followed another," said Jean.

"Are Val's children close in age then?" I asked.

"Yes, a year to eighteen months between them," she replied. "It's a funny old world."

I nodded in agreement, and wanted to get on my way, but didn't wish to appear rude. The years melted away, as I once more tuned into the unusual rhythm of the way she spoke. The memory of her voice had never left me, as I listened enthralled to what she was saying.

"Would you like to see a photo of Val and her family?" she suddenly asked, rising from her seat.

"Erm... I would... that would be lovely," I replied.

A picture paints a thousand words, and so it proved when I took the framed photograph in my hands. I first looked at Val, and then one by one at her children, and by the time I'd finished, it was too late... he looked much as I remembered... his dark hair was shorter now, with slight traces of ageing, which suited him. His smile remained the same as that which had made my mouth and lips turn dry... that first day when he'd awakened me.

The last thing I noticed was his arm resting around her shoulders, as I handed her the framed image back. "I've no doubt you'll remember him," Jean said, rhetorically.

I nodded. Of course I remembered him, but what I didn't understand was how the situation in the photograph had evolved? I looked up, and re-tuned into her matter-of-fact, chatter, obviously oblivious to the depth of feelings there had once been between him and me.

"You wouldn't have forgotten him, Dawn. The two of you gave us folks plenty to talk about that day at the Fair. You may not realise, but our Val had a liking for him too, even way back then," she disclosed.

I couldn't believe what I was hearing… Val had a liking for him? If she had, she'd made a damned good job of hiding it.

"Of course, she was a much quieter, shyer little girl than you. The confidence just oozed from your pores. You had the guile of an adult, and precociousness to match. Yes, that's the word for it, I believe," continued Jean.

As was he… precocious described him well too. Where's she going with this line of conversation? Val hadn't half played her cards close to her chest that day. I should leave, but on the other hand, I was riveted with curiosity… "How… did they get together?" I asked, trying not to sound too interested.

"Were you aware that the Doubleday family all disappeared shortly after your family left?" she replied.

I nodded, wondering what was coming next.

"Well, years later, Joe came back, nicely dressed, smart, and with a nice car. He rented a cottage on the Green and took over Bailey's old building yard. Folks around here were wary at first, but little by little he met their needs and his business prospered. He must have been here for about two years, when Harry asked him to do a few small jobs for us," continued Jean. "It was Joe who showed us what we could do with our house, and by that time, he came highly recommended."

"How are his... little sisters?" I asked.

"Married with children of their own, and all doing well, I believe. They visit Joe and Val," replied Jean.

She then stopped talking and stood up... "Let's sit next door, Dawn... I'm in need of a soft seat," she continued.

"Oh, actually, I'll need to go," I replied. I desperately wanted to be on my way, but I also desperately wanted to learn more, so followed her next door.

"Stay for another five minutes, love, and take a seat," said Jean. "I'll be back in a jiffy... call of nature, I'm afraid."

Still ever the sleuth, my eyes scanned the room until settling on the family photos, and when she'd left I scrambled up to examine them more closely. There was Brian; he looked very much like Joe, and next to him Shirley. I now knew why she looked so familiar... she resembled Val. The younger girl took her looks from Joe and the little one from her mother. I was back seated by the time Jean returned.

"Where was I?" she asked, trying to gather her thoughts...

"You were telling me about Joe creating your new kitchen," I replied.

"Ah, yes, that's right... Harry was well pleased with the way Joe went about his business, and Val had just arrived back home to stay with us at that time. She'd been away studying at university, but missed us, and came home," said Jean. "You don't want them to be unhappy do you?"

"No, I suppose you don't," I replied. "What was she studying?"

"Law," answered Jean.

I nearly choked... Law? Val studying law seemed absurd, and it was no small wonder she had cracked up and came home. The Val I remembered, wouldn't have been comfortable with the cut and thrust of the world of legislation and litigation.

"Keep it under your hat, but she actually suffered a breakdown of sorts. We kept it well hidden... you know how folks around here like to gossip?" she continued.

Yes, I remember how folks liked to talk, but telling me to keep it under my hat? That's rich... to whom was I going to tell? This all happened years ago for goodness sake, and no one I knew now, would show even the slightest interest in Val's past situation.

"So, he was working here... when she came back from university. Was it... love at first——," I began hesitantly.

"Oh, no, not at all," she interrupted. "In fact, they took quite a while before they got together. He didn't seem to bother with girls, with Joe it was work, work, and even more work. Val would bring him the odd cup of tea or coffee, and sometimes he'd join us for a meal. I often had to insist, as he would've worked right through without a meal break otherwise. He got to know her slowly... and then things took their natural course... I couldn't have asked for a better son-in-law."

"I'm glad it's all worked out so well... now I really must get going, as I want to get everything sorted before my family arrive home tomorrow," I said, rising to my feet.

We suddenly heard a noise from the hall, looked towards the door and in she came... heavens, her disposition hadn't improved with time... she was as torn-faced as I'd remembered.

"Look who is here, Silvia," said Jean, "do you recognise her... think long hair instead of short?"

She frowned in my direction and nodded her head, "Dawn?" she answered, somewhat surprised. "I thought it was Joe's car parked outside. It's strange you having similar cars, as they're not the most common of vehicles."

"I'm just about to remove my one," I said. "Thanks for the chat and the tea, Jean, it's been lovely."

I then headed for the door with Jean at my tail. "Look in again, Dawn... don't be a stranger. I'm sure Val would love to spend some time with you, as you will have so much catching up to do," she urged.

I rushed to my car before she asked for my address, telephone number... that kind of thing. If she had, then I didn't hear, for I departed at speed. My head was buzzing and reeling from what I'd just gleaned... Val and Joe... Joe and Val? Had he come back looking for me? Had he been waiting for me? I now wished I'd never come back to *Cloverley*, and longed for the safety of James's arms.

My eyes began to water, and the low sunlight was now shining directly onto my windscreen... I reached for my sunglasses and slipped them on... that's better. Suddenly there was a car heading towards me; it looked like a reflection of mine, which threw me for a moment... I then felt a thump, accompanied by a horrible grating noise, as I lurched to one side and then came to an abrupt halt on the grassy verge. Our car wing mirrors had clipped each other; I turned and saw that the other car had also stopped on the other side of the narrow road, and that the driver was heading my way.

I heard his words, "Are you okay?" as I floored the accelerator, and caught sight of him in my rear-view mirror, standing somewhat astounded by my sudden departure!

*

Joe Doubleday walked back to his car, shaking his head in disbelief, "Damned stupid woman, I should report her to the police," he muttered, "she was much too far over the road. How damned ignorant is that? Imagine driving off?"

"She was over on your side of the road, Dad," agreed Brian, "I recognised her, she's the same woman who was at Charlie and Charlene's house yesterday."

"How do you know that?" he asked.

"I recognised her car... it's the same as yours, and I've never seen another like it before," answered Brian.

"She was at Charlene and Charlie's, over at the old Weekender?" repeated a puzzled Joe.

"Yes, Dad... I saw her too," chipped in Shirley, "Charlie and Charlene introduced us to her. They said her mum and dad used to live in their house a long time ago."

"Do you remember her name?" asked Joe.

"Erm... Mrs Brennan," he replied.

"Charlene said she liked the lady's other name," added Shirley, "it was Dawn."

"Listen kids, when we get to Grandma's, don't mention our little bump as it may upset her," suggested Joe.

CHAPTER FIFTEEN:

Joe's mind was in a whirl as he parked his car outside his mother-in-law's. He followed the kids as they raced into the house, but saw them stop in their tracks when their Auntie Silvia came into view, "Joe, you've just missed Dawn Pearson, although she's called Mrs Brennan now," she said.

Joe noticed Brian and Shirley were about to comment, so he quickly gestured to them with his finger held to his lips. They gave him a puzzled look, shrugged their shoulders, and turned their attention to their two little sisters, who were now excitedly showing their Auntie Silvia pictures they'd drawn. Thank goodness they didn't appear too upset by the bump, or at least it did not seem as important as their pictures, he thought.

As she glanced at their drawings, Joe could feel her eyes trained on him. He'd never taken to his sister-in-law, and struggled to hide his emotions, as he returned her icy gaze. Silvia had never taken to him either, so the feeling was... mutual.

"That would have been an interesting encounter, if Joe had arrived earlier, eh, Mum?" said Silvia, "I can still remember that day at the Fair!"

Jean despaired. Silvia loved to get her teeth into Joe whenever an opportunity arose. This made it difficult for her, as she loved her son-in-law, but Silvia was her daughter. "I'm sure they would've loved to have met again as friends. For goodness sake, how long ago was that Fair?" she replied.

"It may have been almost thirty years, but it's stuck in my mind, so I'm sure it would've stuck in Joe's too," she answered. Then turning to stare at him, asked, "Any special reasons for visiting Mum?"

"I was just going to ask you the same thing," he replied.

"You can both visit anytime you wish, and I'm never too tired to see my lovely grandchildren," said Jean. "Now everyone settle down, and we'll have a cup of tea or a glass of juice. Could you manage to arrange that for us please, Silvia dear? There's also a lovely big cake in the kitchen that's far too much for one person."

Silvia disappeared into the kitchen followed by little Brigitte, who liked to help. Silvia popped her head back into the lounge after a minute, "Before I make a start, where's our Val?" she asked.

"Mum's in bed, she taken one of her headaches," replied Shirley.

"I wonder who or what causes her headaches?" Silvia asked, looking directly at Joe.

"Doctor McKay's looking into possible causes," he replied, with a shrug of his shoulders.

Silvia then disappeared back into the kitchen after giving Joe yet another one of her disapproving looks.

"Joe, don't let her upset you. She's always been that way, causing trouble wherever and whenever she can. We just have to accept her for the way she is," sighed Jean, "at least, that's what Harry always used to say."

I don't need to accept her, the moody cow! She doesn't make much of an effort to accept me, thought Joe. He however disregarded his thoughts and gave Jean a hug. Life would be far more pleasant around here without Silvia in the picture. There was no more mention made of Dawn, for which Joe was relieved, and the atmosphere soon returned to normal. The kids enjoyed the cake, juice and their grandma's company.

When they were piling into the car to go home, Silvia grabbed hold of Joe's arm, "Are you going to tell, Val?" she asked.

"Tell her about what?" he replied.

"About Dawn blinking Pearson, you—," she replied.

"That's my business," he interrupted, "and I thought you would've learned to finish off your sentences by now."

"If the children weren't here, I'd have finished it off, and added a whole lot more as well," she snarled.

Joe left her and crossed over to kiss Jean goodbye. He lingered an extra moment with his arms around her… he loved his mother-in-law, as she had accepted him into her family from the very outset.

Harry, his father-in-law, had been fine with him during the building work on the house. However, when Joe took up with Val, he'd taken him aside to ask his intentions towards his daughter? Once this had been clarified, the two men went on to have an excellent relationship, which constantly niggled Silvia each time she saw them together. Her husband Don was the senior son-in-law, but for some reason, was not Harry's cup of tea. He liked the feel of dirt under his fingernails and boots, as did Joe, whilst Don presented the image of soft delicately manicured fingernails and perfectly spoken English.

Silvia's resentment of their relationship continued long after her father's death, and she'd snipe at Joe at every opportunity. When he tackled her over her remarks, he would be told he'd a vivid imagination, as she didn't have a clue as to what he was referring? Joe decided to let things be, as life was too short.

Val felt ashamed of her sister's attitude, but as Joe had told her that it didn't bother him, she too tried to ignore her unreasonable attitude.

However, the reality was that Silvia's continual sniping truly bugged him!

CHAPTER SIXTEEN:

Joe and the kids sang together in the car as they drove home, when Shirley suddenly remembered something just as home came into sight, "Dad, why didn't you want us to tell Grandma what happened with Mrs Brennan and our car?" she asked.

"Because Auntie Silvia would have made a great fuss and blown it out of all proportion," he replied. His answer appeared to satisfy, and a relieved Joe relaxed as he drove along the lane to their bungalow.

Val was still in bed when they reached home, and the children rushed straight for the fridge. "For goodness sake, I saw you lot stuff yourselves with cake at Grandma's," said Joe.

"Oh, Dad, will you never understand that cake's not proper food," replied Brian.

"True, enough," he agreed, then went to look in on Val. She smiled as he pecked her on the forehead, "What can I get you, babe," he asked, "how's the headache?"

"Hot milk would be great," she answered, "and my headache's a little better... was everything okay over at Mum's?"

"That's good... yes, everything was fine, but your dear sister was there," he answered, "which was the only blot on the page."

"Now Joe, you know she means well," said Val.

"Does she heck," he replied, "she's a... a vindictive bitch."

"Joe, I wish you wouldn't speak like that," scolded Val.

"I'll make your drink, and then see to the troops," he replied. He could only say so much to her about her sister, before she became defensive. "Damn, damn, and triple damn," he muttered, as he made his way back to the kitchen.

CHAPTER SEVENTEEN:

I drove for what must have been an hour, before stopping for a break in a convenient lay-by. I'd done many stupid things in my life, but that was up there with the worst. Within the space of a few minutes, I'd twice driven off at speed, with a total disregard for the thoughts or feelings of those left in my wake. Furthermore, the reality that Joe had been within touching distance had just sunk into my thick skull, making my insides feel as wobbly as a jelly clinging to the flimsy edges of a soggy cardboard plate.

I walked around stretching my legs until a lorry drew in, whereupon I once more departed at speed. My nerves still raw, I continued for a few further miles until I saw a number of cars parked outside a large service station... surely no one would find me in the middle of that lot, I mused?

Once parked, I darted inside to answer a call of nature, and to buy a nerve settling caffé macchiato.

"Had a long drive, love?" asked the cashier, "You look kind of tired."

"No, not too far," I replied. I wasn't going to give any clues as to where I'd come from or to where I was going, and certainly not to her. She continued to stare, as she waited for a more forthcoming answer. "Have a nice day," I replied, as I collected my tray. That was all she was going to get out of me, as I recalled the contents of the newsletters I'd received from the Junior Sleuth League. I wasn't going to let anything slip that could be held as evidence against me at a later date.

I found myself an empty table, where I sat with my hands around my mug of hot coffee, lost in my thoughts, until I heard a high-pitched voice directed towards me... "Excuse me, dear... do you mind if I sit here?" asked a stout set woman, wearing a high-necked blue coat.

"Pardon?" I replied.

"Do you mind if I join you?" she repeated, hovering above my temporary sanctuary.

"Join me... join me?" I repeated. "Why?"

"Because there are no other free tables, and you looked the nicest person I could see who had an empty seat at theirs," she haughtily explained.

I saw she was embarrassed, but that didn't stop me, "Well, I'm not that nice," I replied.

"Oh, sorry to bother you, and I must say," she huffed, as she turned away to look for pastures new.

I gulped down what remained of my coffee, stood up and speedily headed for the exit. I felt her eyes firmly fixed on my back, but didn't give a damn as to what she thought of me. I wasn't a nice person, not today anyway. I'd have to make myself look less nice, less approachable to members of the public in future... I must remember to wear a scowl.

Once back in the safety of my car, I phoned James, "I just wanted to... hear your voice," I sobbed.

"Dawn, what's wrong?" he asked. "I can hear something's wrong, there's a quiver in your voice."

"James, I'm perfectly fine," I sniffled, before bursting into tears.

"Dawn, Dawn, what is it," he repeated, "come on love, tell me?"

"I've just gone and got myself a little upset... it's over nothing really, absolutely nothing... in fact, I shouldn't have phoned in this state," I answered. "I'll call you back in half-an-hour... I'll be fine by then... bye, love."

I cut the call short. Damn, I thought, James would be worried sick now. What's wrong with you Dawn? You

didn't need to upset him on top of everything else… that was
nothing short of blooming selfish!

CHAPTER EIGHTEEN:

Leaving the service station was a relief in more ways than one. My inner tension gradually subsided, and I soon felt I was back on a straight track. After a few miles, an emptiness gnawed inside my stomach. "Of course, I hadn't eaten since breakfast," I muttered, and decided to stop at the next eating-place.

A few minutes later, I entered the Barley Bree Inn, and made straight for the serving counter, "Do you do food?" I asked.

"My, we've a hungry one here," remarked the elderly man behind the counter to the woman working alongside. He was of my father's generation, so to my mind, it was acceptable to make that kind of off-hand comment.

"I've had a hell of a busy day, and it's just dawned on me that I'm hungry," I replied, with a half laugh.

"Well, you are a happy chicken," he replied beaming, "what's so funny?"

"I said that hunger had dawned on me, and Dawn just happens to be my name," I giggled, vainly trying to explain.

"You take yourself over there lass, while I ponder what you've said," he replied. "I'll send someone over to take your order."

"She meant her name was Dawn, and that it had just dawned on her she was hungry," explained the woman alongside him.

"I don't know how you worked that one out, Nell," he answered, "is she right, lass?"

I nodded to him in response, and took myself off to a comfy seat beside the crackling fire. It was a nice and cosy place, one of those friendly pubs that one often hears about, but have difficulty finding. Nell then arrived to take my order, and gently guided me through the menu until she had eased me into ordering what was still available.

We immediately struck up a trusty girly friendship, and I found myself asking her to bring herself a coffee and join me. While I ate, I poured out a few of today's events, while she nodded and made the appropriate noises of understanding, "You could always send the lady flowers," she suggested, "to the one you drove off from so rudely, I mean. That would do the trick for me."

"Yes, that a good idea," I agreed, and immediately phoned my secretary. "Mona, will you send a bunch of flowers to a Mrs Jean Brown in *Cloverley*?"

"Is there an address?" quipped Mona.

"I've just told you the address," I replied.

"There's usually a street name and number, Dawn," she queried.

"It's a very small place; believe me it will reach her," I replied. "Wait, Mona… it's 5 Briar Terrace… send her a message to say that it was lovely to see her, and that I'm sorry for being so rude. Oh, and add that I'll be back in touch soon."

"Rude? What in heaven's name did you do or say?" asked Mona.

"That's my business Mona… now just sign the card Dawn… just Dawn," I answered.

"Just Dawn?" she repeated, somewhat puzzled.

"No, Mona… Dawn, not just Dawn," I stressed.

When I came off the phone and turned to Nell, she appeared fascinated by the call. "I wish I'd a secretary," she commented. "I'd think I'd made it, if I had my own private secretary to do my every bidding."

"No, you wouldn't, not if that secretary happened to be Mona," I hurriedly replied.

Nell poked at the open fire, "Dealing with the guy however, will be a little more difficult," she said slowly. "You see, my old man's a copper, and it's just as well he wasn't around when you had that little… how shall I say… entanglement."

"How is it… being married to a policeman, I mean?" I asked.

"Let's just say it has its moments," she replied, with a smile. "You could always leave a message on the guy's answer phone."

"What sort of message?" I probed.

"A sorry-for-what-happened type of message, I suppose… ask your secretary to make the call, that's what I'd do," she replied.

She had hit a nerve talking about 'the guy'… I somehow didn't think so… this conversation had now run its course.

"Bill, can you be a love and clear the plates, and bring us over another two coffees? Dawn is in need of some advice," she called over to the man behind the counter.

"Well, she's scraping the bottom of the barrel, getting any advice from you," he quipped back.

"Come on, chop-chop, let's be having a tidy table here," she joked.

We watched as he cleared away the dishes, and then she rose to collect the coffees herself. I asked her to only to bring one as I didn't want another. "I don't care to over exert Bill. We're lucky he's still here, but that's another story," whispered Nell. "When I come back with my coffee, let's get back to your problem."

"I'm not going to leave a message; it might not reach him, if you see what I mean?" I replied. "Listen, Nell, it's been lovely meeting you and for your company and advice, but I really need to be on my way. Could you fetch me my bill, please?"

I appreciated the fact that she didn't protest, and brought my bill over without further delay. I duly paid, including a sizeable tip, and thanked her once more for her time. I then grabbed by bag and jacket, and departed at speed.

When I got into my car I had to smile, as I imagined what the chat would be in the Barley Bree Inn. "Look out for a bouquet arriving," Nell would no doubt be telling Bill, who once again would be left in the dark to ponder why on earth they'd be receiving flowers.

I decided that wouldn't be the case however, as Nell had already received a handsome tip.

CHAPTER NINETEEN:

Mrs Jean Brown was most surprised when she took delivery of an expensive bouquet, only a few hours after standing open-mouthed at her front door. "What's with her," she muttered, "nice thought though, as they must've cost a pretty penny?"

She soon separated the flowers into three suitable vases, stood back to admire them, then picked up and read the message on the card once more. Rude? Had Dawn been rude? Perhaps a little, but not this much!

She then phoned Silvia to tell her of the flowers, "Dawn always was a waster with her money... and with other things," she replied.

"I didn't know that," exclaimed Jean. "Heaven's above, Silvia, she must've been only eleven the last time you saw her... just a child."

"I can always tell how children will turn out. That one shone out at five years of age as having precocious and wayward tendencies," she replied.

"She was rather forward I must agree, but I found that somewhat refreshing and cute," answered Jean.

"Everyone's entitled to their own opinion," said Silvia, "I have to get on now, Mum, so see you tomorrow."

"Bye… Silvia dear," replied Jean.

*

Val felt fine the next morning and at eleven o'clock headed into *Cloverley* with her youngest. Daisy was a few years younger than her other children, but catching up fast. "Can we visit Grandma?" she asked.

Val looked at her. She was the last child Joe and she would ever have, and this thought reminded her of her dad and the conversation he'd had with Joe, some years earlier. "There are ways to stop it from happening," he'd told him. "Our Val's given you more than enough of a family… three children, with another on the way, is plenty enough for anyone." Joe had repeated this to Val, whilst in the next breath, told her the date of his… impending appointment at the Health Clinic!

"Yes, we can visit Grandma. You won't be able to come with me so often, once you start school," Val answered.

"Is that soon?" asked Daisy.

"In September," she replied. "Do you know how long that is… how many months?"

Daisy grinned at her mum with her cheeky face, "No, I don't… it's too hard. You can just tell me when I need to go," she answered.

"Come on then lazy-bones, if you can't count, then let's find out how fast you can run… I'll race you to Grandma's," Val replied.

They arrived at the gate of number five, sweating, red-faced and puffing loudly, "I won, I won," yelled Daisy, as she knocked on the front door.

"Come in… it's open," Jean called out. They trooped in and Daisy rushed to give her grandma a hug. They were very close, with her having been born within weeks of Harry's death. The little scrap that was Daisy, had helped Jean enormously to cope during her darkest hours.

Val plopped herself into an armchair, sniffed the perfumed air, and looked around the room for a reason? "What's with all the flowers, Mum," she asked, "you've… let me see, three vases full?"

"They're lovely, aren't they? They were delivered from a visitor I had yesterday," she replied, "delivered only a few hours after she'd left, they were."

"What visitor was that?" asked Val.

"Did Joe not mention I had a visit from Dawn?" she answered. "Silvia looked in for a bit too while she was here."

"Dawn? Dawn who?" asked Val.

"Your childhood friend, Dawn Pearson... although her name's Brennan now, and it was lovely to see her," answered Jean.

Val didn't know how to respond, and hoped her face wasn't giving too much away. "I was still in bed with a headache when Joe came home yesterday," she explained. "Was she still here when Joe and the kids arrived?"

"No, she'd gone before they arrived," answered Jean.

"What's she like... now... I mean?" asked Val.

"You'd recognise her; she hasn't changed that much, but her hair's cut into a shorter style. What I can say is that she was surprised about you and Joe being married," answered Jean.

"Is she married?" asked Val.

"Yes, as I just said, her name's Brennan now, and she has three children of her own. She said she couldn't imagine you with four," laughed Jean.

"Do you want a cuppa, Mum?" asked Val, suddenly changing the subject.

"Yes, that would be lovely. I'll speak to my clever little girl next door while you make it," she replied.

Val was relieved to reach the privacy of the kitchen. She wished she was back in bed nursing her headache... however, whilst headaches come and go, she had always hoped Dawn Pearson or whatever her name now was, had gone forever...

CHAPTER TWENTY:

James Brennan was seated, belted and ready for take-off, with his two daughters on either side, Lorraine in the aisle seat and Angela next to the window. His son Sean was seated a few rows in front, alongside two attractive young girls, so he was happy.

"Mum will be dying to see us, Dad. I hope she's not been too sad, with us being away," remarked Angela.

"Mum's been busy, but she's fine, and I'm sure she's missed us," he replied.

"Did I hear you say she'd gone on a memory trip or something?" asked Lorraine.

"Yes, well sort of… she went back to visit the place where she used to holiday with her folks when a young girl," he answered.

"Why would she do that, Dad? Was that where she went on holiday before Grandma Madge and Grandad Frank were divorced?" asked Lorraine.

"I think it must have been… but I'm not too sure," he replied.

James pressed back into his seat and closed his eyes. Why had she gone back there? Perhaps some unfinished business or was it mere curiosity? Would he go back somewhere? He didn't think so, as he couldn't think of anywhere he'd want to revisit.

"Dad," asked Lorraine "is everything good between you and Mum?"

James opened his eyes and turned towards her, "Lorraine, of course," he whispered, and looked to see if Angela was showing any interest in their chat, but her nose was pressed hard up against the tiny window as she watched the last of the passengers baggage being loaded into the hold. "Lorraine," he added, "believe me, everything's fine between me and Mum. I'm so looking forward to seeing her."

"Good," she replied, giving him a smile and squeezing his arm. She then reached for her magazine.

"We're moving," shouted Angela suddenly, as she pulled herself up as far as she could, "we're moving. Sean, we're moving," she called out to her brother.

Sean turned and smiled at his little sister, and the two pretty girls beside him turned and smiled too.

"Sean? Mmm, that's a nice name," one of the girls whispered to the other, "he's nice to his little sister too, which is unusual."

Sean was secretly pleased... he was making an impact! His time on board flew by, as did Lorraine's, but for Angela it wasn't nearly long enough. An hour-and-a-half is simply not long enough when you're having fun.

James felt nervous at the thought of seeing Dawn, yet couldn't understand why? Something was niggling... a lost phrase perhaps or a slipped word... there was something, something he'd forgotten, but something which Dawn hadn't.

*

"Come on, Dad, just push your way forward," urged Angela, once the debarkation process had begun. A few people tutted, but Angela didn't care. If Dawn had been here, she would've undoubtedly commented that she was a chip off the old block.

"Angela, don't be rude," scolded James, as he allowed a few people past, much to his precocious daughter's annoyance.

"Oh, Da-a-ad," begged Angela, "let's go."

He made no mention regarding her behaviour when they finally left the plane, and secretly admired his daughter's blunt forwardness, which reminded him so much of his wife. Angela now bounced up and down in anticipation of seeing her mum, while Sean continued to chat with his new friends. James's pride swelled, he had his beautiful elder daughter Lorraine on his arm.

*

"Mum, Mum," Angela yelled, rushing to greet me.

I lifted her and whirled her around, "I've missed you my little pumpkin," I said, my eyes searching beyond Angela, first taking in the sight of Sean and his new lady friends, before coming to rest on Lorraine and James. Our eyes met with a shyness that made us feel a certain vulnerability.

Hugs and kisses were exchanged all round… Sean said goodbye to his new friends who coyly turned and gave little waves as they left. He smiled and gave them a tentative finger wave back.

James took my hand and squeezed it tight, "Okay lad, not so tight please, I'm not going anywhere," I said.

He looked at me, "Have you missed me?" he asked.

"What do you think?" I replied. "I'll show you how much later, and then tell you all about *Cloverley*, that's if you want to hear?"

"What! I wouldn't miss it for anything," he replied. "I want you to spit out every teensy-weensy detail."

I gave Sean a peck on the cheek and teased him about his new friends, whilst I slipped my arm through Lorraine's. "James, will you keep an eye on Madam please?

You too Sean, I don't want her getting lost, you know what she's like." I said, then turned to Lorraine, "Have you enjoyed yourself, darling, you weren't bored were you?"

"No, I love going to Ireland, but wish you'd come with us, I missed you," she replied. "What have you been up to, it all sounded a bit strange, according to Dad's description? Are you and Dad happy enough together?"

"Of course we are. What in heaven's name has he been saying?" I asked.

"Nothing, it was just strange with you not being with us, that's all. Gran and Grandad remarked about that too," she replied. She then let go of my arm and turned her attention to her phone. I saw that Sean was already deeply engrossed with his, so this time it was my turn to squeeze James's hand.

"Where the devil is she?" I asked, scanning the Arrivals Hall. "Next time I'm going to put reins on her, or a dog lead. From where did she get all this bad behaviour, not to mention her insubordination?"

"I have no idea," replied James, with a smirk.

"What? What are you inferring?" I asked, my smile trying to disguise itself, but rather unsuccessfully.

We eventually got hold of our wayward daughter, and I drove my family home to our spacious and comfortable house. James and I having professional vocations meant we could afford life's little luxuries, and I must say, we did like to indulge ourselves. Later that evening I told him my tale, albeit, omitting a few bits and bobs which I considered unnecessary, but overall I gave him the full flavour of my adventure.

"Whatever possessed you?" he asked.

"Whatever possessed me to do what?" I queried.

"To go stay in a grotty B&B, and look up folks from thirty odd years ago," he asked.

"Twenty-eight, to be precise," I replied, defensively. He looked at me in a strange way.

"I liked *Cloverley* when I was a child... anyway, what's wrong with that?" I continued.

"Nothing, I suppose. But don't you realise, you're probably romanticising about something that in reality is most likely mundane," he replied.

"I wasn't romanticising about anything. The village is a living place, with real live breathing people," I protested.

"Yes, but if it was such a good place, you'd have taken us to visit years ago," he countered.

This statement shocked me. None of my family belonged there, it was my place and my precious memories would be destroyed if I took them there. "James, I think I'll have an early night, are you coming?" I asked.

"I'll be right up, Dawn, I just want to check up on this place of yours on the Web," he replied.

"Whatever for? It's mine James, not yours," I half protested.

"Okay, okay, I'll not look it up then," he replied, "you can keep your precious village all to yourself."

We then went to bed and no mention was made of it again, at least not until the following morning.

*

Joe Doubleday's building firm was busy, with three large-scale renovation projects in *Cloverley* alone. He kept a tight control over each of them. Quality workmanship was what he required and wished it to be synonymous with the name **'Doubleday Builders'**.

He rose early each morning to check each site before his workers arrived, pro-actively looking for snagging and any other potential cock-ups, knowing how to show his displeasure when necessary.

*

Joe had left long before Val and the kids surfaced. Once washed and dressed, they gathered noisily around the breakfast table. "Mummy, do you remember when you were in bed with your sore head, and Daddy took us to visit Grandma?" began Brigitte.

"Yes, I remember, why?" she answered, wondering what was coming next.

"Well, Daddy bumped his car, and I got my knee scraped," she announced, raising her leg. "I thought you'd want to see it and I forgot to tell you yesterday."

"Of course I'd want to see it," replied her mum. "Did you not have your seat belt fastened?"

Brigitte nodded, in typical Brigitte fashion, which meant Val didn't know if she meant yes or no.

"It wasn't really much of a bump, and it wasn't Dad's fault," explained Brian, as he glared at Brigitte in such a way that her bottom lip began to quiver.

Okay, thought Shirley, Dad didn't want us to mention anything about the bump to either Grandma or Auntie Silvia, but didn't say we couldn't mention it to Mum! Brigitte had let the cat out of the basket anyway, so she felt free to wade into the fray... "It was with a Mrs Brennan... her car's exactly the same as Dad's," added Shirley, "and it was only the car mirrors that touched."

Only the car mirrors touched, resounded inside Val's head... that's more than enough of a touch for me!

"Mrs Brennan drove off when Dad went to check on her," continued Shirley.

"She went fast," added Brigitte, who had now recovered her composure.

"Let me get this straight kids, are you telling me that she drove off before your dad could even speak to her? Is that what happened?" she asked.

"Yes," answered Brian. "Dad didn't know who it was until we told him."

"And how come you knew the lady's name?" asked an even more puzzled Val.

"We spoke to her earlier and noticed she'd the same kind of car as Dad. Charlene and Charlie told us she'd been at their house visiting," explained Brian.

"Charlene and Charlie's house belonged to Mrs Brennan's mum and dad a long time ago," added Shirley. "Her other name's Dawn, and I told Dad after the crash that the driver's name was Dawn Brennan."

"And what did he say to that?" she asked, noticing that the original 'bump' had now turned into a 'crash'… Shirley and her vivid imagination!

"Nothing, he just stood in the middle of the road and watched her disappear," answered Shirley.

"And fast," added Brigitte, "she went really fast."

"I got a bump too," joined in Daisy, "but Brian kissed it better."

Val smiled at her, "That was nice of him," she replied, "whatever happened next?"

"We went to Grandma's for cake, and Auntie Silvia was there. I helped her in the kitchen," answered Brigitte.

"Grandma told us she'd a visitor called Dawn Brennan. Dad asked us not to tell them about her car and ours," explained Shirley. "Auntie Silvia's never nice to him, and I don't like her, so we never said a word."

"All this fuss over nothing," replied Val. "Now move… the lot of you, or you'll be late for school. Daisy, can you help me clear the table, please?"

They cleared up the breakfast dishes, and then Val made herself a coffee and poured a fresh orange-juice for Daisy. Sitting opposite each other at the table, Val looked around the ghost town that now surrounded them, and smiled at Daisy. "This is great, Daisy, it's so quiet and peaceful with just the two of us," she said, with a sigh of relief.

Daisy continued to sip her orange-juice…

What will I do, Daisy, she mused…why didn't Joe tell me when he brought me my hot milk the other evening, or even last night when we had time to ourselves once everyone was in bed? I remember he was on about the Johnson's extension, and how he thought it was something special… he also mentioned that we could have one too, once he had more time… I can't remember if he talked of much else, other than asking if anyone was in need of new shoes, clothes… in fact, he behaved as he did most nights. Was there any tension? It's hard to say, as he's always so sweet. But why didn't he tell me about the car, and the news that my childhood friend… his childhood sweetheart, had visited Mum? Why didn't he mention anything?

Daisy had now finished her orange-juice, and was sitting watching two birds chasing each other around the garden. Val looked at her and smiled, and an image of Joe, when he was a boy, entered her mind... she had his easy ways... should I tell him that I know all about it and act nonchalantly, or should I forget the whole business, she wondered once more? I can't do that though, as everyone else knows, and it will surely raise its ugly head again, of that I'm certain.

"Daisy, please tell me what I ought to do?" sighed Val suddenly.

"We could have ourselves an ice cream," she replied, still looking out into the garden.

*

The next morning, I didn't rise to the sound of singing birds, but to the sound of an electric razor. We hadn't communicated with each other during the night, and not one touch had we exchanged, but this was the start of a new day. I sprang from our bed and made my way into the shower room, "Good morning," I began——

"And to you," he replied. "Sorry about last night, I didn't mean to prod you for information, but you must see it from my side?"

"Afraid not," I replied, turning on the shower, "I didn't pry into what you'd been doing over in Ireland."

"Oh, give me a break, Dawn... the two things are completely different," he protested.

115

I could see he was upset and I suppose I could understand why, "Yes, you're right, James, two different ball games, with two different teams," I replied.

He didn't know how to answer and so I gave him a hug. "James, I've slightly damaged the offside mirror of my car," I confessed, as I hopped into the shower.

"That'll be most upsetting, knowing how much you love your car. What happened?" he asked.

"Oh, it was really nothing… just an idiot on the wrong side of the road… it could've been much worse," I answered, from the safety of my steam closet.

"I hope you gave him one of your famous mouthfuls?" he said, through the glass door.

"No,… I didn't think it would serve any purpose," I replied.

"Perhaps not, but it would've given you the satisfaction of getting it off your chest," he suggested.

"No, James, I wanted to do the exact opposite and get myself away as far as possible," I replied.

"That's not like you, Dawn," he exclaimed, and left it at that… for which I was truly thankful.

*

James later asked if I wanted to use his car, and offered to take mine to our local garage to get the mirror replaced. "That would be great," I replied. "Do you still trust me to drive your beast?"

"Why wouldn't I," he answered, "by the way, did you get the other guy's number? We should report him."

"No, I never thought about getting his number," I replied, "I just wanted to put distance between us."

"So, it was definitely a guy?" he asked.

"Eh, yes," I replied, "I… saw him."

"How could you see him properly?" he queried.

"Because he got out of his car and was coming towards me," I replied.

"Coming towards you? What a strange thing for him to be doing… unless he was coming to threaten you?" said James.

"No, I don't think he was going to threaten me… it would probably be to see if I was hurt or something," I replied. That answer didn't sound right, and I regretted saying it as soon as it left my lips.

"An idiot isn't usually in the habit of doing that," he said.

He made me feel guilty with that remark, right to the pit of my stomach. "Well, this idiot must've been different to your normal run-of-the-mill idiot." I replied.

James said no more, picked up my car keys and blew me a kiss. "Sorry Dawn, there I go again, analysing the actions of a stranger," he said, "just ignore me darling."

Relief spread over me, as I heard him drive away. It had sounded like an interrogation, or rather an inquisition, although I knew he meant well. I then got the kids off to school, and thanked the Lord that Angela didn't play up today, or give me any of her wisecracks. I then finished dressing, and set off for my office. Fortunately my first appointment wasn't until ten.

*

I felt unsure about driving James's car, but arrived safely and without incident. Mona was sitting behind her desk with that smarmy smile she often put on, printed across her face, "Did you have a nice time, Dawn," she chirped, "what's the story with the bouquet?"

She rose from her seat and was now following closely behind me, as I made my way towards my office. "Oh, for goodness sake, Mona, let me take my jacket off, you're right up the back of my heels. You must have been mighty bored last week, with me not being here?" I said.

"I'm just taking a healthy interest," she replied.

"You tell me, you're far more up to date on these things than me," I answered. I wanted to choke her… I was her boss, which had somehow escaped her somewhere down the line.

"You don't often send flowers to people," she continued, "in fact, I can't remember you ever sending anyone flowers."

"And probably won't again. It was actually someone else's crazy idea, not one of mine," I replied.

"I just knew it must have been someone else's idea," she said, "tell me more?"

What a remark to make, just what kind of scrooge did she think I was? I decided to send flowers to a few other people without further delay… "Mona, can you arrange for a bouquet to be sent to my mum… you have her address, and can you do it this morning, please," I said, "it's urgent."

"Urgent," she replied, "has she suddenly taken ill or something?"

"No,… just do it, please," I answered, "but not before you've made coffee."

She huffed as she left to make the coffee, whilst I lifted a file from my desk and tried to get to terms with my first patient of the day. The file wasn't making much sense, so I knew I'd need to wing it. "Oh, hurry up, Mona or she'll be here before I get my innards reinforced," I muttered.

There was a rattle of china, and it arrived resplendent on a tray. I always insisted on having china cups and saucers in the office, although at home we used our old favourite mugs.

I now only had five minutes left to myself, five minutes in which to think things over and to sleuth my way through the maze that was my emotions.

CHAPTER TWENTY-ONE:

The extension on the rear of the Johnson house was indeed exceptional, and the architect told Joe that it was worthy of an award. In Joe's own mind, everything was taking shape. He'd taken on board what he'd learned on this job and would apply it later to his own house extension. Val hadn't enthused over his plans, which wasn't unusual, as she wasn't one who readily jumped with joy. No, she was a more of a steady-as-you-go, loyal kind of woman.

His mind then wandered… she would've shown her approval for his schemes in her vocal, gregarious manner. He could picture her… bouncing around… laughing and chattering… of course, she could be different now, she was a grown woman, and doing, he knew-not-what with her life. She was now… Mrs Brennan, but that didn't tell him much. He'd waited in vain for her for so long, and had even returned to *Cloverley* in the hope that her folks still owned their Weekender, but alas it was not to be.

Then Val had come along and saved him from a wasted life. He learned to love her dearly... so must let those memories of Dawn go, once and for all...

Joe went to wash his hands and face before he left for home. He had always been a hands-on boss, mucking in whenever he could, and as he stood in the cloakroom of his client's house, he looked deep into the mirror above the wash-basin... *suddenly she appeared in front of him, and they were back at their special place beside the river, where he remembered how she always came up with a cheeky answer, always unafraid to get herself dirty, and yet scrubbed up, oh, so...*

"Forget her," he muttered, and looked away. But, try as he might, questions and memories continued to flood his mind... imagine her having the same model of car, the same colour... perhaps even the same year? It was not that common a model either, what did that show? It showed their good taste!

However, that car had driven off at speed... if she had been at the wheel, then why would she have done that? If she was the woman in the car, why couldn't she have waited to say hello? Perhaps she didn't recognise him or worse, didn't wish to see him? He'd never know for sure... his thoughts then turned to Val... and remembered that she had been there that day, that glorious day of the Fair...

"I love Joe," Dawn had told her, *"and he loves me."* He often wondered how Val felt about Dawn's frank

revelations, but had never dared ask. They always tried to avoid potentially confrontational situations. "Let's start our relationship from now, with no looking back," she had said when they'd first set out on life's journey together.

But, why hadn't he told her of Dawn's visit to her mum, and the incident with the cars? Plenty of opportunities had come and gone. He was in no doubt that she'd have heard of it by now... but crucially, she hadn't heard it from him.

*

Val laughed at Daisy's ice cream suggestion, "Daisy, I think ice cream would curdle the fresh orange juice in your tummy," she replied.

"What does that mean?" she asked.

"It means it would make it all choppy... you know, like the way the sea has waves," explained Val. "Why don't we wait until after lunch, then I'll give you a great big bowl of ice cream... would you like that?"

Daisy maintained her I'm-not-too-pleased look on her face. "I'll put a chocolate stick in with it... one of those flaky ones," she added.

That did it... Daisy came over and gave her a cuddle. Val bent over and kissed her tousled hair... hair that felt and looked like Joe's... what was she going to say to him?

Suddenly, her thoughts were broken by the sound of her front door bell... "It's only me," rang out an all too familiar voice, and not one she wanted to hear at this particular moment. "Ah, good, you're home. I forgot to call first," added Silvia. "Hello, Daisy, are you and Mummy having a lazy start to the day?"

"No, we're not. We've been tidying and getting things done before we dress," replied Val. "It's how we like to do things."

"Whatever you say," said Silvia. "Daisy, it's my birthday next Saturday, do you want to come to my party?"

"Just me?" she queried.

"No, silly works, everyone's invited," she replied, "with the exception of your daddy, who will no doubt be busy working on that big flashy job of his."

"No, Joe won't be working as that project's almost finished, so he'll manage," replied Val.

"Oh, all right, I'll look forward to the pleasure of his company as well then," said Silvia sarcastically. The two sisters exchanged momentary glances, and although no words were spoken, each was left with their own thoughts...

"Are you not at work today?" asked Val.

"No silly... you've obviously forgotten that I'm part-time now, because of the IVF treatment. Surely you haven't forgotten about that?" she replied.

Alas, Val had, and Silvia could see that was the case.

"I told you that Don wanted me to go part-time, to give me a better chance," she continued, "of course, you can't possibly understand, as you've had it all so easy."

"I've had it easy? You try bringing up four children, Silvia," snapped Val, "I can tell you, it's far from easy."

"Hmm… I wish I had just one," she sighed.

"Oh, I'm sorry," replied Val, "I wasn't thinking."

"Yes, that's the trouble with everyone, nobody ever thinks how it is for Don and me," she huffed. "Mum feels sorry for me, you feel sorry for me, and to tell the truth, probably Don even feels sorry for me."

"No, we don't," replied Val. "I don't think of things in that way, neither does Mum. It's not something we even discuss."

"Yes, I can understand that too… just sweep it under the bed or the table, forget about it, and it will go away," said Silvia, "out of sight… out of mind."

"No, not at all, Silvia… your problems are personal to you… and Don," replied Val.

"Well, just make sure you keep it that way. I don't want to hear anything that might upset me… next Saturday's my next big day," said Silvia, "and I can't wait."

"Then let me wish you both every success," replied Val. She loved Silvia but found her exceedingly hard work. She'd never taken to her husband Don, and Silvia had always detested Joe. However, because of family loyalties, they continued to muddle through life together.

"Did the 'gypsy rover' tell you?" asked Silvia.

"Did he tell me what," asked Val, "and please stop calling Joe by that name?"

"Did he tell you about Dawn Pearson's visit to Mum's the other day?" she replied. She could see he hadn't… the no good weasel, she thought.

*

When Joe arrived home, family life was back in full swing. Brian was riding high as top-scorer for the *Cloverley* Junior School football team in their match against their arch-rivals. "Four two, four two, Dad, and guess who scored a hat trick?" he sang.

"I've no idea… whoever that could have been?" answered Joe.

Shirley also wanted to tell him of a concert her class was planning, and the little ones were playing on the floor and giggling over nothing in particular. Joe looked at Val, desperate for a word, but she was far too busy to be disturbed.

"Later, Joe… own up to your crime later," he mumbled to himself.

"Daddy's talking to himself," said Brigitte.

"That's the first sign of madness," added Shirley.

"Thanks for that, Shirley," he replied, as he looked over once more to Val.

This time she looked back, and smiled, "Your dad's always talked to himself, so we needn't concern ourselves unduly," she said.

"Thank you, Mummy," he replied, with a shake of his head.

"Auntie Silvia was here," piped up Daisy, "she's asked me to her birthday party on Saturday."

"Lucky you," said Shirley, laughing.

"We're all invited," clarified Val, "even you Daddy."

"No, not me," said Joe, "I want to press on and finish the Johnson extension, and then make a start on our own."

"Oh, I told her you were coming," replied Val.

He could tell by her eyes that it was important to her, "Right, I know what I'll do. I'll press on with the job on Sunday instead. Brian, you can come and help if you want?" he suggested.

"I'd rather we did it on the Saturday, Dad. I don't really want to go to Auntie Silvia's silly party either," he confessed.

"If I can stomach it, then you can too. We'll be pleasing Mum if we go," replied Joe.

Brian frowned, but conceded defeat for his mum's sake, just as his dad had done.

"I don't like going to Auntie Silvia's much either," added Shirley.

"Well, we all have to do things at times we don't like," replied Val.

"What's wrong with going? I want to go, 'cause I like parties, as there's always lots of ice cream, birthday cake, and fizzy drinks," gushed Brigitte, "what's wrong with that?"

"It's all right sweetheart, we're all going to the party," replied Val, "and that means everyone!"

*

After tea, the two little girls went outside to play, while Brian and Shirley tackled their homework. Joe saw his opportunity, and put his arms around Val… "How's your day been?" he asked.

"Fine, it's been a good day, except for Silvia's visit. You know how she winds me up, Joe," she answered, "and thanks for agreeing to come to her party with us?"

"You don't need to thank me for that, that's nothing… look at what you do for me," he replied. "Val——,"

The phone rang at that moment and she rushed to answer it, "Hi, Mum, it's fine, we've all had our tea. I'll go and find a quiet corner and we can have a good old natter," she replied. She then smiled at Joe and mouthed 'Mum' to him.

He, in turn, pointed out to the garden and she nodded. Once outside, he sat on a bench and watched his little daughters giggling and capering as they enjoyed themselves in the warm evening sunshine. When they saw him, they rushed over and cuddled into him.

Joe loved his family so much.

CHAPTER TWENTY-TWO:

The phone on my desk rang during my first appointment after lunch. "Please excuse me," I said to my patient. I turned away from Mrs Dawson so I could speak in a less than pleasant tone to my secretary, "What is it, Mona," I asked, in a quiet but stern voice, "you know my rules?"

"It's your mum, Dawn," answered a solemn Mona.

"Oh no… when, Mona?" I asked.

"When, what?" she replied.

"She's not died, has she?" I asked, sensing Mrs Dawson moving closer towards me…

"No, she's not dead! Why would Madge be dead? No, she's demanding to speak to you now, so what am I supposed to do? She's not accepting my usual flannel about you being in consultation," she explained.

"But I am in a consultation, so it's not flannel," I hissed, whilst smiling at Mrs Dawson, who appeared very interested in my line of conversation. "Put her through, Mona, I'll talk to you later," I continued, "Mrs Dawson, I'm sorry about this, there appears to be an emergency. Please help yourself to coffee and biscuits."

She nodded, and I got the distinct feeling she was enjoying this far more than her consultation.

"Mum, what is it?" I whispered.

"You sent me flowers?" she replied. "It upset me, dear. I never get flowers, so I needed to speak to you. Are you terminally ill or something?"

"No, I'm not terminally ill, I'm absolutely fine. Does my doting step-dad not send you flowers?" I asked.

I was in shock… what a thing to have been asked, but I managed to nod to Mrs Dawson. I was not so much in shock however, to fail to notice her plate piled high with chocolate biscuits. The devil in me was tempted to say something rather rude, but I changed my mind. Behave yourself, Dawn, you're meant to be a professional, for goodness sake!

"No, Alexander doesn't have any time for perishable items like flowers. It must go back to his days in the grocery trade," she replied.

Mum, don't talk about Alexander Sugar and the grocery trade, not now, not ever. Not after what happened, I thought. "Listen, Mum, I'll phone you back later, and then we can have a proper chat about the flowers, and anything else that's bothering you," I suggested.

Mrs Dawson looked a trifle disappointed, and I almost regretted not having put the phone on loudspeaker, to enable her to eavesdrop on both sides of our conversation.

"Sorry about that, elderly parents can be difficult," I explained, after I had hung up.

"Difficult? Nobody can tell me anything new about elderly parents being difficult, Dr Brennan. They're an absolute nightmare," she replied. "How old is your mum?"

I looked at her, stunned by her question. How old was my mother? I could always lie, but why should I? I heaved my chest, breathed out, "She's almost fifty-nine," I said, with a straight face. I wanted to laugh; fifty-nine wasn't even old, let alone elderly.

"Oh, I thought she would have been much older," she replied.

I took a sly glimpse at the file in front of me to refresh my memory of her date of birth. I flinched, Mrs Dawson was seventy-three... she certainly didn't look that age and was one of my most stylishly dressed patients. My God, she even wore high-heeled shoes!

"Does your mother perhaps suffer from... premature ageing?" she then asked.

"I'm not sure," I replied, "I don't pay that much attention... you know how it is when you see someone lots?"

"You mean in these circumstances, you don't notice subtle differences in people? Your mother appears to be suffering from more than subtle changes, Dr Brennan, if you think of her as being elderly at fifty-eight," she said.

"When I was calling her elderly, I was using it in the medical context," I waffled, with a broad smile, vainly trying to side-step the issue... God help me, I had now lied to a patient!

"I see... I'm not up on that sort of thing or I wouldn't need to see you, would I?" she said.

"No indeed," I replied, glancing at the clock, "We'd better return our thoughts to you, Mrs Dawson... you are my patient after all." I laughed as I said this, perhaps a little too loudly for my own liking, but thankfully, she never noticed my little joke.

*

"Don't you ever put me in a position like that again! You've no idea how embarrassing that was," I ranted to Mona after Mrs Dawson had departed. However, I could see from her expression that she did have an idea. "What were you playing at, Mona? You know damn well my rules on phone calls during consultations. That was not an emergency, so I would've expected you to have dealt with it without involving me."

"Well, your mother made it seem like one. If you had sent her flowers more often, it might not have been such a shock," she replied. Mona always talked as if she was my equal, sometimes even my superior. Why was I so fond of her? I glared at her whilst she glared back at me.

"They were very fast," I huffed.

"Who were very fast?" she asked.

"They were very fast in delivering the flowers, whoever they were," I clarified.

"Well, what did you expect… a Wells Fargo delivery, three days later by stagecoach?" she said, smiling.

"I need to prepare for my next patient," I replied, as I turned and went back into my consulting room, slamming the door behind me. I immediately re-opened it, and then slammed it shut once more… that felt much better! I then relaxed and settled into my comfy chair, ready to open my next file, when the phone on my desk rang… I let the damned thing ring and ring before I grabbed it… "Yes?"

"Dawn, did you hear that banging noise just now? Have you any ideas where it came from?" asked Mona.

"Get back to your work," I snapped, through my laughter.

*

James and I always exchanged our take on the day during the early part of the evening, when relaxing and unwinding with our glass of favourite red. "Something's happened to you today," he said, "I can see it in your aura."

"Come on, James, none of your airy-fairy talk, although I must admit to my blood temperature rising sharply today," I replied.

"Mona?" he asked.

"Partly her... and partly my mother," I replied.

"Your mother? My goodness you haven't been anywhere near her for a while," he exclaimed.

"That was the problem," I replied, "and the flowers, of course." I wished I hadn't mentioned the flowers, as it stemmed from my visit to *Cloverley* and would now make the whole explanation rather more tricky.

"Flowers? I'm intrigued," said James, perking up.

I covered my tracks well, blaming Mona for sending the flowers and then blaming her again for not dealing with Mum's call... James was fascinated...

"And?" he asked, expectantly...

I continued along on my wavy path with my tale, trying to moderate what had transpired.

"So, let me get this straight... you thought she was dead, and she thought you were terminally ill," summed up James. "No wonder your blood was heated... the pressure would have been soaring too." I detected a splattering of amusement in his reply, and hated it when people didn't take me seriously, especially my beloved.

"We must visit her at the weekend. Go tell the kids that they're going to visit Grandma Madge tomorrow, and be prepared for any backlash," I replied.

"Oh, no... you tell them... it's you who wants to spoil their weekend. For heaven's sake, Dawn, why did you send her flowers? You never send anyone flowers," he replied.

"I've just started to... I've thought it over, and I think it makes a lovely gesture," I said, trying to justify my actions.

"After this morning, how can you possibly say that?" he replied.

"This morning was all Mona's fault," I stated.

"Then sack her. She's always winding you up; that's what I'd do, if it was me," he said.

"Sack her? Don't be so ridiculous, James, I like Mona. It just wouldn't be the same without her," I replied.

"No, but it might be a damn sight better," he stated.

"Mona stays, Mona's mine, end of story," I replied. "How about another glass before you tell the kids where they're going at the weekend?"

*

We arranged to take two cars on the Saturday morning. Sean now had his provisional licence, and James agreed to allow him drive there and back. I would take the two girls with me in my car.

Lorraine wished to bring her best friend, but I told her it was only family today. I dipped my hand into my purse, and magically had a happy and contented elder daughter onside. Our Angela, on the other hand, had no choice in the matter, as she'd shown in the past that she couldn't be trusted to be left with anyone. Anyway, this outing would be of interest to her. She hadn't visited for a while, and liked nothing better than to poke around other people's houses.

*

We stopped on the way for coffee and a snack. "How's the learner doing?" I asked.

"Very well," answered James, "he's about ready for his test."

"Thanks, Dad," said a beaming Sean.

"I'm so proud of you, Sean," I said. "By the way James, I never thanked you for taking my car to the garage to get the mirror fixed."

"No, problem… but now that you mention it, the funny thing was that the mechanic who ordered the new mirror from the specialist supplier, mentioned that it was the second one that the specialist had been asked for that day," he replied.

"What's wrong with that, Dad?" asked Sean.

"Well, your mum's car is one of a very limited edition, and the supplier had never been asked for any mirrors at all before," he replied.

"It's maybe just like buses... there are none for ages, and then two come along together," I chipped in. All joking aside, my stomach was in knots, so I excused myself and headed for the ladies. Sitting in the cubical, my mind relived my unfortunate tangle with Joe's car, and in my heart of hearts, I knew that the other mirror was for his car.

I then heard a familiar voice... "Mum, are you in there?" called out Lorraine.

I didn't answer, but unlocked the door, and the next thing I saw was Angela down on her hands and knees, with Lorraine standing beside her, "What in heaven's name are you're doing down there?" I asked. "No, on second thoughts, don't even bother trying to explain, I already know the answer. Get up Angela, and wash your hands."

Lorraine and I caught each other's eye and howled with laughter.

*

We took two and a half hours to reach Mum's house. She and Alexander Sugar had moved into his childhood home after the breakup of his and my parents' marriage. Mum greeted us with tears running down her face… "What's with all the emotion, Mum?" I asked.

"Oh, Dawn, I'm so pleased to see you. The arrival of your flowers gave me such a shock," she sniffled.

"Not one of my better ideas," I agreed. "It was all Mona's fault."

"How is she?" Mum asked.

"Mona," I replied, "the same as usual, I suppose?" God, I hadn't travelled all this distance to discuss Mona's wellbeing!

I could see Alexander Sugar seated in the living-room ready to greet us, and noticed the kids already checking out their likely escape routes. I would probably want to join them, as the man still gave me the creeps, much the same as he had done twenty-eight years ago. "Dawn, how are you, my dear?" he asked, with outstretched arms.

I wondered if another Dawn had entered the room, but that was unlikely. "Working hard," I replied, making no attempt to surrender to his disgusting grasp.

He put his arms back by his side and glanced at Mum to show he'd tried to comply with her instructions. "Pulling in lots of money no doubt. I don't approve of private medicine," he commented.

And I don't approve of you, I thought. "It's the way my speciality is frequently conducted, that perhaps gives it a poor press," I answered.

"A speciality best left well alone. You'd do better getting off your butt and back into real medicine," he growled, lowering his tone back to normal.

"You'd do better just getting off your butt!" I replied, and made my escape. He deserved that remark, as I knew he had Mum dancing service on him all day long. Once a nasty bit of stuff, always a nasty bit of stuff. What she ever saw in him remains a complete mystery... and I now remembered why we didn't visit often.

Mum had laid on a meal of soup and sandwiches, and we sat together around the table, much the same as any extended family would.

"The little one's missing," announced Alexander.

"I'll look for her," I replied, relieved to leave the table. Nice move by Angela, hoping that nobody would miss her presence. My baby and I were kindred spirits, and I knew where she'd be.

Mum kept my childhood dolls stored up in a spare room, and Angela being Angela, would not have forgotten about them. So I took this opportunity to have a nose around myself, my sleuthing habit never having left me. Boy, they must still enjoy their wine, as there were bottles stored in every nook and cranny. Mum had never been particularly tidy, and I noted that things hadn't improved.

As a family, we would have made an effort to visit more regularly, if it hadn't been for old man Sugar. I recalled that Joe used to call him that, and could still hear his voice saying these very words... I went to the upstairs hall window and stared out onto the front garden... *his voice floated on the air and I could see his reflection in the glass...*

"Mum, what are you doing?" asked Angela.

I looked around and was momentarily shocked to see myself as I was back then. I quickly pulled myself together, "Looking for you, young lady, but I somehow got distracted," I blustered, as I put my arm around her shoulder, and together we walked back to where the others were gathered.

*

That evening James and I sat with a cafetière of black coffee, with little cups taking the place of our usual large glasses. We were strained and tired. James had found it stressful sitting next to and supervising Sean, whilst he on the other hand loved driving and had hogged the wheel for the whole journey home. "He was grand, Dawn, but I like driving myself... and it was a long trip," he sighed.

"I'll supervise him next time, to check on his readiness," I offered.

"You're very welcome to take over the whole supervision of his driving if you like. You'll be more relaxed with him than me," he said. "You weren't exactly relaxed today though, especially with Alexander."

"Did I go too far," I asked, "you know me, whenever I see a goalpost, I shoot?"

"Twenty years of marriage in June, is it?" said James. "I've seen you score plenty of goals and quite a few hat tricks in that time."

"Actually, it's nineteen years in July," I corrected him.

"Okay, I was close and may have struck the post," he said, continuing with the football analogy.

I moved closer and kissed him, "I do love you, my darling," I said.

"I know you do, and I love you too," he replied.

CHAPTER TWENTY-THREE:

Joe Doubleday decided to leave things as they were with Val. It was too late to tell her now, as it ought to have been mentioned at the time it happened. Silvia's dreaded birthday party was looming, and it was the last place he would choose to go, but as Val had insisted, he would oblige… he'd do anything for her.

*

As the days passed, Val accepted that Joe hadn't deliberately avoided telling her of Dawn's visit, and it had just been down to circumstances. She knew he would've felt awkward, as she understood how his mind worked. Furthermore, she too wished they could avoid Silvia's impending party, but it was a family occasion and her mum always delighted in seeing her family together.

*

It was a lovely evening and Joe was feeling on top of the world, as they watched the little ones play in the garden. "What should I buy as a present for Silvia?" asked Val.

"As little as possible as far as I'm concerned," he replied, his pleasant evening taking a sudden dip.

"Oh Joe, don't make it any more difficult than it already is, please," pleaded Val. "It's not an easy situation for me with you and Silvia constantly at war."

"Look Val, just buy her whatever you want. I don't honestly care," he replied, "and I'm not at war with her. I do try to get on, but she doesn't make it easy."

She kissed him, and the girls shrieked with laughter as they came running over, "Daddy, Mummy, come and play with us," they begged.

"Why not," agreed Joe, looking at Val?

"You girls play with Daddy, I've lots of other things to do," she replied.

He looked at her a trifle dejected by her refusal to join in with them. "Come on Daddy, you'll do," the girls replied in unison.

As Val watched them run around acting crazy, she wished she had agreed to join in. Why did she always say she was too busy? And why did she mention Silvia's birthday present? She was more than capable of picking something herself, and Joe wouldn't object to anything she bought, irrespective of price. He loves me, she concluded, but I'm not worthy of that love, as I often spoil his enjoyment of those precious times over stupid little things that just don't matter.

Val cried inside, but held back the tears so as not to upset the others. She rose, went indoors, and when she remembered that her house was empty, Brian and Shirley being over at Charlene and Charlie's, she let her tears flow.

*

The present for Silvia now lay wrapped taking pride of place on the sideboard within the lounge. "What is it, Mummy?" asked a curious Daisy, who'd been with her when she'd bought it, but distracted by something else when the actual purchase was made.

"It's a surprise for Auntie Silvia, and a surprise for everyone else," she answered.

"But not from me?" persisted Daisy.

"Yes, and from you too," replied Val, "and as you're about to start school soon, you should be the same as the others."

Daisy didn't like the sound of that, not one little bit, and the expression on her face told her that this conversation could be tactfully challenging. "I don't want to go to school. I want to stay little," she huffed.

"Everyone grows up, Daisy, so just accept it," replied Val.

"I don't want to become a big girl. I'll ask Daddy… he won't want me to grow up, 'cause he likes me as I am," insisted Daisy.

"What a good idea, you ask Daddy as soon as he comes home," replied Val, as she watched her stomp from the room. Val was certain she would be lying in wait for Joe when he came home that evening. The joys, the joys, she thought. She also knew that it was mean to push all the onus onto him, but that was too bad. He'd no doubt come up with something and put Daisy down more gently than she could ever have done.

"Is that a present for Auntie Silvia?" asked Shirley, when she arrived home from school. "It's big and looks rather expensive."

Val was ironing whilst watching TV, "Yes, who else," she replied, "and she is my only sister, after all?"

"I'd rather not have a sister than have Auntie Silvia," she replied. "What have you bought her… a box of dynamite?"

"Shirley Doubleday, what a thing to say," scolded Val. "It's a surprise, but what I will say is that it's not dynamite." Although that would please Joe… gone forever in a puff of smoke, she thought.

"You can tell me," begged Shirley, "I won't tell anyone."

"Let me say, if I was going to tell anyone, it would be you, Shirley dear," replied Val, "but I'm not."

146

"Not even, Dad?" she asked.

"That's right, not even him," Val answered.

"Well, that's not fair. He earns the money, but it's you who gets to spend it. It's always you who's spending his money, never him," groaned Shirley.

"Shirley, apologise right now," said Val, "what do you think Dad would say if he heard you talking that way?"

"He'd agree with me," answered a defiant Shirley, who then stomped off to join Daisy in the queue to greet Joe when he arrived home from his hard day's work.

It's all Silvia's fault and mine... I'm not fit to be a mother, thought Val.

*

Tea-time arrived and to Val's surprise, everyone appeared happy and chatty. Good old Joe must have weaved his magic once more? However, she got the distinct impression that everyone was pussyfooting around her and watching her every move. Was it happening, or was it her imagination? She gave Joe a what-have-you-told-them look, which managed to find its way through the cross chatter, but he only winked and coyly smiled back. What in heaven's name has he told them, she wondered?

Joe winked lots, and nobody else she knew winked as often; well not to the extent that he did. Val had always found this cute until one day, Silvia remarked that this habit was some kind of genetic throw back. At this very moment, she wished she could throw Silvia as far away from her as possible. She then glanced over at her sister's parcel, standing guard on the sideboard, and wanted to hurl it after her... both as far away as possible, and more importantly, out of sight and mind.

When they'd finished their meal, she was surprised when the kids asked her to sit through in the lounge, so that they could clear away the dishes.

"I'll bring you through a coffee, Mum," offered Shirley.

"And I'll bring you a biscuit, Mummy," added Daisy, her words creating a whistling sound caused by a gap in her front teeth. She had prematurely lost a baby tooth in an accident with her brother's knee a few days ago.

During their chat earlier that morning, Val hadn't noticed, but this evening, her toothless gap gave her a strange sinister expression that she hadn't detected earlier.

Val went into the lounge and switched on the TV. The news came on and it was all doom and gloom, so she switched it off and picked up a book from under the coffee table. After staring at the first page for a few minutes, nothing registered, so she closed it and laid it back from whence it came.

Shirley then appeared with her coffee, together with Daisy, carrying a plate bearing one lonely biscuit. Brigitte then followed with the sugar bowl and spoon... "We couldn't remember if you took sugar or not?" she explained.

Val heard herself thank her daughters, who then beat a speedy retreat, with Shirley pulling the door firmly closed behind them. She sipped her solitary coffee, nibbled on her lonely biscuit, and felt as though she had been unwittingly incarcerated in her own lounge.

Joe, on the other hand, hoped she was enjoying her peace and quiet, as she often told him of her need for a quieter life.

*

Earlier, when he'd arrived home from work, he'd been met with dissension from his young troops. He responded by telling them the score, exaggerating Val's need for peace and quiet by making out that she was verging on some sort of illness brought on by her lack of rest. Whilst their speedy agreement had somewhat surprised him, he took it as a token of their love for her.

Once the domestic chores were completed, the kids went out to play with their friends and Joe quietly opened the door, and made his way into the lounge. He found Val fast asleep. He raised her legs onto the couch, collected her dishes and tiptoed from the room.

He went through into the garage and spent time washing, polishing, and pampering his beloved car. Whilst so engrossed, he took a moment to wonder if Dawn had managed to get her wing mirror fixed... he hoped she had. Joe's garage was his sanctuary, and after he'd finished valeting, he sat at his workbench and looked over his work schedules. He liked to keep ahead of the game, by having the answers to his men's queries on tap.

Once finished, he called on the kids but no one answered. He knew where they'd be, and set off for the Warners' house, which had once been Dawn's parents' Weekender. Whilst there had been significant changes over the years, many of its old features still remained. For example, the path to the front door was the same as the one he'd trodden as a boy…

"Hi Joe," greeted Brenda, "Tony isn't home yet, another one of his late nights."

"Well, he is bringing in the bacon, Brenda," he replied, with a smile.

"If you say so," she answered, as he followed her through into the kitchen.

"Have the kids been okay?" he asked.

"Fine, as always. You should be proud of them," she replied.

"I am," agreed Joe.

"Got time for a cuppa?" she asked.

"No, not really," he sighed, "I need to get the kids home and things organised… but thanks for the offer." He just wanted to pick the kids up and get home to Val. He should have checked on her before coming here, as time this evening had flown by.

"Anytime, Joe," she replied, "by the way, I'd a certain lady visitor recently. I haven't had a chance to talk to Val before now, but her parents used to own this house, years ago."

"I know, it was Dawn," he replied, "she apparently looked in on Val's mum before she left *Cloverley*."

"Oh, so she knew Val back then?" said Brenda. "You wouldn't know her though, would you?"

"Val and her used to play together when her folks came for their weekends here. This place was their Weekender. Yes, Val and Dawn were the best of friends back then," he replied, "and yes, I did know her."

"How's that?" she asked.

He wished now he hadn't mentioned he'd known Dawn, as she looked at him wide-eyed, awaiting his reply. "I used to live here too, remember. I told you before, how we used to live on the site where my new house sits. My old man owned the land," he answered.

"Ah, did you have much to do with Mrs Brennan back then?" she asked.

Mrs Brennan? For heaven's sakes… no, I didn't have anything to do with a Mrs Brennan, the girl I knew and had much to do with, was Dawn Pearson, he thought. "A bit," he answered.

"Which bit?" she asked, laughing at her little joke.

All of her, he wanted to say; I loved all of her. How could you ever begin to understand what Dawn meant to me, he thought?

151

"So, you've known Val since you were a boy," continued Brenda. "Did you have a crush on her then... or maybe it was Mrs Brennan who took your fancy? She's still a looker. I could see her turning all the little boys' heads and teasing them."

How dare you talk about my Dawn in such a manner. He wanted out of here, as Brenda could never understand how he would always feel about her? "I'll fetch the kids... Val's not feeling too great this evening," he replied, changing the subject.

"Oh, sorry to hear that. I'm looking forward to chatting to her about Mrs Brennan, especially since they were the best of pals. I'm sure she'll be interested," she replied.

Why does she keep going on about Mrs Brennan? It's Dawn, damn you, call her Dawn, he thought. He then went to collect the kids. Daisy and Brigitte should have been in bed ages ago, as the light was now fading fast. Where had the evening gone?

*

The lounge was empty when they got back, so Joe switched on the lamps, then rushed to make sure Val was in bed. He came back with his finger up to his lips, "Right everyone, get yourselves a drink, or whatever you want, but do it quietly and then off to bed," he whispered.

"But Daddy, my legs are still dirty," groaned Daisy.

152

"Shirley, can you give her a quick wipe with a damp cloth, but do it quietly, we don't want to disturb Mum, do we?" he said. "A quick wipe for you all will do for one night." He then kissed the little ones and gave Shirley and Brian a hug. "Thanks everyone."

"I'm going to clean my teeth Daddy. Mummy says it's important," announced Brigitte.

"Yes, I agree. Everyone clean their teeth, please," replied Joe. "Brigitte's right, Mum would want you all to brush your teeth."

CHAPTER TWENTY-FOUR:

Mona was sitting with her head bent over her desk when I arrived at the office. The place had that Monday morning lingering smell of disinfectant it always had after the weekend. I suppose that was appropriate for me today, as I needed to disinfect my thoughts towards my step-dad.

"Just be thankful you've your own lovely dad to make up for Alexander Sugar," I muttered to myself, as I walked through the foyer to my office.

Mona looked up and smiled. It was forced, I could tell... let's hope I could tell; it is my profession after all! "What's up doc?" I asked flippantly.

"Everything," she groaned.

That wasn't the answer I wanted to hear, especially not on a Monday morning. "What's happened, for goodness sake woman, spit it out?" I said, biting my tongue as the words left my mouth. Where's your humanity, I asked myself?

"I'm lonely," she replied.

"Lonely?" I repeated. "How?"

"How?" she replied, "Because I don't have anyone, that's how. The weekends are the worst of all. You go home to James and the kids; everyone else goes home to their families. Dawn, I'm a single woman of forty-three... do you know what that means?"

I was forced to answer "No," to her question... I felt... impotent.

"Well, I do, it means I'm lonely," she replied.

I realised this was serious, as Mona never brought her private woes to work. In fact, I'd never heard her speak this way before now... my mind was racing, as I heard myself begin to speak... "Next weekend, why don't you stay with us? I think you'll fit in a treat Mona. I can visualise you there as we speak," I lied.

"Can you, Dawn? Why that's wonderful... you've cheered me up no end, and given me something to look forward to," she gushed.

I was shocked... she had actually agreed! How had that happened? Why had I issued that invitation? I hadn't even consulted my diary or, more importantly, my husband. Oh Christ, Mona at my house… staying over… sleeping in one of my beds, and using my… facilities!

I dumped myself on a chair, whilst offering her a forced smile. She rose from hers, came across the room, and gave me a hug. I could feel her sincerity, which moved me… in opposite directions, at the same time.

*

"You told her what!" exclaimed James.

"I told her that she could stay this weekend with us. She's desperate and lonely, James, where's your heart?" I explained.

"I'm all heart, Dawn, but my weekends are my weekends to spend with my wife and children," he snapped back.

I couldn't think of an appropriate answer, and knew damned fine I was out of order, but this was Mona we were discussing. We sat in silence for a long time, and it was becoming ever more painful… "Well?" he eventually asked.

"Well, what?" I answered.

"Dawn, stop it. You've got us into this mess, so it's up to you to get us out of it," he replied. "Don't imagine I'll feel bad about this, because I won't."

"I always thought you were someone with whom I could depend upon to support me," I offered.

"How dare you say something like that to me," he responded. His anger was upping the temperature in the room, whilst his mouth had gone into a certain set position I'd rarely seen throughout our nineteen year marriage. It was not a pretty sight and it reminded me of a firmly drawn drawbridge...

I rose to re-fill his glass, but he covered the rim with his hand. This was a first, and this action made it serious. "Stop being petty," I said. I was becoming angry... talk about taking things too seriously... what a way for him to react, "I'm sure Mona will be very useful," I added.

"What exactly are you thinking of having her do?" he managed to utter.

"I didn't mean anything in particular, just little things, like passing the salt or peeling the fruit or veg, and she'll probably bring us flowers," I replied.

"Aw Gawd... you take the cream cracker for that last remark. Flowers? Look at the damage you managed to do with a bunch of flowers," said James. "The time has come for you to become one of your own patients... physician, heal thyself."

"That's a damn silly thing to say. I don't think there's anything wrong with me," I huffed.

"You never do, that's the problem," he huffed back.

"Do you mind explaining that last remark?" I asked. "This is something new I'm hearing from you."

"It means exactly what I said, take it on-board and get off your blooming high horse," he snapped.

"Get off your own blooming high horse, you've been on it for long enough," I replied. I didn't understand why I'd said that to him. In fact, I'd no idea why I was saying any of the things I was saying to him?

I left the room in an almighty huff and headed for the bathroom. Once inside, I ran a bath and stood looking into the rising steam. If I stripped and entered the bath, there would be no going back to James that night. I would head straight for bed, and he wouldn't join me, but would sleep through in the spare room. Everything in our happy home would lapse into turmoil. Thank goodness, Sean and Lorraine were out, and Angela was staying over with her best friend. Oh, what a darned mess! This ought to have been a happy, romantic night, just my beloved and me, instead, he'd turned into a monster by not wishing to welcome my dear Mona into our family midst.

I stripped off, soaked, or rather stewed in my bath for a while, and then went straight to bed with my current book in tow. Joe momentarily floated into my mind, and I remembered how caring he'd been towards his little sisters… he would've welcomed Mona into his house, particularly in her hour of desperate need… of that I had no doubts.

*

James sat and watched TV, as he waited for his two older children to arrive home. "Where's Mum?" asked Lorraine, when she popped her head into the lounge.

"Early night," he replied.

"Are you sure, Dad," she asked, "you two haven't fallen out, have you?"

"Don't be so silly… it's just that your mum found her patients extra difficult today," he lied. He hated doing that… he should have told her the truth, and brought the Mona situation out into the open in the late evening air.

"I don't know why Mum does that job of hers? Grandad Sugar had a point. I wish she'd get herself back into mainstream medicine too," she replied.

"Your mum chose to specialise in her field, Lorraine," he said. "You wouldn't like anyone telling you what you could or couldn't do, would you?"

"That happens to me every day… think about it, Dad." she quipped.

"I meant when you'd grown up," he clarified, but when he looked at his sixteen-year-old daughter, she looked pretty grown up to him, especially as she'd dolled herself up to go out with her boyfriend.

"Do you want toast and cocoa, Dad?" she asked, changing the subject.

"Yes, thanks," he replied, "Lorraine, if it means anything, I already think of you as my grown up daughter."

"Thanks for that. It opens many possibilities for me, and means you'll accept what I want to do with my future," she answered.

That was not exactly what he'd meant, and he might live to regret his words. At that moment, Sean arrived home and dived straight into the kitchen. After five minutes, he looked into the lounge and tried to say good night with his mouth full. They knew what he meant and waved him on his way.

"Lorraine, Mum and I did have a falling out of sorts this evening," confessed James. "I'm sorry for not telling you the truth earlier."

"Its fine, Dad, I knew the truth anyway, I'm your daughter after all," she replied.

James wasn't sure what she'd meant by that, but was pleased with her response. "She's invited Mona to stay with us this coming weekend," he continued.

"Who's Mona," asked Lorraine, "not Mona, her secretary, surely not?"

"Oh yes, the very same," he replied.

"Whatever for, Dad? She's, well, she's a bit of a frump as far as I remember, although I haven't seen her for a while," she stated. "Maybe she's had a makeover?"

"No, the last time I saw her she hadn't," he replied.

"Why for the whole weekend, and not just for a meal or a coffee?" she asked.

"She told your mum she's lonely and in need of company, that's why," he replied.

*

The next morning, I was having breakfast when James joined me… "Morning, darling," he said, "I'm going to phone around and arrange for a new super mattress for the spare room bed, and try to have it delivered before Friday. I don't want Mona to be uncomfortable."

This statement made me look up for the first time since he arrived in the room. "Does that mean what I think it does?" I asked.

He nodded, grabbed some cereal, and sat beside me. He moved his chair close, so I could feel his arm touching mine…

"What's happened to change your mind?" I asked, turning and planting a kiss on his cheek.

"Lorraine pointed out the error of my ways. She's grown up Dawn, and we each have to remember that when dealing with her in future," he replied.

"I've known she's been grown up for ages," I said. "Was the new mattress her idea?"

"No, I managed that all by myself," he replied.

"Thanks James, and sorry for the way I treated you last night. But if I hadn't, we wouldn't have found out how bad the mattress in the spare bed was, now would we?" I said. I then cuddled up beside him, sorry to have put him through such a rotten night.

Still, he had identified the need for and taken on the task of researching and acquiring a new mattress. It had therefore been a worthwhile exercise.

CHAPTER TWENTY-FIVE:

Back in *Cloverley*, Val rose to see Joe off to work... however he just asked how she was feeling? Neither mentioned the previous evening. "Love you," he said, as he gave her a kiss.

"And I love you," she answered; very much indeed, she thought, as she stood by the door and waved as he drove off. Whilst each were now wearing happy smiles, Val realised that he had to be kept happy at all costs, and it was her job to make sure it happened.

She had a little time before she needed to get the kids up, so she sat on the doorstep to take in the fresh morning air. She wouldn't allow anyone to find out how she truly felt, especially Joe. Yesterday's wobble wouldn't happen again; this cross was hers to bear and hers alone...

After a while, she rose and went back into the house. The quietness soothed her, but was spoiled by the thought that it wouldn't stay that way for long. Their noise was so difficult for her to take... their endless questions and their continuous childish bickering.

She couldn't tell her doctor as it was sure to leak into this close knit community. Here, people were small-minded and fed voraciously on the miseries of others. Her thoughts returned to years ago when she had suddenly and unexpectedly arrived home from university... firstly, the gossip had centred on the possibility she was pregnant, but when nothing came of that, the focus changed to the state of her mental health. The black cloud of depression was quickly seized upon, discussed and dissected at length, or at least she imagined that to be the case.

However, despite repeated reassurances from her parents, that their neighbours and friends only wished her well, it was something she hadn't been able to accept. In retrospect, that thought hadn't been at all fair, as these folks were also kind and generous. It was her mind that had distorted and darkened.

She could always confide in her parents once more, as they knew first-hand how she'd been previously... when she'd walked away from her university law course and come back home to hide. They hadn't got mad with her, instead they had eased her back into a better place with love and understanding. Alas, Mum was now on her own, and with no dad to share the burden, she decided to conceal any tell-tale signs from her.

The house began to stir... and she could hear the different noises it made, just little tweaks of movement, and then it came rushing towards her, the sounds of them rising to face a new day.

*

"Strip that down and do that again, Pete lad," Joe instructed one of his workers.

"Why? Nobody will ever fuckin' know," he replied.

"You and I will both know," stressed Joe.

"Boss, you know it doesn't matter... it'll do the fuckin' job well enough," he replied.

"Listen here you... I'm not standing here, wasting my fuckin' time telling you the bloody score. Just because you've been out drinking to the point of no return, don't think I'm bloody impressed. Either do the damn thing over and properly, or pick up your jotters! I don't give a tinker's curse how sore your head is, just do the job you're paid or clear out," snapped Joe, as he walked away.

Pete watched him go, and realised he had meant what he'd said. He couldn't remember ever hearing him swear until this morning, and knew he was right. He was part of his top-team and there were many who would've loved to have such a position, and a man like Joe as their boss. With him it wasn't solely about the money, it was his reputation to deliver first-class workmanship and service that mattered. Christ, he thought, I've let him down big time, and by swearing in front of him too. There was a Company rule, to respect others by not swearing... Pete resolved not to let his work suffer again... and there would be no more drinking sprees during the week for him.

*

Joe thumped the heels of his hands on the desk in his makeshift office. He hated when one of his employees let him down badly, and Pete was now hanging on to his job by his fingertips. Worse than that, he had lowered himself and spoken words he'd been no stranger to in the past. However, he'd only endured listening to such language in order to learn and progress in his trade. He would have to keep an eye on Pete, as customers didn't want to hear that kind of language, particularly in their own homes...

Their homes... that made him think of his home. What had been wrong with Val last night? She would surely tell him if it was anything serious, or would she? Val was not like his sisters, who phoned regularly with details of their latest family news. Indeed, Nicolette had phoned him just the other day, to say she'd bought new pots and pans of all things! He couldn't imagine Val ever phoning Silvia with such trivia, as she liked to keep things close to her chest.

Last night he'd sent the kids to bed unwashed, and if Val ever learned of that, she would be horrified and there would be hell to pay.

He then remembered back to his boyhood days... when washing wasn't considered such a priority, which was one of the main reasons he'd liked his secret place... that special spot beside the river. Over the years, he'd taken it upon himself to instil a sense of hygiene into his little girlies, and recalled how clean he used to feel himself after bathing in the river's icy waters. He'd taken Dawn there, and she'd joined him in the river… together, they'd drank the water of life…

*

Joe went to find his lieutenant Steve, and asked him to take over for a while. He then jumped into his van, drove off in the direction of the river, and on arrival, searched for the footpath… not any path, but his special path. When he came upon it, he saw that the long grasses showed freshly trodden signs … someone had walked this way… could it have been her?

When he arrived at the riverbank, he somehow sensed she had recently been there and wondered if she had also dipped in their river? The waterfall confirmed he was right. Joe quickly striped off his overalls and jumped into one of the deeper pools, splashing and ducking his head under its icy waters. Once back on the banking, he looked for his secret cup… it was still there, but he didn't fancy drinking from it after twenty-eight years of it having survived the elements. Instead, he cupped his hands and drank straight from the waterfall. Why hadn't he come here before? For the same reason he would probably never return. But that wouldn't spoil this moment as he lay in the warm morning sunshine to dry, and drifted off to sleep…

*

She looked so pretty in her pink shorts and white top with delicately embroidered pink flowers. He looked

167

down at her tiny sandals and then up at her unruly dark curls, which framed the face he loved...

"Come on Joe, I'll race you across and back," she yelled, already on her way.

"Come back, that's not fair," he called, as he splashed after her.

He loved her cheeky ways; she was his girl... she was one who would tackle anything. She was laughing so much, that he soon caught up and was about to pass her, when she caught hold of his shirt... and they ended up tumbling into the water's bosom together, choking on their laughter...

That was the Dawn he remembered... that was his Dawn.

Joe awoke with a start... at first disappointed, but then remembered Val and his children whom he loved so much. His jeans were still damp, but his overalls had dried, so he changed into them and left.

*

The house fell quiet once more after Brian, Shirley, and Brigitte had left for school, leaving Val and Daisy in peace once more. She loved this time when there was just the two of them, as Daisy was a sweet placid child who only brought her pleasure. "Let's walk over and visit Grandma; you'd like that wouldn't you? It's a lovely day," suggested Val.

168

"Yeah," replied an excited Daisy, jumping up and down on the spot.

It wasn't far, and Val would enjoy the walk with her fingers entwined with Daisy's. Her spirits rose and then plummeted, when she remembered that this situation could not last. Daisy would soon be off to school and most likely change into a loud boisterous child, much like her siblings. Brian at times, showed a quiet sentimental side, and Brigitte could still demonstrate moments of sweetness. However, Shirley had turned into a prepubescent know-it-all, not unlike her Auntie Silvia, although not nearly half as bad.

Grandma Jean welcomed them warmly and was soon busying in the kitchen with Daisy's help. A little later, Daisy could be found preoccupied, examining Grandma's assortment of ornaments. Jean looked over to check on her, then lowering her voice, and asked Val a certain question. She was at a loss as what to do, confess or cover-up?

"Val, don't keep it to yourself, tell me and it will begin to get better," she suggested.

Val checked on Daisy, and found her still absorbed with Jean's trinkets, "Mum, I do need help," she whispered, "I fear it's… come back."

"I thought it perhaps had… I can always tell, it's intuitive," she replied. "Come through into the bedroom where we can talk privately," she whispered. "Daisy will be fine on her own for five minutes."

They went into Jean's bedroom and pushed the door until it was almost closed, "Do you know what's brought it back?" asked Jean. "Are you and Joe… fine?"

"Yes, but——," replied Val.

"Val, I may be an older woman, but I still have feelings. I may be well off the mark here, but was it Dawn's visit that's suddenly set this off again?" she asked. "The past often lives as bright in our memory as the day it happened, or at least that's what we tend to think. In reality, it's often laced with a rose coloured glow."

"Mum, it might have been. I was at the Fair all these years ago when my husband and Dawn declared undying love for each other. I know they were only twelve at the time, but it still hurts," she confessed. "I don't know if you remember, but I told you I loved him then, and you're the only person I've ever told."

Jean remembered having mentioned this to Dawn and felt disloyal. She hated to be weighed down with guilt about anything and felt the need to confess, "Val, I mentioned to Dawn that you'd always loved Joe, even way back then," she disclosed.

"Why did you do that?" exclaimed Val.

"No particular reason, it just came out naturally in normal conversation," she replied.

"And what was her reaction?" asked Val.

"Surprise, that's all, just surprise," replied Jean. "Val, Dawn's a grown woman with a husband and three children of her own; she's not the little girl you remember."

Despite what her mum said, Val still felt betrayed, betrayed by her own flesh and blood, her last bastion of support.

At that moment, Daisy came running into the bedroom and climbed up onto the bed. "You've lots of bedrooms, Grandma. Could I stay here with you sometimes?" she announced.

"I've not that many, but there's enough room for my little daisy flower anytime," replied her grandma.

"Can I stay now? Daddy could bring my pyjamas. I'll need a bath though, as I didn't get washed properly last night... Shirley just wiped the mud from my legs," she disclosed... then looked at them both with a toothless smile, waiting for a reply.

"If it's all right with Mummy, I'd love you to stay, and I'll make sure you get a proper bath too. Grandma knows how to look after her little daisy," replied Jean.

And I don't, thought Val, the tears welling up inside of her? Daisy and her mum looked the perfect picture of happiness, sat together and making plans that seemingly excluded her.

"She can stay, Val, and that'll give you a little peace and quiet," agreed Jean.

"Grandma, Mummy had peace and quiet last night. Daddy looked after us. He collected us from Charlene and Charlie's. We were late 'cause he was talking to their mum," said Daisy. "We also had to keep quiet when we got home as Mummy was sleeping."

"Well, that explains why you didn't have time to get properly washed," said Grandma.

"Not to me it doesn't. Joe ought not to be spending time gossiping to Brenda Warner and neglecting his children," snapped Val.

"It's hardly neglect, Val. They'd just be catching up on things," replied Jean.

"Yes, they probably would and without me," added Val. "Daisy, you can stay over with Grandma; Daddy will bring over your pyjamas later along with Teddy Fred."

"Are you sure love, maybe I shouldn't have suggested it?" queried Jean.

"No, Mum, it's all fixed, Daisy can stay," she replied, as she rose to leave. "I'll get off to my peace and quiet now… have fun you two."

She then left after a quick kiss to both, and had only walked a short distance when her tears began to flow again.

*

Joe began work earlier each day so he could finish sooner and spend more time with his family. That was the way he liked to organise his schedule. That evening, when he arrived home, he headed directly for the kitchen... "Where's my little pumpkin pie?" he asked Val.

Pumpkin could usually be found waiting to meet him as soon as he came through the front door. "She's over at Mum's. She wanted to stay overnight, so I told her you'd fetch her pyjamas later," replied Val.

"That's our baby... she's practically all grown-up now," sighed Joe, with a smile. She looked at him in horror. "What? What did I say that was so wrong? It was only a throwaway remark," he protested. However, she started to cry, so he rushed to take her in his arms, "What's wrong, darling," he asked, "tell me please, I can fix anything for you?"

"You can't fix this, Joe," she sobbed. "Go and take Daisy's pyjamas over and ask Mum... she'll manage to explain things much better than me."

"I can't leave you like this," he protested once more.

"Of course you can. See, I'm much better already," she sniffed. "Joe, I'd prefer to have a little time on my own... please."

"If you're sure?" he replied, somewhat taken aback. "Do you want me to make you a coffee or a cup of tea first?"

"No, off you go, I'm fine. Mum's bound to have a slice cake for you, you know what she's like?" she answered.

Joe left to collect Daisy's pyjamas and toothbrush from her bedroom, and wondered what else she might need? "Val, what else will Daisy need, I have her P.J's and toothbrush?" he called to her.

Val arrived in Daisy's room, seemingly recovered, and pecked him on the cheek. "Underwear, socks, Teddy Fred, and a clean dress for tomorrow. That ought to do it, and don't forget to tell her I love her very much, from me," she replied.

"Good thinking to include Teddy Fred," said Joe, "I wouldn't have thought of that, and I'd probably would have missed out one or two of the other things too. You're a champ, Val... my champ."

"Hardly, Joe, that was child's play," she replied, then quickly turned away so he couldn't read what she'd meant by that remark.

"Val, why can't you accept a compliment when it's given, and stop being so humble? You're a very special lady, only you refuse to believe in yourself," he said. He now had a desperate need to get to his mother-in-law's so that she might shed light on Val's peculiar behaviour. It was fast becoming too much for him to handle on his own.

*

"Daddy! Daddy! Here's my daddy, Grandma," shouted Daisy. "I can see his car coming."

"Let me take a look, Daisy... Oh, yes, that's his car," agreed Jean.

"Grandma, I'll hide behind the couch and surprise him," she suggested excitedly.

"If you want to darling, but you'll have to keep very quiet," replied Jean.

"I'm good at that... Brigitte showed me how," she answered.

"Nice one, Brigitte," replied Jean, with a smile.

Joe came straight in through the unlocked door and gave Jean a hug, "Behind the couch," she whispered, giving him a knowing nudge.

"I happened to be passing, so I decided to visit my favourite mother-in-law," said Joe, loudly.

"Oh, that was nice of you. I've a lovely piece of cake waiting through in the kitchen," replied Jean. "I was hoping someone would visit, so they could share it with me. We can have half each."

"That's a great idea, I'm so glad none of my greedy children are here," he answered loudly once more.

"Did you hear that noise, Joe... it sounded like a... puppy?" enquired Jean.

"A puppy? Come to think of it, I did hear something… yes! I think it's coming from over… there," he replied.

Something that sounded like giggling, grew louder and louder, until it sounded more like a snorting piglet…

"My, my, it must be a big doggie," exclaimed Jean, "what a strange noise!"

"It's not a big doggie… it's me," yelled Daisy, "it's Daisy, Daddy!"

"What are you doing here, Daisy? You don't need to answer pumpkin, I know why, and here are your things," said Joe, picking her up and swinging her through the air.

Daisy then peered into the bag he had brought… "Grandma, Daddy's brought Teddy Fred," she gushed. "Thanks, Daddy."

"It's thanks to Mummy for Teddy Fred," he answered, catching Jean's eye.

"Let's take the bag and put it in your room, then we'll cut you a big slice of cake while I make Daddy a hot drink," suggested Jean. "Do you want to watch television, Daisy, it's almost time for one of your favourite programs?"

"Yes, thanks Grandma," she answered. "I'm also going to have a bath here tonight, Daddy."

"That's lovely pumpkin," replied Joe.

"Joe, Daisy was telling us this morning that there hadn't been time for a proper wash last night," said Jean, "which, I can tell you, didn't impress Val, as you can well imagine."

"Shirley did wash my legs," chipped in Daisy, pointing to her knees

Joe smiled at her, she was so cute, was his little Daisy. She then went off to collect her slice of cake and to watch TV. Joe slipped into the conservatory, followed by Jean with a tray of tea and cake...

"Jean, Val said to ask you to explain what's wrong with her? I know there's something going on, but I'm finding things too difficult to deal with by myself," he said.

"Oh, Joe, where do I start?" she replied, with a sigh.

"At the beginning," he stated.

Jean did her best to explain Val's condition and how she had suffered in the past, whilst Joe listened intently. When she'd finished, he added, "She never offered me any reason for her giving up university, so I never pressed her. I didn't wish to intrude as we both wanted to start from where we were, and not from where we'd been. When we got together, our relationship began from that moment. Val never asked what had happened during the years I was away from *Cloverley* either, although she could piece together quite a bit now."

"I hear what you're saying about not looking back, but can I ask you something that's come into my mind recently?" asked Jean. "Did you come back to *Cloverley* in the hope that Dawn would be here, or at least to find out if the Pearson's still owned their Weekender?"

He looked at her and then out into her garden… what could he say to her? How could he put it? "Yes, I did. A little part of me hoped that through all the years, somehow or other we would meet up again once more… as two grown up people," he answered, "but it wasn't to be. I got to know Val, and as they say, the rest is now history."

"The thought of Dawn being back here may be a factor in making her depression re-occur," suggested Jean.

"I love Val, you know that Jean, but it's so hard to make her accept that, and to get her to believe in herself," he replied.

"I understand completely. My Silvia's far too over-confident, whilst Val lacks self-belief," agreed Jean.

She then asked him to try to understand how Val might have regressed due to some deep-seated fears over Dawn, and he said he would. He was desperate to help her, and yet just that morning, he'd relived his brief time with Dawn down by the river. His clothes still lay damp in the laundry-room at home… guilt was taking a huge bite, but sweet memories were also being tasted!

CHAPTER TWENTY-SIX:

I arrived home on Friday afternoon with my weekend guest in tow. Mona had been giving off an air of sweet contentment all day at the office, which was not her usual Friday demeanour. "Let's go straight into the house Mona; James or Sean will collect your luggage from the car," I suggested. Luggage it was indeed! We had struggled to get it all into my not very generous car boot back at the office.

"Yes, that's okay... what a beautiful house you have... oh, it's just wonderful!" she exclaimed.

"Mona, stop going on... it's only a house for heaven's sake. If it hadn't been wonderful, we wouldn't have bought the damned place," I replied. My day had been hard, and I now needed time to relax. I suppose that was why my use of language had dipped below par?

"Dawn, please don't use such expletives when talking to me, I'm not used to them," Mona announced.

"Bloody hell, give me a break," I muttered, as I led the way indoors to find James, seated in the lounge. He'd deliberately arrived home early to greet Mona, having taken advice from his elder daughter. "James, this is Mona," I said, "Mona, this is James… my husband."

"Dawn, there's no need for such formal introductions, I've met James many times at the office, and I've also met your children," she replied.

Nice one Dawn, I thought, get a grip, it's only Mona, so don't let it rock your boat too much. "Of course you have, what an idiot I am," I agreed.

"I'll second that," piped up Angela, having newly arrived in the room. "Hi, Mona, I don't know why you want to visit for the whole weekend, but, if that's what you're into, then good luck."

"Hello to you too, Angela. You've grown so much taller," replied Mona, "you're almost fully grown."

"Fully grown? Where did you get that notion from?" I asked.

"It's common knowledge, Dawn. I'm surprised it somehow bypassed you," she answered. "You've probably been too busy with other things to notice."

"Good answer, Mona," agreed Angela. "I've always thought of you as a right gormless geek, but you're really okay. Way to go, Mona!"

Mona smiled smugly, seemly choosing to ignore the 'gormless geek' remark, and sat next to James. He smiled at her with interest, and I could tell he was wondering how we ever managed to spend our working days together?

James continued to utter pleasantries in Mona's direction, so I decided that this was the opportune moment to broach the subject of her generous luggage... "James, my darling, will you nip out to my car and bring in Mona's luggage, please?" I asked.

"Luggage?" he replied, with a questioning expression.

"Yes, James dear, her luggage," I reiterated.

He pulled a face and left the room. A little later, he returned looking somewhat red-faced and stunned... "Mona, how long exactly are you here for?" he asked.

"Two nights, if that's all right with you, James? I don't want to put any of you out. That was not my wish when I accepted Dawn's kind offer," she replied. "I can call a taxi now, if you wish?"

I remained silent, waiting pensively to see how this would develop, as I wasn't sure how James was going to get out of this.

"No, no, Mona... of course you're welcome to stay for two nights, in fact stay longer... stay as long as you want," he flustered.

James, stop for goodness sake, I wanted to scream, and if I'd still been our Angela's age, I probably would have. But life, and most likely my profession had taught me to consider carefully the consequences before exploding feelings onto the world.

*

Lorraine and Sean arrived home after attending their post-school activities... I wasn't sure exactly what activities these were? "Look who we have here," I announced.

"Mum, we can see it's Mona," answered Lorraine. "Hi, Mona, how are you? I haven't seen you for ages."

"Fine dear, what a lovely daughter you have, James," she purred.

She's also mine, I was bursting to say.

"And look at this young man, he looks taller than you, James," she continued.

I knew for a fact, Sean was two inches smaller than his father... I must remember to make a note to send Mona for an eye test!

"It must be the weight of carrying Mona's luggage, that's taken a good few inches off your stature, James. You were taller than Sean this morning," I tried to joke. "I wouldn't want to lug that lot again, as we had a devil of a job humping it into the boot of my car earlier."

All eyes were suddenly on me, although I didn't think I'd said anything out of turn.

"He may have sprouted up during school today, Mum," suggested our Angela, who had re-joined us. "You didn't allow for that, did you?"

I felt I was now being picked upon by my nearest and dearest, but at least up until now James hadn't joined in with them. Then it came... "Mona's right, I probably look smaller because I don't stand up properly. I must remember to consider my posture in future," he announced.

"I like you the way you are," I replied. All eyes fell upon me once more. "Well, I do... and James, you needn't think about your posture as far as I'm concerned," I hastily added.

"Mum," replied Lorraine, "that's a stupid thing to say. Dad should always consider his posture, as should you."

If looks could kill, my daughter would be no more. Whilst our Angela at least was a child, and perhaps could be forgiven for her outspokenness, Madame Lorraine, on the other hand, was no longer a child in my books, and ought to know better!

I announced I was off to make a start on preparations for the evening meal, and headed for the kitchen. On the way, I admitted to myself that I was not enjoying Mona's visit, not one little iota... my God, and she'd only just arrived! Mona on the other hand, looked so smug and content, and to make matters worse, there was just the outside chance of her taking up James's offer of what sounded like permanent residence!

Having no memory of ever having been like this before today, I concluded that I was suffering a physical sense of inner distress. Suddenly, I linked this painful sensation with my recent trip to *Cloverley*, and my reliving of past times. Could I perhaps be going through an early menopause? "Surely not," I said aloud, addressing the contents of my fridge.

"Surely not, what?" asked James, who'd followed me into the kitchen.

"Yes, surely not what?" added Lorraine, who had followed her dad.

"I could lie," I said, "but instead, I'll tell the truth. What you heard me saying was that, I'm surely not going through an early menopause."

In that brief moment, it dawned on me that James and Lorraine had torn themselves away from Mona, choosing my company instead. I stood momentarily happy as I waited for their response. "You might well be love, but don't worry, I'll still love you," said James.

"And so will I," added Lorraine.

I looked at their faces, and saw their sincerity. These were not, however, the answers I'd wished to hear.

For goodness sake, they most certainly were not! James was meant to say, "Oh, no, not you my love," and Lorraine, "Mum, you're far too young for that sort of thing."

My James however, came and put his arms around me. He could see I was upset, as could Lorraine, who reached out for my hand.

"Mona's intruding," I bleated. "I don't feel comfortable with her in the house, especially not when you both think I'm menopausal."

"Dawn, we didn't say you were menopausal, we both just thought it might be a slight possibility," replied James, as he raised my drooping head to kiss me.

"Mum," added Lorraine, "we understand that you work with Mona every day and we don't. But the fact is that you're seeing her out of context, and we now realise how difficult that may be. What she's doing is invading your personal space."

"Yes," agreed James, "and we realise this house is your sacred sanctuary from life outside. Perhaps your reaction also shows that your job is becoming too demanding and distressing? You have such a heavy load to bear with many of your patients."

I sprang from his arms… "I can cope, I can cope," I cried out.

James put his finger to his lips, and Lorraine instinctively shouldered the kitchen door closed.

"What we'll do is dine out tonight and tomorrow night... the whole family, plus Mona. Then you can relax and unwind the same as the rest of us," announced James. "Lorraine, you take Mum back through and see to coffee and nibbles, while I book us into *Chez Jules* for the early sitting tonight."

"Come on, Mum, let's go," said Lorraine. "We can't leave Mona alone with our Angela. You never know what she'll say to her, especially as Sean will have escaped upstairs by now."

I thanked them both... James with a tender kiss and Lorraine, by slipping my arm through hers and pulling her tightly towards me. I now felt heaps better and any lingering thoughts of the menopause were retreating fast.

*

The meal was progressing nicely at *Chez Jules.* We were frequent patrons, it being one of our favourite restaurants, and because of this, the owner lavished extra attention on us. I could tell Mona felt rather special.

"This is simply lovely, Dawn," she said. "Let me thank you once again."

"Our pleasure, Mona," I replied, and for once, I meant it.

This evening was turning out to be an amusing affair, and thoughts of an early menopause had now well and truly left me. I knew Mona wasn't a drinker of wine before tonight, but that was changing fast, as my naughty husband recharged her glass at every opportunity. As a consequence, her tongue became looser and looser with every additional sip... suddenly, she unzipped all her inhibitions and began to tell Lorraine about a boy she'd once been in love with when her age. Lorraine sat enthralled by this revelation, as did Sean, and I noticed that even our Angela was cocking an ear in Mona's direction...

James was chattering on to me about cars... "Sh... let me hear what Mona's saying," I whispered.

"You surely don't want to listen to that old mush?" he whispered back.

"Yes, I most certainly do," I whispered, "actually, I'm fascinated."

James tossed his head backwards in disbelief.

Words tumbled faster and faster from Mona's lips, as she told a tale of a boy and a girl who'd met, loved, and parted. The boy, whose name was Daniel, had sworn eternal love for his Ramona... blah, blah, blah...

James nudged me... "Ramona, now that's what you'd call a good old-fashioned name," he whispered, a trifle loud. "Ramona, I hear the—,"

"No, James, no renditions please, not even one chorus," I hissed straight into his ear.

"Dad, don't be so rude, we all want to hear about Ramona and Daniel, even if you don't," chided Lorraine.

187

"That's you told," I said, as I nudged him in the back, big time.

"Will you two stop showing us up," scolded Angela. "Mona, let me apologise for my mum and dad, they can act childishly at times."

"It's fine, Angela dear, remember I work with her, and see her every day," she replied.

At this point, James excused himself and headed for the gents, to have a good old fashioned belly laugh... amongst other things. I would have gone to the ladies to do the same, but was finding Mona's tale far too enthralling, so crossed my legs and sat tight!

"What happened after you parted?" asked Lorraine, who was in the first throes of a romance herself with a boy from Sean's year at school.

"He found himself someone new," sighed Mona, with a glazed, faraway look in her eyes.

"And what about you, Mona... what happened to you?" asked our Angela, being as forward as ever.

"I carried on loving him, of course," she replied, with a shrug of her shoulders.

"What do you mean by that?" pressed Angela.

"Just what I said, Angela dear; I carried on loving him. In fact, I still love him to this very day, and expect I always will love him," she replied, with tears threatening to break loose at any second.

My God, I thought, I don't believe I'm hearing this! It could be straight from a Bronte novel or some Victorian tale of a young maiden who'd died from a broken heart due to unrequited love. I realised I was perhaps over dramatising, as Mona was still with us. This woman, who'd shared my office and worked shoulder to shoulder with me for, let me see, coming up for almost ten years, had never uttered one single word about her dear Daniel. In fairness, I realised that during that same period, I hadn't mentioned Joe to her either. However, I quickly justified to myself that the reason for this, was because I was her employer!

*

When I awoke the following morning, I was surprised to find James had prised himself out of bed without disturbing me. I stretched and grinned. He hadn't been gone long as his side was still lovely and warm, so I nestled in and thought about my baby girl... Angela was a chip of my old block. She was a sleuth in the making, and had interrogated Mona in style last night. The girl was frighteningly akin to me when I'd been a child... so much so, that I rose from my comfy bed to escape her.

There was only one seat left at the kitchen table when I arrived downstairs. I had hurriedly washed, combed my hair, and slipped into a smart lounging outfit, remembering we had a house guest. As it transpired, I needn't have bothered, as everyone else was dressed in their PJ's except for Mona, who sat resplendent in her floor length, outsized, candlewick dressing gown...

"Oh, Dawn, James is indeed a lucky man to start his days with a glimpse of you," groaned Mona.

"I agree, I am a lucky man, a very lucky one indeed," he replied, greeting my eyes with his.

"Mum, where have I seen something like Mona's dressing gown before?" asked Angela.

It came to me at once, and I knew exactly to what she was referring... "Think about last weekend," I replied, giving her a look with my eyes.

"Last weekend, where were we last weekend?" asked a puzzled Angela.

"Remember, we were dragged over to visit Grandma Madge and Grandad Alexander's pad?" answered Sean.

"You've changed your tune, Sean. You were up for it then. Have you forgotten that you were allowed to drive?" asked James.

"Oh, sorry Dad, I forgot. Thanks for that, I appreciate it very much," he replied.

"And so you should... so you should," said James.

I noted James was beginning to talk in the same way as his father... spare me never to talk like my mother...

"Mum, you've never answered my question," said Angela.

"Sean, told you... at Grandma Madge's," I replied, with a nod of my head to reinforce my reply, and in the hope of jogging her memory. Angela kept on looking at me, with that familiar frown she often applied. "On their bed, their... candlewick cover," I whispered.

"Oh yeah, that old thing," replied Angela, "why don't you buy her a new one?"

"She doesn't want a new one. My mother's happy with the one she's got," I answered.

"They've had it on their bed for as long as I've known them," said James, "so that must be at least twenty years."

I looked at Mona. She wasn't reacting, so I wouldn't either... for the moment anyway.

The doorbell suddenly rang and Angela rushed to answer. "James, please go after her," I asked, "I don't want her answering the door in her PJ's."

"Why don't you go Dawn, you're the only one here who's dressed half-decent," he replied.

As I scurried after Angela, I noticed Mona check herself for decency. I returned a short time later, with my arms full of flowers, which I must admit, looked a rather tasteful bunch. I glanced at James, before I read the card...

"They'll be from, Mona, I guess," he said.

"Yes, you're right, they are from, Mona," I replied, relieved to see her name on the card. My husband and his remarks!

"They look expensive," commented Angela, "how much does Mum pay you each week, Mona?

"Not enough," I answered, giving Mona a hug and a big thank you!

CHAPTER TWENTY-SEVEN:

Brigitte wanted to go with her daddy to collect Daisy on Saturday morning. "That's fine Brigitte, as long as you're ready to go now," agreed Joe. She nodded and smiled, making his heart beat faster. She was only a year and a few months older than Daisy, but seemed far more grown-up. I suppose that's what school does to kids, he thought?

During the short journey, Brigitte chatted continuously, as was her norm, "I'm looking forward to Auntie Silvia's birthday party," she gushed. "Why does she not have any children, Daddy?"

"I don't know, Brigitte, maybe Mummy knows why?" he answered.

"She doesn't," she replied, "cause I've already asked her, and she told me to ask you."

"What are you going to wear to the party," asked Joe, changing the subject, "have I seen the dress you're wearing?"

"No silly, it's new… so it'll be a surprise. You've seen Daisy's though, she's wearing her turquoise one," she replied, "you know, the one with white bits around the neck and arms."

"I think I know it," replied Joe, "not sure, though." The reasoning behind Brigitte's logic eluded him… why was he silly, and why did Brigitte have a new dress, whilst Daisy didn't? He smiled and patted her head. "Right, we're here, out you get," he said, as he pulled up outside. Brigitte shot out of the car and met Daisy half way, as she came running to meet them from the house. They hugged, which pleased him, as it reminded him of Mel, Mandy, and Nicolette, and the way they always loved to hug each other.

Next, both girls came, took hold of his hands, and skipped alongside him into Grandma Jean's. She already had the tea trolley laden with juice, teacups, biscuits, and the obligatory cake. The girls ran towards her, and she stood proudly with her arms around their narrow shoulders. Joe smiled warmly as she looked up to welcome him.

The freshly baked cake looked irresistible, however Joe glanced at the grandfather clock in the corner… it wasn't yet ten o'clock, so he shouldn't, but as the cake looked delicious, he decided he would. From next Monday, he also decided to eat more sensibly. Lately he'd spotted a couple of stray greys in his black mane, and the last pair of jeans he'd bought had been a size larger than his usual.

The girls sat on the floor whispering and laughing. Daisy then took Brigitte by the hand through to her bedroom, and at that point Jean beckoned to Joe to sit beside her, "How's Val?" she asked, in a hushed voice. "Have you made any progress with her?"

"She's avoiding being alone with me, but other than that, seems fine. You'll see for yourself this afternoon," he replied.

"This afternoon?" queried Jean.

"Yes, at Silvia's birthday party," replied Joe.

"Oh, yes... I suppose I will," she agreed. "I do wish Silvia wouldn't have these birthday parties; they're out of all proportion to the occasion now she's no longer a child."

Joe then remembered what Brigitte had asked. Perhaps the two things tied together or perhaps not? He then rapidly tried to drive all thoughts of that Silvia women from his mind.

"Get stuck into the cake Joe, it's not like you to hold back," added Jean. "A man who does physical work needs extra feeding. From what I hear, Silvia's man sits on his backside for most of the day."

Joe smiled and got stuck into the cake. This afternoon, he would've liked to have body-swerved the whole affair altogether, but he wouldn't for Val's sake. He decided he would grin and bear both Silvia and Don.

*

All too soon the girls were kissing Grandma Jean goodbye, whilst he was already seated at the wheel, in readiness for their return journey. "Come on you two, you'll see Grandma again this afternoon," he called out, as they came swaying down the path towards him hand-in-hand, turning, and waving to Jean after each step. He felt so proud of them.

Dawn and her children then came into his mind… Jean had mentioned she had three… boys or girls, he wondered? He should've asked whether they were like her or her husband? He didn't know who the man was, only that his surname was Brennan. She however knew all about him and Val. What a shock that must've been for her, and he wondered just how much of a shock?

"Come on then, Daddy, let's hit the road," urged Brigitte.

Hit the road? From where did she glean that phrase? He was not inclined to ask, as Brigitte's explanation would just muddy the waters even more.

"Come on Daddy… hit the road," repeated Daisy, with a toothy smile. What else could he do, but hit the road.

*

196

Val asked Joe to collect Silvia's present from the sideboard and put it into the boot of their car. He'd looked at it all week, trying to work out what could possibly be under the fancy wrapping paper? Whatever it was, it was in a box; that was the only thing that was obvious. Val hadn't told him or any of the children what the box contained, and on moving it into the boot of the car, found it rather weighty. The mystery deepens...

Joe always thought Val indulged her elder sister far too much at birthdays and other special occasions, with overly expensive gifts. It was never reciprocated, and this annoyed him immensely. He'd asked her more times than he could remember, why she continued to do it, as in his opinion the woman didn't appreciate it? She was a taker not a giver!

This was one of the few things that regularly caused strife between them. The other was Val's lack of self-confidence. He was forever critical of her self-deprecatory nature, but nothing ever changed.

*

The Doubleday children were finally dressed, polished, and ready to go. Brian must have had a sudden growth spurt, or his newish trousers had shrunk. Apart from that, he looked very smart, or as smart as anyone could look who shared Joe's head of unruly hair. Shirley looked different, but Joe couldn't work out what it was... "Val, what's with our Shirley?" he asked.

"She's eleven," she answered.

"Right, eleven," he repeated, still none the wiser? That had been Dawn's age back then… and he slowly realised what Val had inferred. Whilst Shirley's looks mainly favoured her mum, there remained a lot of him in her.

Brigitte and Daisy next appeared waiting for his reaction. Joe looked at Daisy's dress, and couldn't remember ever having seen it before. He then looked at Brigitte's; he certainly hadn't seen hers before today. "My little princesses," he said, "Brigitte, come over here, the price ticket's still pinned to the underside of your dress. Come here, and I'll snip it off."

Val went to fetch a pair of scissors. "How much?" exclaimed Joe, as he peered at the label. "I don't believe you paid that amount for a child's dress, Val."

"Joe, stop making such a fuss, you do want her to look nice, don't you?" she replied.

"Nice dresses cost money, Dad," chipped in Shirley.

"Let me see the tag, Dad. I want to see how much it was?" asked Brian.

"Too much," shouted Joe, "and it's none of your business."

"What's wrong with my dress?" asked Brigitte, who was now crying.

"Nothing's wrong with your dress, darling, it's just Daddy making a fuss," replied Val.

"Here we go again," groaned Shirley, "for goodness sake Dad, get to grips with how much things cost in the real world."

"I beg your pardon, young lady?" he replied. "This has nothing to do with you. Now get into the car as we're running late... you too, Brian."

The two stomped out, and when Shirley turned to spout some more, she caught her dad's eye, and quickly thought better of it.

Val tried to comfort Brigitte, as Daisy looked on, unsure of what exactly was happening? "Joe, say sorry to Brigitte," she said, "and don't bring her out until you've sorted out the distress you've caused. Daisy, you come out to the car with Mummy." Daisy started to cry as she left, still unsure of what was happening?

Joe then picked up Brigitte, "Honey lamb, I'm so sorry. It's all my silly fault. I know nothing about the price of dresses," he whispered in her ear. "All I know is that it is beautiful and so are you... will you please forgive me?"

She looked at him, face to face.

"Please honey lamb... forgive Daddy; he loves you so much," he continued.

She suddenly smiled and kissed him on the nose, "Okay," she agreed. Joe put her back down, and they walked out to the car hand-in-hand.

"I'm sorry," he whispered to Val, as he climbed into the driver's seat, and she could see he meant it. "I'm sorry everyone," he added, this time aloud, and was pleased to see that Daisy had also recovered.

"And so you should be," grumbled Shirley from the rear, a remark which he chose to ignore.

*

The bunting was out on the driveway at Silvia and Don's imposing house… a Victorian villa, with large rooms, high ceilings and original features… points which she always went to great lengths to stress. Silvia could never countenance living in a new build, as in her opinion, they lacked the features she sought, and would often remind Val each time the subject came up when in each others company.

Don had already picked up both Jean and his parents. This was the way Silvia's birthdays were always organised. She liked everyone to arrive in plenty of time for the three o'clock kick-off.

Don's brother Mike and his wife Janis, made up the remainder, and had arrived under their own steam.

Val, Joe, and family were now running late. He glanced at the fuel gauge and saw they needed to fill up, so stopped off at the local petrol station. "Joe, could you not have filled up yesterday?" groaned Val. "We'll now be late, and she'll get most upset."

"For goodness sake, Val, we've got four children to get ready, 'Fanny Fruitcake' has only herself," he replied, "and I don't give a toss if we're a little late," he muttered under his breath… so that no one overheard. "And if I had my way, I wouldn't be going either," he added.

"For goodness sake, just get the tank filled and stop bickering," scolded Shirley.

"Yes, Shirley's right, let's stop it, Val. If Silvia thought we were bickering it would make her birthday for her," agreed Joe, "and we don't want to do that."

He then went to pay for the fuel and Shirley tapped on her mum's shoulder… "Mum, don't make such a fuss about Auntie Silvia. You know how rude she can be to Dad. I hate hearing what comes out of her mouth," she said. "You really ought to put her in her place, or she'll just get worse."

"I agree with Shirley," said Brian, "sock it to her."

Val didn't answer, but when Joe returned, she pecked him on the cheek and they continued on their way… harmony restored once more.

CHAPTER TWENTY-EIGHT:

Lorraine was a gem and asked Mona and me if we wished to go shopping? I knew full well that the shopping excursion would be an expensive affair as Lorraine would need plenty of cash to spend, so made my excuses by saying James and I had a prior engagement. She probably had her eye on something specific, and would no doubt guide Mona accordingly.

"What about me," asked Angela, "am I included?"

No, you most certainly are not, I thought. "Sean dear, can you take your little sister to the cinema this afternoon?" I asked, giving him a wink.

"I'll have a look to see what's on," he replied, "as 'Titch' isn't allowed to watch big boy and girl films——,"

"I can always dress up, and go as your girlfriend, then I'll get into anything," interrupted Angela. "Come upstairs and I'll show you, Sean."

She was growing up fast! She hadn't reacted to the 'Titch' comment, and had shown maturity in thinking her way around the cinema predicament. I winked at Sean, and nodded my head in approval as they left the room together.

"Dawn, should you be encouraging Angela?" asked Mona.

"With what?" I asked.

"I thought that would be obvious," she replied, "to go to those sorts of films of course?"

"It's not obvious to me Mona. For goodness sake, we all did exactly the same when her age," I replied.

Mona looked at me, as did James, and even Lorraine raised her eyebrows…

"On the other hand, perhaps not," I quickly added, "although I did, and it didn't do me any harm."

"Hmm, that's a matter of opinion," said Mona.

I turned to James for support, and my darling husband didn't let me down on this occasion… "Mona, I don't think it matters too much, children these days can see everything they want on the internet, should they choose," he replied.

"Not if a parental lock is applied," Mona quickly retaliated.

"Mona, I have considered things in my professional capacity, and concluded that it's absolutely fine for Angela to go to the cinema with her brother this afternoon," I announced. "Anyway, they usually keep all the more risqué movies until the evening."

"In that case, I stand corrected," sighed Mona, "Lorraine, what time are we going shopping dear?"

"After lunch, or if you wish, we could go out for a spot of lunch?" she suggested.

"Yes, I think I'd like that very much, but I insist lunch is on me," agreed Mona.

I mouthed the words 'thank you' to Lorraine. I was so glad our Angela was not present or she would have started on about the level of Mona's salary once more. Lorraine and Mona then trotted upstairs to ready themselves, whilst James and I sauntered through into the kitchen to begin preparations for lunch.

Suddenly, Sean and Angela came bursting into the room, "Will she do?" he asked.

"Of course, I'll do," replied Angela.

I nodded and turned to James, who looked at me, and then nodded his approval too.

"Just do me a favour, Angela, and stay upstairs until Mona and Lorraine leave," I asked. She nodded; she was smart this daughter of mine, and reminded me so much of myself at her age.

"How much do you need for spending, Sean?" I asked, offering him some folding money. "Will this be enough?"

"Yes, that should cover it just fine," he replied, and then with a smile added, "You two behave yourselves, now that you've the house to yourselves."

"We may or we may not," replied James.

*

In actuality, we spent a lovely afternoon sitting out in the garden talking over our week with each other, whilst watching our friendly neighbourhood birds at play. The shattering of our idyllic peace occurred when Sean and Angela returned from the cinema…

"The film was great, Mum… what's for tea, we're starving?" asked Angela.

"Nothing," I replied.

"What do you mean, nothing," queried Sean, "we're starving?"

"Mum means nothing, because we're going out again tonight. I'm not having her cooking while we've Mona staying with us," replied James.

"That's fine about going out for a meal, but how much longer is she going to be here? Enough is enough," groaned Angela.

"She probably feels the same way about us," replied Sean.

"No she won't, 'cause we're cool, Sean… she's just a pain in the butt," stated Angela.

"Angela, that's enough of that; now get changed please, before they come back," I scolded.

"But Mum, I'm fine as I am," she replied, smoothing down her clothes.

"Just let her stay as she is, Dawn," relented James. "We're not going to jump through hoops just to please Lady Mona."

"You're right, after all she's only the hired help," I replied, just as I saw them come out into the garden to join us. If she'd overheard, she didn't let on. I hoped she hadn't, because it wasn't meant to come out in the way it sounded.

*

That evening we were booked to eat at *Franco's*, another of our favourite haunts. It's charm was its informality, and it usually attracted a mixed clientele. As it was a 'BYOB' establishment, James and I selected a couple of nice Italian whites to take with us.

"That ought to be enough," I said, looking at Mona.

"Don't look at me, Dawn, I had enough to drink last night to do me for the rest of the month," she replied.

"A month? How can you be so precise, Mona?" I asked, with a smile.

"You know what I mean, enough is enough," she answered.

"I think I've heard that phrase already today," I replied.

Mona frowned, and I could tell she was trying to work out my meaning? Then she turned her attention to our Angela, who looked three or four years older than she had the previous evening. She stared at her and then looked at me. I pulled up my shoulders and raised my palms in the air, to communicate that what she was wearing had nothing to do with me.

"I'll go and freshen up," said Mona, departing indoors, taking her dissatisfaction with her.

"How did it go?" I asked Lorraine, once she was well out of earshot.

"To tell the truth, Mum, it was hard going. How can you work with her, she's so old-fashioned?" she replied, "I never bought anything, as every time I fancied something, she'd tell me she didn't think it suitable. I've done my best, but I don't want to do that again."

"Right," I said, "thanks for today… and I know what you mean, believe me I do."

*

That evening, James phoned for a couple of taxis to take us to the restaurant, and when we arrived, I could see from Mona's face that this was not her kind of place. I can fully understand that bare distressed wooden tables, half-melted candles stuffed into empty wine bottles, and noisy patrons, were not everyone's ideal, but we liked it, so tough!

I found myself sitting next to Mona and opposite James, which was not how it was meant to be arranged, but she was my guest, and I suppose I ought to take responsibility for her.

During the meal, I coaxed her to have a glass of white with her pasta. James then leant across the table and topped her up at every opportunity and, strangely enough, she didn't protest. I pictured James frequently leaning across the table with a bottle in his hand, when suddenly I sensed Mona's body relax. Then, in the midst of all the loud conversations, I felt the dead weight of a sleeping head drop onto my shoulder, pinning me to the spot. I closed my own eyes and let my mind stray…

There was an earthy smell in the air. Joe said it was because the farmers had been working their fields mixed with the recent rainfall…

"The flowers are as pretty as they are wild," I commented.

"You say the most strange, but lovely things," he replied.

"It sounds nicer than saying, the wild flowers are pretty," I said.

"Yes, it does," he agreed.

Joe tickled me and I slipped. He slipped too, and joined me on the bank beside our river… he then took my hand, and we stared together into the pools of dark water…

"One day we'll sit here when we're grown-ups, Dawn. You and I will be grown-ups… you and I will be grown-ups…"

"Dawn, Dawn, wake up, you've dosed off," said James, giving me a gentle nudge under the table.

"What…?" I replied, a little disorientated.

"You dropped off and were muttering to yourself," he said, "something about being grown-up?"

"Really?" I replied. I looked around and saw that Mona's head now rested on Lorraine's shoulder, "James, can we go home," I asked, "some of us appear to be… overtired?"

"Sure, but how you both could drop off with all the noise in here, I don't understand," he replied, shaking his head.

He gently wakened Mona; she pretended she hadn't been asleep as she wiped the sides of her mouth. James ordered a round of coffees and after phoned for a couple of taxis.

Once home, everyone seemed keen to get to bed, and the house was soon in darkness…

*

Early next morning, Mona announced that she needed to get home directly after breakfast. "Dawn, you know how it is? I've so much to do at home with having been away, and I have to prepare for work tomorrow," she explained.

"Right," I replied, "whatever you say. James will take you home, and Sean will help with your luggage."

"I can always call for a taxi," she suggested.

"No, you can't… just do as you're told," I replied.

She thanked us all for a lovely time, and then produced a large box of hand-made Belgian chocolates.

"These look expensive," remarked our Angela. "Mona, you never did tell me how much Mum paid you?"

"And she never will," I quickly interjected.

*

James and Sean wrestled with Mona's luggage but eventually managed to stuff it all into the boot of the car. I had offered him mine, but he insisted his was more than big enough, and I saw him glancing back at the lounge window to see if I was watching. I was not, as I'd gone upstairs to one of the bedrooms to catch a better view!

After they'd gone, I sat on the bed, and contemplated the last few days. In some ways, Mona's visit had been better than expected, and in other ways... much worse. It had shown my two elder children up in a relatively good light, and Angela to be on track to be what I thought she would be... me at her age! She would need to be watched as carefully as I had been in my pre-adulthood period.

Ramona and Daniel? Now that had been a revelation... "I will love him forever"... what a statement to make in the circumstances... what a waste of Mona's life, stuck being a dogsbody with nothing else on which to focus her love and attention. If I could get hold of Daniel whatever-his-other-name-was at this moment, I'd cheerfully string him up... but then, that would probably upset her even more.

I felt guilty over Joe. Oh, so guilty! Our circumstances had been different, but the ghost of him lingered.

*

Later that day, we all tucked into Mona's large box of hand-crafted chocolates. "She wasn't that bad," commented James, as he stuffed another into his mouth. "Her house looked a shade dingy from the outside, and although we offered to carry her luggage in, she didn't allow us over the threshold. I felt kind of sad leaving her there."

"Yeah, me too," added Sean, "how the other half live, and all that?"

211

"Do you think I should pay her more salary than I do?" I asked.

"That depends on how much you pay her now. I've no idea; it's not something we've ever discussed," answered James.

"I pay her as per the current NHS rates. I suppose I could always promote her to the next grade?" I said.

"You're working in the private sector, Dawn, you don't have to keep to NHS pay scales," suggested James.

"I'm not obliged to, but it's an unwritten rule which we, in my profession, like to keep. We're all doctors after all, public or private, and work often entails a bit of both," I replied.

"Pay her what she's worth to you," chipped in Sean, "only you know that figure."

"I agree, it's your problem to resolve, my love," replied James.

I turned away thankful that our Angela wasn't within earshot. "James, do you think the same as Lorraine… that I should perhaps go back into general medicine?"

"Dawn," he answered, "decisions about your work are yours to make and yours alone. I'll support you whatever you decide."

What a fat lot of help that was, and a cop out… wait until he wants advice from me. Mona's visit had dislodged a few stones which now lay on my path, and which needed fixing...

*

It was twenty-five past three when the Doubleday family finally arrived. "For goodness sakes, Val," scolded Silvia, "Mum and my in-laws have been here for the best part of an hour."

"Sorry, we had to stop on the way for petrol," replied Val.

"If we hadn't, we wouldn't have arrived at all," added Joe, with a grin.

"Most sensible people would've organised themselves better, and filled up in plenty of time," huffed Silvia. "Never mind, you're all here now."

She then moved to the centre of her lounge, where everyone had gathered and clapped her hands together... "Quiet, everyone please, and find yourselves a seat... and that includes you Daisy and Brigitte. Joe, can you see to your girls please?" she announced. "Don, once everyone's settled, pass my presents to me one at a time to open, but before you begin, fetch me a chair please."

Every time Silvia mentioned the name Don, Joe felt his stomach churn. It was as if she was taking the name Dawn in vain, and he wanted her to stop. "I think he better suits his given name, Donald," he called out.

213

"I don't think it's important what you think, Joe, he's my husband and I like him to be known as Don, thank you very much," she replied, "and not flaming 'Donald Where's Your Trousers', after that ridiculous song."

"I only said Donald," protested Joe, still with a grin, "nothing about his trousers, flaming or otherwise!"

"We all know how one thing leads to another," she sniped glaringly, and then turned it into a weak smile, on the pretext it was a standing joke between them.

Val was about to nudge Joe, when it suddenly dawned on her why he might have said what he had. She couldn't tell from his face if what she was thinking was correct or not?

Don dutifully handed Silvia her presents one by one as instructed, and she made a great display of removing the gift wrappings, showing them off, and then thanking whoever the giver was... it was a truly embarrassing procedure.

"How can anyone feel comfortable with this pantomime," whispered Joe to Val, "especially when I don't even know what's in our package?"

"Oh God, I forgot... it's still in the boot of your car. Can you nip out and bring it in please," she whispered?

Joe lifted the girls from his knee, and made to go. "Where are you going now, Joe?" called out Silvia from the centre of the room.

"To fetch your present… it's still in the boot of our car," he answered.

"Sit and wait until I've opened the others," she replied, "I can always open yours last."

"It isn't from me, it's from your sister," he muttered, as he sat back beside Val.

"Stop winding her up," whispered Val.

"Why should I, she winds me up enough?" he whispered back.

The little girls had now moved, and were sharing Grandma Jean's generous armchair, from where they waved from across the room. Joe took Val's hand, squeezed it, and they each waved back to their daughters.

The time had now arrived for Silvia to receive her final present. She sat majestically on her seat, amidst a sea of discarded wrapping paper, wearing the resplendent flashy necklace she had received from her doting hubby… "You may fetch in your present now, Joe. I'm very much looking forward to opening it," she declared.

We can pick our friends but not our bloody sister-in-laws, thought Joe, slowly rising to do her bidding. She stared at him with her cat's claws out, and with a sickly grin pasted across her face. Joe gave a little shiver as he let go of Val's hand… if Silvia were a bloke, he would be wrestling on the floor at this very moment… "The conceited bitch," he mumbled under his breath, as he left the room.

Nobody detected what he was mumbling, except for Val. In the meantime, Shirley and Brian moved over beside her, "It's the moment of truth, Mum," whispered Brian, as they took their seats in the gallery.

"Yep, your big secret will soon be out, Mum," agreed Shirley, with a smile.

Val felt stupid for having kept it secret. The fact she had done that, made this whole occasion even worse. Why had she kept it hush-hush, there had been no reason, and it didn't make any sense? Furthermore, she'd used Joe's hard-earned cash to buy the dashed thing, and then kept it from him. What was wrong with her?

When Joe returned, he didn't hand the parcel to Silvia, but placed it at her feet. She bent to pick it up, and was surprised to discover just how heavy it was... "You damned 'tink'," she muttered, as she heaved and pulled at the package. No way was she going to ask for any help. Finally, she managed to struggle it up on to her lap.

He just smiled, resisting the temptation to rise to her bait, and when he retook his seat, Val slipped her hand into his, "I'm so sorry, I've mucked up well and proper this time," she whispered.

"No, you haven't. I hate her, Val. I'm sorry to say that to you, but it's the honest truth," he whispered back.

"Val thanks, it's just what I've always wanted, and in the right colour too," puffed Silvia, as she laid her top-of-the-range coffee machine on the floor. She then rose, came across and planted an affected kiss on Val, Brian, and Shirley, totally ignoring Joe.

Shirley and Brian crossed over to look at their parent's present, "Brian, that's the very same coffee machine Dad said he liked the last time we all went into town," whispered Shirley.

"I remember seeing something similar... you're right," he agreed.

"Dad, the coffee machine's the same as the one you liked in town," called out Shirley in his direction.

Joe turned and looked at Val... surely not? She had said it was a waste of money when he'd pointed it out to her. He had fancied the machine, whether it was a waste of money or not. He rose to his feet and said he needed to pop outside for a spot of fresh air. Brigitte and Daisy ran after him, when they saw him heading for the door... "Can we come with you, Daddy?" they called out.

"Come on then," he answered, "but first let Mummy know you're going outside with me."

Once outside, Joe sat on a bench, whilst the girls ran around and played a hopping game on the large expanse of paving. He felt betrayed. What was it with Val? Why can't she see through the bloody witch?

Just then, a man came and asked if he could join him? Joe knew exactly who he was but had never exchanged more than a few passing words, or exchanges about the weather. He was just a relation who continually appeared at Silvia's various doos.

"It's Mike," said Don's brother, introducing himself.

"I know you're Don's brother, but that's about all," replied Joe.

"I know slightly more about you Joe, you've a great reputation in these parts, as has your business," said Mike. Joe looked at him wondering what was coming next? This was unexpected. "I was hoping for an opportunity to talk with you this afternoon. It's always difficult to even breathe, let alone talk when Silvia's in charge. In fact, I don't think I can face many more of these family affairs as she calls them. I've always found her to be a pain in the butt. What my brother sees in her, I have no idea," he continued. "Listen, I'm sorry… I'm talking out of turn, she is, after all, your wife's sister."

"For my sins," replied Joe, shaking Mike's extended hand. "Nice to find an ally in the camp. How does your wife find her?"

"She agrees with me, but she's rather better at disguising her feelings," said Mike. "Listen, I want to put a proposition to you, but before I start, let me say that I thought your suggestion that Don better suited the name Donald, hit the mark. That's what we all used to call him before he met her."

"I'm not going to repeat what Silvia called me, and still does," said Joe "but listen mate, you can speak to me anytime——"

"Daddy, can we go inside now, it's getting cold?" interrupted Brigitte.

"Sure, come on you two, let's get you back indoors. Mike, can you come around to my house tomorrow... say around six... you do know where I live?" said Joe.

"I do and I will. I'm going back inside too," he answered, "and looking forward to us doing a little business."

*

The birthday party continued in its usual format. The little ones enjoyed it, as Silvia had gifts for them, and the dining-room table appeared to sag under the weight of food. The cake had been specially baked and decorated, with the theme for this year being golf, which Silvia had recently taken up, and was in the throes of receiving lessons. Consequently, many of her presents were, unsurprisingly, golf related.

Joe had told Jean earlier that morning, that she'd be able to see for herself how Val was at the party. She didn't look well to her wise eyes, as she kept watch at every opportunity. She was concerned when Joe left to go outside, but Daisy told her that it was because he hadn't known what the birthday present was. "Only Mummy knew," she whispered.

Jean crossed the floor to sit beside her daughter, "Is everything all right, love?" she asked. "Are you enjoying yourself?"

"I'm fine Mum, just fine… well not really," she sighed, "I've made a big mistake."

"What was that, Val," asked Jean, "I hope it's not to do with Joe?"

"No, what makes you ask that?" she replied. "Has he been telling tales?" She wondered why she had said that… with Joe, it would never be tales, only concern.

"No, he was just sharing his concern for you, with me," said Jean. "Val, I don't think this is either the time nor the place. I'm going to come home with you after this fiasco's over, and then we can have some honest, straight talking." She then crossed back over the room, before Val could offer any objections.

At that moment, Joe returned with the girls and Mike in tow, "Val, Mike's coming over tomorrow evening to talk over a spot of business," explained Joe.

"That's good of you Mike, nice to keep it in the family," she replied.

Mike raised his eyebrows in Joe's direction, who acknowledged his gesture. When Mike departed, she apologised to Joe.

"It's fine, there's no need to explain, I understand," he said, but she knew he didn't.

"Can we go home early," she asked, "I'm not really in the mood for much more of this?"

"We can go home this very minute if you wish," he replied, "just tell her."

Val then went to pass on their excuses to her sister, "Silvia, can I have a word with you in the study please?" she asked.

"Sure, lead the way," she replied. They went into the study and Val closed the door. "What is it, Val?" she asked.

"I'm not feeling too good, and need to go home," she replied.

"You say you're not feeling good... what in heaven's name's wrong with you now? It's all in your head, if you ask me," snapped Silvia.

"Then I'll not ask you," replied Val.

Silvia was not best pleased with her little sister adopting this manner. "It's my birthday Val, you might have made more of an effort to stay longer," she huffed.

"I've made a tremendous effort; I picked up on your loud hint regarding which coffee machine you'd like, and what colour it had to be," replied Val.

"My loud hint? How dare you speak to me in that manner, I'm never brash and loud, not like a certain other person I've had the misfortune of knowing," she snapped.

"And who would that be, Silvia, as if I didn't already know?" queried Val.

"You should know… you married him," she replied, "and once a 'tink', always a damned 'tink'."

"Silvia, why do you dislike Joe so much? Is it because he's everything Don isn't?" asked Val.

"I don't dislike him… I hate the damned man! He's wormed his way into our family and fooled everyone including you, that he's changed. But these types don't ever change," snarled Silvia.

"Everything all right in here?" asked Joe, as he popped his head into the study, "I've gathered the kids, so we can get off home whenever you're ready."

"Everything's fine in here, why wouldn't it be?" sniped Silvia. "I'm surely allowed a few minutes to say goodbye to my only sister on my birthday?"

Joe didn't answer, but took hold of Val's hand, led her from the room, and with their family gathered, said their collective goodbyes…

"Where do you think you're going, Mum?" gasped Silvia.

"I'm going home with Joe, to help with Val. She's not well, Silvia… surely you can see that," replied Jean.

"But that means there will be hardly anyone left," she groaned.

"I'm sorry, but we've to leave early too, Silvia," added Mike, "and if Mum and Dad, can come away now, I can give them a lift home with us."

"Just go… just go, the damned lot of you, but don't expect me to lay on a family party again. This is the last time I'll share my birthday with any of you," shouted Silvia.

"Thank the Lord," whispered Joe to Val as they made their way out.

CHAPTER TWENTY-NINE:

When I arrived at the office on Monday morning, Mona had yet to turn up. I placed her favourite mug on her desk and boiled the water in the kettle.When she did appear, there was no, "Good morning Dawn, how are things?" from my receptionist, just a furled frown.

"What's going on, Dawn?" she asked, looking more than a trifle suspicious of my modest gesture.

"Nothing's wrong, I'm just being nice, and thanking you for your generosity towards my family at the weekend," I replied. "I also found myself in earlier than usual, so had time to boil the kettle for a change."

"But it was you and your family who were generous to me," she said.

"Oh, that was nothing. You sent flowers, bought us chocolates, and treated Lorraine to lunch," I replied.

She didn't answer and as I poured the tea, didn't seem totally convinced either. She sat behind her desk and then announced that my first patient was due at nine-thirty... "Yes, it's Mrs Shand," I replied, "I know, because I've already checked the appointments diary."

"You'll soon not need my services if you continue to organise things by yourself," she commented.

"Oh, for goodness sake, Mona, I only looked to see who my first patient was. If I've overstretched my authority, then I'm sorry," I replied.

"Don't speak like that, Dawn... I recognise condescension when I hear it," said Mona.

"Mona, drink your tea, and listen to what I have to say to you," I replied. "I think you deserve a pay rise; what do you say to that?"

Mona took a sip of her tea, followed by... silence...

"Well, aren't you going to say something, are you not pleased?" I continued.

"I don't know, I'll have to think about it," she replied.

"Suit yourself," I said, "I'm off to my office, and please show Mrs Shand straight in when she arrives."

I went into my consulting room, closed the door, and thumped the desk. I had to get rid of my frustrations before my first patient arrived. After all, Mrs Shand was paying top dollar and deserved my full attention while she poured out her innermost secrets.

However, Mona still lingered in my mind, and had not responded to my thump in the way she usually did, so I thumped my desk once more to get her out of my hair. "Right, that's me sorted for the rest of the morning," I announced at the top of my voice... still no response... tough... let her sulk.

*

Drained could not describe how I felt by lunchtime. This job was becoming more and ever more demanding. The words, *'she gave them her all, but still they wanted more'*, would make a nice commemorative plaque above my desk...

Suddenly, there was a knock on my door, so I crashed my head down on top of my hands, which were resting on my desk. Which one of my patients had returned, I wondered? The door opened and as I peeped through my fingers saw Mona... "Thank goodness, it's you. I thought for a minute, one of them from this morning had come back to haunt my poor battered soul," I said, somewhat relieved.

"Don't be so morbid and melancholy, Dawn. I bet your parents were driven to distraction with your imagination when you were a child?" she replied.

"Imagination? My imagination...?" I said.

226

"Dawn, I'll gladly accept the pay rise you offered. I don't want to cause you anymore grief than that you've already suffered," she announced. "I was just acting silly beggars earlier."

"That's fine, Mona, and thanks for that. I'll see to the financial side of things in the morning," I replied. "Could you leave me alone for a little now, and if you wouldn't mind, buy us both soup and a sandwich from the kiosk on the corner?"

She stood and stared at me…

"What?" I asked. "What? Oh, sorry… PLEASE!"

I smiled and she smiled back… we'd be back on track by the afternoon session… at least I hoped we would.

*

Mid-afternoon came, and I found time to begin writing up my notes. I wrote a few headers, but then my mind began to drift… "my imagination?" I mumbled, "my imagination?"

Mona may have unintentionally shown what lay at the heart of my innermost feelings. I had never considered that my memories could be mixed up or even tainted by my imagination! I had gone to *Cloverley* because I still felt a lingering guilt about a broken promise to Joe Doubleday all those years ago. What had I promised? What memories were factual, and what others were laced with my imagination?

Jean Brown... she'd sat in front of me and was real enough... I'd chatted with her in her house a few weeks ago, and she seemed as I remembered, albeit a little older... I remembered her house... and recalled which things had remained the same, and which others had changed... these were true memories, not my imagination... then there was Silvia... she was definitely the same nasty bit of stuff that I'd taken an instant dislike to as a young child! What about the river, with its waterfall at our special place? It remained as I remembered too... it's air hung with the same fresh scents and atmosphere as then...

But, these memories and the way they made me feel... were they wholly real or were they influenced in part by my apparently vivid imagination?

The office phone rang out shrilly, which startled me back into the present, "Yes?" I said, with a shiver.

"Dr Brennan, Mrs Charles has arrived with Melanie. They're a shade early, but wonder if it would be convenient to see them right away?" asked Mona.

I glanced at the clock; they were only fifteen minutes early... I suppose the sooner I started, the sooner I'd finish... "Yes, send them in, Mona," I answered, remembering to say *PLEASE*.

CHAPTER THIRTY:

As Joe drove home, Jean decided she'd rather go straight to her house instead, as she felt drained and tired. Joe made the short detour, and the kids waved her goodbye. Val promised to call her later, to check on how she was.

The kids were now desperate to get out to play, so as soon as they arrived home, good clothes were discarded and replaced with items far more suitable.

Val and Joe found themselves alone at last. He held out his arms, and she ran straight into them, "Joe, I'm so sorry. I don't understand… why I did that," she stammered, her voice breaking.

"Did what?" he asked, pulling her tighter.

"Bought that damned coffee machine," she sobbed.

"Because she told you that was what she wanted, that's why," he replied.

Val looked at him, wondering how he knew.

"Shirley told me how Silvia works," he replied. "She makes sure you don't make random choices. Our Shirley's a good little sleuth."

"Joe, from where did you produce the word sleuth?" she asked.

His face reddened, and now she had her answer... "It's a word that's somehow stuck, and it's only stuck with me because I found it a strange word at the time, and not for any other reason," he explained. "Now, let's get back to your sister."

"She frightens me, Joe. She's always dominated me, and made me feel inferior," confessed Val. "I grew up and have changed in many ways, but Silvia... she's remained the thorn which makes me bleed."

"Once a bully, always a bully," replied Joe. "It's true in her case anyway. Remember Val, I only saw her from a distance when I was younger."

"How do I sort this? Please help me," she asked. "It's Silvia who's making me ill again and———"

"Say it, Val. Say what you're thinking," interrupted Joe. "That's the first step in trying to make things better."

"I can't, not to you. I've never told you before that I loved you back then... when you loved... her," she sobbed.

"Val, the trouble is we never talked to each other about our pasts," he replied. "You've never even asked me what happened after my family left. I've asked my sisters, and they've told me that you've never asked them either."

"Joe, can you tell me now?" she asked. "I'm asking you now."

"We'll talk about it, but not today. That was twelve years of my life, and I can't just spout it out in half-an-hour. I don't have the strength to face that today. That sister of yours has hurt and insulted me once too many. You must hear what she calls me at every opportunity," he replied.

Val nodded, "Joe, I'm partly to blame, I let her use these despicable words to describe you, and I don't know why?" she replied. "Joe, help me please..."

"I'd wrap you up in cotton wool and keep you safe from the world, but I can't. If you can't be strong for yourself, be strong for our children. Focus on them, forget it's you who's standing there and imagine it's them," he answered.

"And what about... her?" she asked.

"What's her name, Val," replied Joe, "say to me her name?"

"Dawn," she whispered...

"Thanks for saying her name," he replied. "I can't change the way it was between Dawn and me back then. I can't forget words like sleuth or destroy what memories I have. All I know is that I've tried to show over the years, how much I love you. For goodness sake Val, we have our lovely children, a great life and you're allowing the past and your sister to spoil it. From now on, I'm not taking any more of her evil tongue. I'm sorry if it hurts your mum, but I'm not taking it any longer from Silvia."

"Joe, I'll try to be stronger too. You and the kids must come first, but... how do I come to terms with... Dawn?" she asked.

"There's nothing to come to terms with, but if you think there is, then it's for you to resolve. I've done everything I can," replied Joe. Why can't you just accept me as I am, here and now, he thought? Dawn's a distant memory, and the only member of the Junior Sleuth League that I've ever met... that last thought still made him inwardly chuckle.

CHAPTER THIRTY-ONE:

"James… do you think I've, what you might call, a vivid imagination?" I asked.

"How vivid is vivid?" he responded cautiously.

"Just answer my question," I replied.

"You're far more qualified to answer that than me," he said, cocking his head in my direction.

He did have a point. Once again, *physician heal thyself*, floated by on the wind. "You're right," I replied, "I am."

"Why were you asking anyway," he asked, "I'm interested now?"

"That's tough on you then, as the moment's past," I replied.

"Aw, that's not good enough, I'm really, really, interested," he repeated, "you've whetted my appetite."

"I'll wet your whistle instead," I replied, pouring him a glass of red.

"Imagination can play funny tricks you know," said James. "Are you going to tell me why you were asking?"

"It was just something that Mona happened to say earlier today," I replied.

"Ah, the lovely Mona, our sweet house guest. You and her are becoming quite a cosy team," said James.

"What do you mean by that?" I asked. "James, stop this nonsense, I have a serious question for you."

"Do I need to lie on the couch?" he joked.

"What's going on in here?" asked our Angela, as she skipped into the room. "Why does Dad need to lie down? What are you two thinking of doing?"

James and I looked at each other, wondering if we should react, or ignore our baby daughter? However, she was expecting an answer, I could tell that much…

"It's okay, I'm not staying, so there's no need to think up a story," she continued, as she skipped back out of the room.

"That child's precocious; where did we get her from, the other two were never like that?" I remarked.

"Hmm, I wonder," replied James, with an almighty grin.

"What? What are you grinning at?" I asked.

"Like mother like daughter," he answered, smugly.

I surely was never as bad as our Angela, I thought? "Surely not, James," I exclaimed.

"Afraid so, my dear... both cast from the same mould methinks," he replied.

*

Later, Dawn sat thinking... out of the same mould, James had said? Was I similar to our Angela at her age, so brash in my speech, so in-your-face with the things I would do and say? I had never been shy, but can't remember being so up-for-everything, although, if I'm honest... what I mean is that I can't really complain about our Angela.

Val wasn't a child like me. Shy and quiet, she didn't like to do the exciting, risky things I enjoyed, lest it got her into trouble. In fact, we didn't have much in common, except that we were the same age. Her mum was friends with mine, so for years each time I arrived for the weekend, or for holidays, I'd run down to the village and knock on her door. That was... until there was Joe. He was different, so sure of himself, so exciting to be with, and so in tune with me… and now married to the shy, quiet and retiring Val.

I'd married James, a lovable, clever, and generous man who, with his easy ways, was my rock, my dependable best friend, the father of my children, and more importantly… the man I loved.

Life was indeed strange!

CHAPTER THIRTY-TWO:

The following evening, Mike arrived as arranged. Joe had spent his Sunday at work, catching up on the time he'd wasted at Silvia's birthday party. He'd intended taking Brian with him, to break him into what a full day's work actually entailed, but then remembered how his old man had expected him to help and bring in cash at that tender age. Consequently, he decided Brian wasn't going to suffer in the same way he had… little by little, he thought, was the more preferred approach.

"Daddy, that man who was at Auntie Silvia's party is here," announced Daisy.

"Sorry, I forgot you were coming… my time clock's knocked out by yesterday's affair," apologised Joe. "However, I'm glad you've come. Thanks pumpkin, can you run and tell Mummy that Mike's here, please?"

"Joe, I'll not keep you long, I just wanted to quickly run something past you. I want my house completely remodelled, then I want to split my large garden into two and build a small bungalow for Janis's dad on one part. He's a good bit further down the road than you and I. After that, if we work well together, I have various other parcels of land dotted about upon which I should secure planning permission for more upmarket, bespoke homes. Do you see where I'm going?"

"I'm your man, Mike," said Joe. "What do you do yourself?"

"If I said I'm what you might call a wheeler dealer… would that make sense to you?" he replied. Joe nodded and grinned… he understood precisely what he meant. "But I'm also a qualified architect," he added.

"Ah, even better," replied Joe, "in fact, much, better."

Just then Val came into the room carrying a tray with coffee and cake. Joe noticed that she had only brought two cups, and quickly nipped to the kitchen to fetch a third. She hadn't spoken much to Mike in the past, other than the usual small talk.

"Val, come and join us. You need to hear all about Mike's proposition," invited Joe, gesturing her to take a seat beside them. Mike then went through his ideas once more, and she could see that Joe was delighted with his outline proposals. "Mike's a good guy; I was chatting to him yesterday at Silvia's," added Joe. "Talking of Silvia, what are we going to do about her?"

Val looked at him with horror in her eyes. "It's fine, Mike can't stand her either… he's with me on the Silvia topic," he said reassuringly.

"Val, I'm sorry to confirm what Joe says. I know she's your sister and all that, but as they say we can't choose our relatives, especially our in-laws," agreed Mike. "Listen, I'll have a word with Donald. Heaven knows what I'll achieve, but at least it'll be a start."

"That would be a good place to start, wouldn't you agree, Val?" said Joe, looking to her for a response.

"Yes, that would be helpful. Thanks for that, Mike, and I hope your business venture with Joe works out fine," she replied. "Joe will do an excellent job, as he's a grafter is my man, a perfectionist who keeps his troops well in check."

"Which often is the hardest of all the jobs in the building trade," added Joe.

"I've every confidence in his abilities," confirmed Mike.

Joe looked at her and could read her mind, "I've an extension to put up here before I can start any of this new work, Mike," he said, "I'll get on to that within the next few days."

"Do you want to show me what's involved?" asked Mike.

239

"It's really just a variation on the Johnston's extension," explained Joe. "It worked out really well there, and this place is not that different."

"Actually my friend who designed it took me to visit your handiwork," said Mike, "and that's what persuaded me to ask you to work with me on this new venture."

Joe took Val's hand and squeezed it gently. "As I told you, Val… little steps grow into bigger ones," said Joe. "Mike will speak to Don, sorry I mean Donald, and that'll be our first little step on the journey towards sorting out your sister."

Mike sensed relief in Val's expression. How different she was to her arrogant sister, he thought.

*

Later that day, Val took the opportunity to tackle Joe on the delicate matter they'd been discussing earlier, "Joe, let's make time to sit down and talk over your past," she suggested.

"Right, I will, but I'll have to ask my sisters over to assist," he replied, "that's if you don't mind?"

"Will that not seem rather strange to them," she asked, "it's not as if we're recently married? We've four children, and they'll think I'm daft."

"No, they'll not, they'll think that you love me so much, that nothing else matters," he replied.

240

"Really?" said Val.

"No," replied Joe, laughing, "but they'll love to come over. It'll give them an excuse to talk over the good old days with us."

"You make it sound so lovely," said Val.

"Good," he replied, "that's it settled; we'll both get a laugh with the girlies."

Val nodded in agreement, while Joe mulled it over. He decided that he'd have to tread carefully, enclose it in a rosy glow, which the girlies will love... with just a few snippets of the harsh truth interspersed here and there with dollops of poetic, imaginative licence.

*

Nicolette and Mel agreed to come but not Mandy. Joe had forgotten the birth of her third baby was imminent. "Sorry, it's too far down the road at the moment, Joe. I'll come to stay with the kids after this little one's arrived," she said, as she stroked her enlarged waistline.

"We'll speak about that later, in fact, we might come and visit you instead," replied Joe.

"Joe, you love babies. I keep on waiting for news of number five," she teased.

"You'll have a long wait if you are," he answered, with a chuckle.

"Oh, no, Joe... have you really?" she asked.

"I'm saying nothing," replied her big brother.

"Can you perhaps speak to Frank about… you-know-what, the next time we come to visit?" she asked.

"I'll certainly speak to him, but I don't know what I'll say to him," he replied.

"Oh, Joe Doubleday, you know you'll do anything for one of your little girlies," she cooed.

"We'll see… let's forget about that for the moment, and concentrate on this baby. Sorry, but I need to get on… take care… love you," replied Joe, as he closed the call. He laughed when he came off the phone… his little girlies? The fact that they needed and relied upon him, had pulled him through some of his darkest nights… two will be enough, as it's only a fairytale anyway.

*

Over the next week, Val tried her best to avoid Silvia. She visited her mum when she was sure her sister wouldn't come marching in, and didn't answer her phone when she saw her number on the caller display.

A new air of contentment flowed over her, which pleased her husband. Joe's sisters were coming to visit, the foundations were about to be laid for their new extension, and Joe and Mike were making good progress with their future plans. Things were definitely on the up… and sometimes she even found herself repeating the name Dawn to herself. It was an empowering tonic… little steps… little steps, Joe had said. "Dawn... Dawn," she repeated over and over, as she busied herself.

*

"Why aren't the children coming, we hardly ever see them?" Brigitte asked her mum.

"It's only a quick visit to talk over some things with me and Daddy," she replied. "When Auntie Mandy's had her new baby, we'll make time to see the children then."

"I'd like a baby," announced Daisy, "can we get a new one too, Mummy?"

"Daisy, we are getting one, that's who'll be sleeping in the new room, once it's finished," replied Brigitte.

"It's not for a baby, it's for all of us to use," corrected Val, trying to suppress her blushes.

"I'd much rather have a new baby than a silly room," replied Daisy.

"Well, that's not going to happen," said Val. "Now get on with the things you've got to do."

They then left the room chanting, "We want a baby" as Val closed the door after them. She was not in the mood for any of their nonsense today. A few moments later, she re-opened it and listened. The chanting had stopped, having been replaced with the sounds of giggling from their bedroom. Val shook her head and closed the door once more. She didn't want any more children, but the girls had given her a funny sensation with their comments. Daisy was soon to start school, so she'd be on her own. What would she do? I know, I could work with Joe, she concluded.

CHAPTER THIRTY-THREE:

I decided to take James for a drive in the country the following weekend in my pride and joy. He needed to experience my car's interior, the garage having done a top of the range valeting job along with the repair. I had struggled to keep it in this condition, so could put it off no longer. My messy husband could not help but be impressed.

"You love this car, don't you, Dawn," he announced, as he stretched back in the front passenger seat.

"It is rather special," I agreed, "and rare... that's why I love it so much."

"That is true, " he agreed. I noticed him taking in my spotless interior, and felt smug. We sat for a moment with our own thoughts. "Not... that... rare... though, " he slowly stated. We do know of three others... and not too far from here." He turned and gave me a smug smile.

Damn the man, I thought, always looking to score a bloody point. "James you know full well that they are just ordinary models in the most common of colours," I replied.

"Suppose… that is true," he replied. He turned his head, and looked at me. "Tell me, have you ever seen another special edition in the same colour as yours," he asked? "I don't think I have. "

I was unsettled by this question… and wondered if he knew my guilty secret? I furtively glanced sideways… his eyes were closed in a relaxed way, and he didn't seem unduly concerned. "Well, I have seen one similar if the truth be told… and when I phoned to check if mine was ready for collection, the man from the garage mentioned his supplier had told him some tale of another of these models needing a repair," I replied.

"Hmm… but was it the same colour?" James asked now with his eyes closed as he relaxed deeper into his seat.

I looked at him closely to check if his eyes were fully closed, "I believe so," I replied, "well, if the truth be told, I know it was the same."

His eyes suddenly opened wide, and he stared at the car windscreen, then closed them again, as he settled back into his seat. "What's all this if-the-truth-be-told business, Dawn? You're sounding rather furtive," he said.

"Furtive? I'm never furtive," I answered.

"Oh, yes you are," said James, opening his eyes wide, and this time turning his head in my direction. "If you only heard through the grapevine of a similar car being somewhere or other for repair, how do you know it to be the same colour?"

"Because I was told it was the same colour. I was also told by a young boy that his dad had a similarly coloured one... in his garage at home," I replied. What was all this, I thought? I take him out for a nice relaxing drive in the country, and find him squeezing me dry.

James now appeared more alert, although still reclining in his seat. He then leaned forward, twisting his shoulders like someone waking up in bed would do, "What boy told you... do I know him?" he asked.

"Hmm... no, I don't think you do... in fact I know you don't," I replied. "What's with all the questioning anyway?"

"To get answers, and to get to the bottom of this furtive business which is intriguing me, Dawn," he replied. "Let's examine the facts... a boy told you what?"

I looked at him with dismay. Why could he not just accept, shut up, and close his eyes again? I wouldn't even mind if he dropped off to sleep.

"That his dad had a similar one at home in his garage," he continued. "Do we know if this account is accurate? What age was this boy, and where were you when he told you?"

I drove my car into a lay-by, which luckily had conveniently appeared and stopped. My blood was doing funny things, and I felt James's cross-examinations had put me on trial. "James, how can I drive safely, when you're continually interrogating me?" I asked.

"I was just taking an interest in things... doing a little... what you would call sleuthing," he said, with a smile, "like the way you so often do."

"I don't sleuth... at least not anymore," I vainly protested. I didn't like the way James's sleuthing was going. "I'm not even nosey," I added.

"Don't make me laugh, Dawn... not nosey!" he exclaimed.

"James, just because I'm a psychiatrist, doesn't mean that I indulge in unnecessary sleuthing or nosing," I replied.

An eerie silence fell inside the car, and not being too sure where we were exactly, I turned on my sat-nav, waited for it to boot up, and then punched in the word 'Home'...

"That was unnecessary, I could've told you the way," said James, now sitting upright in his seat.

"You have already told me where to go," I replied.

"If you say so," he sighed.

I could see his thinly disguised smirk, as he sensed victory against his nearest and dearest. He then closed his eyes once more, reclined his seat, and not another word was spoken until we reached home. Once indoors, I headed straight for the kitchen, and was surprised, but delighted, to find preparations for the evening meal had already begun.

Lorraine suddenly came into the kitchen with a young man in tow, "Mum, meet Simon, he's a good friend of mine," she announced, with a wave of her hand.

"Ehm, nice to meet you Simon, did you do this for me?" I asked.

"No, I did it Mum, what a strange thing to ask him," answered Lorraine.

"Sorry," I said, winking at her. She frowned at me with her brow deeply furrowed. I wanted to say what we always said about the wind changing… but kept my mouth firmly shut, as it had been a decidedly bruising afternoon for me already. "Thanks, Lorraine… just my little joke, Simon," I hurriedly proffered. "Do you want to join us for our evening meal?"

"That would be very nice, Mrs Brennan," replied Simon, "or is it Doctor Brennan?"

"Just call me Dawn," I said, "it suits me better than Mrs Brennan or the other."

"She means it makes her feel younger," quipped Lorraine.

"What a thing to say," I remarked, with a forced smile. "Have you introduced Simon to your father? If not, you perhaps should, or he'll wonder who's sitting next to him at the dinner table."

That was perhaps a stupid thing to say, but Lorraine had thrown me with her 'makes-her-feel-younger' remark. I was only being friendly to the young lad. Seems I couldn't win… well, at least not today anyway.

Sean knew Simon as they shared a few class subjects at school, and appeared friendly enough. Lorraine sat on Simon's right and our Angela grabbed the seat on his left. Having shown a keen interest in this visitor, she looked him over with her usual thoroughness… "Is Lorraine your girlfriend, Simon?" she suddenly asked, whilst looking directly at him.

Simon seemed momentarily caught off guard and turned to Lorraine for a clue as how to answer?

"That's private, Angela, you'll be told of our status when you need to know," interjected Lorraine.

"Lorraine, it was a perfectly good question, and I was looking forward to hearing the answer myself," countered James.

"Oh, Dad, don't embarrass me, please," replied a now flush-faced Lorraine.

"I'd love Lorraine to be my girlfriend, Mr Brennan," the bold Simon, announced.

"Don't tell them things like that, Simon... we'll never hear the end of it... you don't know what they're like," flustered Lorraine.

"That'll do, Lorraine," cautioned James.

Lorraine grimaced, while James turned to Simon and asked what subjects he was studying at school? He duly listed them, while Lorraine continued to sit in silence. I wondered why she had brought him here today, if she didn't want us to engage him in conversation?

"That's pretty much the same subjects as our Sean," concluded James.

"What do you work at, Mr Brennan?" asked Simon, relaxing a little.

"I work at the University and my good lady wife is a doctor... of sorts," he answered.

Simon looked confused, and I couldn't blame him. James had told the poor lad nothing or at least, very little. "Simon, James is a Professor of History, whilst I'm a Doctor of Psychiatry, which I hope better answers your question," I clarified.

James smiled across the table at me. I softened, and decided to put this afternoon and talk of motor cars firmly behind me.

"Your mum and dad must be brilliantly clever," concluded Simon.

"You wouldn't think so at times," piped up our angel of a younger daughter.

"I'll second that," chipped in Sean.

James kicked him under the table. His foot caught the edge of my shoe, which was how I knew.

"What?" asked Sean, looking over towards his dad...

"They want you to say nice things about them to make them feel good," huffed Lorraine.

"What's so wrong with that?" asked James.

"Nothing, Dad," she replied, "I'm sorry."

Afterwards, things at the table improved. Slowly I could see Simon becoming more comfortable, and Lorraine returned to her pleasant self. I wondered if our Sean had a girlfriend? He'd never brought a girl home, but I would like him to be comfortable with us whenever he decided the moment was right. Surprisingly, our Angela behaved not too badly either, and I reckoned that we had the beginnings of a young lady on our hands. My impression was that it would not be too long before she brought home a boyfriend... although I hoped not for a year or two yet.

After the meal, James and I found ourselves alone. He went to make a cafetière of coffee, whilst I switched on the fire and lit various scented candles in order to create a certain ambience in the lounge. Our lighting had been specially wired to enable us to create an adjustable ambient backdrop, and I considered myself a dab hand at creating just that.

When he arrived through with his tray, he sat beside me on the couch, "Nice mood you've created, my love," he said.

"Just for you, my dear," I responded.

"My apologies for pulling your leg this afternoon," he next said.

"It didn't feel as though it was just my leg that was being pulled," I replied.

We both laughed, and then James poured the coffee.

"James, how remiss, I've forgotten the music," I said, then selected some convivial background music. When I returned, I sat on the opposite couch so I could fully stretch out my legs. After a few minutes, I reclined and closed my eyes… "This is the life," I sighed contentedly.

"Yes," James replied, appearing to agree. However, something in his voice struck a note of discord, which prompted me to open my eyes and look over in his direction. His eyes were upon me.

"Yes?" I asked.

"Nothing," he replied, which really meant the opposite.

I then partially rose, propped myself up on my elbow, then sat up properly, "Spit it out," I said.

"It's nothing, Dawn… only it's just occurred to me that you never fully answered my questions this afternoon," he answered. "It's you who ought to spit it out… whatever it is."

I rose slowly and switched off my carefully selected playlist, "There's no need for soothing music anymore," I announced. "I thought my interrogation was over, but I'm obviously wrong as the inquisition has started once again. I would have thought better of you, James."

"And I would've thought better of you, my love," he replied.

"Don't call me your love using that tone," I said, rising to switch on the main overhead lights.

"Why have you done that?" he asked, shading his eyes from the sudden harsh glare.

"Because, you don't deserve nice soft lighting," I replied. "Answers? You want answers, so put me on trial. Stand me in the naughty corner and I'll give you your answers." My bosom was heaving, and heated blood now coursed through my veins. What had come over my James, treating me in such a manner?

"You're crazy," he said.

"Crazy? How dare you call me crazy! I should've expected that though. What was it you said at the table this evening? Oh, yes, I remember… my good lady wife here is a doctor of sorts," I replied.

"Oh, Dawn, I meant nothing by that, I was only playing with the lad," he protested.

"Our daughter brings home a fine young man for the first time, and you find nothing better to do than play him like a salmon on a line?" I replied.

"I've never fished in my entire life, and you know that. I wish you'd calm down and stop exaggerating," protested James.

"I'm crazy remember, and us crazy people don't know how to do calm… that's why we're crazy," I replied.

We went silent for a period; even I could see the ridiculousness of this fast developing situation. However, I had my professional reputation and my good name to uphold. I was known for my clear thinking, my incisive problem solving, and my understanding nature…

"James, let's calm down, and sort this out," I began, "I don't understand why the colour of some car, the age of a boy, et cetera, et cetera is of importance. But if it is, then allow me to furnish you with the full facts. The boy in question was aged about twelve years, had a good knowledge of my car model, and I was in *Cloverley* at the time."

"Ah ha!" he announced, "I knew there was more to this than you were letting on. You're telling me that a twelve year old boy from *Cloverley*, told you that his dad had a car exactly the same as yours in his garage? I find it remarkable that in the entire motoring world, an identical car... as rare a model as yours, is garaged in a small place like *Cloverley*."

"I don't understand why you're making such a big fuss, James. Coincidences do happen," I replied.

"Switch off that damned light would you please, my dear," said James, "it's interfering with my thinking process."

I switched off the bright lights, went back to my couch, and waited for his next move. He sat and rubbed his chin, the way that some people do when deliberating... then the next onslaught came... "Did you know the boy?" he asked.

This question was the one I hadn't wanted him to ask. "I didn't know him... but I did work out who he was," I cagily replied.

"So, you managed to sleuth your way to this boy's identity?" pronounced James.

"Well, yes... I suppose I did... his name's Brian," I replied.

"And did you manage to sleuth his surname too?" he asked.

"Doubleday... it is Doubleday," I replied.

James clapped his hands and smiled, "My, my, now we're making some progress," he said.

I was confused, and guilty. I wanted to say, please don't ask me anymore questions, but how could I explain?

"So, we have a twelve year old boy who lives in *Cloverley* named Brian Doubleday, who has a dad with a car exactly the same as yours sitting parked in his garage," he summarised. "Well, well, this *Cloverley* place of yours seems to be a far more interesting place than you've ever given it credit. I think we ought to take a trip there, and sometime soon... in fact, you can show us all the sights."

"Yes, and why not?" I replied, defiantly.

CHAPTER THIRTY-FOUR:

Two of Joe's three sisters were on their way for the arranged visit. Nicolette had picked Mel up in her car, and it would take them around three hours.

"It seems a shame to drag them all this way, to tell me something that you could've told me yourself," said Val.

"It will be an opportunity to see them. It doesn't happen very often these days, as we all have busy lives to contend with," replied Joe. "I'm sure you'll enjoy their visit though… they're full of nonsense."

Val was doing well at managing to steer clear of Silvia, and it was paying dividends. Joe could see steady progress as she tried to concentrate on her family. He wanted her to re-gain her self-confidence and face the world squarely in the face. He also hoped she would enjoy the girls' visit.

*

Nicolette's car pulled into the driveway and both Brigitte and Daisy ran out to greet them.

"Wait for Mum and me," Joe called after them, but to no avail.

"Joe, let's just wait in here for them," suggested Val.

Joe realised she was apprehensive about Nicolette and Melanie's visit… of course, she didn't know them as he did, they were his sisters. He smiled, took her hand, and a few minutes later, they trundled in… Joe's girlies.

"Oh, Mel, look at the two love birds… four children and still holding hands!" exclaimed Nicolette. "Val, what's your secret?"

"Yes, Val, you need to let us into your secret. My Steve hasn't held my hand since——," began Mel.

"Oh, Mel," interrupted Val, "I am so sorry."

"Don't be, Val, she needs putting back in her box. The two of them were holding hands and kissing just before we left this morning," replied Nicolette.

"Oh?" said Val, a little confused.

Joe squeezed her hand and planted a kiss on her lips, "Val, they can't help it, they've been badly brought up," said Joe, with a grin. "Come here you two." He hugged and kissed them as he always had, and it never ceased to amaze Val at the emotion they shared with one another.

"How's Mandy?" he asked. "I spoke to her on the phone, but she's always so cheerful, it's hard to tell what's going on with her."

"Joe, it's been hard. She's not been too well throughout this pregnancy, but nothing specific," answered Mel. "Hopefully this will be her last baby."

"I think she feels the same way too, if what she said to me was true... I'm supposed to have a word with Frank," said Joe, screwing up his face.

Val looked at him; she knew what he meant, but was surprised that he'd been so direct, but there again, it concerned one of his beloved sisters.

"Joe, you don't mean... you've had the snip?" giggled Nicolette.

"I only said that I'd have a chat with Frank," he laughed, "and no, I haven't had anything snipped!"

Shirley and Brian arrived through with tea, biscuits, and sandwiches on a tray, which surprised Val, until she quickly realised that Joe had organised them. Together they laid the table and everyone took a seat.

"What have you two got there?" asked Joe, of his younger daughters.

"We've new tee-shirts and so have Shirley and Brian. But theirs have a different picture from ours," replied Brigitte. "Thank you, Auntie Mel and Auntie Nic."

"You're most welcome," replied Mel and Nicolette, in unison.

"Thank you," added Daisy, giving them one of her special smiles.

"It's a pleasure," they replied.

Shirley and Brian were then hugged, thanked for the refreshments, and in turn, they thanked them for their presents.

"We've something for you too, but we'll give them to you later," announced Mel, looking over towards Joe and Val. The four adults then gathered themselves around the table, and tucked into their snacks. All too soon the girls would have to leave for their long drive home, so they wanted to make the most of their short visitation.

"Mel and Nicolette, I have to apologise for having you drive this distance. If I'd not thought it important enough in twelve years of marriage to ask Joe to explain," said Val, "then there really was no rush."

"Val, this is the right time. It will do us good to think back and realise just how far we've each come. It's a pity Mandy isn't here, but that can't be helped," replied Mel.

"Let's get on with this, there's no apologies needed," added Nicolette.

"Well, if I can perhaps begin… we left here over twenty-seven years ago…" began Mel. "I can still smell the stench of our old dump of a home, as it was razed to the ground… I hated him that day."

"We all hated him that day," stressed Joe.

"I still don't understand why he had to do that?" revealed Nicolette. "I remember my hankie being soaked with tears."

"None of us know, Nic," replied Mel, "and I believe you tried to stop him, Joe?"

"Yes, I did try, but my own father would've set me alight if I hadn't backed off. He was on a roll, with glazed eyes that blazed like some crazed animal. 'You get back in the van or take what's coming to you,' I remember him shouting and screaming," added Joe. "I was just a boy at the time, and was powerless to stop him, so I just got back into the old van which was packed full with our junk… and us."

"Mummy was silent, she was like a ghost, and I think part of her died that day, as she was never the same afterwards," stated Mel. "I can still see the marks on her face and shoulders where he'd lashed out at her for crossing him. Joe, do you remember Mandy being sick and us having to hide it from him?"

Joe nodded, he remembered only too well.

Val looked at their faces, and the terrible torment shocked her, "What did he hope to gain from setting your house alight?" she asked.

"Val, you lived in the village, so you must've seen our lousy shack back then?" said Joe. "It should have been condemned. I'm not sure why he burned the place down though; maybe to stop the villagers from torching it themselves?"

"I remember looking over when I walked to—," began Val.

"Dawn's house?" interrupted Joe.

"Yes, I remember, Dawn," exclaimed Mel. "You really liked her Joe, didn't you?"

"He told Mum that he was going to marry her… it was Dawn's parents who looked after me that day, when we all went to the Fair," said Nicolette.

"That's right, I remember you trotted off with them hand-in-hand," said Joe, "which saved me money. I'd saved up enough to give you girls a treat, and Dawn's dad gave her some to share between us too. So, all in all, we ended up quite flush."

"We had a great day. The Fair was the last thing I remember that was good in my life back then," confessed Mel. "You and Dawn took Mandy and me on the 'Waltzers', and I remember the man didn't take money for us little ones. We sat between you and her, and I was so scared when it started to go fast."

"But, you loved it anyway, and don't try telling me you didn't," said Joe. "We went back on the 'Waltzers' lots of times."

263

"You know we loved them," replied Mel. "I had Mandy holding my right hand, and Dawn my left, and with you and her sitting on either side, it made us feel safe being in the middle."

Val was unprepared for the major role Dawn had played in these girls' memories. Joe reached over and put his hand on top of her's as it lay on the table. This surprised her, as she thought that with all this talk of Dawn, his mind would be drawn elsewhere?

She looked first to Joe, then up at the clock and rose from her seat, "Listen everyone, I'll need to make us something to eat. I'll keep it simple so I'll not be too long," she announced.

"No, you don't need to, because I've ordered fish 'n' chips from the café in the village. George will deliver them straight from the fryer as a special favour," said Joe. "We've got half-an-hour before he's due... buttered rolls as well, girls, you know how you always liked your buttered rolls."

"Joe, you're the best brother ever," replied Nicolette. "You always seem to know exactly what we really want."

"He's the best brother any girl could wish for, Val. He used to do everything for us, kept us clean and tidy, kept us out of mischief, bought us treats and loved us... Joe knows how to love," agreed Mel.

Val felt she needed to leave the room, so excused herself and went through to the cloakroom, where she washed her hands and then allowed the water to run cold, before tackling her face. She'd be happier when all their recollections of Dawn had subsided, and moved their memories well away from *Cloverley.*

*

The kids came running back into the house when they spotted George from the chip shop arrive. "Here you are folks, fresh hot fish, chips, and buttered rolls for eight. I wish I had customers like this every day, Joe. It would give my dinner-time trade a right good shot in the arm," he said. "I've also brought paper plates and plastic forks. You don't need to use them, but I'm all for keeping to a minimum the work for the little lady of the house."

Nicolette and Mel looked around to see who in heaven's name the little lady was, then began to giggle when they realised he meant Val.

"That's great, George, and thanks for being so thoughtful," replied Val, with a straight face.

"I'll see you out," said Joe. He could that see his sisters were finding the whole situation amusing, although in reality, it never took much to set them off. He hurried George along, thanking him once again for his kindness, and when he came back into the room, it was noisy, smelling strongly of fish, chips, brown sauce, and vinegar. He looked over and it warmed his heart to see Val chatting and laughing with Mel and Nicolette.

After lunch, they cleared the table, and resumed their memoirs… time was passing far too fast.

"What happened once you left *Cloverley?*" asked Val.

The three of them paused, wondering what to say. "It wasn't very nice, Val," answered Mel, looking at the others. "We drove for a couple of hours, then he pulled over to the side of the road. He told us that we had nowhere to go, and I recall Mummy shouting at him, but he took no notice."

"So, what did you do?" asked Val.

"He drove us along some country track… to a place by a river with trees and told us to get out and make the best of it. There was nothing else we could do, so we… made do," added Joe.

Nicolette began to cry, "I don't want to do this anymore, Joe… it's brought it all back to me. I was so frightened that night; the memory had sunk so deep, and had all but disappeared," she sobbed.

"We had to live like animals for over a week, until some men came and moved us on," added Mel, with watery eyes.

"Nic and Mel, go and see to the kids, this has been a bad idea," suggested Joe.

"No, it's all my fault," added Val.

"And mine," agreed Joe. "I should've fed you little snippets over the years when it came up naturally. It's all too

266

much to handle in one big dollop like this. That time was truly horrendous for us."

"Look, stop," said Val, "all I really wanted to know is how you learned your trade?"

"He learned from Uncle Pete, of course," said Mel. "Joe, do you two never talk? I'm sure Uncle Pete must've come up somewhere in conversation over the years?"

Val looked vacant, her expression said it all.

"Obviously not," said Nicolette, "Joe, for goodness sake, why not?"

Nicolette had now recovered, but the occasion hadn't turned out as they'd hoped. Perhaps they thought things would seem different; that the past would somehow be enveloped in a rosy haze? However, that was not the case.

"Right," said Joe, "I think we've finished. I'll tell about the good times later, I don't think any of us should linger on the bad or the sad bits anymore."

They then all went outside into the sunshine. For the remainder of their visit, she watched them interact with Joe, the kids, and even managed to join in herself. She genuinely hoped, it wouldn't be too long before they could all get together again. Compared to her own sister Silvia, they were like a breath of fresh mountain air.

CHAPTER THIRTY-FIVE:

"James wants us to visit *Cloverley*," I confided in Mona, during a quiet spell in between patient appointments.

"Is that good?" she asked.

"I don't know… you tell me?" I replied.

"Me, tell you? I know nothing about this *Clover…* place. For a supposedly clever woman, you do ask some dumb questions," said Mona.

"Supposedly clever? How dare you Mona, what do you see hanging on these walls? What do they tell you?" I asked, turning to point out my hard-earned collection of professional qualifications, memberships, degrees, and diplomas…

"Personally, they don't tell me anything. I've always thought they were rather pretentious, if you must know," she replied.

"Well, that takes the biscuit, and empties the barrel right to the bottom," I remarked.

"Trust you to turn the conversation towards biscuits, barrels, and bottoms," she retorted.

I wanted to laugh, my mirth vibrating inside, but I couldn't let her win, at least not so easily. "You may think that a clever remark, Mona, but I view it as childish. Only children make remarks about bottoms," I said.

"Jokes about bottoms? I'm not making any such jokes… it's you who's gone to the bottom of the pile with that last remark," she replied.

I turned for the sanctuary of my office, closed the door and let my laughter escape as quietly as possible. Then I crept through into my cloakroom, and chortled where I knew she couldn't overhear. I knew she'd probably be outside my office door listening, as was her normal practise. Mona was a caring person; my welfare was her top priority, not her job!

Back to reality, I was nervous over James's plan for a family visit to *Cloverley*. He wanted me to show him our Weekender, the local sights, including Alexander's old shop, and introduce him to some folks I knew back then. This could be potentially embarrassing, and I couldn't tell him why. We were due to visit my dad next weekend, so I decided to get him to put James off this *Cloverley* idea.

*

During the week, Mona had shown herself to be utterly useless at coming up with plausible excuses or reasons, which I could use to stop us visiting *Cloverley*. I think it gave her perverse pleasure to see my distress, so when Friday afternoon arrived, I waved her goodbye and headed home, relieved that my week's work was over, although not my dilemma.

The following morning we headed off to visit my dad, my step-mum Barbara, and their two boys. We wafted along the motorway, lost to the outside world in the comfort of James's car.

When we finally drew up alongside their front door, I noticed Dad looked happy and relaxed standing on the doorstep with his arm around Barbara's shoulder. This second marriage had been a successful union, and not just because of the arrival of my two half-brothers. I lowered the car's electric window, and stuck my head out, "Hi guys," I called.

"Sorry, the boys aren't here, Dawn, they're committed to a rugby tournament this weekend. However, they send everyone their love," said Dad, "so, you're stuck with us two oldies."

Lorraine and Sean groaned on hearing of the boys' absence, but I managed to cover their disappointment by telling Dad and Barbara, that they were just fishing for compliments, over their looks or how much older they looked… that sort of thing.

Nevertheless, Sean and Lorraine's groans focused my mind on the fact that they would not be accompanying their parents for too much longer. Our Angela, however, had merely shrugged her shoulders at the news of the boys' absence. They were obviously not on her agenda for today. Our Angela, always had her own agenda.

"It can't be helped," I said, "people should always stick to their commitments."

"I hope you're remembering we're off to *Cloverley* soon, Dawn. We're committed to that visit," said James, as we clambered from the car. "I'm intrigued to meet the folks from your bygone times."

He'd said this in an artificially loud voice, which, when he put it on, always annoyed me. Furthermore, Dad would be certain to have overheard and would grasp it by the short and curlies. I was going to be embarrassed, about that there was no doubt, and I could see the clouds of discomfort closing in around me…

"*Cloverley?* I've not heard anyone mention that place for a long time. I've some good memories of *Cloverley*," said Dad, "and some bloody bad ones too, as you well know, Dawn?"

"Yes, Dad, I know. Now let's all get ourselves indoors to freshen up," I suggested, giving both him and Barbara a hug.

*

271

As we lay in our bed that night, James mentioned that my dad had quizzed him over his sudden interest in *Cloverley*. I knew it! I thought Dad might let it pass, but I should have known better. "Why all the sudden fuss about a hick village?" I asked.

"A hick village? Now that sounds wonderful! I wish I'd thought of us going there sooner. The kids would've loved holidaying in a but-and-ben when they were younger," he answered.

"Our Weekender wasn't a but-and-ben, as you've described... it was a proper house, set in its own land just outside the village," I replied.

"But you did get to run around wild in your bare feet, half clothed, with uncombed hair and jam smeared on your face," he said, desperately trying to suppress a snigger.

I'd briefly worried about my over active imagination not that long ago. However, mine was nothing compared to his! "From where are you getting all his claptrap?" I asked.

"It's not claptrap, it's how your dad described it... just slightly embellished, that's all," he replied, moving closer...

I eased myself slowly towards the edge of the bed... I wasn't quite finished with this discussion yet... "And what else did Papa dear relate to you?" I asked.

"I asked if he remembered anyone by the name of Doubleday?" he replied.

"And did he?" I asked, already knowing the answer.

"Oh, yes, nothing wrong with his memory," replied James. "He remembered them alright, in fact, he also mentioned a young lad called Joe, who would undoubtedly have led you astray if circumstances hadn't been that your folks divorced and never went back. Old man Sugar also came from *Cloverley*, and the place reeked with sourness as far as your dad's concerned."

Sugar, sourness? He thought he was so smart, did my James. I decided to concentrate on Alexander, which would hopefully allow me to gloss over any references to Joe... "It was not my fault that Mum fell for the charms of Alexander Sugar," I replied, "and anyway, he's now well removed from *Cloverley*."

"I'm more interested in this Joe bloke... how old was he?" asked James.

"Twelve-ish," I replied, in rather hushed tones.

"Twelve?" he repeated. "The way your dad ranted on about him, I thought he was old enough to lead you astray romantically. Heavens, there's nothing wrong with a bit of tree climbing and childish mischief."

I inched back closer to him, until *Cloverley* was no longer uppermost on his mind, and decided that I'd have a word with my father in the morning...

273

CHAPTER THIRTY-SIX:

A few days after Mel and Nicolette's visit, Joe and Val returned home having delivered Daisy and Brigitte to Grandma Jean's. Brigitte had suggested they both stay over with her, as she would enjoy having them both, much more than Daisy on her own.

"Brigitte's good at organising things to her advantage," remarked Joe.

"She was pretty upset when Daisy got to stay over on her own the last time. It wasn't deliberate; it was just one of those spur of the moment happenings," replied Val.

"Well, she's now managed to turn that around," said Joe. "As I said, she's good at organising."

"So are you," she replied. "You'll need to take her into the business when she's older."

"I'll get you settled in first," he said, with a grin, "one girl at a time... Val, I'm delighted that you want to become involved."

"Talking about your business, can you tell me more about your Uncle Pete?" she replied. "How come I've never met him?"

"Because he's dead," replied Joe, turning off the car engine.

"Oh, I'm sorry to hear that, when did he die?" she asked.

"It must have been a year or so before I came back to *Cloverley*. He suffered a sudden heart attack... here one moment and gone the next," replied Joe. "He was a good man, one of the best."

"What exactly was his relationship that made him your uncle?" asked Val.

"His relationship? Well, he was my mum's eldest brother, that's how," replied Joe. The moment had arrived to finally come clean and tell her the whole sorry tale. She had a right to know about her husband's dark past...

"Val, we ended up living in a dump of a flat in the city. Things were always stormy between my folks as you've gathered, when one day he attacked Mum... I can't remember the exact reason which sparked him off, but it turned out to be for the very last time. When he'd finished his frenzied attack on her, he turned and caught me with his fist, then left, slamming the door behind him."

"Did he hurt the girls?" asked Val.

"No, but they witnessed it. They were still young, but I'd turned fourteen, and had become his new target," he replied. "The girls were wailing and his punch stunned me. I realised Mum had been hurt badly… she was moaning and calling out to me, and I managed to struggle her up onto the couch."

"Did she need treatment?" asked Val.

"She probably did, but because she could still speak, that clouded my judgement," answered Joe. "She sent me out to phone this Pete person for help. She told me he was my uncle, and that she'd kept his phone number in the front of her purse. I found the piece of paper with his number scrawled on it, and hoped it was the right one. I then went next door, and asked Mrs Thompson if she could lend me some coins for the public kiosk. She didn't ask why, but gave me some loose change. I must've convinced Uncle Pete of our desperate situation, as I remember someone calling out and thumping on our front door. Mum recognised his voice, so I opened it to a complete stranger… a burly man, a little older than Mum. He pushed past, knelt beside Mum and gently tended to her bruised face.

Val… this act of tenderness shocked me. I'd never met this man before, in fact, I didn't even know he existed. However, I found out later that Mum had been too ashamed to keep in contact with her family after she'd married… yet he still came to her aid. When Pete saw the state of her, he took control. He told me to gather everyone's stuff together as we were leaving——,"

"So, what did you do?" interrupted Val.

Joe recalled everything in his mind as clearly as the day it had happened, "I went back to our neighbour Mrs Thompson, and asked if she'd any spare rubbish bags, and she had. I suppose, looking back, they must've known our desperate situation... they must've heard Mum's screams, and it must've been terrible hearing everything else that went on, but they never intervened or knocked on our door."

"Surely they should've helped your mum?" said Val.

"No, they were a frail old couple, but kind. Mrs Thompson pushed a fiver into my pocket along with the rubbish bags. I think they were trying their best in the circumstances," he explained. "We stuffed the bags full with everything we could lay our hands on, which wasn't much... then Dad came back————"

"What did you do then," interrupted Val, "what did he want?"

"I suppose he came back to either say sorry, or create more hell, who knows? That's what he always did... he always thought that if he came back and said sorry, it made everything okay... until the next time," explained Joe. "This time the girls had ducked down behind the couch to escape him, and I felt like joining them."

"Oh, Joe!" gasped Val, visibly shocked.

"Dad demanded to know what that bastard Pete was doing in his house, and if it was Mum's doing? I didn't know what to say, and recall his eyes burning into mine, waiting for me to explain... and then turning to the hurriedly stuffed bags which lay in the middle of the room. I froze when it dawned on him what was happening. He lurched in my direction, pulling off his belt from around his waist. Mum screamed at him, as she knew what he was about to do, when Uncle Pete grabbed him and pushed him to the floor. Dad struggled back to his feet, his eyes blazing with rage, and took a swing at him. He missed and then Uncle Pete hit him with an almighty punch, which landed him on the floor with a thump."

"Joe, what a terrible experience... your mum, how...?" began Val.

"She was lying sobbing, the moisture from her tears smeared the dried blood on her face, making it sticky and streaked. Pete asked me to help drag Dad, who was thrashing and kicking into the other room. Mandy quickly produced a key from somewhere, and we locked the door," explained Joe. "Pete thanked her, and I remember how pleased she was with her little self, her face lighting up in the midst of this horrific drama which was unfolding all around."

"Joe, I can't imagine how you could all live in a world like that?" replied Val.

"We just did. It wasn't living, it was more like existing... you know deep down that everything's wrong in your life, but you carry on trying to cope for yourself and for the people you love," he answered. "Pete saw that the girls were upset and confused, and gently explained to them that he was Mum's brother, and here to help."

"Were they not upset because he'd fought with their dad?" asked Val.

"No, it was the state of Mum that upset them," he replied. "Pete explained that she had agreed we should all leave and go home with him."

Val reached out and took hold of Joe's hand.

"It was just chaotic; Dad was cursing and kicking at the locked door with all his might. Such was the racket, that Pete felt sure the neighbours would call the police. I told him that I didn't think they would, as they were on our side. He understood and asked me to get him a pencil."

"A pencil, what for," asked Val, "and did you?"

"Yes, we'd plenty of them, Nicolette used to acquire pencils at every opportunity," replied Joe, with a short laugh. "Pete wrote an address on a scrap of paper, then took us out into the street, and I remember us standing outside like lost souls. It felt unreal, like some surreal dream. Pete stopped a passing cab, gave the driver the slip of paper with the address, along with some money. Our instructions were to sit tight outside the address until he arrived in his car with Mum and our stuff."

"Joe, you did what he told you, even although you didn't really know him… why?" asked Val.

"I desperately needed someone to take the responsibility from me. I couldn't manage on my own anymore. Pete was Mum's brother, our uncle, and if she trusted him, then there was no reason for us not to do likewise," he replied. "Dad's behaviour had gotten much worse recently, making our time in *Cloverley* when we lived in the old run-down shack, seem good in comparison. It was the thought of what life could be like here that kept my dreams alive."

"What happened next?" asked Val.

"Well, the taxi driver left us outside the address he'd been given, and we stood there huddled together. We'd waited for what seemed ages, and then it began to rain, so we found shelter under the front porch of the house, where we continued to wait," said Joe.

"Did you begin to think he perhaps wasn't coming?" asked Val.

"The longer we waited, the more I worried, then Nicolette started to cry, and this started off the other two," explained Joe. "I was at the stage when I wanted to cry myself when luckily they arrived. Pete passed Mandy the key to his front door, then carefully picked Mum up from the back seat of his car, and we all traipsed inside out of the rain."

"What was Pete's house like," asked Val, "did he not have a wife?"

"No, he'd never married. His house was on the outskirts of town, in a neat and tidy street, each with

280

individual garages and large back gardens. It wasn't a mansion, but to us it appeared huge," answered Joe. "Inside was warm and furnished with proper furniture and real carpets. Pete laid Mum out on the couch and asked me to help make her a bed through in one of the other rooms."

"Did you manage," asked Val, "to make up a bed, I mean?"

"I copied what he was doing with the sheets and things, it wasn't too difficult. Pete then showed us the upstairs bedrooms, which I don't think he used much, if at all. Mel and I got one whole empty room each, whilst Mandy and Nicolette shared another," said Joe. "Despite the emptiness of the rooms, we felt safe. Back downstairs, I helped Pete move Mum into the room we'd prepared, and I sponged her face with warm water. I still remember the state of her bruised frame. Uncle Pete fetched some aspirin for her pain——- I'm sorry Val, that's it for today; I'll tell you more some other time."

"Joe," replied Val, "of course, and thanks for sharing your pain."

They had arrived home and had been sitting outside in their car talking for some time. Suddenly there was a knock on their car window, "Are you going to stay outside all night?" yelled Shirley.

"We're just coming Shirley sweetheart," replied Joe. "Come on Val, let's get ourselves back to the here and now… it's where I want to be."

CHAPTER THIRTY-SEVEN:

The next morning my sweet James never mentioned the dreaded 'C' word, and we went down to breakfast hand-in-hand. Once there, I carefully stirred the breakfast conversation around and around. Dad and I ate whilst discussing his garden, the boys sporting achievements and his and Barbara's upcoming holiday, whilst James and the kids seemed content to gobble up Barbara's delicious breakfast fare.

Barbara and I got on extremely well, and in truth, I preferred her to Mum for conversation, advice, comfort… in fact, for all the times when talking was good therapy. Let me add, that I do love my own mum more than I do Barbara… but it's a funny old world, full of relations, that in reality, one cannot stand or can only bear in small doses.

Barbara finally stopped seeing to our needs and settled at the table with us, as we drained the remaining dregs from the coffee pot. Dad then came out with Alexander Sugar's name… for reasons unbeknown to me. James then assumed the mantle, which made my heart sink… "We visited him and Dawn's mum a few weeks back," he said, "and he certainly wasn't looking as good as you."

"He never did look as good as me, that's what I could never understand," Dad replied. "What did you think Dawn, you were in the perfect position to judge?"

"Dad, I was only young when it all kicked off, give me a break," I replied. I wanted to rise and leave the table; thoughts of old man Sugar were more than enough to give me acute indigestion…

"You may have only been young Dawn, but you were such a precocious child. You surely had an opinion or at least an observation?" he continued. "Come on, don't disappoint me."

I could tell that our Angela had now tuned into our conversation… once a sleuth, and all that. James too sat smirking and smiling, and I've never come across anyone who could do that as well as him. I needed to gather my wits about me, and quickly…

"Dad, the whole thing wasn't about looks. You were always a good looking man and Sugar wasn't," I replied, "it must've been something else about him."

"But what was it she saw in him?" he asked, peering at me. "You're the best qualified person here to answer my dilemma."

Heavens, this happened twenty-eight years ago, why this morning, Dad, why, I thought? "The mystery of love, is exactly that… a mystery," I replied, with a shrug of my shoulders.

"Is that the kind of deduction you get paid all that money for, Mum?" asked Sean. "Non-committal statements like that are a load of rubbish."

I hadn't realised he was even listening to our conversation… family members supporting each other… that'll be the day! "People have to hand over big bucks to get my professional opinion," I replied haughtily.

"But Grandad's your dad," piped up Angela, "surely even you, wouldn't charge him for advice?"

'Surely even you'… these words stung… where had I gone wrong with that child?

"Angela, your mum's trying to tell Grandad gently, that she doesn't want involved, as the truth's too close to home," answered James, still smirking in my direction.

"Yes, Daddy's got it exactly right," I replied. Why am I calling him Daddy, for goodness sake?

"Methinks my father ought to be the psychiatrist in this family," muttered Sean.

I glared at my only son…

"Dawn, I don't know why Frank's brought up the topic of your mum today? You'd think because he and I have been married for twenty-four years, he would've moved on by now," offered Barbara, taking more of an interest in the way this discussion was heading.

"I was just thinking back Barbara, after James and I chatted about *Cloverley* last night. It's nothing to do with us, you do realise that, don't you?" explained Dad.

I'd been going to rise and excuse myself, but suddenly found myself developing an interest in where this line of conversation may go, so sat tight.

"I don't think I do, Frank. I've given you two sons, and looked after every single one of your needs, and yet you still appear to lust over Madge," she replied.

Lust? Now that was a strong word, especially coming from Barbara. Lust? She was talking about my parents, and I'd never realised that this whole sorry mess had arisen out of... well, lust?

"Don't talk nonsense, Barbara. Lust? When did you start using the lust word? It must be from the influence of these books you read," replied Dad.

My, this had the potential of becoming rather serious... I'd clearly failed in my professional capacity, as I must've somehow overlooked the brewing evidence... this explosion of words could be laid squarely at my door... "Come on kids, and you too, James, I'd like to have a look around the garden to see Dad's handiwork while the sun's still shining," I hurriedly announced.

"But——," protested Angela.

"You too, Angela, this is not a sitting-on-your-butt-day, not even for you," I quickly added.

James took my hand on our way out to the garden, and we found ourselves alone, as the kids decided to go to the nearby shops instead. He was full of excitement, as his expectations of *Cloverley* had now, in his mind, reached a new high. "This hick village has taken my imagination to new heights," he said, "especially with the inclusion of this lust ingredient in the mix."

I dropped my hand from his, "James, for goodness sake! Don't let that word go to your head," I hissed, barely taking in the garden sights as we strolled along.

"Why not my love, it just adds to the intrigue of the place?" he replied, with a grin. "I just can't wait to go."

"I never put you down as being… a lustful man," I countered.

"Who, me? I only lust over you, my love," he replied, still grinning.

I went to turn back to the house, when he took hold of my arm, "Dawn, what's wrong with you? Where's your famous sense of humour?" he asked.

He was right… lust in *Cloverley*? It was just too funny to contemplate seriously… or was it?

"James, it would be comical if I wasn't personally involved, but it's my folks that are being made fun of," I huffed.

James then put his arms around me, "You're right, Dawn. I'm sorry. Let me apologise to you here and now… but it's still all quite amusing, you must agree?" he replied.

I nodded, as I stood there in his arms, and we began to giggle. I loved this man.

*

We survived the rest of the weekend without any further mention of Alexander Sugar, lust, or my folk's relationship. Furthermore, the dreaded 'C' word was never mentioned either. As a result, I arrived back at my practice on Monday morning, a refreshed woman.

"My, my, what have we here?" asked Mona. "You're actually smiling this morning."

"I always smile," I replied, with a degree of aloofness…

She looked at me with widened eyes.

"What? I do always smile. Are you trying to tell me otherwise?" I added. The cheeky besom, she took more liberties than the famous statue. I was pleased I had thought this, as even I didn't think it would have sounded too clever a throw-away remark. "Mona, don't you have any work to get on with?" I asked. "It's after nine o'clock, you know."

"So you're late then?" she instantly answered.

I stomped through into my consulting room, slamming the door behind me. I lifted my hand to thump my desk, but decided not to give her any further satisfaction. Moreover, I'd hurt my hand the last time I'd vented my frustration out on my desk.

We still had twenty minutes before my first patient arrived, so I waited impatiently for a couple of minutes, then tip-toed back to the door. I listened for any signs of activity... but nothing... nothing at all. I then grabbed hold of the handle and yanked the door wide open... and there she was, standing frozen to the spot, with her hand raised in the air...

"I was just about to knock," she said.

"Well, have you a problem?" I asked.

"No, have you?" she replied. "How did it go at your dad and Barbara's?"

"It started badly, but then recovered," I found myself replying.

"Do you want to tell me about it?" she asked.

"Have we time?" I answered, glancing over at the office clock.

"I don't know? It all depends on how much there is to tell," she smugly replied.

"I suppose, I could squeeze it in, if I leave out the naughty bits," I said. Her little face looked as if it had been dealt a cruel blow. "Right, you get the coffee poured and I'll begin. If you're in luck, my first patient may be running late."

*

James called shortly after lunch with the news I'd been dreading. He'd managed to book us into some plush hotel not too far from *Cloverley*, "I decided to go for it, as there was no point in hanging around waiting for the snows to clear completely," he said.

"It's not winter, James... and why in heaven's name are you saying that?" I replied.

"Oh, my grandad used to say that all the time. It just kind of slipped out," he answered.

"You'd better watch what else you let slip out in future," I replied.

"What a strange thing to say, Dawn, but never mind," he said with a chuckle, "are you pleased?"

"Ecstatic, can't you guess?" I replied, biting on my lower lip.

"Now my darling, don't be like that. I'm sure you'll enjoy the trip, the hotel and the other," he said.

"I'm sure I will enjoy the trip... and the hotel," I replied, "it's the other what bothers me."

"What, re-visiting dear friends? How come? You felt drawn to them yourself only recently," he said.

In a way that made sense… I suppose… "You're right, I'm just being stupid," I replied. "It'll be great, and thanks love."

I said goodbye, and buzzed Mona to send through my next patient. Be professional Dawn; don't fall into a heap on the floor until you've sorted out your patient first. Remember to apply the skills you've been equipped with through many years of study, training and experience.

*

"Dawn, you look drained," said Mona, later that afternoon. She placed her arm around my shoulder, and I knew in that instant why I employed her. She could read me like a book, from cover to cover. "If it would help, would you like me to stay on so that we could talk for a while, it's not a problem?" she suggested.

"No, it's fine; off you go home, I'll finish up in here," I replied.

After Mona left, I sat at my desk with my eyes closed, and considered my options… it was odds on, that I'd probably have to face Joe sometime, and I felt such a fool. I didn't have the words to express to James what I felt for him… not the Joe as he is now, but how he'd been then. If we did meet again, as the Fates appeared to be conspiring, there existed the distinct possibility that my memories from the distant past risked being shattered…

Why did he marry Val of all people? I would have to face her and their children, albeit I'd spoken to two of them already. They'd remember me for sure, in fact, I might have bumped into some or all of them, when I'd had that stupid car altercation... these cars which were related had briefly kissed in the passing. How could I now face him? He'd stood in the middle of the roadway and watched me make my get-away... and then there was his son, Brian, he'd definitely recognise the car if he'd been with him that day...

Furthermore, there was Mrs Brown... Jean may not want to see me again, because I'd hurriedly driven off from her too? Okay, Mona had sent her a bunch of placatory flowers, but I'd still driven off from her and from Joe... was that my subconscious *modus operandi*... to run away from reality? So many questions and yet so very few answers...

I rose, switched off the office lights, locked up and headed home... mentally drained.

CHAPTER THIRTY-EIGHT:

Joe gradually filled Val in with the remaining aspects of his past life over the next few days. She learned from him that his Uncle Pete, a lifelong bachelor, had agreed with the rest of his family, that his sister Katerina shouldn't marry Daniel Doubleday. Their opinion however hadn't bothered Katerina, in her eyes he scrubbed up well, and she adored all the things her family disliked. Whilst Daniel regularly boasted he'd inherit land and a house in the country, they hadn't taken kindly to his aggressive attitude, swarthy appearance, and found his honesty and integrity somewhat dubious.

Katerina was the only daughter in her family, sandwiched between two brothers. Her father's strict rules often created problems, and it didn't help matters that her mother invariably backed her husband's every move.

"Was your Daniel a 'tink', as my dad used to say?" asked Val.

"Kind of ways," replied Joe. "He was on the edge, although I never got to the bottom of what he was."

"I apologise for the past, Joe. Years ago, my dad called you that name, before he got to know you," said Val. "When we were young, you frightened me, yet despite that, I loved you."

"Do you mean, back in the time of Dawn?" asked Joe.

"Yes," she answered.

This revelation shocked, as he'd hardly noticed her back then, and wasn't a leading feature in his picture. She stayed in the village, and was always a background character, unlike Dawn, who floated in and out injecting fresh excitement…

"Please, not a word, Joe. I know you were in love with her then, and I believe she's the reason you came back to *Cloverley*," she continued.

"I had the land to come back to, but I'll not lie to you Val, I did come back in the hope I might find Dawn here, although I knew it was a long shot," he replied.

They were sitting alone outside on their favourite bench in the garden, their children having gone to the Warner house to play. Brenda's husband's absence from home had become ever more frequent, and she found having extra children around, kept her mind off him and her troubles.

Val and Joe sat in silence. Was it his imagination, or had she moved further away from him? After a few minutes, she rose and told him she had things to get on with in the house. He, on the other hand, lingered on the bench, full of lonely dread and racked with guilt...

That night as they lay in bed, Joe held Val close and soon felt her melt in his arms. "Thank you," he whispered to her in the darkness.

"Joe, the past is over; I was just being childish earlier," she whispered back.

Later, when sleeping and breathing softly beside him, he finally closed his own eyes... a weight had been lifted from him, but his conscience was still tortured and torn. He'd not only come back to *Cloverley* hoping to find Dawn, but had also found his memories of her remained very much alive. Over time, as he'd made the transition into manhood, her memory clung on, spurring him to be evermore successful, to make her proud of him... eventually, he fell into an uneasy sleep.

*

He swaggered along the lane, in defiance of Dawn's dad. Would she be back? He now didn't think she would... at least, not for a very long time!

Dawn had always spoken of her dad as if he was the original Mr Good Guy. For sure he'd gently taken

Nicolette's hand at the Fair, but today, to his eyes and ears it had been a wholly different story. Joe kicked stones into the long grass at the side of the path in frustration. The anger that Mr Pearson had displayed towards him, showed him to be far less than friendly.

He looked back to the Weekender hoping for a glimpse of Dawn, but their shapes had now melded into one indistinguishable blurry mass... He was on his way along the track which led to his shack, when he heard the sound of a car as it drove past the top of the lane. Dawn was being carried away on the breeze... she was going and would soon be gone, perhaps forever,... why couldn't it have taken him too?

Joe dragged his feet, as he got closer and closer to the ramshackle converted bus that was his home... he should've been there this morning, and not at the river with Dawn. His old man had told him not to wander off, but he had... it was now done, and he would have to face the inevitable consequences... but despite this, he wouldn't have changed anything.

He knew what was coming; there would be no homecoming smiles and kisses... he just prayed his girlies where not around to see him humiliated... those sweet girlies... where had they come from?

"Hey you, pretty boy, get yourself over here! Where the hell did you skulk off to this morning? I told you to fuckin' stay put. I needed you, so where were you?" he yelled. "In the fuckin' river I   see... you're soaked, you stupid, bloody fool. Get out of my sight."

Joe couldn't believe his luck, he'd been expecting a brutal beating...

"Joe, you're soaked," said his mum. "Go inside and change right now. Have you been in that river again?"

"Of course he's been in the fuckin' river, you stupid bitch," snarled his dad. "Leave him wet, it'll teach him a bloody lesson. Come with me boy, I need you to stack wood, right now."

Joe was busily stacking wood when the girlies arrived by his side, "Joe, why are your clothes wet, and why are you shivering?" asked a concerned Mel.

He couldn't answer or control his shivering... "Mum, Mum, I think Joe's ill... he can't stop shaking," yelled Mandy.

His mum ran over to the woodshed, and called on his dad, "Look at what you've done now by leaving him soaking wet... he'll catch his death," she scolded.

For once he didn't answer, but came over, lifted Joe in his strong arms, and carried him into their shack. For the first time in his life that he could remember, he was fussed over by his dad. He was dried, wrapped in warm blankets, made hot drinks, and allowed to stay in bed all day. The girlies came and played hospitals with him, and for a moment, saw the all too briefest signs of affection between his parents...

Joe awoke with a start, tears running down his cheeks. Val stirred and took his hand, as he quickly wiped his eyes with the back of his other…

CHAPTER THIRTY-NINE:

Love was in the air for our Lorraine, and whilst James found it amusing, I did not! "She still has two years of education and exams to go through before she leaves school, and now she's talking of engagement rings and all the rest," I exclaimed.

"Dawn, he's a nice boy," replied James.

"Boy, that exactly the issue! He's the same age as our Sean, for goodness sake. He's not going out with girls or thinking of buying rings... no... he has brains... he's intelligent," I protested.

"In some quarters, he might also be seen as being a shade backward," replied James.

"Backward? That's our son you're talking about," I remarked.

"Precisely, I was far more advanced than him at his age," he replied.

"Advanced? At what... exactly?" I countered.

"What do you think?" he answered. "I was a red-blooded male... I lived for love."

"You lived for love?" I exclaimed. "Explain, in detail please... if you can?"

"Come on, Dawn, I never took you for being a prude," he replied.

"I've been called many things over the years, but never a prude. That to me suggests that I'm a poor relation to a prune," I huffed.

"No, you're not as wizened as a prune," replied James. "Sorry, what I mean is that you're not wizened at all!"

Too little, too late... I felt wronged, and tonight I'd make my solitary way to the spare room.

*

My next working day had reached its end, when Mona and I struck up a conversation. I had managed to contain within myself what had happened last night, that is until now...

"He compared you to a prune?" remarked Mona, "How strange."

299

"Nothing's stranger than a man... you know nothing about men and these sorts of things," I replied.

"What sort of things, Dawn?" she asked, defensively.

"The things that can happen between men and women... the sort of things that have eluded you, Mona, my dear," I replied, perhaps on reflection, rather too sanctimoniously?

"What gives you the right to judge and tell me that certain things have eluded me?" she snapped.

A defensive silence suddenly descended upon us, with each encamped in the middle of our own self-righteousness. The kettle whistled in the background, not realising that whistling or singing was inappropriate at this time...

"You make the tea, Mona, I'm the boss, and you're my employee, a fact which often escapes you," I heard myself saying.

She glared at me, and then stomped about making the tea without another word. It was duly placed in front of me in an unceremonious fashion, slurping its contents over the rim of the china cup into its saucer.

"Start again, Mona, please dear. I see that I'll have to go back to basics with you," I said. I just couldn't stop myself...

"You're the one who should go back to basics... the basics of manners," she replied, "I can no longer work with you, Dawn."

"Suit yourself, but don't expect me to keep your seat warm," I answered... plenty of other fish in the sea.

On a roll, I marched into my office and as usual in these circumstances, slammed my door shut. Then it happened, a strange dullness took over me, and I received no satisfaction at all from my actions. I tiptoed back over to the door and pressed my ear to one of the panels... nothing. On returning to my seat, I buzzed through... again nothing. In desperation, I rose, retraced my steps to the door, and threw it open wide... but to my astonishment, there was no one there... Mona had vanished!

It was fortunate for me, that it was the end of our working day. I would've been hard pressed to even look at a patient, let alone talk to one. I sat back at my desk, making no attempt to set off for home... what a darned mess I'd got myself into. I hadn't spoken to James all day, and it was really hurting that he hadn't attempted to contact me. In addition, my relationship with Lorraine had taken a massive dip, when I'd allowed my disapproval of her proposed engagement be known. Now this unnecessary upset with Mona, simply added to my increasing woes...

I made my way to the cloakroom, splashed my face with cold water, and then retraced my steps to my desk. Looking around at the degrees, diplomas, and awards affixed to the walls, I suddenly felt decidedly stupid and unworthy of any of them. I was a force for destruction!

Lifting the phone I dialled James's number... "About time too," he answered, "have you been very busy today?"

What he really meant was, had I not had the time to call, due to patients? "Yes," I lied. I was not worthy of him either. "James, Mona's left..."

"Left what?" he asked.

"Left her job... here, at the practice... with me," I replied.

"That was very sudden, especially after we were good enough to have her stay for the weekend. Yes, Dawn, I'm most surprised to hear that bit of news," he said. "Need to go now though darling... see you when you get home... love you."

"Love you prune, you mean?" I replied.

"Dawn, get back to normality by the time you come home, or I'll take myself off for the weekend," he said.

"That sounds like a veiled threat?" I replied.

"It is!" he affirmed.

*

When I arrived home, I found Lorraine busy in the kitchen, trying to act all grown-up by making a start on the preparations for our evening meal. In truth, she was acting far more grown-up than me, who hadn't even given food a thought.

"Mum, are we okay? I know that you and Dad have fallen out over me, and I hate that," asked Lorraine.

"No, we haven't... it was because he called me a prune," I replied.

"No, he didn't. He told me he hadn't thought you were a prude... not a prune," she corrected.

"But he did say I was wizen," I snapped back.

"He got his words muddled, that's all. This is Dad we're talking of here, you know fine well he adores you," she replied.

I said nothing as Madam lectured me. I'm the person who's meant to help people, be empathetic and understanding, not her! It was a difficult task being a psychiatrist in this house...

"Mum, did you ever fall in love with anyone before you met Dad? Perhaps when you were around my age?" she asked.

"Not around your age," I replied.

"Then what age were you?" she asked.

"Mine was a proper romantic love, not like you and Simon, if that's what you're driving at?" I answered.

"What makes what you do always so blinking special... always so much better than anyone else?" she next asked.

"I'll leave you to get on with the cooking… it's nice to get a break from the monotonous drudgery of kitchen domesticity," I replied. I wasn't going to rise to the cheap jibes of a mere slip of a girl.

When James came home, he found me in the lounge. He sat beside me, and I offered a smile that was big enough for him to forgive me. "James, I've solved our Lorraine problem," I said, "once she's been stood peeling potatoes in these high-heels she has on for the past half-an-hour or so, she'll soon go off this engagement lark."

James looked at me.

"What?" I continued.

"Where's the romance in you, Dawn," he asked, "were you never young and in love?"

"Yes, I was young… and in love once," I answered.

"Well, give our Lorraine a break. Think back to how she must be feeling, and respond accordingly," he replied.

Lorraine came in to check what, beside vegetables, we wanted to have with our meal? James informed her that I'd had a rethink over her and Simon's relationship, and I felt obliged to agree. "Thanks, Mum," she said, hugging me tightly.

"By the way, who was this young man who captured the heart of the fair maiden Dawn?" asked James.

I tried to look nonchalant, but probably failed miserably, "I was never a fair maiden, I've always been dark," I replied, "and can you two stop harassing me with your incessant questions… you'll be setting our sleuthing Angela onto me next? I wish some people would mind their own business." I then rose and headed for the door, amidst peals of laughter.

"Touchy, touchy… good performance though, Dawn," said James.

"Someone's got something to hide," called out Lorraine.

Their laughter continued to ring in my ears as I left the room… guilty as hell!

*

The next morning, I asked James if he would accompany me. "Come with you where?" he asked.

"To Mona's; I must try to get this sorry, unfortunate mess sorted," I replied.

"That is women's business; you can manage without me, and in any case, I've paperwork to finish. I'll meet you for lunch or you can pick me up here, depending on the time?" he suggested.

It was his support I wanted; the knowledge that he was seated outside in the car, ready to comfort me in case things went pear-shaped. "Fine," I replied, "I'll get off on my own then… straight away. I'll probably phone when I'm done… is there anything else before I go?"

"Only that Lorraine wants Simon to come with us next weekend," said James.

"Come with us to *Cloverley*, you mean?" I said, somewhat astounded.

"Yes, that's where we're off to next weekend, I believe. He can share Sean's room," replied James. "I've told her it'll be fine, as long as there's no… monkey business."

I nearly asked him what exactly he meant by monkey business, then remembered it was along similar lines to what had caused me such trouble with Mona. "Well, Simon can be yours to look after," I said, "he's definitely not mine."

He didn't reply, so I kissed him and told him I'd see him later. Go on James, wish me luck… squeeze it out, from behind that darned newspaper you're hiding behind. I was extremely nervous, but at least I knew it didn't show. He re-engrossed himself in his paper, so I slipped out of the room, out from the house, and into the sanctuary of my lovely car…

That was something else to look forward to… having Simon in tow in *Cloverley*… was there no end to my cruel torture?

*

After a short drive, I turned into the street where Mona lived, and stopped outside her house. I knew where she resided, as I'd dropped her off on a handful of somewhat happier occasions, and had actually been over the threshold twice. I rang her doorbell and waited, and then waited some more, before I eventually heard movement from inside coming my way…

"Oh, it's you," she said, avoiding direct eye contact.

"Mona, I've come to apologise, and ask you to reconsider what you said about your job," I replied.

"You'd better come inside for a moment, I hate talking to anyone on my doorstep," she said.

Come in for a moment, and only because she didn't like talking on the doorstep, not because she wanted me in her house? Things were even worse than I had imagined! "Thanks," I mumbled, as I followed her indoors.

The house was as I remembered, small, old-fashioned, but tidy. We went into the sitting-room, where a man lay stretched out comfortably on the sofa, sipping from a mug. He nodded and smiled slightly as I entered. Mona however, made no attempt to introduce him, and she being the person who had dared to spout off to me on the subject of basic manners!

"Mona, can we have a word together… in private?" I asked, hesitantly.

She didn't answer, but led me through to the kitchen, which was tiny and had nowhere to sit. So we stood beside the sink, and when I glanced downwards, I noted two dishes waiting to be washed… I just can't help myself from sleuthing. She saw that I'd noticed, but gave no explanation, which did nothing for my heightening curiosity.

"I accept your apology, and I'll see you on Monday as usual. Perhaps if you could modify your behaviour, things might remain on a more even keel," she replied, in a hushed tone.

I'm the one who's supposed to say these sorts of things, Mona, I thought, but never mind. "I'll be off then, now that we've sorted things out, and I'll let you get back to your… friend, see you on Monday," I said.

"Thanks," she replied, without further comment.

Well, that was a doddle, I mused; it had gone much better than expected, in fact, less than five minutes in total from beginning to end.

I drove off to relate to James what I'd just encountered. As soon as I arrived home, I rushed to tell him my news, but before I could, I met our Angela in the hallway, "I'm coming for lunch with Dad and you," she announced, "I told him I was bored."

"You're coming with us, because you're bored?" I replied. "If you're coming with us, then please keep your boredom to yourself, because the last thing I need right now, is a large dollop of pre-pubescent boredom."

"Is something wrong, Mum? Do you want to talk it over with me?" she asked.

"Why not, at least you've offered," I replied. "Angela, let Dad know I'm back, and that we're going to have a chat through in the conservatory, before we leave."

She nipped into the lounge, then came and joined me. Right, I thought, let Angela be privy to the whole story... she at least cares. For around an hour, we huddled together in the chilly glass-house. It was the wrong time of the day to be sitting there, but my temperature was riding high by the time she left, so I hadn't noticed. Angela had turned into an excellent listener; she was indeed a counselling genius, as she displayed understanding, nodded where appropriate, and put herself in my place by gently prodding and leading me to see where I may have overreacted, made an error of judgement or assumption.

All joking aside, she helped me understand Mona, and in doing so, myself. I was in awe of my younger daughter. Of course she was welcome to dine with her father and me. I even dabbled with the thought that it might be better if James didn't come.

Angela skipped out from the conservatory, announcing that she too had enjoyed our little discussion and was no longer bored... yet another patient helped by me. Life is a two-way process; that was what our Angela told me, and she certainly brought that home to roost.

I hadn't strayed from the conservatory, when James popped in on the pretext of rescuing me. I told him I didn't need rescuing, but thanked him for his concern.

"Dawn, you'll get a chill sitting in there at this time of day. I must look into having heating installed, especially if you're keen to use it at such inappropriate times," he said. "By the way, did Angela mention, I've asked her to join us for lunch?"

I looked up at him.

"The child was bored, what else could I do?" he added. "I knew you wouldn't mind, you being a romantic at heart. It would also be nice for me to have lunch with my two darling ladies. As you know, romance produces certain end results... like our Angela."

He then stretched out his hand, which I took and allowed him to pull me to my feet. I then gave him a kiss and squeezed his hand. "Of course, it's all right," I replied.

"How did things go with old Mona," he asked, "everything fine?"

"Oh, yes," I replied, "it was a doddle."

"Good," said James.

After my chat with Angela, who'd told me to never jump to conclusions, I felt no need to tell James anything about my visit. Angela and I, both sleuths by nature, had reviewed the evidence in relation to what else I had deduced... the presence of a strange man in the house, the fact that he was stretched out on the sofa, the evidence of the unwashed cutlery and crockery in the sink, and last but by no means least, Mona's lack of formal introduction.

We concluded that there had been nothing to indicate that this man was anything other than a neighbour with whom she'd breakfasted with that weekend... that will be right! I could not wait to get hold of her on Monday morning, when I would squeeze every nuance of truth out of that little madam!

*

That afternoon, back in the comfort of our lounge, James was sitting, nodding pensively…

"James, what's going on inside that head of yours?" I asked.

"Oh, I was just pondering the fact that you and Angela were—," replied James.

"Intellectually on the same wavelength at lunch today?" I interrupted. "I have to admit she's certainly coming along very nicely. No surprise there, as she is, after all, our daughter."

CHAPTER FORTY:

Val had not seen or spoken to Silvia for over two weeks. This was most unusual, and her mum told her that Silvia was fuming, "Val, she's just about to combust. She hates it when people are not at her beck and call," said Jean. "I'm surprised she's not been around, hammering on your door."

"So am I, Mum. It'll be because she thinks Joe might be behind the door," she replied. "Mum, why does she hate him so much, because the funny thing is, she loves his kids?"

"Even she couldn't resist the kids, Val," said Jean. "As far as Joe's concerned, she's just plain old-fashioned jealous… the old green-eyed monster, and who wouldn't be? Don, and I'm not exaggerating here, is a wimp of a man, with no looks or personality, whilst Joe has everything… strength of character, personality and such good looks."

"Mum, she insists on calling or referring to Joe as a 'tink' at every available opportunity. I remember Dad used to call him that too, when I was young," said Val.

"And he was ashamed of himself in later life. You know that Joe and him got on so well, and he ended up being tremendously proud of his son-in-law and what he'd achieved," replied Jean. "Yes, your dad was so ashamed of himself, that the night you gave birth to Brian, he sat in this very room and blubbered like a baby."

She looked at her late husband's picture with glazed eyes… "Val, your Dad's opinion when you were young, was based on Joe's father, Daniel Doubleday. He was a nasty piece of work, and it was the old like-father-like-son chorus. Silvia tagged onto her dad's words and the rest is history," she added. "I haven't heard her saying these things to Joe though. That means she's being sleekit, which demonstrates she knows she's in the wrong. Leave it with me, I'll have words."

"Mum, don't get yourself upset, that's the last thing Joe would want, he loves you," said Val.

"And I love him too," replied Jean. "It'll give me pleasure to get my teeth into her ladyship. She can't hurt me anymore than she has already."

"If you say so," said Val.

"I do," replied Jean.

*

313

The extension at the rear of the Doubleday's house was taking shape. Joe had as many workers as was feasible working on its construction. Once finished, the team would move on to work on their first project for Mike, the architect. Joe and Mike respected each other and their fledgling joint future looked promising.

"I had a word with you-know-who," said Mike. "First, I told him that Mum and I were reverting to calling him Donald. Then I told him I was most embarrassed at the birthday party. I told a little white lie, when I said I'd overheard his wife being less than polite to you."

"Do you think it'll do any good?" asked Joe. "Not that I care, but it's for Val's sake. She's always been loyal to Silvia, but I hope she's now seeing the error of her ways?"

"Well, let's give Donald a chance, my brother's not that bad a guy," he replied.

They had been standing talking in Joe's garden, when they decided to move back into the kitchen to have a cuppa with Val. During their conversation, Mike asked about Joe's apprenticeship in the trade.

"Val and I have been discussing my past recently. I hadn't reached that part, so I can kill two birds with one stone, as they say," said Joe. "Suffice to say that my Uncle Pete, my mother's brother, had his own building company, or we wouldn't have been sitting here today. I worked hard and Uncle Pete used to say that the trade was in my blood. When he died, he left his business to me, together with a quarter share of his house. That set me up here, and the rest, as they say, is now history."

Val and Joe exchanged looks; they both knew there was a lot more to be said on that particular subject. At that point, the door opened and Daisy ran into the kitchen and jumped up on her daddy's knee...

"Who have we here?" asked Mike, "I think I know this little princess."

"Daisy," she replied, looking over, "I'm Daisy."

"I like your name," replied Mike.

"So do I," she answered.

They laughed, and she smiled, pleased with her little self.

"Are any of the girls due for a future in the Firm," asked Mike, "or is it only Brian?"

"I don't know about the little ones, but something tells me our Brian has other ideas," replied Joe.

"That just leaves, Shirley," replied Val, "I can see her working alongside you."

"Perhaps you're right, Val, and then she'll be following in her mother's footsteps, won't she?" he said. "Val's coming to work with me, once Daisy begins school."

"Doing what?" asked Mike.

"As my unofficial apprentice... I want her working alongside me every day," replied Joe.

"My, you two must have it bad," laughed Mike, shaking his head.

*

Two days later, Joe having completed his early morning inspections of the current sites, returned home to share breakfast with Val and the kids. He showered and changed out of his work clothes, ready for his meeting with Mike to go over the designs for their new joint project. He drove into *Cloverley* and parked outside his office. This was his Firm's hub, located in what had once been old man Sugar's shop when Joe was a boy. He could still picture it as a grocery store... the window displays had remained unchanged over the years, and during renovations, he'd found the old dummy tins and packets from the displays, lying discarded in a corner. This was a bittersweet moment of discovery in the premises he'd picked up on the cheap. The value of the renovated real estate meant nothing to him, as compared to the memories it rekindled... especially of Dawn.

As he approached the door to his offices, a figure suddenly stepped out in front of him from under the shadow of the canopy, causing him to snatch himself an extra intake of breath.

"What do you think you're doing hiding in the shadows?" he asked, now recognising Silvia.

"I'm waiting to see you, brother-in-law dear. I want a word and far away from where it could upset my sister," she snarled.

"You, not wanting to upset, Val? Now that would be a first," he exclaimed.

"Don't give me any of your smart arse talk, you——," she hissed, "Don't you think I can't see through you, and the vile poison you spread against me?"

"I've never poisoned anyone in my whole life. You're the poison expert in these parts," replied Joe. "For goodness sake Silvia, come inside or leave. I'm not discussing anything with you on my doorstep. If we really need to talk, then we'll do it inside."

"Acting the big man as usual?" she sniped back.

"Look, Silvia, either come in or get lost... I don't give a damn what you do," he answered.

She followed him inside dragging her feet. She hated being told what to do, especially by the likes of him. It surprised her when they entered a light filled, airy open-plan office where two employees were already at work. Off to the left was a door marked 'Private'... the whole place surprised Silvia, as it was by no stretch of the imagination, a grubby works office.

Joe said his good mornings to Judy and Bert, and checked with them that everything was running smoothly, before heading for his office. She followed, and was once more surprised by the tasteful decor. He took off his jacket, hung it on a peg, and sat himself behind his expansive desk, "Silvia, if you please," he said, inviting her to take a seat with a gesture of his arm

The dark green leather chair, with its comfortable padding, looked tempting... she had been standing outside for some considerable time, waiting for Joe to arrive but...

"You've not been in here before, have you?" added Joe.

She looked at him; the smug-faced git is not getting the better of me today, she thought. He cocked his head, with an air of anticipation, and waited... then smiled a polite smile and waited some more... Silvia turned, then walked out the office and the building.

Once outside, she didn't know what to do. Her head was pounding with anger, and her first reaction was to cry. The encounter had certainly not gone the way she'd hoped. On impulse, she crossed the road and headed towards Peggy's coffee shop. Once inside, she nodded to a few of the people she knew, before slipping into a vacant booth, well away from the window, and the gaze of other customers.

"Morning, Silvia, we don't see you in here too often," said the owner. "Have you come for breakfast?"

"Morning, Peggy, no, not breakfast, just a plain coffee," she replied. "I'm not in here very often because as you know... I'm a very busy lady."

"Oh? But I did hear you'd been at home recently... resting I believe?" said Peggy, with a knowing smile.

Damn, does this whole village know every blasted move I make, thought Silvia? "Whatever, Peggy," she replied. "Can I have a latte please?"

"Good to see you're keeping up the calcium levels," said Peggy.

At that, Silvia wriggled out of the booth, and stomped out. "Sorry, Peggy, cancel my order, I've just remembered I've somewhere else I need to be," she said as she left.

All eyes in the café watched her cross the street towards the Doubleday offices...

CHAPTER FORTY-ONE:

On Monday morning I found myself running late, and when I finally arrived at work, was disappointed to find my surgery still locked. "Where the devil's...," I mumbled to myself, "God, I hope she hasn't changed her mind? I couldn't imagine working with anyone else." Mona's antics kept me sane. For sure we have our little games we play with each other, but we also had mutual respect... well, I hoped she had respect for me, at least.

Once inside and settled, the phone rang and rang, and then it dawned on me that I was the only person here, so it was up to me to answer, "Yes, this is Dr Brennan speaking... to whom am I talking?" I asked. "Right, tell her we'll see her when we see her then, I suppose... bye."

"Blast and damn... okay Mona, you've made your point," I yelled. "I'll get everything set out myself." I next scurried around checking everything was in order, and then went to make myself a coffee. "Hell's bells Mona, how am I meant to drink coffee without milk? It's Monday morning and the fridge is bare," I screeched, "fetching the milk is your job."

"Hello? Hello Doctor Brennan... eh-em, sorry I'm early... am I interrupting something?" asked my nine-thirty...

"No, of course not, I was just rehearsing," I hastily lied.

"Oh, are you theatrically trained?" she asked.

"Um, yes, I'm... no... well... sometimes. It's a new play which I've been asked to road test, and I find it difficult to review these things without hearing the actual words ringing in my ears," I replied. "But enough of me, it's you who's the patient, Mrs Saunders."

She smiled at me, reassured, "No Mona, today, Doctor Brennan?" she asked.

"Um, I'm afraid not, although I expect her in later," I replied, "I think?"

She looked at me a little unsure with my last remark and I fully understood why. I'm one of the few people in her life whom she expects to know what's happening at all times, and to be in control of every situation. At half-past ten, Mona did arrive, just as Mrs Saunders was leaving. I decided to keep myself calm, and give her time to explain about Saturday morning...

"Morning, Dawn... sorry about not getting in until now, I——," she began.

"Mona, forget about that, just tell me who the guy lying on your couch was on Saturday?" I demanded.

"Is that part of my job description?" she asked.

I was astounded; this was tantamount to mutiny... "Mona, I tell you what I get up to, so I'm entitled to know what you've been up to... surely that's only fair?" I replied. "Surely?"

"Dawn, I don't see it that way at all. I'm a private person, while you're——," said Mona.

"While I am what?" I asked tersely, although I didn't really wish to hear her reply.

"Not so private," she replied.

"Just tell me, Mona, get it over with, you know you want to," I urged.

"Here's the milk, I suppose you'll be gasping for a coffee by now?" she replied.

"Look, stop being so blinking stubborn, you know that I'll keep going until you tell me. If you tell me now, I'll make the coffee," I suggested. I couldn't offer her a better deal than that at this precise moment.

"And if I don't tell," answered Mona, "I'll have to make the coffee as usual... is that what you're saying?"

"You understand fine what I'm—," I replied.

Just at that moment, my second patient arrived... also early. What was wrong with them this morning? Why could they not arrive when they were supposed to arrive?

"Good morning, Mr MacDonald, would you like a coffee since you're early? My assistant Mona was just about to make one," I said, in as a professional tone as I could muster.

"Thank you, Mona, that would be lovely," he answered, turning towards her.

"Mona, will you bring mine through, please, while I finalise preparations for Mr MacDonald," I said. "I'll be ready for you in around ten minutes Mr MacDonald. I trust you understand that I have certain things to prepare before I can see you. I run things by the clock in this clinic."

"No problem, Doctor Brennan, I understand completely, and let me apologise for being a shade early," he replied.

I smiled at him and took myself into my room sharpish. Making patients feel they needed to apologise for being early? I was beginning to wonder just what kind of doctor I'd become? I hoped Mona would put me out of my misery when she brought through my brew, so I could give Mr MacDonald my full attention. Otherwise, I concluded, it would be her, and not me who'd fallen short in our professional patient-practice standards. This was something to which I'd draw to her attention, in due course.

Glancing at the clock, I saw that three minutes had already gone by, each one eating into my private coffee time. I placed my hand upon the phone to tell her to get a move on, when she duly arrived... "About time too," I whispered.

"About time? You're obsessed with time. Imagine telling off that nice patient for being early," she hissed back.

"I didn't tell him off, you're not concentrating, Mona. You've so many secrets on your mind it's interfering with your work and doesn't suit you," I replied, whispering louder this time, if such a thing was possible?

"And that's the way it'll remain," she hissed back in return.

"I've gleaned that his name's Tom," I replied in a semi-raised tone.

"Trust you to ask him his name when he called in on my behalf," said Mona.

"For goodness sake, that's normal procedure... I couldn't bloody see who was calling, could I?" I whispered extremely loudly, if ever one could do such a thing?

"I take a completely different view. So you've found out that his name's Tom. I hope that will satisfy you," she hissed back. Mona was good at hissing... much better than I was at this whispering lark. Her's took on a far more menacing tone.

"No, it does not—," I began, when someone knocked on the door, interrupting us. We both looked around. "Ah, come right in," I shouted, relieved at last for not needing to whisper.

In came Mr MacDonald, "That's me right on time now, Doctor Brennan. I know you'll want to get started so you can keep your schedule on track," he announced.

"Right, Mona dear, that will be all for now," I said politely, somewhat shocked.

I glanced at my untouched coffee cup sitting neglected on my desk. Mr MacDonald must have finished his, and I wondered if it would it be acceptable for me to drink it in front of him? He must have sensed my predicament, for he pointed out that my coffee would be getting cold. I thought swiftly of offering him my chair behind the desk, but quickly recovered my professional composure, and set about the man with my usual flair.

*

Two hours later, when Mr MacDonald left, I stayed glued to the chair in my consulting room. I could hear Mona banging about next door. What in heaven's name was she doing? Suddenly, there was a knock on the door...

"Come in," I called out.

"Can you open the door for me, please?" she called back.

I obliged, and there she stood with a tray, and a broad grin. She crossed the floor and plonked the laden tray on my desk, "I've ordered us a takeaway from the local Italian down the street," she announced.

I looked amazed. Where had she found the cutlery, and the glasses for the bottle of white wine perched on the tray? "What's the story with all the banging?" I asked.

"I was looking for the plates and things; I knew we had them somewhere," she replied.

"Why would we have such things?" I asked.

"You should know; you brought them from your house a few years back. You must remember when we used to order in quite a few meals back in the days before you bothered about your figure," replied Mona.

"You're right, Mona, I'd completely forgotten about that. We used to indulge our little selves in a variety of treats back then," I concurred.

"Only until you decided that you were approaching middle-age, and got all fussy about your ageing body," replied Mona.

"Mona, what a cruel thing to say," I said.

"Which part?" she asked.

"I'm not too sure, it's a toss-up between my ageing body and the bit about me being middle-aged," I replied.

Mona was no longer listening, as she dragged her favourite chair over towards my desk, "Get stuck in before I change my mind and give it back to Gino," she said.

"You always do the right thing in the circumstances," I replied. Why had I said that to Mona of all people? "This is truly lovely, but when is my next appointment?" I added, glancing anxiously at the clock.

"There was only your three o'clock this afternoon, and as she usually only stays for three quarters of an hour, so I took it upon myself to cancel her, and squeeze her in tomorrow instead. Did I do right?" asked Mona.

I now had a mouthful of food, and had poured my first glass of wine. What could I say? "I'll have to think long and hard about that one, Mona," I finally replied.

"I take it, that'll be a yes then," she said, with a gleam in her eyes.

We indulged ourselves. She had certainly gone to town on my petty cash, "Can I take it that this is to make up for the torment you've been causing me?" I asked.

"What torment would that be, Dawn?" she replied.

I made no comment, but my face showed the level of my enjoyment had overtaken any previous level of torment. We sat, assessing the meal, whilst we ate and drank our fill.

"It is good," I said, in between mouthfuls.

"Is it not very good?" she replied, cocking her head to one side.

"Yip, that's what I meant, very, very good," I agreed.

"Not perhaps verging on excellent?" she ventured.

"Let's drink to excellence," I said, raising my glass.

"You never told me what your trip to that, *Clover* place, was all about?" she suddenly announced.

"Surely that isn't the reason why you're keeping details of your Tom a mystery?" I countered. I could tell from her face that it was. How childish! "Well, I never! I would've told you anything you wanted to know, Mona. Ask away, there's no secret; it was just a spur of the moment decision to revisit... my childhood haunts," I continued. How simple it sounded when glossed over so quickly.

We continued to eat companionably... no etiquette, no standing on ceremony, not us, we just gobbled until it was all gone. I then topped up our glasses to the brim, and we sat back in our chairs, allowing time for our feast to digest.

"Mona, to show my appreciation, I'll make the coffee, but not right now though, a little later," I offered. "Who is he then? Tell Dawn. If you think it over, you'll realise that no one else in the whole world is as interested in your Tom, as me."

"Well, if you must know, Tom's my brother. His wife died a few years ago... you will remember I told you at the time? Well, he at long last decided to make the two hour journey to visit his little sister," she revealed. "We got on far better than I could ever have imagined."

"Your brother?" I replied. "What a blinking swizz, Mona! You led me up a juicy path with that one, only to lead me back down the other side again. He doesn't even look like you."

"I can't help that. You're not pinning that one on me," she said. "I'm efficient, but even I have my limitations."

"No, you don't," I replied. "Wait until I tell James. I bet he says, nice one, Mona."

We laughed until she stopped, looked straight at me, and said these fateful three little words… "Out with it!"

CHAPTER FORTY-TWO:

Joe had no time to ponder Silvia. Mike was due any minute to discuss the design possibilities of their new joint project, otherwise he wouldn't have been in his office this morning, but out on site. Mike arrived promptly, parked his car next to Joe's and sauntered in, looking forward to their meeting. "I've always admired that car of yours, Joe, you don't see many of them around," he said.

"No, it's a rare breed, especially in that colour," agreed Joe. How did she get hold of her's, Joe wondered?

"I had a word with Donald the other day, regarding Silvia. I put it as tactfully as I could, which wasn't easy," continued Mike. "My brother impressed me for once, and promised he'd speak to her. I'm sure he will, if the deed hasn't already been done."

"You could well be right, because I've just had her pay me a visit. She verbally assaulted me outside the office, and then came in, looked around, and promptly left," sighed Joe.

"My goodness, that's enough to sour anyone's breakfast milk," answered Mike. "Glad it wasn't me."

The door opened at that moment and in walked the brazen Silvia. She'd been so wrapped up in the moment, that she'd not spotted Mike's car parked outside, "Oh," she gasped in surprise, "what are you doing here?"

"I have a valid reason… have you?" replied Mike.

"Look, Silvia, take a seat, please. You obviously have something on your mind or you wouldn't have come back. If you care for Val, sit down please," asked Joe.

She looked scared, like a rabbit caught in the headlights of a speeding car. Mike stood up and fetched over another chair… she looked at him somewhat confused, but accepted the offer.

Joe was at a loss. "I'll make us coffee," he suggested. "Silvia, I'm ashamed to say this, but I don't know how you take yours?"

"With two sugars," she replied, in a hushed voice.

"I'll come and help you carry them through," offered Mike. Once outside, he followed Joe into the small kitchen. "What are we going to do?" he whispered.

"I don't know, my friend. The only thing I can say is that she appears to be… let me phrase it as… not quite herself," Joe replied. "First of all, stop whispering, and go back and ask her if she wants a biscuit?"

"Me?" he protested.

"Yes, you, because you don't know where I keep the sugar and things," replied Joe.

"I could always ask one of your staff?" he suggested.

"Off you go and stop wimping. You're her brother-in-law, for goodness sake," replied Joe.

"I hate to tell you this, but you're her brother-in-law as well," said Mike.

"But you're older than me," rallied Joe.

Mike did not return to the kitchen, so it was tray-carrying Joe, who returned to his office, together with a packet of biscuits stuffed in his pocket for good measure. All was quiet when he re-entered, and Mike had his arm stretched lightly around Silvia's shoulders. He looked over to Joe and pulled a face. There was an unfamiliar noise in the background. My God, thought Joe, that's the sound of her sobbing. He laid down the tray, poured out the coffees, and noticed that Mike's arm had taken on a rigid appearance…

"Would you like a biscuit, Silvia?" asked Joe, tentatively.

"Yes…,"she sobbed, "please."

Joe passed her the packet, first taking one for himself, and then sticking another into Mike's wide-open mouth. Silvia took the packet and prised herself out a handful... her eating my biscuits... that must be a first, mused Joe. He then motioned for Mike to join him outside his office to discuss what they ought to do next, when the phone rang. Joe answered, and was delighted with the news he was given, that his sister Mandy had given birth to a boy... everything had gone to plan, and mother and baby were fine and healthy.

"Thanks for getting the news to me, Val. A baby boy, now that's great news! Mandy will be so relieved he's arrived safely. She's been on my mind, as I still worry over these girls, as if they were my responsibility," said Joe.

He laughed at whatever was being said at the other end of the line, and was about to reveal who had unexpectedly dropped into the office, when he saw Silvia's finger shoot up to her lips. He respected her wishes...

"Mike's here with me, holding me back from my proper work. Love you too, Val... I will," said Joe, replacing the receiver. "Val, says hello, Mike."

They looked at each other as Mike gently lifted his protective arm from around Silvia's shoulder, although her sobbing continued to throb in their ears. "Silvia, would you like me to drive you home?" he asked.

"No, I don't know," she sobbed.

"Silvia, can we talk? It's obvious things are not right," asked Joe.

"Was that Mandy, your sister, whose had a baby boy?" she asked, in between sobs.

"Yes,... she's just had her second little boy," he answered.

"You loved your little sisters back then," she sobbed, "I remember... it seemed strange to me at the time."

"Why was that?" asked Joe.

"Well, it just wasn't done... a boy like you... spending time with and caring after his little sisters," she sobbed.

Joe went and sat alongside her, "Silvia, what do you mean by, a boy like me?" he asked.

"Well, you were a——," replied Silvia, "you know what you were."

"I only know that I was a boy who loved his little sisters," he replied.

"And her," she sniffled, "you loved her too."

"Do you mean, Dawn? Yes, I loved her, but none of that was a crime," said Joe.

"Your father was a——," replied Silvia.

"I'm not my father, Silvia," stressed Joe.

"Silvia, Joe's a top guy. Why don't you try to be friends? Why don't you and I be friends too?" suggested

Mike. "I know Janis would like to be your friend, and Val too."

"Val's my sister for goodness sake, she doesn't need to be my friend," replied Silvia.

"Oh, yes she does," said Joe. "You don't appreciate what a good sister and friend Val is to you. She's on the edge of stopping being your friend though, and you surely don't want that?"

"No, she's not," she snapped.

"Oh, yes she is. Val told me that too," added Mike.

"You must've noticed that she's been avoiding you recently?" said Joe.

Suddenly Silvia flared up in anger, "That's because of you... you 'tink'...you've been bad mouthing me to her," she snarled. "You're the lowest of the low."

Mike thumped the table, astounded at her outburst, "Silvia, apologise to Joe this minute, or I'm calling Donald," he snapped. "You're sitting in his office, drinking his coffee and eating his biscuits and you're behaving like—,"

She was back sobbing again. "Why is it that Mandy can have babies, Val even has four, whilst I can't have any?" she wailed.

"Janis and I don't have a family either," Mike reminded her.

"You don't want any, that's why," cried Silvia.

"Who said that? Where did that bit of misinformation come from?" he replied. "The very opposite is true... only we don't take it out on the people we love, like you."

"Don't phone Don...," sobbed Silvia, "I beg of you."

"Don't beg me... ask Joe, he's the one you've wronged," replied Mike.

"Silvia, you don't need to beg for anything. Here's my hand of friendship, it's all I have to offer," said Joe.

The tension in the room could be felt like a chilled fog, as Silvia began to cry hysterically once again, "Joe, help me please... I'm so very sorry," she cried, her body vibrating uncontrollably.

He reached over, helped her to her feet, and held her close. "It's all right, I do understand," he whispered. He stood with his arms around his sister-in-law, looking over to Mike, both men feeling well out of their depth... he wondered what Judy and Bert must be thinking was going on in his office, and just at that moment, there was a gentle knock on the door...

"Everything okay in there, Joe?" asked Bert.

"Everything okay, Silvia?" asked Joe.

She nodded, clinging on to him ever tighter.

"It's fine now, Bert, and thanks for your concern," replied Joe.

"We thought that we'd been invaded by a green-eyed monster, didn't we Joe, but it was a false alarm," added Mike.

Silvia lifted her head, and they both detected a faint smile through her waning tears.

CHAPTER FORTY-THREE:

Whilst Mona had asked me to confess all, I managed to side-step her that afternoon, as we each sloped off home as soon as we'd finished our meal. I did have to promise her a full confession the next day though.

*

As we sat relaxing that evening, I told James the tale, "What's wrong with telling her what you did when you went to *Cloverley*?" he asked. "She can then relate it to me, as I was too mannerly to ask you myself, and the information has never been offered."

"It's private," I replied, which sounded to my ears as being both childish and rather petty... what a thing to say to my James.

"It was also her own private business who the man in her house was, but you wheedled that out of poor Mona. I think she deserved something in return," said James.

Talk about Mr Nice Guy? My husband, Professor halo-above-his-head Brennan. "There's nothing to tell. I went and I returned... end of story," I replied.

"And the band played believe-it-if-you-like," piped up Angela, who'd been sitting with her head in a book. Both James and I were surprised, as neither of us had ever heard anyone use that phrase for years.

"Where did you get that saying from, Angela?" I asked.

"I must have just sleuthed it from somewhere Mother dear," she replied, with one of her special grins.

"It's good that our Angela has an aptitude for picking up words, phrases, and such-like," said James.

Could this man not see anything wrong with anybody or anything? He always looked on the bright side, which could be so bloody annoying!

"We're going to *Cloverley* next weekend, so any secrets will come tumbling out then. I'm looking forward to this trip Dad, aren't you?" remarked our smug-faced baby daughter.

"Yes, I am... very much. I was hoping to keep my anticipation from your mum, but I must agree with you, it'll all come tumbling out next weekend," agreed James.

I made my way out of the room as fast as I could, retreating into the chill of the conservatory. A little later James came through and sat beside me, taking my hand in his. "Is there anything I ought to know before we set off to you-know-where next weekend?" he asked. "Like… what was his name?"

I sat and bit my lip, moving my teeth over and under my lips. I knew he was laughing inside, as I could feel the vibrations through the hand I knew so well… "Joe," I whispered.

"Joe? You mean the twelve year old Joe?" he asked. "Do you mean the one your dad told me about, the one whom he feared would lead you astray… Joe Doubleday?"

"Y-Yes…," I replied, still rather subdued.

James burst out laughing. "Our Angela will have herself a field day this weekend," he chuckled.

CHAPTER FORTY-FOUR:

Joe helped Silvia to his car. He couldn't remember her ever being in his car before, and momentarily swithered whether to sit her in the front or in the rear, and plumped for the latter. "Comfortable?" he asked, before driving off. Silvia nodded and gave him the slightest of smiles. Mike then followed in his own car. Joe thought Val would get a real surprise when he arrived with this unexpected package! On the way, Joe switched on the radio and found a station with restful music to lull her.

When they arrived, he was about to get out of his car, when... "Joe, I like sitting here in your car, can I stay a little longer?" she asked.

"Sure, be my guest," he replied, "I'll leave the radio on if you wish?"

She nodded and this time smiled a proper smile. Mike pulled up behind, and the two men went into the house together to bring Val up to speed with the fast developing situation. After a while, she went out to check on her sister, found her fast asleep, and returned indoors.

"Well, I'll be damned," said Joe. "Val, you'll never believe it, but she clung to me and allowed me to put my arms around her on the way out to the car. She even managed to raise me a smile!"

He then relayed the whole story, chapter and verse, to her, "Do you think she's maybe had some kind of breakdown, Joe?" she asked.

"I don't know about any breakdown, but I may have made a breakthrough," he replied. "We'll have a better idea once she awakens."

CHAPTER FORTY-FIVE:

The following morning, Mona got her promised account of my short stay in *Cloverley*. "And you're going back there this weekend... with James?" she exclaimed. "Will this Joe character be there along with this Val woman?"

"How am I expected to know that?" I replied.

"But you are secretly hoping Joe will be there?" she pressed.

I knew there were signs of flushing on my face, as I hastily thought of an appropriate answer, "It might be nice... to see how he's turned out, that's all," I replied, "and Val too, of course."

"Of course, let's not forget about good old Val," teased Mona, with a knowing smirk.

I quickly tried to change the subject... "Mona, let's get back to work and no more of this nonsense," I suggested. "We've a busy day ahead; well I have anyway, as I now need to fit my three o'clock in from yesterday, along with a full house today."

I tried to concentrate on my patients, but my mind kept straying back to Mona's talk of Joe and Val. Their names echoed back and forth inside my head, until I came up with a plan, which I thought might ease my situation... "Mona, can you look up the telephone number for Valerie Doubleday, in *Cloverley*, please?" I asked.

"Right now?" she enquired.

"Yes, please... as soon as possible," I said.

"What are you going to say to her?" she asked.

"At this very moment, I haven't a clue," I answered, "but try and get me her number."

Mona got right onto the trail of the phone number, and a few minutes later, buzzed through to me. "I've found your friend Joe's number... there's a building firm's number together with a house number for a Doubleday in *Cloverley*. As far as I can see, there's only one, so I can only presume that'll be Valerie's number as well," she intimated.

"Right, can you call the house number for me, please?" I asked.

"You'll be asking me to speak to her next?" she replied.

"Spot on... I'm far too busy," I answered, with a tone of smugness.

"For goodness sake, Dawn, I don't know what you would want me to say. I can't speak for you," she groaned.

"I only want you to check if a woman answers; he should be at work," I replied.

"You're barmy," said Mona, having come through to my office, to speak with me face-to-face.

"Mona, mind your language. Barmy is not an appropriate word to use within these four walls," I cautioned.

She glared at me, "I believe in telling the truth," she huffed. "Right, I'll go back to my perch and make your call."

I rose from behind my desk, and took a seat in the armchair beside the couch... there still remained ten minutes of my break. As I awaited developments, I drummed my fingers on the arm of the chair, firstly with one hand and then with the other, and had worked up quite a head of steam before she returned.

*

Joe went out to check on Silvia, in time to find her stirring from her slumber. The gentle purring sound of her breathing had now lost its regular beat. Joe turned off the car radio, which was also humming in the background. "Silvia, wake up, Val's waiting to see you. Here, give me your hand," he said, and to his surprise, she readily obliged.

He continued to hold her hand as they entered the house, and he felt it tighten its grip in a similar manner to a vice. Through the tightness, he detected a tremor, which grew stronger with each step they took...

"Silvia, are you okay?" asked a concerned Val.

"Oh, Val... I've missed you," she answered, as she released Joe from her grip, and lunged forward to give Val a hug. "Joe's been so good to me," she sobbed, then returned to hold Joe's hand once more.

Val couldn't believe her eyes, "I've put the kettle on," she said, "let's take a seat and make ourselves comfortable."

"Could one of you phone Don, and ask him to take me home? I can't remember where I've left my car, or if I perhaps walked?" asked Silvia.

"Silvia, once you've had a hot drink, I'll drive you home myself, then I can check on the whereabouts of your car. Leave it with me," replied Joe.

"Thanks, and I'm sorry for the hurt I've caused each of you in the past," she said with genuine contriteness, looking at both him and her sister.

"There's nothing to be sorry for," replied Joe... that'll be right, he thought, but at that moment, nothing she'd said in the past seemed to matter anymore.

*

The phone suddenly rang, and a woman asked if a Val Doubleday was available?

"Who's calling?" answered a puzzled Val.

"I'm calling on behalf of a Doctor Brennan," replied Mona. "Doctor Dawn Brennan." The devil had popped into Mona's head, and she couldn't resist stirring the *Cloverley* pudding...

"Oh? Right, just a moment, I'll take the call next door," said Val.

"Pick up please, Dawn, that's Val Doubleday on the line for you," announced Mona, in her mischievous tone...

"What the hell have you done, Mona? I said for you to make sure a woman answered, that was all," I hissed under my breath. I had just wanted to know if Val would be likely to answer the phone. I wanted time to sit and compose myself, before I made the actual call. However, the damage had already been done, so I reluctantly picked up my handset... "Hello, Val... do you remember me?" I asked, trying to sound as cheerful as I could in the circumstances.

"I actually recognise your voice, although it's dropped a little," she replied.

Dropped? My voice dropped? Oh, never mind, it's not important, concentrate, Dawn. "Did you hear that I'd called in at your mum's recently? I recognised her by chance in the street when I was passing. It was lovely to see her and so strange to be back in your old house again," I began, my mind furiously searching for my next line...

"Did she show you her new extension?" asked Val.

Why on earth is she mentioning the extension, I thought? "Yes, in fact she did... it's apparently her pride and joy," I answered.

"Joe built it for her," she next revealed,"... and for my dad."

"I was sorry to hear about your dad, Val... your mum told me that you and Joe got together when he was working on the extension," I replied, in as much of a matter-of-fact-way as I could muster.

There was a short awkward silence; it was clear she too was choosing her words carefully, "Yes, during that time, Joe and I did get to know each other... very well," she agreed.

"That was nice," I replied.

"Yes, it was," she agreed.

"Good," I replied, "what it is... the reason why I'm phoning... is to say that my husband James and me and our family are intending spending this weekend near *Cloverley*, and James would like me to show him the sights... like where our old Weekender was, my childhood haunts, you know, that sort of thing? Whilst we were there... I was also hoping to take him to meet your mum..."

There was a slight delay, and then she answered, "I'm sure she'll like that very much... I'll tell her you intend popping in and I'm sure she'll have a cake specially baked," she replied. "Dawn, perhaps you'd care to bring your family to visit us too… that's if you've time? You know where we are, just down the lane from your old place. If you're definitely going to see your old Weekender, then I'd enjoy meeting your family… and you of course."

"Well, that's settled then, I'd enjoy seeing you and your family too; I believe you've four children?" I replied.

"Yes, and Mum told me that you've three yourself," she replied, "albeit, all a bit older than ours."

"Yes, two are, but my youngest… our Angela, is an eleven year old toe-rag," I said.

"Who does she take after?" asked Val.

"Well, it's not after my James, that's for sure" I said, as I began to laugh.

"You were quite outspoken as a child, as I recall… full of confidence and up for anything," she replied. "Dawn, are you a doctor? The reason I ask is that the lady who put you through, called you Doctor Dawn Brennan."

"Yes, I am for my sins. I don't suppose you ever thought I'd go into medicine?" I asked.

"No, not medicine in particular, but I knew that whatever you eventually decided, you'd undoubtedly succeed," she replied.

"Oh, thanks, Val, that's a really nice thing to say," I said.

"What does your husband do for a living?" she next asked…

"He's a… Professor of History… at the local university" I answered.

"A doctor and a professor! You two won't want to mix with the likes of Joe and me," said Val.

"Of course we will. I'm just the same person you've always known, and my James is… well, he's just James," I replied, "and I think you'll like him."

"Wait until I tell Mum… you never mentioned to her you were a doctor," she said.

"Didn't I… well, it's not a big deal as far as I'm concerned. Val, I'll have to go now as my next patient's due any minute. I'm so looking forward to seeing you all at the weekend… bye for now," I replied.

I then pressed the intercom on my desk…"Thanks for that, Mona," I said, "now show in my next patient, please."

CHAPTER FORTY-SIX:

"Who was on the phone, Val?" asked Joe.

"I'll tell you about the call later, let's get her ladyship settled first," she replied.

"Yes, I agree, let's get Silvia home," said Mike.

"I want to stay here with Val. She knows me best, and she'll look after me," said Silvia, "and Joe too." She was sitting with her hand still clasped in Joe's, and her head had now rolled onto his shoulder. The sight was one of the strangest Val had seen in a long time. What's come over her, she wondered?

Daisy, who'd been playing in her bedroom, came skipping into the room, "What's wrong with Auntie Silvia?" she asked.

"I'm fine, Daisy, your mummy's looking after me… and your daddy too," replied Silvia, who then squeezed Joe's hand, which he found alarming… in fact, this whole scenario was rather bizarre.

"Why are you holding Daddy's hand, when you don't like him?" asked Daisy.

"From out of the mouths of babes, and all that," whispered Mike to Val.

"I… like your daddy… now," replied Silvia.

"Well, that makes me feel better, Auntie Silvia. I didn't like it, when you were horrible to him," she answered.

"Oh, Daisy," sobbed Silvia, as she burst into tears once again.

"Mike, can you phone Donald… this is too much for Joe and I to handle?" whispered Val.

*

It seemed forever before Donald eventually arrived. However when he finally did, he was stunned at the scene which greeted him, namely his wife sitting holding Joe's hand with her head on his shoulder, and Val stroking her other hand.

Silvia still had the traces of tears on her cheeks and he became quite emotional. "Silvia, what is it, my darling? What's happened?" he asked.

"I don't know," she sobbed. "Everything's just fallen apart…"

"I'll sort it for you, my love," he replied.

The other three adults looked at each other with raised eyebrows. None had ever been quite sure of the depth of their relationship before, but they were now. He gently separated her from Joe, and led her to their car, "Thanks for everything folks, we'll speak later," he added, before driving off.

They watched them go, "Good luck," muttered Mike, "you'll need it, my boy."

"Val, can we stay and look over Mike's designs?" asked Joe.

"Sorry Joe, I've left my brief-case back at your office," replied Mike.

"That's fine, we can head back there, now that all the excitement's subdued," suggested Joe.

Val took Joe to one side, "Thanks for that. If you think that was weird, wait till I see you later… and you'll find out just how weird a day it's been," she whispered.

"I can't wait… was it the phone call?" he asked.

Val nodded, "It can wait until this evening, though," she replied, with a smile.

"Can I come with you, Daddy, I haven't seen Judy or Bert for a long time?" asked Daisy.

"Why not, if that's okay with Mummy?" asked Joe.

"Wonderful, that means I can catch up on some reading," replied Val.

"You just relax dear… love you," said Joe.

CHAPTER FORTY-SEVEN:

"Well, that turned out well… Auntie Mona knows what's best for her Dawn," said my grinning secretary.

"Occasionally you do," I answered. I was happy enough now that I'd finally spoken to Val, particularly as she'd invited us to visit. Things were perhaps not going to be as bad as I first expected? I was now looking forward to the weekend, except for the fact that I was still nervous about meeting Joe… I wondered if he'd even recognise me… or I him?

Yes, I would recognise him… I'd seen recent photos in Jean Brown's house, not to mention that distant view in my rear-view mirror, as I'd made my escape from the scene of my crime…

*

That evening, I told James of my conversation with Val.

"We could've visited these people in *Cloverley* years ago, if I'd known it was so important to you," he concluded.

I felt him searching my eyes with his, looking for clues. I looked at him with a blank expression, and put on an extra special front in an effort to entice him away from his current thoughts. "James, as our Lorraine has invited Simon, I was wondering if Sean has a girl he'd like to bring? If he has, she could share with Lorraine. Has he told you if he has anyone special?" I enquired.

"Well, I know for sure he isn't going out with anyone at the moment, so we can't ask him to just bring any girl. I suppose he could always bring another boy?" replied James.

"Another boy can't sleep with our Lorraine," I remarked.

"Dawn, if anyone wants to sleep with Lorraine, it'll be Simon," he answered.

"Simon? Oh, I see what you mean… behave yourself, James. But if he did bring a friend, then our Angela could share with Lorraine, and the three boys could bunk down together," I suggested.

"I'll change the booking to a room with three beds then," he replied, "that's what I'll do, if he decides he wants to bring someone."

"Who's going in which car?" I asked.

"Well, I'll take Sean and his friend, that's if he brings one, then Sean can drive part of the way if he wants. I'd also better take our Angela," replied James. "If she goes with you, she'll no doubt plonk herself in between Simon and Lorraine, and I can just imagine how that'll go down with them."

"That might be a good idea, as it would save me having to check my mirror, to see what they're up to in the back seat," I said.

"Oh, Dawn, leave them alone. You were young once yourself," he replied, with a wry smile.

Now was the time to change the subject yet again. His looks and remarks were cutting into the surface, and no way would I wish these to go any deeper... "I'm quite looking forward to going now," I said, changing tact. "It'll be nice to catch up with my old friend Val again. She told me that her mum, Jean Brown, was going to bake us a special cake. How good is that of her?"

"Very good indeed, although it'll have to be a big cake, if it's to satisfy our lot," replied James. "You may be looking forward to seeing good old Val, but I'm more interested in meeting her husband..."

It was all a big joke to him, and I could appreciate that, as nobody enjoyed a joke more than me. But this was me and Joe he was laughing at, and that had never been a subject for people's mirth. Joe and I had laughed together, and what we'd between us was fun and laughter, but not for the amusement of others...

... The river gently meandered along its timeless journey with its waterfall lacing the droplets with the waters of life. The sun shone high above, as Joe handed me a cup from which I tasted its contents, dripping drop by drop on its journey deep inside of me. He promised me his love forever, and I promised mine to him... forever...

"Dawn, Dawn, are you okay?" asked James. I can hear that his concern is sincere, as I nod and smile. James is now my rock, the rock on which I've built my life...

CHAPTER FORTY-EIGHT:

Donald called their family doctor and insisted she visit Silvia at their home. She was sleeping when the doctor eventually arrived, so they discussed downstairs what could be the possible problem. "Doctor, as you know, we're about to go through what will be our last try at IVF treatment. Could Silvia's anxiety over this, be what's causing whatever this turns out to be?" he asked.

She sat and listened, saying little, just giving a nod here and there, "Can you gently waken her for me?" she then asked.

"Yes, she was actually like a baby when I put her to bed, not her usual self," he replied.

They each exchanged a smile, knowing she was no baby. "When Silvia's awake, I'd like to talk with her in private," said Doctor McKay.

"Of course," replied Donald "you'll find me downstairs in the kitchen when you've finished."

The doctor then spent a good half-hour with her, before re-joining Donald. "Cup of tea, or coffee?" he asked.

"No, you're fine, thanks," she replied, "I've a few things I want to check on back at the surgery. I'll phone you around three o'clock this afternoon."

"Does she not need any medicine prescribed?" enquired Donald.

"I'll tell you that when I call. Just give her liquids until then... water preferably," replied the doctor. "Can you stay with her? The best thing for her at the moment is for you two to be together."

He saw the doctor out, and then bounded upstairs, where he sat on the bed with watery eyes. Silvia smiled at him and took his hand. He then lay down beside her, and shortly afterwards, they both fell asleep...

The sound of the phone ringing, awakened Donald. He glanced at the bedside clock; it would be her! He ran to take the call in the adjoining room, and by the time he came off the phone, was in shock... He hurriedly made a few phone calls and asked the immediate family if they could come to see him that evening?

"We'll have to bring Brigitte and Daisy with us, we can't leave them," said Val. "Donald, can't you tell me anything about Silvia before then, if only to put my mind at ease?"

360

"No, Val... wait until this evening please," he replied.

*

That evening, Brigitte and Daisy rushed into their Auntie Silvia's house, as was their custom, "We're here," called out Brigitte, "where are you?"

"Sh, she's sleeping, girls. Do you want to watch TV, while I have a chat with Mummy and Daddy?" asked their Uncle Donald. The girls looked at each other, each carefully considering their options...

"Just get into the lounge and behave yourselves," interrupted Joe, "you've got to be firm with children, Donald."

"Just like Joe's firm with his?" joked Val, shaking her head.

"I do try," he replied, with a grin, "although I'll be the first to admit that I don't always succeed." He then took his girls by their chubby little hands, settled them in the lounge, and switched on the TV. He then skipped through various channels until he found one which they wanted to view. "There's a treat in it for you, but only if you are good," he whispered.

The girls clapped their hands, and he gave them each a kiss, and waved as he left.

Mike and Janis arrived in the wake of Joe and Val, "What is it, Donald," asked Mike, "what's wrong with her?"

"Can you go through into the dining-room please, as the girls are watching TV in the lounge," he suggested. "I'll check on Silvia, and then I'll be right with you."

They went into the dining-room and sat around the table, drumming away with their fingers... "This isn't looking too good Val, I'm sorry to say. It must be serious given the way he's behaving," remarked Mike.

"Mike, what do you think's wrong with her?" asked Val. "I feel terrible, as I've been deliberately avoiding her ever since that fiasco of a birthday party."

"Let's just wait and see what Donald has to say, before we jump to any wrong conclusions," suggested Janis.

"I agree, let's not get too ahead of ourselves," said Joe.

Donald joined them at that moment, and looked around the table, only to find that nobody looked him directly in the eye. "Thanks for today Joe and Mike. I can only apologise for Silvia's behaviour," he began. "It wasn't her fault, I should've realised that she was in a bad place——,"

"For goodness sake man, it was nothing this morning," interrupted Joe.

"Donald, you can't be held responsible for someone else's actions," added Mike. "Even those of your dear wife."

"No, but I should have noticed she'd changed. There was something different about her," he replied. He then rose and checked the door was firmly closed, which made Val shudder.

"I know you all think she's loud-mouthed, meddling, and tough, but in actual fact, she isn't. What I mean is, she's vulnerable, sometimes like a lost soul trying to make sense of things going on around her," he continued. "You don't know her as I do."

The others each had their own thoughts, as they ventured a quick glance at each other... Joe squeezed Val's hand under the table.

Donald then began to sob uncontrollably... whilst the others sat rigid in their seats as they considered how to deal with him, and whatever was coming next? Joe felt out of his depth and motioned to Val, for them to slip out of the room. Once outside, they clung to each other for a moment in silence, "Joe, I'm so scared... let's go upstairs and see Silvia," she suggested.

"Do you think we should?" queried Joe.

"You stay here then, and I'll go. I'm her only sister, so he can't stop me from seeing her," she replied.

"I don't think he'd ever do that," replied Joe.

She kissed him and left for Silvia's bedroom, whilst Joe stood with his hands in his pockets. He then remembered about his girls, went through into the lounge and sat beside them as they continued to watch their programme, "Daddy, this is a good bit... watch this," said Daisy.

"Joe, sorry to disturb you. Please come… you'll never believe what he's just told me," said Mike, poking his head around the door. "Where's Val?"

"She's gone upstairs to see Silvia," he replied.

"That's fine, but come through and hear this," he urged…

CHAPTER FORTY-NINE:

James mentioned to Sean that he might want to consider bringing a friend to *Cloverley* at the weekend? "Leave it with me, Pops; I'll see if anyone's interested... it's not exactly a weekend in Paris though, is it?" he replied.

"I'm glad to be going to *Cloverley* and not Paris," replied James. "It'll be far more interesting."

"Maybe for people who are easily pleased," he answered. "I don't understand why Mum wants to go back, just because she used to stay there as a child?"

"Sometimes you come across children who are a little more advanced," replied James.

"What, like our Angela?" he asked.

"Yes, I hadn't thought of that until you mentioned it," agreed James.

Sean went on his way and James sat in his favourite armchair by the window to relax. He gazed out on the greenery, as he let his mind wander... Sean and Lorraine both favoured him and had similar temperaments, but Angela, now she took after her mum, and appeared to have more of her genes than his... when is an eleven-year-old girl not a typical eleven-year-old girl... when that eleven-year-old girl is Angela... or Dawn?

Dawn joined James at that moment. He snapped out of his daydream and smiled. "Hi, James, what were you daydreaming about, my good man?" she asked.

"My good lady," he replied, with a grin.

"And was it a pleasant daydream?" she asked.

"Yes, and very interesting too," he replied.

"Well, what was happening, what was I doing?" she probed.

"I'm not too sure," he replied, "I'm just not too sure..."

CHAPTER FIFTY:

Joe followed Mike through into the dining-room, his feet being forced to take each leaden step. On entering, they found Donald seated at the table, with tears streaming from his eyes, and braced himself for the inevitable. It didn't matter how much he'd previously disliked Silvia, as the events of this morning had swept all that away. He wouldn't have wished for this, whatever it was, on anyone... even his worst enemy.

"Donald, can you tell Joe?" asked Mike. He looked up to where Joe was, and opened and closed his mouth, unable to find the appropriate words. "Come on Donald, you can do it, I don't want to spoil it for you by telling him myself," he continued.

Spoil it for him, thought Joe? Spoil it for him? What a strange thing to say...

"Come on Donald, you can't keep him in suspense all day," urged Mike.

Donald motioned for Joe to sit, which he did, watched by an exasperated Mike. Joe reckoned he couldn't take much more, as the tension in the room was suffocating; he could feel his throat closing... and he now was fighting for each and every breath...

"Donald, for Gawd's sake, tell the man, before his heart gives way or something along these lines. This is your last chance or I'll do it for you," stressed Mike.

"Joe," began Donald, "I'm so sorry about all of this, it's just so overwhelming, I'm finding it hard to get the words out."

"Donald, from where I'm standing, it's not just hard for you, it's nigh on bloody impossible!" said Mike.

"No, it's not Mike, don't be so impatient," he replied, "you're not allowing me time to steady myself."

Well, good old Donald, he's managed to get these two sentences out okay, thought Joe.

"Sorry, Donald," replied Mike. "I'm really sorry."

"It's okay," he answered.

Mike put his arms around his brother's shoulders, as Val opened the door.

"Joe, can you come with me, please?" she asked tentatively.

"Delighted," he replied... anything to get out of this room, he thought, as he rose and left the brothers to themselves. "What is it, Val?" he asked. "I've been going through a nightmare, with these two chumps."

"Has he not told you then?" she asked.

"Nope, he seemingly can't get the words out," replied Joe.

"Oh, for goodness sake, men!" she snapped.

"Val, can you tell me, as you appear to know what this is all about?" he replied.

"Silvia's almost two months pregnant! She's been concentrating so much on the IVF treatment programme, she never thought about anything else. Her hormones have been all over the place, and with all the stress she's been feeling as a consequence, she's simply lost her way," she explained.

"Is that all it was? My God, I thought she was dying or something. What's the matter with Donald? I think they've both lost their way... what a performance I've just had from him," replied Joe. "What happens now? Who do I congratulate first?"

"Let's go and see Donald; Silvia will have dosed off again by now," suggested Val.

"Val, before we go in to see him, come and give me a big hug. I'm glad you never reacted like your sister on receiving such good news," answered Joe. "I'm so glad you're you."

CHAPTER FIFTY-ONE:

Sean's friend Zac intimated he'd like to come with us on the *Cloverley* trip. James, Angela, and I were in the lounge when he told us the news. "I've Zac coming with us at the weekend. I thought I'd have to coax someone, but he didn't seem to mind. To be honest, I tried to put the poor guy off the trip, but nope, his parents have seemingly never taken him away for a weekend before," said Sean, "so to him, the *Cloverley* trip sounded really cool."

"Oh, how lovely James, don't you think? A seventeen year old boy who voluntarily wants to spend a weekend with you and me," I replied.

"And me… make sure you remember that I'm included in this shindig," spouted Angela.

Shindig? From where did our Angela unearth her words? I wondered if she even knew what it actually meant?

"Angela, it's not so much of a shindig, it's more a hootenanny," I replied, continuing with the metaphor.

"I disagree, Mum. You're not getting me up to sing," Angela replied. "I'd much rather a shindig."

I smiled at her, and decided not to further this conversation. Instead, I would discuss our Angela with my James later…

"He's not an odd guy, this Zac… is he, Sean," asked James, "or troublesome?"

"No, he's not; he's a friend of mine, and to put your mind at rest, a regular guy," replied Sean.

"Right, that's it settled then," I said, "but this will be a strange outing."

"How's that, Dawn?" asked James.

"It's just that I don't want to disappoint everyone," I replied.

"I'll not be disappointed, quite the opposite," said James. "I'm so looking forward to meeting your friend… sorry, I mean, friends."

I knew exactly to whom he was referring! This was one thing that James and I were approaching from entirely different ends. To him it was all so very amusing, but to me it was far from funny. Far from funny? It was more like an emotional roller coaster! Was I the same as yesteryear, or had I lost myself somewhere along the way?

I was now alone in our large empty lounge. I typed the name of Nat King Cole into the device thingy, and selected the song *Somewhere Along The Way*. It played the haunting melody, followed by his dulcet tones delivering its sentiment. I lay out on the couch, closed my eyes, and floated off to a land of... *green fields, woods, and sparkling clear waters...*

Nicolette had her little chubby hand in mine. She always loved to hold someone's hand did Nicolette. Mandy came and took my other, while Mel was in front with Joe enjoying a piggyback ride.

"You really like our Joe, don't you Dawn," chirped Mandy. "He loves you, the same as he loves us."

"But he can marry Dawn... he can't marry us," replied Nicolette.

"I'd like to marry someone with fair hair," said Mandy.

"Not me, I'd rather marry someone like Joe," announced Nicolette.

"I suppose that might be better," agreed Mandy.

I walked between them, watching their little faces as they tugged on my arm whilst they continued to discuss this subject. They were ever so cute...

"Right, Mandy, its now your turn," Joe called, as he bent over to allow Mel to slither down from his back.

"Don't forget, I've not had my turn," called out Nicolette.

I wanted to laugh at her intense little face, which the next moment was smiling once more.

"I haven't forgotten my little pumpkin," said Joe, with a smile.

Mandy ran to take her turn, whilst Mel came over to take my hand. Joe turned and winked at me.

"Mel, what colour of hair do you want your husband to have?" asked Nicolette.

"What?" replied a surprised Mel, "I don't care, as long as he loves me, and is good to me and my children."

I could tell in that moment, that the extra year she had over Mandy and the two years she had on Nicolette, made such a difference to her answer. I saw where she was coming from. I too didn't like the look of their dad, not one little bit!

"My turn, my turn," called out Nicolette, after a few minutes.

"Why don't we give Joe a rest," I suggested, "after all, he must be tired?"

"Joe's strong, Dawn," she replied.

"Dawn's right, Nicolette. We know he's strong, but let him have time to be with Dawn," agreed Mel.

374

"I want my turn now," replied Nicolette, with a slight frown.

"Nicolette, you'll get a longer piggyback than us, as Joe will be much fresher later," explained Mel.

She nodded her head, smiled as she let go of our hands, and ran to Joe. "Joe, I'll get a longer piggyback ride, won't I?" she asked.

"Of course you will pumpkin, once I've spent some time with Dawn," he replied.

We sat on the grass, while the girls frolicked around us. Our shoulders were touching and he felt so close. "Joe, I think you're like a shepherd and they are your lambs," I ventured.

"One day, they'll be your lambs too," he replied.

"We could perhaps have some more lambs, I'd like that," I said.

"So would I," he replied.

We sat hand-in-hand, shoulders touching and watched the girlies as they played, wholly content in each other's company...

CHAPTER FIFTY-TWO:

Val and Joe congratulated Donald, who apologised profusely for his emotional state. "Donald, you don't need to apologise, it's only Val and Joe," said Mike, "they fully understand how you feel. They've been there themselves, and remember, they've had four babies of their own."

"That's right, Donald, Joe and I have been there, and know it can be rather overwhelming," agreed Val.

In your dreams, thought Joe. I've not been to the place he's been to, and neither has my Val.

"I didn't realise it could be so stressful," replied Donald.

"Yes, but you're over that now. Your job now is to look after Silvia," said Val. "so, no more stressing."

Just then, the girls came hopping and skipping along the corridor and into the dining-room. "Mummy, Daddy, can we go home?" asked Brigitte. "Please——,"

"Yes, can we go home, pleeese," added Daisy. "Our TV program's finished, and we want to go home to play outside."

Well done, Brigitte and Daisy, and with that, the Doubledays made their fortuitous escape...

*

When they arrived home, Joe and Val sat in shell of their new extension, whilst the girls went out to play. Joe opened a bottle of red; what a day it had been for them, as they firstly raised a glass to toast Mandy's new arrival... "I hope Silvia's baby will solve most of her problems," said Val.

"I hope it solves all her problems," replied Joe.

"Joe, she's always been a moan, even when she was younger, so I'm not looking for perfection. A miracle might just happen though?" she answered.

"Here's hoping," he replied, lifting his glass to make another toast, "Here's to the poor little mite..."

"Yes, here's to Silvia's baby," repeated Val.

Joe closed his eyes for a moment to picture Silvia when she was a youngster...

The familiar sounds of the Fair hung in the air. The bright colours of the rides and stalls, sparkled in the rays of the summer sun. Joe stood hand-in-hand with Dawn, watching Val leave them to go around the Fairground with her sister Silvia...

"Joe, I think Val's telling her about you and me. Look at her face, it's gone that funny twisted way it sometimes does. She doesn't approve of me, and she certainly doesn't approve of you. Quick, wave our joined hands to her and then hold me close. That'll make her day!" said Dawn.

"You're a bad influence on me, Dawn Pearson," he replied, with a broad grin.

"As you are on me, Joe Doubleday," replied a smiling Dawn.

They turned away, and Joe walked as close as he could to her. One arm was around her shoulders, whilst the other tightly held her hand. They went on their merry way until Mandy and Mel squeezed in between them. They didn't mind, the girlies were their family. Once Nicolette was back with them this afternoon, their family would be complete...

"What is it, Joe, what's wrong," asked Val, "you looked miles away?"

He opened his eyes and smiled. Val had been in his memory, but not as she is now. Back then, she hadn't been his leading lady... "Things move along life's road in a strange way, Val. We've changed, so why not Silvia?" he replied.

Val answered a call from Donald first thing the following morning. "No, Donald, you can't expect me to tell her," she replied, to his suggestion. "No, you can't just phone her, and it definitely can't wait until Silvia's allowed out of bed either. In such a small village as this, the news will quickly get out soon enough, and it will hurt Mum if she's not told first. Yes, I'm positive, it's not my place to tell her. Thanks for thinking that I'd be good at it though. No, definitely not… you'll want Joe to tell Mum next," she added. "Donald, go and do it right now, and for goodness sake, make it the great and exciting announcement that it is. Don't water it down into something resembling a bland chore."

Val bit her lip and wished she could take back the last bit she'd said, "Donald, I'm sorry, I'm sure you'll do a wonderful job of telling Mum. Just do it right away please."

Later that morning, Val and Daisy called over to visit Jean. They found her bursting to tell Val her news, so she played along with her. "I hope motherhood brings out a nicer side in our Silvia? Donald was a bag of nerves when he told me this morning. You'd think I was a monster or something… I'm not Val, am I?" she asked.

"No, of course not, Mum. I only hope that fatherhood brings to the fore a few new qualities in our Donald too," replied Val.

"What are you talking to Grandma about, Mummy?" asked the ever inquisitive Daisy.

They exchanged glances, "Auntie Silvia and Uncle Donald are going to have a baby," said Val.

"They don't look like a mummy and daddy," she replied.

"Well, mums and dads don't all look alike," said her grandma.

Daisy looked at Donald and Silvia's wedding photograph, which stood on the bureau. Jean and Val wanted to laugh at her serious little face, as she studied it. She still didn't seem convinced, "Can I please have a biscuit, Grandma?" she asked.

"You can, if you give me a hug first," replied Jean.

Daisy ran and put her arms around the top of her Grandma's legs. Jean smiled down at this precious little flower… Val and Jean then settled down with a coffee. She told her mum that Silvia had come to terms with Joe, at long last… at least she hoped she had.

"Thank the Lord," exclaimed Jean, "Joe certainly didn't deserve to hear any of that cruel rubbish."

"Joe wants to make a fresh start and forget the past," replied Val.

"That's my special boy," said a happy Jean.

CHAPTER FIFTY-THREE:

I awoke to find James's eyes upon me, and wondered how long he'd been standing there? "James, what on earth are you doing?" I asked.

"Watching my wife in her slumber," he replied.

"And did you find it entertaining?" I asked, checking my mouth hadn't dribbled.

"Very," he replied. "How sweet she sleepeth my lady fair, in dreams of times gone by. How sweet the smile upon her lips, of what, I will not pry…"

"Why that was beautiful, James… sometimes I believe you've been born in the wrong century. You ought to belong to a time when men were chivalrous and ladies were——," replied Dawn.

"I am no noble knight my lady, but a simple man who only lives to please his fair maiden," interrupted James.

I jumped up and kissed him. This man was something special... my knight and my day. "Alas, my dear James, you are sorely mistaken, I am no longer a maiden," I replied, with a wicked smile...

*

I dealt with two urgent appointments before we closed the clinic at lunchtime on Friday. Mona and her brother Tom had apparently re-bonded, and she was off to visit him for the weekend. I was pleased for dear Mona.

Cloverley now awaited. I picked Lorraine up from the house, and we set off to collect Simon. I needed to reassure his parents that I'd take good care of their seventeen-year-old. It would be nice if they reassured me in return, about their son's care of our sixteen-year-old daughter! I then met up with James, who'd rounded up Sean, his friend Zac and our Angela.

"Can't I come with you in your car, Mum?" asked Angela.

"No, you go with Dad. You can sit up front, as long as Sean isn't driving," I replied.

Angela was a smart cookie and pointed out she could also sit up front with me in my car. She had a point, so I relented. I disliked anyone sitting beside me whilst at the wheel, but I could give Angela the job of monitoring the pair in the back... then she wouldn't get in my way. I could rely on her to do this task with vigour. This whole situation of us taking two cars was entirely Lorraine's fault. If she hadn't brought Simon along, then Sean wouldn't have needed to bring Zac, and we could have travelled together as a family in one car. If the truth were told, I had no wish to take my car back to the scene of my indiscretion, but now I had no choice. Were things not embarrassing enough?

We arrived at the hotel, and I must admit I was rather impressed. James had excelled apart from the fact that he had Angela sleeping in our room. In heaven's name why, I asked? She was supposed to share with Lorraine. When I discovered this, I communicated my displeasure to him, only to find that he thought the whole situation rather amusing. "Dawn, it's only for two nights, and there are three beds," he said.

"Two nights too many," I replied, "and when did you and I start sleeping in separate beds?"

"Look upon it as a novelty," he answered, with a silly grin.

"I'll give you novelty," I replied. "If you want separate beds then say the word, and it can be arranged... permanently."

"Oh, Dawn, think of the welcome I'll get if I'm kept out of your reach for two whole nights," he said.

"It's me who might like it too much," I replied.

"Like what?" he asked.

"The grand isolation of course. I could lie in peace, consider my patients, review their cases, knowing that no one or nothing will disturb me," I replied. "I think that may well be the way to go in future... by devoting myself, my mind, and my body to my profession."

James was frowning by now, as there are times when he just isn't sure if I'm pulling his leg or not, "We could always push two of the beds together?" he suggested.

"There's no point in that," I replied, "we'll still have Angela sharing with us, and have you forgotten how inquisitive our little Madam can be?"

"Okay, I'll try and get Angela her own room," he sighed.

"Then why didn't you do that in the first place?" I replied. "No, just leave the arrangements as you saw fit when you booked the rooms."

James looked like a dog whose little waggly tail had been cut off. I felt sorry for him, but tried hard not to show any weakness, "James," I continued, "why can't she share with Lorraine?"

"I booked her into a single room, in case Simon got any funny ideas," answered James.

"I don't think a single room will put him off any ideas, funny or otherwise... but had our Angela been sharing the room——," I said.

"Dawn, I've done my best," he replied.

"I know you have darling, I know you have," I agreed. This was not the start I needed for this visit, estranged from my husband, alone in my bed, haunted by my patients, the ghosts of *Cloverley*, and our Angela watching my every move...

Oh, Joe, what have I done? This shouldn't have happened... I shouldn't even be here.

When two Universes collide...

CHAPTER FIFTY-FOUR:

"What time are they coming tomorrow," asked Joe? "I'll take the day off work, and catch up on Sunday."

"Thanks, I need you by my side," replied Val. "I told Dawn that it would be best if they visited Mum first, and then brought her with them over here for a buffet lunch."

He could see the strain on her face and the watery sadness which filled her eyes... He knew the reason, as part of him wanted to cancel this visit for her sake, but the rest of him wanted to see Dawn, and put things between them to bed... once and for all. "Val, it's only Dawn. You and her were the best of friends once," he said. "People often worry over something that often turns out to be nothing."

"She was more than a best friend to you though," she replied.

"Oh, Val, that was a long time ago. I was only twelve," he protested.

"I suppose so," she replied.

Joe pulled her close and told her that she was his wife, nothing would ever change that, and that he loved her and their kids very much.

"Joe, I'm just being stupid, aren't I?" she asked.

"We all feel stupid at times. We're all vulnerable," he replied. He would make sure he supported her tomorrow; Val was fragile, as well as vulnerable.

*

On Saturday morning, Joe awoke to a feeling of nervousness. Val had already risen, and he found her in the kitchen, busy with preparations for the buffet lunch.

"Are you okay?" he asked. "Can I help with anything?"

"Make us a coffee please, I've not had one yet," she replied. "We can sit and hold hands while we drink."

"We certainly can," he agreed, "only coffee?"

"That'll do for starters," she replied, "then if you can organise the kids, that'll be a great help?"

There wasn't much else said between them, as they sat with their coffees and their fingers entwined.

"What's going on?" asked Brian, eyes half shut and hair sprouting in all directions.

"I'm just holding your mum's hand… you don't mind do you?" replied Joe. "Val, has he got taller or is it my imagination?"

Val looked Brian over, got up, and stood next to him. "Yes, I do believe he has," she replied. "That's one of Mother Nature's mysteries, how someone suddenly grows like that overnight."

Brian helped himself to cereal and milk, and then got tore into his breakfast. He looked at his dad, "Were you as tall as me at my age, Dad?" he asked.

"He was about the same height and build as you," replied Val.

"You must've had quite a thing about Dad to remember so well, Mum?" said Brian. "Did you like her too, Dad?"

"I've always liked your mum, Brian," replied Joe.

"He liked someone else better though," muttered Val, under her breath.

Why did she have to say that, and why did Brian have to ask that today of all days, thought Joe? His heart rate noticeably increased.

"Who was that?" asked Brian, who had overheard his mum.

"My friend, Dawn," she replied. "That's the lady who's coming to visit today with her family."

Brian gave out a low long whistle. "Interesting, I'll make sure I hang around to meet her... and her family," he said. "Wait till I tell Shirley." He then supped up the remnants of his breakfast, and left to get ready for football training. "I'll be back in plenty of time for lunch," he added, as he left the kitchen.

A little time passed, before Val and Joe spoke, "I'm saying nothing," said Joe, "but I could've done without that being discussed today."

"Things are better out in the open, and not kept behind closed doors," she replied.

"I'm not keeping anything behind closed doors. All I'm saying is that what happened back then is nobody's business but ours," stressed Joe.

"He's your son, he isn't just anybody," replied Val.

"I know he's my son. Who do you think's giving him a lift to his football training? Me... his dad," he said.

Val turned her back on him, and he left the room without another word...

CHAPTER FIFTY-FIVE:

I found my night in the single bed surprisingly refreshing, and rose with a spring in my step the following morning.

"Dawn, I missed you," whispered James, as our Angela lay gently snoring. "She's done that for most of the night."

"I missed you too," I whispered back. "Our Angela's lying on her back, that's what's making her snore."

"She's not sharing a room with us again," he replied, giving her a gentle poke. "Time to get up sweetheart, it's big breakfast time."

I said nothing, but smiled. Breakfast was a happy, help-yourself-to-as-much-as-you-want affair. Just as well, as Zac's mum must have starved him in anticipation of this trip with us. I made a mental note to get my slice of cake at Jean's, as soon as she placed the plate on the table.

Simon had better manners, or perhaps he was displaying them for our benefit, trying to show he was sound son-in-law material? I decided to give our Angela the task of monitoring his behaviour. I glanced at her; she was a strange child, with her wild sleuthing ways, and her dark striking looks. She somehow looked older this morning, and I nudged James as I whispered this in his ear...

"I think you're right, Dawn. She gets more like you every day," he whispered back.

"Manners you two," chirped Angela, with her cheeky grin. "We can't take you two anywhere."

"Angela's right, Mum always lets the side down," agreed Lorraine.

"Come on Lorraine, Angela was only joking. Mum's always good for a laugh, and you're just Dad's pet lamb," said Sean.

Hurt and pleased at the same time, I looked over at Sean. "We wouldn't change Mum for the world," he said, sensing my feelings.

Did he mean that they'd gotten used to my brash, loud ways, and would miss my humour? I gave him the benefit of the doubt, and Sean shot to the top of my affection list... my other knight... my lovely son.

"Mum's great, Lorraine, that was a mean thing to say," chipped in Angela. "Dad, can be equally embarrassing." My youngest daughter's remark pleased me.

Lorraine suddenly rose from her chair, came around, and gave me a hug, "I'm sorry, Mum, you're the best. I didn't mean anything by that," she said.

"No offence taken, Lorraine, I knew all along you didn't mean it," I smugly replied.

After breakfast, we headed the few miles into *Cloverley*. James pecked me on the cheek, and said sweetly for me to go first as this was my M-O-T. I pecked him back and told him it wouldn't take us long to get to Jean's, although not being quite sure what he meant by the M-O-T remark? Probably something to do with his perception of my often erratic driving technique?

Mine was the lead car as I knew the way, and as I drove along, I opened my driver's window wide. "Mum, it's chilly in the back," protested Lorraine, as she rubbed up close to Simon.

"Rubbish, just breathe in the good clean country air," I replied, with a laugh.

"It's more countrified than I'd imagined," announced our Angela, holding her nose.

"It's not countrified at all," I replied, "it's real, genuine countryside." Emotions were rising inside of me…

"I suppose it is nice and green, Mum," conceded Lorraine, "there are plenty of trees... look Simon, the branches are touching each other over our heads."

"Just because the trees are touching each other, that's no reason for you two to touch," remarked Angela. My head spun around at speed, but wouldn't turn far enough for me to see what was going on, so I reverted to concentrating on the road.

"Split, right this minute... one at one side, and one at the other. Angela, you watch them, that's how accidents happen," I screeched.

They all began to laugh. "Accidents happen when nosey people take their eyes off the road," replied an indignant Lorraine.

I have always brought my children up to be free spirits, so their backchat, I suppose, was partly my own fault. "Damn!" I shouted... it had just struck me what James's comment of M-O-T actually meant———.

"Child present," interrupted our Angela.

"Sorry, darling, something just popped into my head," I replied.

"Is this *Cloverley*," asked Lorraine, "it looks as if there's a village ahead, although it doesn't look like there's much life there?"

"There may not be much life, as you put it, but I loved this place when I was young, so there," I replied...

Moment of Truth… James was right, in more ways than one…

"We've just passed a nice looking café; we could always go there if we get bored, Simon," yawned Lorraine.

"Let's just wait and see what's happening, before we hear the bored word please. Why can't you look upon this as an adventure?" I asked.

"I am," replied our Angela. She put her hand on my leg, and I dropped my hand for a moment to squeeze hers.

"Thanks," I said, as I indicated to turn into Briar Terrace…

*

The two cars parked bumper to bumper in the lane outside number five.

"Nice scenery," said James. "I saw the Doubleday name on a building we passed back in the village. Is that anything to do with our man… sorry, our boy?"

"Yes, that's his place… the irony is, it used to be Alexander Sugar's grocery store when I was young. That's where Mum's big romance had its roots," I replied. "That's where I had to endure innuendo after innuendo between them."

"Poor you," he replied, with one of those little smiles he often produced. "The building didn't look as if had once been a shop."

Jean came out to greet us at that moment with out-stretched arms. "Thanks for coming back to see me again, Dawn," she said, "and for bringing your family." She made no mention, thank goodness, of my hasty retreat the last time, the one which had led to my dastardly crime.

"This is James, my lovely husband," I said, by way of introduction.

"Nice to meet you, James," she replied, shaking his hand and giving him a quick once over.

"Jean, I must apologise for bringing an extra two bodies with us— ," I started to say.

"Dawn, there's no need to apologise, everyone's welcome here," she interrupted. "Now introduce me to the rest of your family."

"This is my son, Sean, and his friend Zac," I said.

"Hello, Sean... hello Zac," she replied.

"And this is my daughter, Lorraine, and her boyfriend, Simon," I added.

"Welcome Lorraine and Simon, and you don't need to tell me that this young lady is your daughter. She's exactly how I remember you, that last time you came to your Weekender with your folks. The resemblance is quite remarkable... and what's your name?"

"I'm Angela. I'm Mum's last baby, they won't be having any more," she replied, with a wry smile in my direction.

Too much information, Angela... Jean however merely laughed.

"James, do you know that's the sort of reply Dawn would've given at her age?" said Jean. "You're very welcome, Angela."

As we trooped inside, James kept making funny faces towards me, "I didn't know I had twins," he whispered, as he nudged my arm.

Jean took us through into her extension, and I expected her to announce that Joe, her son-in-law, had built it for her, but thankfully she didn't. She had our elevenses already laid out on the table... "I do hope there's enough cake to go around," she said. "Oh, and I'll need two extra cups and plates."

"I'll get them for you," replied Angela, as she scarpered off into the kitchen.

"But you'll not—," began Jean.

"Don't worry, she'll find them, Jean. She's a sleuth," I replied.

James gave a little cough and Jean looked at me blankly. Had Jean heard me correctly? Sleuth or sloth? Oh, whatever, what's done is done! Angela was back in a tick, with the required cups, saucers and plates, and the conversation moved forward.

"There will be plenty enough cake, Jean, we've just had an enormous breakfast, haven't we folks?" I said, looking around to everyone. I had wanted to add, especially Zac, but refrained from doing so.

We ate and drank, as Jean began to relax in our company, "I've never had a professor in my house before!" she remarked.

"What about a psychiatrist?" asked Angela…

My God, couldn't you not have just said doctor, I thought?

"A psychiatrist… who in heaven's name's a psychiatrist?" she asked.

Everyone looked at me, except for Zac, who had his eyes firmly fixed on the cake.

"Dawn? My goodness, what possessed you to become one of those," she exclaimed, "does that mean you're a doctor, too?"

I nodded in a nonchalant manner.

"Dawn was drawn to psychiatric medicine, which is just as well, Jean, as someone's got to do it," said James. He was enjoying his little self, and smiled at me once more, with another one of his annoying, cheesy smiles. "One usually ends up doing what suits one best," he continued.

"You were drawn to ancient history, Dad, so does that makes you an old fogey?" joked Angela. There were giggles and sniggers all round, and I noticed Jean almost choked on her coffee. Nice one Angela; that will have put Mr Smug back into his box.

"Enough about us, Jean, what's been happening with you?" I asked.

"One piece of good news that I do have for you, Dawn, is that Silvia's pregnant," she announced. I could see how pleased she was at the news. Heaven help the child, was my first thought, but that was not fair, so I immediately put it out of my mind.

"Great news," I said, as convincingly as I could manage.

"Who's Silvia?" probed our Angela.

"My elder daughter... I've two daughters, the other is Valerie, whom you'll meet later. She has four children," answered Jean.

"How many children has Silvia already?" asked Angela.

"This will be her first," answered Jean.

I knew instinctively what was coming next... "If Valerie's ages with Mum, then Silvia must be in her... forties?" remarked Angela, who then glanced over, and saw the look of horror written across my face. "Well, Jean did say her elder daughter, so she must be in her forties," she continued, reiterating her point...

"That's a clever one you've got, Dawn; I wonder what she'll end up being?" stated Jean.

"Probably something between a psychiatrist and an old fogey professor," I answered drily.

CHAPTER FIFTY-SIX:

Joe dropped Brian off at football training and headed back home to deal with the girls. "Morning, Dad," said Shirley, when he arrived.

"Morning, darling, I'm surprised to see you up already," he replied.

"We're all up, Dad. Mum got us up early and we've all had breakfast too," she announced.

"Oh, right," he replied, then looked into the kitchen to tell Val he was back home. "Need any help?" he asked.

"No, I'm fine, everything's under control," she sighed.

"Do you want me to take the kids to watch Brian play football? They always finish the training sessions with a kick-about game," suggested Joe.

"That would be grand, thanks," said Val.

Joe wanted to put things back to normal with her, but Brigitte and Daisy caught sight of him, before he could say anything further, "Daddy, Daddy," they called out, as they came skipping towards him.

"Daddy's taking you out, so Mummy can get things ready for our visitors," said Val, trying desperately not to look too harassed.

They gleefully jumped up and down clapping their hands, and Joe found himself committed before he could say anything else to her. "Shirley, come on, we're going to watch Brian play football," he called out.

The girls weren't at all interested in the football, but found a grassy knoll to play on. Their friend Charlene Warner came over as soon as she saw them. Charlie, her brother, played for the same team as Brian. "Charlene, is your dad not with you?" asked Joe.

"No, but my mum is," she replied.

Joe looked around until he saw Brenda. He waved from across the pitch and she waved back. Unusually, she did not attempt to come over beside him, and he needed to stay where he was, so he could keep watch on the girls. He wondered if there had been any further developments between Brenda and her husband Tony?

Joe had one eye on the game and one eye on the girls, with his mind elsewhere. Why did he need to have that trivial upset with Val? Why today of all days, when they rarely ever fell out with each other? She must be nervous, because he knew he certainly was. Did he wish that Dawn wasn't coming? He did, and he didn't; the truth being, he really didn't know. Why was he making such a fuss? She would come and she would go, and that would be the end of their story... or would it?

His analysing was suddenly disturbed by the sound of a whistle being blown.

"Girls, that's the game over, time to go home," he called out.

"Can Charlene come to play at our house later, Dad?" asked Brigitte.

"Not today... we've visitors coming later, remember? Sorry, Charlene, you can come tomorrow or any other day, just not today," said Joe.

"I soon won't be able to come ever again," she replied softly...

"How's that?" he asked.

"We're leaving our house and *Cloverley* forever. Mummy says my dad's been bad again," replied Charlene.

Joe had been right. He'd sensed Brenda had been acting strangely; he usually couldn't get rid of her, as she'd chatter on, yet today was avoiding him. Poor woman… what a bloody rat you are, Tony Warner!

"Charlene, ask your mum to drop you off at our house, and Charlie too. It's fine with me if it's okay with your mum," he relented.

"Thanks, Mr Doubleday," replied Charlene, with a beaming smile.

"Thanks, Daddy," said Brigitte, giving him a smile too.

Daisy also gave Joe's legs a hug, and he smiled down at her. Brian was in dire need of a shower when he got home.

"Where's Shirley?" he asked.

"We dropped her off at her friend Denise's. I'll fetch her in a moment. I just want to give Mum a call first," he answered. Joe didn't want to be at odds with Val. Tiny things could grow out of hand if left to fester… she was pleased to hear his voice. "We're on our way back, Val and sorry about earlier," he said, "I love you… Oh, by the way, our Brian's in need of a good scrub."

"Joe, I'm sorry too, and hurry back, I love you," she replied. "Don't worry over Brian, I'm used to him and his dirt."

Joe then turned to the kids, "Right you lot, into the back of the car, and that includes you too, Brian. It'll be easier for Shirley to just slip into the front seat," he said.

"It's this stupid two-door car of yours," said Brian, "you should have brought Mum's instead... it's far more suitable."

"Don't call my car stupid. This is motoring the way I like it to be, so tough. Even you must agree it beats having to walk," he replied. "I get little enough opportunity to drive my baby, as most of the time I'm either in the van or truck."

Brian left it at that and a few minutes later they reached Denise's house. Shirley came running out, and jumped into the front of her dad's pride and joy. "Did you win, Brian?" she asked, looking over her shoulder... "Hi there, my two sweetie pies."

"It wasn't a match," replied Brian, "just training." He then leant forward and whispered something into Shirley's ear, the one furthermost from Joe. Shirley said nothing, but glanced at her dad with interest. He was engrossed in his own thoughts and didn't notice, nor did he hear the giggling of the little ones in the rear when Brian began to tickle them.

Joe was busy trying to form a picture of Dawn in his mind... she wasn't big, or small, just a nice size... she was smart, and had her own way of doing things. Her black wavy hair was similar to his own, but he remembered her eyes were not as dark as his. Was her hair black? He reconsidered... perhaps... or maybe dark brown... but definitely dark. She was up for anything, afraid of nothing, and so full of fun... in looks, she could have been his sister, but then on the other hand, nobody had ever called Dawn a 'tink'!

He wasn't that anymore; he had forged a successful business and was now well respected... a family man who loved his kids, and who had a wife he loved and adored.

All was thanks to his Uncle Pete, his mum's eldest brother. who after his mum died, had taken on her four children and turned them into what they were today. In his head, Joe offered up a little prayer... *God bless Mum, and God bless dear Uncle Pete...*

"Dad, we're home," said Shirley. "You've been in dreamland, but you needn't have worried, I kept my eyes on the road for you."

He smiled at her. What a damn stupid thing to have done, driving the kids without due care and attention... "Thanks for that, Shirley, I'm sorry," he replied.

"It's fine, Dad, I understand," she answered, with a knowing look...

CHAPTER FIFTY-SEVEN:

Angela laughed at my remark concerning her future being somewhere between an old fogey professor and a psychiatrist, for which I was thankfully relieved... when would I stop being the big mouth that I was?

"Have you two been courting long?" I heard Jean then ask Lorraine and Simon.

"Jean means, have you two been going out together for a long time?" I jumped in by way of an explanation.

"Mum, you don't have to explain... Simon and I know what courting means," replied Lorraine.

"Sorry, Lorraine, I had the impression that courting was a word from the distant past, which nobody used anymore," I replied. James continued sipping his tea, whilst persevering with his smirk... damn Mr Smarty Pants. "I was just trying to be helpful," I added, giving him a look.

"Mum, maybe we don't use it on an everyday basis, but we know what the word means," clarified Lorraine.

Daughter of Smarty Pants, just wait, I'll get my own back on the two of them!

"I know what courting means, Mum... what about you, Sean?" piped up Angela. He nodded, and she then checked with Zac, who also nodded.

"Courting is mentioned lots in books we study at school, Mrs Brennan," explained Zac, obviously thinking he was doing me a favour with his tact.

Get back to stuffing your face, you cake-eating monster! The rest of you... Oh, Dawn grow up, I thought. You're meant to be the person who helps people. I knew this to be true but... argh!!

"You've a very lively family," commented Jean.

Lively, why not come out and say what you really mean, Jean, I mused?

"How's your family, Jean? We've heard of Silvia's pregnancy... how's your other daughter?" asked James.

What a big sook, I thought!

"You'll meet Val when we go over for lunch. She's fine, and looking forward to meeting up with Dawn once again," she replied.

"How's Joe?" Angela suddenly asked, with her usual directness.

Good timing, Angela, designed to embarrass until the very end, I thought.

"Who's Joe?" asked Sean, looking around for some clarification.

"Yeah, who's Joe?" added Lorraine.

"He's Val's husband. Your mum knew him well when she was Angela's age. Her family used to come here for weekends and holidays," replied Jean.

All eyes turned towards me, whilst my darling James sat with that silly grin of his pasted over his face. I said nothing, but pressed my lips tight together to keep my mouth firmly shut. Polite conversation ensued from then until just after twelve, when Jean announced that we ought to make tracks…

My body felt numb, having crept upwards from my toes to the very roots of my hair. This meeting of the present with the ghosts of yesteryear was causing me considerable misery. Let sleeping dogs lie… why had I awakened them? My life had been jogging along nicely, and now this!

*

The sound of the troops returning home, resounded along the hall and seeped into the kitchen, disturbing Val's peace. She was enjoying a restful coffee, whilst surveying her buffet spread, when an excited Daisy burst into the room. "Yummy, yummy in my tummy," she shouted, excitedly as her eyes scanned the table.

"Daisy, don't you dare touch anything," warned Val. "Keep it looking nice… please." She looked without touching, but smacked her lips in an exaggerated fashion, which made Val laugh.

"Nice lunch, Mum," commented Brian, "it looks great."

"Brian, take a shower, please," she instructed, "and by the way, did your side win?"

"It was only training," he replied. "Are you looking forward to seeing your friend again?"

"Go and take a shower, right now," she reiterated, "I can smell you from here."

"Stinky, Brian," called out Daisy, pinching her nose.

"Daisy, he can't help it; boys are just naturally stinky," replied Brigitte, who had now joined them in the kitchen.

"Brigitte," explained Val, "boys and girls are only so if they haven't washed."

"Well, I don't think so; everybody knows boys smell most of the time," she replied.

"What's going on in here?" asked Joe, arriving with Shirley on his arm.

"The girls are just leaving to get themselves washed and tidied, before they become stinky," replied Val. "Shirley, can you help them please, I'd like some time alone with Dad?"

"I bet you do," she answered. "I'm really looking forward to meeting your friend, Mum. What's her name again?"

"Dawn, her name's Dawn, and it's not just her whose coming you know, it's her whole family," she replied, "and Grandma Jean too, so don't forget her."

"But Dawn's the main event, eh, Dad?" said Shirley, turning and giving him a wink. "Come on my little girls, let's get you two looking pretty."

"We are pretty; Daddy always calls us his beautiful girls," protested Brigitte.

"But there's a difference between being beautiful and pretty, and I, being clever, know that for sure. So, let's get a move on girls if you want to look pretty," announced Shirley. They left the room in a mist of Brigitte's indignation and Daisy's I-am-pretty protestations...

When they were alone, Joe raised himself up onto the high stool next to Val's, and poured himself a coffee from the cafetière... "Brian must have told Shirley what I spluttered out this morning," whispered Val.

"If he did, I didn't hear him," replied Joe. "It doesn't matter anyway. Shirley will see for herself this afternoon who's the girl for me." He drank up his coffee, and then slipped off his stool after giving her a kiss. "I'd better hurry and get washed too, they won't be long," he added. He kissed her again before he left the room, with Val's eyes following him as he left.

Minutes later, he arrived back again, with two little visitors in tow... "Val, can you look after Charlene and Charlie please, at least until me and the kids are ready? I agreed that they could come to play over here, and Brenda's just dropped them off. I'll explain all about it to you later... thanks love."

Val watched him leave in utter disbelief!

CHAPTER FIFTY-EIGHT:

"Just go around the back," instructed Jean, "they don't stand on ceremony; the back door's usually open."

"If you're sure, Jean," I replied, "will I go first?"

"On you go, lead the way. I'll take James's arm if he doesn't mind?" agreed Jean.

"My pleasure," replied James, offering his arm, "it's a lovely house."

"Joe built it. He's a handy fellow, my son-in-law," said Jean proudly, whose words carried on the breeze in my direction…

"Psst… Angela," I whispered, "Angela, my little sleuth, can you go on ahead, as I'm as nervous as hell?"

"Shh, mind your language; remember where you are," she hissed.

"It's where I am, that's causing me to be as nervous as—," I began.

Angela then squeezed past to lead the way. She was in her element as this was her kind of visiting, and was in no way boring. She disappeared from view as she rounded the corner of the house's gable end. The anticipation made me shiver, but my feet still managed to move ever forward, albeit slowly. When I reached the corner, I peeked around only to be met with... exquisite gardens and open manicured lawns. I also saw that Angela had reached the back door when a boy emerged. I froze and watched... I recognised the boy as Brian, Joe's son... the very same who'd been so interested in my car...

"Who are—?" he started to ask her.

"I've brought your grandma... we're your visitors for today," replied a confident Angela.

Well done, I thought, that's told him straight. "Brian, it's me, the woman with the car the same as your dad's... remember?" I added, as I boldly strode forwards.

He looked me over and slowly nodded, "So, you're her," he replied, as our brief association registered.

"Yes, it's her... she's my mum, and I'm with her," replied Angela.

The others arrived to join us... "This is Brian... my grandson," announced Jean. "He looks as if he's smartened himself up for your visit. He must have known a certain little smasher was coming."

A certain little smasher... that made my Angela sound like an unruly child? However, I knew exactly what she'd meant, and noticed that Angela was busily running her fingers through her tousled waves in an attempt to tidy her hair, whilst continuing to wear a broad grin. Brian didn't have time to be embarrassed by his grandma's remarks, as two little girls suddenly appeared from the house. They looked at us briefly, giggled, and then skipped merrily into the gardens.

"That's Brigitte and Daisy, two of my sisters," announced Brian.

"Two of your sisters, how many more are there?" asked Angela.

"Just one more... our Shirley... Mrs Brennan, you've met her before... on that day when———," replied Brian.

"When what?" interrupted James, his interest suddenly soaring.

"When Dawn last visited, of course," replied Jean. "Now let's all get inside so that James and the family can meet Val and Joe."

She led the way and took us directly into a large light-filled shell of a room, which she told us with some considerable pride, was Joe's latest work in progress. Sitting on the floor were three more children; Shirley, whom I'd met previously, and two others whom I recognised from my old Weekender, namely Charlene and… I couldn't quite remember the boy's name.

"Hi, Grandma," said Shirley. "Mum and Dad are in our old lounge having private time." She then turned her attention to me, as I stood at Jean's side… "I remember you, Mrs Brennan, you're Dawn, Mum and Dad's friend." Shirley reminded me of her mum when she was a similar age, as her eyes gave me the once over, but her confidence remind me more of Joe… "there are lots of you——," she continued.

"Shirley," snapped Jean, "where are your manners?"

"It's okay, Jean," I said. "Shirley, we've brought two friends along with us. The other three are my children… and my husband, of course." I could see from the smirk on James's face, that I needed to shut up, and sharpish.

"Have a seat everyone, if you can find one, and I'll fetch Mum and Dad," suggested Shirley. "Lunch is ready, thank goodness, as it's been ages since we'd breakfast."

"I'll get Mum and Dad," offered Brian, who then looked directly at Angela. "Do you want to come with me?"

She didn't need asking twice and was already on her feet heading for the door. Shirley watched them with a puzzled expression; I also watched them leave, but I wasn't at all puzzled, I knew exactly what was afoot… they didn't look much like children to me anymore…

414

I suddenly began to panic, there was no way I wanted to meet Joe and Val in front of these teenagers and yelping children. "Brian, wait… James and I will come with you," I heard myself saying.

"Okay, Mrs Brennan, just follow us," he replied.

"James, let's go," I urged.

He rose with a puzzled expression, and once out into the hall, Angela pulled the door tightly shut, and turned to me. "Mum, what do you think you're doing?" she asked.

"Dawn, I'm asking you the same question?" added James.

"I can't face Joe and Val with all these people present," I replied. "How have your mum and dad not heard us arrive anyway, Brian?"

"They've probably gone into hiding," joked Angela, "I would if I were them, and had a crazy woman on my tail."

"Angela, that's enough!" scolded James. "Brian, I'm sorry, my daughter can sometimes be a shade—— "

"It's okay, Mr Brennan," said Brian, "Mum and Dad will most likely be in the den. Dad built a room that's totally soundproofed, so we can make as much noise as we want, without disturbing anyone."

"Gee, we could do with one of those in our house… somewhere to go when the olds get out of hand," butted in Angela. "Are your mum and dad by any chance, having a ding-dong in there?"

415

I was horrified, but James and Brian couldn't help but laugh.

"Hi, what's going on here?" said a voice I instantly recognised... I turned, but it was not Joe I saw first, but Val...

"We were just coming to find you," explained Brian. "Your visitors and Grandma Jean arrived about ten minutes ago."

"Sorry," said Val, "we meant to be there to greet you. I thought you'd be along later. Oh, Dawn... I would've recognised you anywhere!"

"I would have known you too, Val," I replied. "Oh, Val, we should've kept in touch with each other over the years."

"I feel that way too," she agreed.

We hugged with genuine affection, and everything else left my mind. We kept hold of each other's hands, and by the time I looked up, James had gone with Brian, Angela, and that... familiar voice.

The door to the lounge was wide open and Val led me in by the hand. As we entered, two little girls squeezed past, and my eyes followed them towards... a seated Joe. I watched as he lifted them onto his knee, and introduced them to my James, neither of whom were aware of my presence. James then began to speak to one of the little girls, and it was then that Joe glanced my way. He gave me a quick wink and then turned back to speak to James. They looked as if they were best buddies already. James stretched out his arms and one of the little ones clambered on to his knee. Well, that's you sorted, James, I thought.

After Val got me seated, I surveyed the room to see how everyone was doing. She left me to say hello to her mum, when Lorraine popped up at my side, "Mum, after lunch, we're thinking of going to that café we passed on the way here. It looked worth a visit," she said, then whispered, "you don't need us hanging around here, whilst you talk over the good old days."

"Who all wants to go?" I asked.

"Just us... Simon, me, Sean and Zac," she replied.

"What about our Angela and the boy Brian?" I asked.

"What about them? I didn't say I wanted to babysit, anyway, they're far too young to be going out with us," she replied.

"Nobody's told them that they're too young," I said.

Lorraine pulled a face; she couldn't see what I could, in fact, none of them could. To me it was the only clear picture amongst this blur of bodies. I felt strangely isolated in this room of happy chattering people, when Val re-appeared at my side, "Dawn, this is the first time I can remember you ever having a lost look on your face," she said. "You were always up for anything, always in charge of the moment."

"Val, it's the first time I can ever remember having such a look showing," I replied.

She sat next to me, took my hand in the same way we'd often done as little girls, as we watched this swirling dance play out in front of us. I was as pleased to be in her company as she was in mine. This was not how I'd thought I'd feel.

"I'll get everyone fed, and then we can have a chat in peace... just the four of us," suggested Val.

I nodded in agreement. She was a thoroughly nice person I concluded, from both a professional point of view, as well as from my own personal one. "I know of four teenagers who want to visit the local café after lunch. I hope you don't think they're being bad-mannered," I said?

"Not at all, Dawn, they're young adults and need their space," she replied.

Why could many of my patients not be as understanding? "What about your Brian and my Angela?" I remarked.

"What about them," she asked, looking around the room, "they're not here, Dawn?"

"Precisely," I replied.

She didn't know what I'd meant, so I decided to say no more.

"Have you spoken to Joe yet?" she suddenly asked.

"No, not yet, he's busy with the little ones, and appears to have found a new buddy in my James," I replied.

"I haven't met James either. I'm looking forward to that. Right, I'll make a start on lunch, and then we'll restore some order," she replied. "Would you care to give me a hand?"

"Delighted, Val... lead the way," I replied.

Val's conversation flowed freely, as did mine. She took the covers from the plates of food, whilst I admired her kitchen... "Who designed this?" I asked. "James has been on at me to upgrade ours for ages. I wasn't keen because of the inevitable mess, but this kitchen's very smart. I might even be able to withstand the chaos, if I knew it would turn out like this."

"Joe and I designed it together, and then he drew up the plans," explained Val.

"Where did he learn to do that?" I asked.

"Joe's a Master Builder, with many related skills crammed under that head of hair of his," she replied, "you were one smart child, and so I bet you also have many skills crammed under that head of hair of yours?"

"Val, what Joe does is useful, whilst there are times, I'm not too sure about what good I do," I said.

"Dawn, I know you're a doctor; is that a doctor of medicine?" she asked.

Yes, and I——," I started to reply.

"Come on everybody, foods ready," shouted Shirley, as she arrived in the kitchen.

"Shirley!" exclaimed Val. "Oh, I suppose we're ready. We may as well let them at it. Ask them all to come through, but politely please."

I found myself a high stool, which I must admit to never having sat on one before, and watched as everyone trickled into the kitchen. A light breeze caressed me from the open French doors, which led out onto a large patio with seats aplenty. Today we were blessed with warm sunshine…

Val was now busily making pots of tea and coffee, and I found myself feeling the kind of affection for her, which I normally kept for Mona and very few others. "Shirley looks very much like you, Val," I called over.

"She may grow out of it, if she's lucky," she called back, with a grin.

"There's nothing wrong with being like you," I replied.

She smiled. Joe was a lucky guy, as Val was both kind and caring, and I doubted if her head was full of the nonsense that weighed so heavily on mine. Jean then arrived, and Val asked her to sit beside me. I would've normally thought this was a plot to keep Joe and I apart, but I wasn't thinking like that… today there was no plot.

I helped her up onto the high stool next to mine, "I don't usually sit on these high chairs, and always refused to try one before, but not today. This is lovely sitting up here beside you, dear Dawn, it's so nice that you've come back into our lives," said Jean.

"What a lovely thing to say," I replied, as I planted a kiss on her cheek.

The teenagers then arrived, and Jean and I watched them load their plates, with Zac's face aglow with anticipation. I was pleased to hear them thank Val for the spread, and then watched as they found themselves a table outdoors. It was as far away from everyone else as was possible, but I wouldn't have expected them to do anything else at their age.

Beyond the French doors, I could see Shirley sitting and munching with Charlene, and her brother, whose name I remembered as being Charlie. These two were the ones who now ran up and down my childhood stairs in our old Weekender. Many things had changed in that house over the years, but not these stairs, which I still considered to be mine.

Joe and James arrived, each holding a little girl by the hand. They waved over at Jean and me, and Joe winked once more... but was that wink aimed at his mother-in-law or at me or perhaps it was meant for us both?

"Jean, it's about time Val, you and I took our plates, and went outside to join the others?" I suggested.

"You bet," she replied, as I then helped her down from the high stool and passed her a plate.

"Grandma, this is good fun," called out Daisy. "I like having visitors."

"Are you going to sit beside me, Daisy," Jean asked, "and Brigitte, what about you, I'd like that?"

The two little girls charged over to hug their grandma. I looked down on Daisy's pretty little head, and saw a smaller version of Val. I then looked at Brigitte, who looked very much like—

"Brigitte, looks the way I imagined you must've looked at her age, Dawn," announced James.

"I look like my daddy," replied Brigitte proudly.

"And also your Auntie Dawn," added James, with a grin.

"James, your Angela looks the way I remember Dawn all these years ago," replied Joe.

"And your Brian looks very much like how I remember you, Joe," I said.

These were the first words we had exchanged in all of twenty-eight years, and they felt... so natural...

"Where's Brian?" asked Joe.

"Come to think of it, where's our Angela?" asked James.

"Together, no doubt," I replied.

"What do you mean together, they've only just met?" puzzled James.

"Sometimes it doesn't take long to get to know someone," I replied.

"Do you know where they are?" asked Joe, his dark eyes looking directly at me for the first time in all these years.

"No, I don't know where they are exactly, but I do know that wherever they are, they will be together," I answered.

"James, stop fretting, they'll be fine, they're growing up fast," said Joe, and this time he winked only for me...

We moved through the French doors and out into the garden, with our cups and laden plates. What Joe had said had been accepted in principle, and whilst Val and James pondered on what he'd actually meant... I already knew.

CHAPTER FIFTY-NINE:

During lunch, I felt moved to sit with Val and Jean. I expected James and Joe to join us, and they did, but only for a short period. The two men appeared to have much in common, if their enthusiastic conversation with each other was anything to go by? We girls had lots to talk about too, but I found I had one eye fixed on them and one ear flapping in the men's direction... this outing was not turning out as I had imagined.

"Dawn love, throw me over your car keys please," asked James, with one of his sweet smiles.

"Whatever for?" I replied, loudly.

Those within earshot stopped whatever they were doing, and looked over at me.

"Same old Dawn," Joe laughed.

"What do you mean by that?" I asked.

"Just what I've said. You were always a questioner of things… what was it you called yourself?" he asked.

"A sleuth?" I replied.

"Yes, that's it… a sleuth, always delving deep into things, and as I recall you had a badge from some sleuthing club from which you also received newsletters," said Joe, with a smile.

This outpouring took me by surprise, and it must have shown, as Val put her arm around my shoulder, "Dawn, he's just showing off that he's remembered," she said. "James, can I ask you why you need Dawn's car keys while in the middle of lunch?"

"Sorry, it can wait,Val. Joe wanted to see inside her car, and we thought we could perhaps skip dessert," James replied.

"Joe isn't that keen on sweet things, and was being impatient, James. He didn't think you'd like dessert either… but would you… like dessert, that is?" asked Val.

James nodded, as I knew he certainly would. He had a sweeter tooth than the proverbial sugar plum fairy. Joe continued to chat to him and didn't look my way, so I walked around to the other side of the table, and tapped James on the shoulder. As he moved to make space for me, I plucked the keys from my bag and gave them to him. He responded by squeezing my hand, whereupon I returned to my seat beside Val and Jean.

After James had scoffed his dessert, he and Joe excused themselves and left.

"I'm sorry, Dawn. I don't know what's got into Joe today," said Val.

"It's fine Val, men must be men," I replied.

We all remained seated, well Val, Jean, and I did, and enjoyed an after lunch coffee. The kids had asked if they could leave the table, and Charlene and Charlie remembered to thank Val for lunch, which I could see she appreciated. I hoped my teenage troops would be as equally polite? I glanced over at them; they were content for the moment, with shrieks of laughter rising from their table...

Jean must have noticed me glancing over at them, "Oh, to be young and in love," she said, with a smile. Val gave me the quickest of sideway glances, which I managed to catch out of the corner of my eye. "You know all about young love, Dawn," continued Jean. "As I recall, you were fast out of the starting blocks when you were a girl."

"As was m'lad," added Val.

"We all grow up in the end though," I replied. I didn't quite follow what I'd meant by that remark, and as neither made any direct comment, I took it that they didn't either.

"How do you find, Joe," asked Val, "what I mean is, do you think he's the same or different?"

I realised she had taken time to build herself up to asking me this question, so I took my time to reply out of respect. It was actually an inappropriate question; of course, he'd changed since he was a lad of twelve. "I'm sure I would have recognised him, Val, as I did you," I replied. "As regards to how you are as adults, I think that you have changed much less than him."

"Becoming a father changes most men," said Jean, rather philosophically.

"For the better or for the worse, Jean?" I asked, with a laugh, trying to keep the mood light. She didn't reply but stared blankly into space…

"What happened to James, when you and he had children?" asked Val.

Gee, this was getting serious… so many damned searching questions, I thought.

"You and I are not likely to understand Dawn's answer, Val… she's a psychiatrist," replied Jean, back with us once more.

"A psychiatrist! Oh, Dawn, you only got around to telling me you were a doctor, which was great news, but I never thought of you as one of those types," Val replied. "I'm shocked… just wait until Joe hears."

As if on cue, James and Joe returned to enquire if there was any coffee left in the pot? "Val, I'll make a fresh pot, while you break the news about Dawn to Joe," offered Jean.

427

"What news is this, Dawn?" asked James.

"I'll let Val do the talking," I replied, with raised eyebrows.

James mouthed, "are you all right?" I nodded, then sat back in my chair, much in the way I did when faced with an awkward patient...

"Before we hear this ground-breaking news, I'd like to tell Dawn, that I admire her choice of car. James told me it was your choice," said Joe, "as it was mine."

"I suppose it's just one of those cases of... great minds thinking alike?" I replied. "And thank you for appreciating my taste... in quality cars."

"I'm sure you share other tastes?" said James, with one of his sweet grins.

"Right, let's be hearing this ground-breaking news, Val," said Joe, swiftly changing the topic.

"First, can I ask James what he does for a living? You both know Joe's a builder and probably have worked out that I'm a stay-at-home mum," suggested Val.

"But that's just until the end of the summer, when Daisy will be off to school. Then, Val will be my apprentice," explained Joe. "We'll be able to spend far more time together, and I know she'll be top notch."

"Well, that sounds really good, doesn't it Dawn?" said James.

"It sure does," I agreed, "James, don't forget Val asked you a question, darling."

"Okay Val, it's nothing glamorous I'm afraid," he answered, "I'm just an old fogey of a history professor... the perk being that I get nice long holidays."

I watched Joe to see if he had already asked James that same question, but from his reaction, the answer appeared that he hadn't. "My goodness, I'd never have guessed that. You seem such a regular, normal, sort of a guy," said Joe.

"He is... a regular, normal sort of guy... he's my regular, normal guy," I replied. My blood temperature having now already risen, and we still hadn't heard the news concerning my vocation...

"Joe, wait until you hear what Dawn does for a living... you'll never guess," exclaimed Val.

"Wait, don't tell me... I think Dawn's a—," he began, then stopped mid-sentence, gave me a look, and tapped his fingers on the table, "a detective... police, or maybe private... I'm not sure, or she could be some kind of forensic scientist?"

Jean arrived back at that moment with a freshly brewed pot of coffee, "If you must know, Dawn's a psychiatrist... have you ever heard the likes?" she spurted out.

"Is this some kind of joke, Jean?" replied Joe, bursting out laughing.

I straightened my back and moved my shoulders to loosen them. I was used to dealing with a variety of people, many of whom harboured very strange ideas about psychiatry...

"It's no joke, Joe," said Val, "and please don't laugh, it's rude... so behave yourself."

I moved forward in my seat, and then settled back again, with my arms loosely resting on the arms of my chair. I had an advantage; I was trained in how to deal with awkward people and even more awkward situations. So, Joe looked upon me as a sleuth... well, the first thing I had sleuthed today, was that Val had addressed him in much the same way as she did her other children!

Suddenly I became aware of bodies approaching, and looked up to a beaming Lorraine... "Hi, everyone, you wouldn't think it too rude of us, if we took a stroll into the village, would you?" she asked. "Thanks for the delicious lunch, we all thoroughly enjoyed it, and it was very kind of you, Mrs Doubleday." The others also muttered their collective appreciation.

"No, of course not," replied Val, "off you go, and if you come across our Brian and your sister on the way... send them back please."

"Sharpish," added Joe.

I felt ashamed, and looked at James with raised eyebrows. I'd forgotten all about our Angela... my dear friend Val had sailed way past me in the motherhood stakes. She was my new heroine... at all times concerned for her children and their welfare… and, whatsmore, appeared to have Joe gripped tightly by the short and curlies…

"James," I called over, "have you a moment please?"

"For you, all the time in the world," he replied, with a smile. He was on his feet in an instant, and over beside me. I spoke to him as discreetly as was possible in the circumstances, "Did you remember that our Angela was absent?" I whispered.

"What a question, Dawn." he whispered back.

"Well?" I whispered again.

"No," he sheepishly replied. I thanked him for that piece of honest information, as it made me feel much better about myself. At least we were putting on a united front, and that's what being a couple meant in my book.

"Dawn… Joe and I are becoming rather anxious, not so much about Brian, but about your Angela," said Val.

"Not just anxious, I for one am bloody annoyed," remarked Joe.

"Joe, there's no need to express yourself in those terms, no matter how annoyed you are," scolded Val. "May I point out folks, that it's our Brian he's angry with, and not your Angela."

My Joe of old would never have put up with anyone telling him what he could or couldn't say. I looked at him with a smirk. He knew what I was thinking, and looked away instantly.

"I thought that the four of us could perhaps head into the village, and see if there's any sign of them," continued Val.

"That would be lovely, as I could show James the sights. Yes, I'd like that. We will keep a look out for Angela and your Brian of course," I replied.

"What sort of girl is your Angela?" asked Joe.

"What a strange question," I replied, "she's a child, and an exceedingly clever one."

"Our Brian's not the brightest spark in our family," said Joe, with a shrug of his shoulders.

"Joe, what a thing to say. Brian's very good at… the things he's very good at," defended Val.

"But our Shirley's more worldly wise, and I think brighter," he countered.

"Perhaps, but Brian's a lovely caring boy," replied Val.

"I'm not saying he's not all of these things, and many more besides, I'm only saying that he's not as mature as our Shirley in certain ways—," stressed Joe.

"Listen you two, this is obviously a private discussion, so James and I will go on ahead and you can follow, once you've resolved your differences. I do remember the way," I interrupted.

I could see that Joe was now angry with me, but I didn't care. What a load of twaddle! I took hold of James's hand, but he resisted, as I was about to take him away from a discussion he was finding increasingly fascinating. "Don't be so nosey," I said to him, when I finally got him moving along the path. "You wouldn't want anyone listening to us when we're flowing like a river."

As we walked towards the village, I couldn't help thinking we were going in the wrong direction. In my mind, I'd subconsciously pictured, not a village, but a river and a certain waterfall... surely, it couldn't happen again?

They however, soon caught up on us before we'd gone too far, "Joe has something he wants to say to you, Dawn," said Val.

Hell, she's not making him apologise, that's the last thing I want to hear from his lips... "I'm sorry, Dawn," he muttered sheepishly.

My, that was short, and to the point, I thought. "Thanks," I replied, "but it really wasn't necessary."

"See Val, I told you she wouldn't want an apology," he huffed, scuffing his feet on the stoney path.

But he'd still made one. It confirmed to me what I'd thought previously, that Val had him well and truly by the short and curlies... about that there was no doubt!

CHAPTER SIXTY:

The men arrived at the café first. Val and I watched as Joe peered in through the window, "It's quite busy inside," he called back to us. "I can see your lot, but no sign of Brian and Angela."

I wanted to remind him that only two of them belonged to us, but I knew what he'd meant and I was just being picky. We headed inside.

"Mum, what are you playing at following us here?" groaned Sean.

"We're not following you, we're actually looking for Brian and Angela," answered James.

"Sorry," replied Sean, "of course you are. We haven't seen them, but we were looking for them on the way over here too."

"Angela needs to be told the score Mum, this is outrageous. Mrs Doubleday put on a lovely spread, and they've bunked off to... who knows where," added Lorraine.

What about the boy Brian, and why does only our Angela need to be told the score? I also noticed that Simon had his arm around Lorraine's shoulder, stroking and massaging her neck as she spoke. This I found irritating, and wanted to wrench his arm away, but managed to stop myself in time. I pictured the headlines in the local rag... *'Mad woman in Cloverley village café assaults teenage boy'*... Mona would know instantly who it was if she ever picked up a copy.

Zac then told me how he shared our concern. Moreover, it was heartfelt and genuine. I couldn't help but take to this boy. He made me want to take him home, as I would a lost puppy. Our dog Jinty had died some time ago, and it had been such a sad experience, that we'd never replaced her. Today, Zac and his sympathies brought her memory to the fore once more...

Joe and James were at the counter, where Joe enquired if Brian had been in today? The staff, who all knew Brian well, told him that they hadn't seen him. We then left the premises, except for my sweet James, who lingered for a moment to make sure the teenagers had enough cash to enjoy themselves.

"What happens now?" he asked, when he rejoined us outside.

"You put your wallet firmly back into your back pocket for a start," I said.

"Are you an old softie, James?" asked Val.

"Yes, he is Val, but let's have a little less of the old, it's embarrassing enough," I replied. Well, spotted Val… I did marry an older man, I mused.

James was grinning at the spotlight being shone upon him.

"How old are you, mate, and may I add, that you're looking good for your age?" said Joe.

"What a contradiction of terms… same old Doubleday flannel," I replied. "My James can give us all eleven years."

"May I say that you look very handsome?" added Val.

"You may, my fair lady," laughed James.

Joe and I looked at each other, with a look that lingered momentarily, and then we also laughed. "They are two of a kind, wouldn't you agree, Joe?" I said.

"I would… a pair of sweeties, and of the soft centred variety," he replied.

I then noticed James eyeing up the village inn across the way… "We could always pop into 'The Wild Goose' whilst we regroup," he suggested, after managing to read the swinging nameplate.

"Why James, is that because you think we're on some kind of forlorn chase?" I asked.

"Nice one, Dawn," replied Joe.

"Joe, stop joking, this is serious. Our Brian and Angela are still missing," said Val.

I could see she was upset; she was giving off vibes of sensitivity. It was an everyday occurrence in my surgery, so I knew that the best thing would be to take her home.

"Val and I are going back to the house. You two can go wild goose chasing if you must, while you work out where they are," I said, "but don't linger any longer than necessary."

"What do you think they're doing?" asked James. I glared at him and left him in no doubt that he had overstepped the mark. "What," he continued, "it was just an innocent remark?"

Before we left, I asked Joe for a quiet word in private, and moved a few paces from James and Val... "Did you ever take Brian there," I whispered, "and don't dare ask me where?"

"No," he replied, "I would've loved to have taken the family, but I couldn't do it, Dawn."

"I understand... I went there myself, that time before our cars—," I began.

"Not long after that, I went there myself too… and found the place to be just as magical," he interrupted. "It's still our place, it belongs to only you and me."

We looked at each other, and in that moment, he was my Joe of old, but I could also see James out of the corner of my eye… "Right, Val, you and I are for the off," I said. "I don't suppose you've got your phone with you James, have you?"

He shook his head.

"Here's mine," I continued, "now keep in touch."

"Joe has a phone," said Val, "they don't need yours."

"No, I don't have my phone with me, love… it's not a work day," he replied.

Val was about to chastise him once more, but I decided to intervene and save the day. After all, my old Joe was still there, despite his recent guise. "It's fine Val, I'm sure they can manage with one phone between them," I said. "It's good to leave your phone at home on the weekends; I tend to do that as well, but luckily not today."

When Val and I arrived back at her house, Daisy and Brigitte came running across the front lawn to meet us. "Where have you been, Mummy?" yelled Brigitte.

"We didn't know where you were," added Daisy. "Grandma wouldn't tell us."

"Sorry girls, we should've told you we were going to look for Brian and Angela," explained Val.

"No, you weren't doing that," replied Brigitte, "that's not true."

Daisy stood with a petted lip, which she always put on when upset and when tears lurked nearby.

"Why are you saying that, Brigitte?" asked Val.

"Cause it's true," she replied, with her arms folded tightly across her chest. "Brian and his friend are here."

I looked at her, who together with her brother Brian and her dad, almost mirrored my Angela in appearance. I'd never realised before now, just how alike Joe and I must have looked when we were young...

"Come on, Dawn, I don't have time to stand listening to all this nonsense," exclaimed Val, as she marched around to the back of the house, with her arm linked through mine. "That's all I need, Dawn... a junior mutiny on my hands."

I didn't get around to answering, before we were interrupted by an all-too-familiar sound.

"Hi, Mum," called out our Angela, "how's things and where is everyone?"

"Hiya, Mum," echoed Brian.

"What the——" began Val, "where have you been, Brian?"

"Nowhere," he replied. "Grandma, told us you'd gone out looking for us. Sorry Mum, but I thought you would've guessed where we were. Going out looking for us was a bit over the top, was it not?"

"It's cool in there, Mum," gushed Angela. "We were in that den room, the one which Brian's folks were in when we arrived."

"Whatever for?" I asked.

"Well, they never heard us arrive, which seemed strange, so I wanted to test it out for myself," she replied.

This made sense to me, as it was the kind of thing I would have done. According to Joe and Val, they hadn't heard any of us arrive, so I could definitely see Angela's point.

"Fair enough then, but why didn't you come out at lunch time. You're always hungry, Brian?" asked Val.

"I took a plate of sandwiches and cakes from the kitchen, before we disappeared into the den. There seemed plenty enough to go around, and I honestly didn't think you'd mind," he replied. "Angie wanted to play loud music to test out the room, so that's what we did. Sorry if we've made a few crumbs, but I've seen it worse."

Val appeared speechless...

"I took one of your jugs of orange juice, and a couple of glasses to wash the food down," chipped in Angela. "Your cakes and sandwiches were ace Mrs Doubleday, nice and fresh, just the way I like them."

"Are you meaning my sandwiches and cakes aren't always fresh?" I found myself forced to question.

"Oh no, Mum, I was being tactful. You're always on at me to be tactful. In truth, to my taste buds, they were no different from your own," was her frank reply.

That was me properly boxed up and dispatched. Where was that child's loyalty to the hand that fed her on a daily basis? Brian beamed in her direction, obviously a smitten young buck, and I couldn't blame him. Our Angela was a special young lady and exquisitely packaged.

"Where's Grandma, and why didn't she phone to say you were here?" asked Val, sinking ever lower.

"Grandma's having a lie down; she's taken one of her convenient headaches, that you say she takes," answered Brian. "Angie told her that we'd babysit the others, which pleased her."

Val stood shell-shocked. I knew she'd be so embarrassed I'd heard Brian's revelations, especially about the crumbs in the den. What surprised me was the amount of empathy I felt for her. I realised that I cared about my friend very much, as I rarely did empathise. I favoured treating most emotions with professional and clinical discipline.

"We would have phoned Dad, but his phone's lying on the sideboard in the hall," continued Brian. "Angie told me her folks didn't use mobile phones at the weekend, which I found strange, but I suppose they're just the same as Dad."

I linked my arm through Val's to show her I understood, which helped her to recover a tad.

"Dawn and I have been into *Cloverley* looking for you. In fact your dad together with Angela's, are still there searching behind every shrub and bush," said Val.

That's a large tube of smarties spilled now, I thought…

"Why are they searching in the bushes for us, Mrs Doubleday?" replied our Angela.

You can't expect our Angela not to pick up on a statement like that Val, I mused. What a gift!

"Yes, Mum, why are they searching the bushes?" repeated Brian, showing solidarity with our Angela.

"Why indeed?" I heard myself agreeing softly…

Val didn't answer the question, as a sudden fast approaching wailing noise interrupted matters and couldn't be ignored. James came around the corner, closely followed by Joe carrying both Brigitte and Daisy under his arms, both of whom were wailing their little hearts out.

"For goodness sake, Val, what did you say to upset them so much?" asked Joe.

"She said—," began Brigitte.

"I know exactly what I said and I was wrong. I'm sorry girls," interrupted Val. "It's all Brian and Angela's fault. Look at them Joe… sitting out in the sunshine without a care in the world, while we've been worried senseless."

Joe lowered the girls to the ground, apparently none the worse after their little upset, and watched as they ran off to find Shirley, and the Warner kids in the garden playhouse. He then turned his attention to Brian, whilst James came and sat by my side.

"Where did you go to, Brian," asked Joe, "tell me the truth and you'll not get into any trouble?"

"Why should I get into trouble when I've been nowhere?" he protested. "I've told Mum already, that Angie and me were in the den eating lunch, and listening to music, that's all. Why didn't anyone not think to check the house first, before rushing off into the village?"

"When did our daughter's name suddenly get shortened to Angie?" whispered James.

"Ask Brian," I whispered back.

"Dad, Angie only wanted a demonstration of the den's soundproofing," continued Brian.

"I can well imagine," muttered Joe.

"Excuse me, you can well imagine what, precisely?" I asked, indignantly, having overheard him.

"You know, Dawn," he replied, giving me a knowing look.

I glared at him, turned, ran back down the garden path and jumped into my thankfully unlocked car for sanctuary. The next moment, the passenger door opened and I found Joe sitting beside me. "Go away," I huffed.

"Dawn, I'm sorry; Angela's not bothered," he began, "she's not taken any offence."

"Good for her," I replied, turning to look the other way.

"I like it when you get on your high horse," he said.

"I'm not for you to like, whether I'm on my high horse or otherwise... now leave me alone," I sniffled.

"Dawn, please," he pleaded.

"Don't Dawn me. I'm nothing to do with you," I continued to huff. "I want my James."

"James is a really nice guy; I like him very much," said Joe.

"Not nearly as much as me," I answered.

"Of course not. You do still like me, just a little bit, don't you?" he asked.

"What kind of stupid question is that?" I replied.

"I'll take that as a yes... a very little yes but still a yes," he said. "By the way, your car's interior is much smarter than mine."

"I'm a sleuth," I replied. "You've got to be smart to be a sleuth."

"I agree," he said, taking my hand loosely in his, "My Dawn's not only a sleuth, but a clever psychiatrist too. I'm so very, very proud of you."

I let him tighten his grasp on my hand; it felt safe, and dare I say, familiar… even after all these years…

CHAPTER SIXTY-ONE:

Joe and I dawdled back along the path at the side of the house, and he let go of my hand just before we reached the corner. When we did, apprehension was written across the faces of the adults. "Listen everyone," he said, "it's all sorted. It was my fault, so let me apologise to you all for everything. Now, can we forget about what's happened and enjoy the remainder of our limited time together? How's about it folks?"

Relief peppered the air. We then gathered around the largest table, and I helped Val serve ice cream, and soon we were back playing happy families once more. Lorraine and Simon arrived back shortly afterwards, but without Sean and Zac. The boys seemingly met a couple of local girls in the café and had decided to stay on with them.

"As long as I can get hold of them when we want to go back to the hotel, that's fine by me," I told James.

He agreed with me as usual, "Are they nice?" he asked.

"They seemed okay," answered Lorraine.

"It's not as if they've got themselves engaged or anything like that, James," I replied. "I don't see if it matters whether they're nice or not." My reply had been much too harsh; I knew that straight away, so I gave James a peck, apologised, and he smiled at me lovingly.

Joe's eyes rested upon us. What was he thinking I wondered? I smiled at him and he winked, probably thinking what a lucky escape he'd had?

We sat chatting in the sunshine. Simon had his arm around our Lorraine's shoulders, and I noticed Brian and Angela moving ever closer together. As soon as my back was turned, Brian pounced, copying Simon. What could I say? Plenty, I can assure you when I got hold of our little Madam later!

Val told us Silvia had intended a short visit today, but had decided against it, not wishing to catch anything from us whilst in her delicate condition. Secretly relieved, I asked Val to pass on our best wishes to her and her husband.

"Would I have wanted to meet this sister of Val's?" asked James.

"No, believe you me you've had a lucky escape," I replied, "she'd have gobbled you up, no problem. It would have been a case of, the man may be a professor but he's no match for me."

Jean had now fully recovered, and we congratulated her again on the news of Silvia's surprise pregnancy. Apart from Sean and Zac, we were now a full house. Nevertheless, I persisted as before, with my eyes well peeled on Brian and his Angie…

"For goodness sake, Dawn," said James, "leave them alone. Were you never young once and in love?"

"Obviously not," I replied. "I'll try for your sake James, although you appear to be well up on this young love lark."

James was still laughing at my last remark, when Joe approached, "James," he said, "Charlene and Charlie are ready to go home. I'd normally let them run along the road by themselves, but I want to have a word with their mum, who I believe has been having a hard time. Do you want to come with me, then I can show you what used to be Dawn's Weekender?"

"Is that where they live, in your old house?" asked James, somewhat surprised.

"Yes," I replied. "I went there when I came on that visit a few weeks ago. I was inside the house and met Brenda Warner, so I'll stay and chat to Val and Jean. This visit's flying by fast enough, and we've still lots to talk about."

"I'll look after James for you," said Joe, "and in return, he can tell me what he was finding so funny just now." The thought of that conversation made me laugh myself.

Shirley then came and sat beside her mum, her grandma, and me. I'd seen very little of her since we'd arrived, as she had been playing with her friends most of the time. "Hi," she said, "I've been meaning to ask you about something my mum mentioned."

"Oh, that sounds interesting," I replied. "How can I help you?"

I noticed Val go visibly pale, and wondered what was coming next...

"Well, Mum said that my dad used to like you more than her... when you were both young," she began, "and I was wondering if you liked him lots then too?"

No wonder Val had paled, and come to think of it, Jean didn't look too good either!

"Shirley, first of all, will you come with me to my car. I've gifts in the boot which I'd almost forgotten about, and could do with a little help," I replied.

"Sure," she agreed.

We trotted out to the car. Inside the boot, I had a mixed case of good quality wines for Joe and Val, and a selection of sweets for the kids, as I couldn't think what else to buy them. Shirley helped me lift out the case of wine, and then I handed her a bottle of liqueur I'd brought for her grandma.

"They'll like these, will my mum and dad," continued Shirley, referring to the wine. "They like a glass or two in the evenings."

"So do we… that is, James and I," I replied.

"Your husband looks much older than you. My dad and you are almost the same age, as is my mum," said Shirley. "Same age or older, which do you think's best?"

I closed the boot of my car, and for once broke my own rules as we leant against it. "What made you ask that question about your dad liking me?" I asked.

"Brian told me. He was in the room when he overheard them talking about you," she replied. "I'm interested in these kinds of things."

If I knew it was still in operation, I would have had no hesitation in introducing this curious child to the Junior Sleuth League. "Shirley, when we were around twelve years of age, your dad and I were… special friends… very special. Now, he loves your mum, and although he and I are still fond of each other, it is in a different sort of way. I love my James, and I don't see him as being older than myself, he's just part of me," I said, "understand?"

"Yes, but why did you stop loving Dad?" she asked.

"Who mentioned anything about love… I thought we were talking about like?" I answered.

"Dawn, I'm eleven years of age; I know when we're talking about love," she replied.

This child was the Doubleday's equivalent of our Angela. Perhaps all families have one? I thought previously that we were the only ones blessed in such a way.

*

Charlene and Charlie ran ahead of the two men, who sauntered behind at their own pace.

"Joe, thanks for giving up your time for us. Val mentioned how busy a guy you are," said James. "She's a lovely lady, very kind and gentle."

"Thanks, I agree with you about Val," replied Joe. "James, your family's visit has been a pleasure. I never thought I'd ever get the chance to meet you all. You're such a lovely man, but I bet she runs circles, not just rings around you? I know what she's like, or should I say, was like."

"You're right, but I love it, and her," he answered. "I'm so lucky she married me because I'm no oil painting, unlike——,"

Joe could hear the emotion in his voice, as he was fighting back his own emotions.

"You and her really cared for each other, and in a way still do, I know that now," continued James. "We were visiting Dawn's dad not that long ago when *Cloverley* was mentioned. He became enraged about this guy Joe Doubleday, who according to him, would've led Dawn astray, if her family had continued to visit their Weekender. When I asked her afterwards and learned that this lad was only twelve years old, I had to laugh, but now I want to apologise for that."

"There's no need to, James. I was not your normal twelve year old," he replied.

"What Dawn and you had between you was not something to be laughed at; I realise that now," said James.

The two men walked on companionably, each with their own thoughts, until they reached the Warner house, where a sign flapped outside in the breeze…

"For sale? Is Dawn's Weekender up for sale?" asked James.

"It would appear so," replied Joe. "Charlene told me this morning that her dad had been bad, and that they'd soon be leaving the village. That's why I told them they could come over to the house today. I was explaining that to Val in the den when you arrived, so I was responsible for your Angela finding out about the joys of soundproofing. That girl is, without doubt, Dawn's daughter."

"She looks like two of your own children. You and Dawn must've looked like brother and sister when you were youngsters," said James.

"I used to tell my little sisters that they, Dawn and I were all one big family," he replied, "but nobody ever called her a 'tink'!"

Joe broke down and James felt sadness for his new friend, "Joe, just let it go… life has moved on," he said. The two men exchanged a hug, and Joe tried to muster a smile.

The Warner children had gone straight into the house, as the outer door had been left open. Joe knocked on the inner door and called out to Brenda… "Come straight in, Joe," she replied.

"I'll wait here," said James. "I'll be quite happy looking around the outside of the place."

"Come inside and meet Brenda first," urged Joe.

They entered the house, each again carrying their own emotions. The thought that Dawn had come through this door, and walked along the very same corridor they were now walking, haunted them.

"Hi, Joe, thanks for having the kids over today. They're both high by the way, and told me you had visitors… like some kind of party," said Brenda. "Who's your friend?"

"I believe you met Dawn Brennan some time back, this is her husband, James. Dawn's over at the house with Val," explained Joe, by way of introduction.

"Ah, the striking lady whose folks once owned this house," she replied. "How do you do James, nice to meet you?"

"What's with the sign, Brenda," asked Joe, "I knew you were upset when we spoke briefly at the football this morning, but this?"

Brenda rose and closed the door, so the kids wouldn't overhear. "My marriage is over, Joe, as Tony's now shacked up with someone new," she disclosed. "This is the real thing, he says and needs the money from this place to furnish his new love nest."

"Tony can't make you sell the house so soon... surely?" replied Joe. "What about the kids?"

"I just want rid of him. I want to move on to wherever that may be... me and my kids," she replied. "I want him out of my head, and out of my hair... for good."

"Folks, I'd really like to have a look around outside if you don't mind, and that'll give you two space to talk privately," said James.

"Feel free," replied Brenda, "it's in a bit of a mess. We had such plans..."

James slipped outside into the fresh air, and took stock of the place with a pair of fresh eyes.

Brenda later came to the door with Joe... "It's a nice place, Brenda," said James. "How much of the land and out-buildings are yours?"

"To the trees over that way, and then around by the lane and along by these other trees on this side. Also all the

454

outbuildings you can see, but they're not much use... falling down, most of them," she replied.

"That's one mighty big plot, Brenda," said James, "probably an acre or more... perhaps even two?"

"Too damned big for me to look after," replied Brenda.

They then said their goodbyes and started back along the track.

"What's your interest in the land and property?" asked Joe.

"What's Brenda's story?" countered James.

*

The two men arrived at Joe's house and were soon back in the throes of family life. Sean and Zac had arrived, feeling a shade guilty for having stayed away so long, but otherwise happy.

"What's brought you two back?" I asked.

"That's not very welcoming, Mum," he answered.

"Did the girls get fed up with you," asked Lorraine, "or did their boyfriends arrive?"

"They don't have boyfriends," replied Zac.

"That'll be right," laughed Lorraine.

"Lorraine, leave them alone, that's cruel," said Simon.

"But probably true," she replied.

"You wait and see, they want us to phone them next week," said Sean.

"It'll be a long-distance relationship then," replied Lorraine.

"That's the best kind, it keeps it fresh," replied her big brother.

*

Joe had ordered fish 'n' chips from the village, which George delivered once more, and for which James insisted on paying. Afterwards, the Brennan's, Zac and Simon, returned to the hotel with the promise they'd return for coffee the following morning before they left for home.

Once back at the hotel, everyone felt happy but ready for an early night.

"Dawn, let's go down to the bar for a nightcap," suggested James.

"Okay, but just the one, I'm tired," I replied.

James warned everyone to be on their best behaviour, and then we took the lift down to the hotel bar. The barman welcomed us as we entered the dimly lit room, which was strangely devoid of patrons... "Where is everyone?" I asked.

"Everyone appears to be tired tonight, Madam," replied the barman. "You know what that means don't you?" He waited for an answer, but none came from us, only bemused blank expressions. "It means that you'll receive my full attention, and that you'll have a quiet atmosphere in which to enjoy your drinks," he continued. "Now what can I get you?"

"Can I be a pest and ask for a hot chocolate?" I answered.

"Certainly, no problem Madam; and you Sir, will it be the same for you?" he asked.

James nodded, and the barman then emerged from behind his bar, and locked his little swing door behind him. The poor man would need to go into the kitchen for the hot chocolates.

"He thought I was a pest, James. He didn't say, 'not at all Madam', instead he said, 'certainly, no problem Madam' and in doing so, was agreeing with me that I'm a pest," I said.

"Wait until you ask for a refill," replied James, "that'll make his night."

"Good thinking, don't let me leave without having at least one refill," I said. "Let's sit over in the corner. If I didn't know you were desperate to talk to me fully awake, I'd have suggested we just grab our drinks and disappear back upstairs to bed with them."

"I need to float something past you tonight, Dawn, and I haven't got a clue as to how you'll react," he replied.

"That's why you have such an exciting life," I said. "You never know what's coming next."

We stayed in the bar until midnight, both enjoying two refills each. A group of people arrived during our stay, which thankfully meant the barman was otherwise pre-occupied, leaving us in peace, and me to ponder James's unexpected proposal…

CHAPTER SIXTY-TWO:

I couldn't sleep, as I wasn't sure I'd be able to go along with James's plans. Half of me embraced his ideas, whilst the other was afraid... afraid of the future because of the past. His plans had rocked me, as had the speed at which he and Joe had bonded. I was no further forward when daylight broke, and realised he'd be expecting my answer.

James was breathing softly with his chest gently rising and falling, as I slipped out of bed and into the bathroom, where I immediately dimmed the lights. There was no chair, so I climbed into the bath and lay back, with a rolled towel under my head. My mind spun around, awash with confusion. Why could life not be more straightforward, I thought?

*

"What the devil are you doing in there?" asked James.

"I didn't want to disturb," I replied sheepishly, as I looked up at him.

"Look, get yourself back into bed for half-an-hour at least. It's still nice and warm," he suggested, "and I'll come and tuck you in tight."

I agreed, as I was now sleepy and my neck ached. After the hard bath, the softness of the mattress and pillow were sheer bliss, and I soon drifted off…

*

"Come on, Dawn, we've all had our breakfast, I've brought yours on a tray," said James. "Come on, sit up, and eat it now. We've got lots to do this morning."

"James, I'm not sure about your plans; I don't know if I can cope with, Joe," I replied.

"In what way cope with him?" he asked.

"He held my hand on our way back from the car yesterday," I confessed, "as we walked up the side-path of Val's house."

"He's held your hand before yesterday," replied James, "so what's new? What's your problem?"

His matter-of-fact reaction surprised me, "I still care about him," I said.

"But not as much as you care for me and our family," he replied.

"Of course not," I said. "How can you ask me that?"

"To illustrate a point. Joe cares for you differently to the way he cares for Val and his family," replied James. "He told me that when you were both young, he imagined you and him looking after his little sisters."

"James, I need to tell you that Joe and I promised to marry each other. It sounds crazy at our age, but we were deadly serious back then. When you and I married, I felt a deep sense of guilt for breaking my promise to him. He came back to *Cloverley* as a grown man, looking for me," I said, "Val, as much told me that."

"Are you trying to tell me, that you don't want me to go ahead with what we talked about last night?" asked James.

"I don't know what I'm trying to tell you," I replied.

"Dawn, you opened the box when you came back here. You must've felt the need for closure," said James. "Joe needed closure too, but didn't know where you were."

"Well, that's it done now, James... closed and over——," I said.

"Or perhaps something new might just have opened," interrupted James.

"What do you mean?" I asked.

461

"It could be the beginnings of something new. You and Val, me and Joe, our Angela and Brian," explained James. "Even Sean and this girl from the village… the possibilities are endless."

I looked at him and saw he was happy, and realised that what I had admitted to him hadn't fazed him in any way at all. As I sat in bed, I felt rather immature by comparison.

"Okay, I can see what you mean, and as long as you understand and don't mind if Joe and I occasionally get sentimental, then go for it and see what happens," I replied.

At that moment, the door handle turned and in came our two daughters, "Come on Mum, this is not like you?" said a surprised Lorraine.

"What have you been doing to get Mum in this state?" asked our Angela.

"Whatever it was Angela, she did it to herself," he replied. "I was fast asleep all night."

"Out, the lot of you; you're keeping me back. Dad and I have lots to do this morning," I said.

"So, she's going to go for it then, Dad?" enquired Angela.

*

A shocked Val couldn't believe what she was hearing when Joe told her what he'd discussed with James. "How can you do this," she asked, "you know I'll feel threatened every time they're here?"

"Did you feel threatened yesterday?" he asked.

"No, but that was different," she replied. "It was one of those one-off occasions."

"You asked them to come for coffee this morning, not me," said Joe. "Was that for an, I'm-glad-I'll-never-see-you-again coffee?"

"No, it was not!" she replied. "I enjoyed having them here, despite whatever might have happened between Brian and their Angela. It must have been the girl's idea, because Brian's never behaved like that before; he had his arm around her shoulder in front of everyone, even my mum."

"Oh, dear, what a crime! Val, they did nothing wrong, in fact I found it nice to see a bit of testosterone coming from him. Please don't blame Angela, because as they say, there's no salt without pepper," said Joe.

"Just what I said," replied Val, "that Angela's hot stuff; she's got that look about her."

"What look is that?" asked Joe.

"You know, she's... she's——," replied Val.

"She's like our Brigitte, she looks like our Brigitte and my sisters. Please think hard before you condemn, Val," he said, but when he saw tears welling up in her eyes, he put his arms around her.

"Oh, Joe, I'm so sorry... you're right in everything you've said," she replied. "I enjoyed having Dawn here, if

I'm honest. I felt I was in the company of a true friend, and I don't want to ever lose her again."

"You don't have to lose her. Okay, I feel sentimental about her, but I love you and my family. Did you happen to like James?" asked Joe.

"He's a lovely man," she replied. "I see what you mean, it would be nice to be able to enjoy their company. It's just their Angela… I don't want her leading our Brian astray."

"My view is that if Brian's going to be led astray, I'd rather it was with Angela than someone else. If you put up opposition to any relationships that he may have in the future, then you'll be the one who'll suffer," said Joe.

"You mean like, better the devil you know, that sort of thing?" replied Val.

"I wouldn't put it like that exactly, but yes," he agreed. "Can I now call Mike?"

"Okay, go on then," said Val. "You've convinced me."

*

Brian was sitting on the front doorstep waiting for us to arrive. When she saw him, our Angela was out of my car before I had time to pull on the handbrake, "You remember what I told you, Angela. I want to know where you are… every moment," I called after her.

464

She rushed to him and their hands slipped easily into each other's.

"You remember now, Angela," I repeated, as I opened my car door. She waved with her free hand, as she turned away.

"Mum, stop it at once. You're making a complete fool of yourself. Don't you ever listen to what Dad says?" chided Lorraine. "What is it you think they're going to be doing, with everyone around anyway?"

"I don't know." I replied, and I didn't.

James just smiled when he came to take my hand.

"I'm sorry," I said.

"Don't worry, it shows that you're a good mum," he replied, "misguided perhaps, but good."

*

Val and Joe were seated at their kitchen table, together with another man, when we knocked on their open back door.

"Morning, come right on in folks," said Joe. "This is Mike, he's Val's brother-in-law's brother, if you get my drift… a good guy, and an architect to boot. Mike and I are partners some of the time."

I noticed a special, good-morning-Dawn, in Joe's twinkling eyes, which made me happy, and was enough for me…

465

"Dawn, are you okay with James's plans?" asked Val.

"I am, if you are?" I answered.

"I am, Dawn, I really am, and I so enjoyed talking with you and James yesterday... not to mention, meeting the rest of your family," she replied.

At the mention of the family word, I edged my way over towards the window, only to find when I turned back, Val was laughing at me, "Dawn, you're over-reacting to my Brian and your Angela," she said.

"It's in my genes to behave in the way I'm behaving," I sighed. I thought back to my own mum and dad, and how they'd have been with me.

Val and I hugged each other, and I helped her carry a couple of jugs of orange juice, glasses, plus a tin of chocolate cookies for our troops outdoors. That'll keep Angela and her new best buddy out of mischief for a few minutes. Luckily, it was another lovely day, and we got peace to sit indoors with our coffee, to discuss the project with very few distractions.

"I can draw you out a plan of the whole plot, if it's still as it was years ago? That place will be etched on my brain forever," I offered. "Is it much the same, Joe?"

"Yes, very little's changed up there, as far as I can see," he replied. "Sketching out plans... how many other talents do you have Mrs Brennan?"

466

"You ain't seen nothin' yet m'lad," answered James. "At times she makes me feel quite inadequate."

"You, my darling, have no need to ever feel inadequate," I replied, with a wry smile. Everyone looked at me with surprise. "What?" I asked.

"Just get on with the drawing, Dawn," replied Joe, with one of his boyish grins I remembered.

"What are you like?" I laughed, as I picked up a pencil. "Excuse them, Mike, they don't know any better."

*

Brenda Warner was not in a good place, when she heard her two dogs begin to bark. "Give me a break you two," she muttered to herself. She knew she had visitors, as her elderly dogs would only bark at strangers, in an attempt to conserve their energy. She dragged herself off the couch, and to her front door, throwing it wide open. "My God, what's wrong, Joe?" she exclaimed. "You've brought an army with you!"

"Nothing, Brenda, nothing at all… is this a bad time for a chat?" he asked.

"No worse a time than any other," she sighed, "you're not all coming into the house surely?"

"No, just these two," answered Joe, pointing at them.

Shirley, Brigitte, and Daisy heard Charlene and Charlie's shrieks coming from the back garden and ran

467

around to meet them. The dogs yawned and then went back to sleep.

*

Meanwhile, back at the Doubleday household, four teenagers and two pre-teens were also enjoying peace, and free from Dawn's ever-watchful eyes, as she had reluctantly left them in Val's charge.

*

"Brenda, would it be all right if Mike and I took a squint around the plot, while we're waiting?" asked Joe.

"Help yourselves," she replied. "Dawn, you know the way; you can show your husband around, while I go and try to make myself decent."

We walked back along the corridor and I hoped James had time to get a better idea of the layout of the place. "This is it," I whispered, as we seated ourselves in the sitting-room. "This is our Weekender but it didn't look like this in our day. It was more old-fashioned. Oh, I don't know, I just liked it better then."

"It's okay, Dawn. I can see beyond the decor," he replied. "I don't think you need to whisper either, the walls look thick enough from where I'm sitting."

Shortly afterwards, Brenda arrived through in her daytime clothes, complete with a tray, upon which stood a coffee pot, mugs, milk, and sugar…

468

"We'll come to the reason for our visit right away, Brenda," I began. "My husband James noticed that the house was for up for sale yesterday, and Joe filled him in with the details of your predicament."

She frowned, which made me wonder if I'd explained with enough sensitivity.

"Mrs Warner, can I explain something which might be of mutual interest to us both," continued James, thankfully taking over from me.

"Give me time to pour the coffee first. Maybe you're on cloud blooming nine, but you would do well to remember that not everyone's in such a happy place," she replied.

She poured the coffee, taking what felt like an eternity. Then she turned to me and it was, do you take milk, how much? Sugar, how many spoonfuls? After me, she then turned to James, and went through the same palaver once more... Thank the Lord there were no biscuits on the tray!

"Right, what were you saying?" she asked, satisfied that she'd completed her hosting duties.

CHAPTER SIXTY-THREE:

Outside the old Weekender, Joe and Mike looked at the layout of the land, the position and condition of the various outbuildings, and then at Dawn's hurriedly sketched drawing. "She's got a useful memory for detail, and puts it on paper well. How long ago was it her folks owned this place?" asked Mike.

"About twenty-eight years ago," answered Joe. "She called herself a sleuth back then, maybe that's why she's remembered it so well?"

"Gee, that wasn't yesterday," remarked Mike. "It's a wonder you even recognised her, sleuth or not."

"I'd always recognise her... anywhere," replied Joe.

Mike left it at that, as Joe offered no more detail, it seemingly being a sensitive subject. "What does she do for a living," he asked, "she doesn't give me the impression that she's a stay-at-home-mum?"

"She isn't, she's involved in medicine," he replied.

"On it, in it, or both?" asked Mike.

"She's a psychiatrist," replied Joe, "one of those swanky, private ones."

"That could be useful... for dealing with Silvia I mean, if she ever gets out of hand again," said Mike, with a grin. "What about her hubby? Is he in the same line?"

"No, he's a university professor of history," replied Joe.

"I doubt if they'll ever need a mortgage," said Mike. "Strange mixture though, but they do say that opposites attract. The funny thing is, she could pass as your sister in looks."

Joe nodded. "Let's get on with the job in hand, Mike, with less chat," he replied, "if you don't mind."

*

At the Doubleday house, Val had Lorraine, Angela, and the boys helped prepare brunch for when the others returned. As the clock ticked towards midday, she changed it to lunch.

"We'll just open a few cans of soup, that'll have to do," said Val. "Listen, I'll have to go and pick up Mum.

She's decided to join us. I'll leave you lot to finish setting out the table and the food... just do what you think's best."

With that, she left them to their own devices, and Lorraine and Angela took over, with the boys pleased to follow their instructions. "Your mum's really nice, Brian, not like ours. You know what Mum's like, Lorraine," said Angela, "with her don't-touch-this, and don't-touch-that routine."

"It would normally pain me, but I have to agree. Dad's a lovely laid-back sort of man, quite the opposite to her. Why is she like that?" asked Lorraine.

"She's the one who's the most streetwise, though. Dad's not, and neither is your mum, Brian," said Sean. "Your dad on the other hand knows the score, but handles it much better than our mum."

"I find it strange to think of my dad ever loving your mum when they were children," replied Brian.

"He was the same age as you Brian. Tell us who the boy-child was who eagerly waited for us to arrive this morning, and who the girl-child was who shot from the car to meet him? Oh, and lest I forget, so eager to slip her hand into his," laughed Lorraine.

"Brian and Angela are just like Mrs Brennan and Mr Doubleday when they were young," suggested Zac, and to his surprise, everyone nodded in agreement, which made him smile.

472

"It's funny how life repeats itself, and how some things never change," added Simon. "It must be in the genes?"

*

Joe and Mike returned to the Weekender after having had a good look around the plot, and knocked on the door. "It's open," called out Brenda, and they made their way through to the sitting-room.

"Hi, what do you think, Brenda?" asked Joe. "Is it a goer? The outbuildings have enough of a footprint for what James and Dawn would be after, and let's face it, that land at the back of the building hasn't been touched for years."

"Are you after an award for selling or something, Joe Doubleday?" replied Brenda. "First of all, it must be done legally, with me not having to do any paperwork. Secondly, you must include a few alterations which I want done in this house, and thirdly, I get the money up front to pay off that damned husband of mine. I also want the yard kept clear of all building materials, and your workers well hidden. Lastly, but most importantly, I ain't being no tea-lady for nobody either!"

"I get the idea," replied Joe. "What alterations are we talking about here?"

"I want a new bathroom and kitchen," stated Brenda.

"Come on, that's pushing it a bit, and you know it," replied Joe.

"We'll add the money to the budget for a new kitchen and bathroom," offered James.

"For goodness sake, it's only a Weekender," I exclaimed. "No, you and I can do without, James. We can always count on getting fed at either Joe's or Brenda's when we visit, and nobody will surely mind us using their facilities."

I looked at their faces to gauge their reaction. Brenda frowned, Joe grinned, whilst Mike looked bewildered, and my James was scanning his brain for a possible solution? I could see nobody knew if I was being serious or otherwise, however, this didn't matter, as I didn't know myself; it was just one of those gems that popped out from my mouth from time to time.

James was now wearing a confused look on his face. He would've agreed to placate Brenda with a whole house full of renovations, if left to his own devices.

"Look, I'm sure we can work something out. You're welcome to meals at our house, and to use our facilities any time you wish, although that's just not always practical. Let's say, breakfast and supper, those sorts of times," said Joe. "Leave it to Mike and me."

"Joe, the wiring in the house looks old and worn to me," added Mike. The two men looked at each other, each knowing that every job done in the house would lead to another. Sentiment was not what was required in business.

"So, is that a done deal then?" asked Brenda. "I don't want to tell the kids, until it's definite, as they've suffered enough."

"Brenda, who got the valuation done... you or Tony?" asked Joe.

"Him," she replied.

"Tomorrow, we'll get an independent valuation done on the property as a whole, and another if it were to be sub-divided. We'll get a full survey done on the outbuildings too, which will give us a better picture as to the overall costs and budget required. Then we can get things sorted out as quickly as possible," suggested Joe. "Can you give me that valuation, together with details of your husband's solicitor, please?"

Brenda rose, lifted a couple of letters from the mantle-piece, and handed them to him.

"Joe, I'm sorry to have sounded so ungrateful earlier. I didn't mean to be so cheeky and ask for all of these things. I know that you'll do your best for the kids and me. The most important thing is that I'll not have to move away. I trust you Joe, but I don't trust that husband of mine," said Brenda.

Brenda's heart-felt trust in Joe moved me. It clearly demonstrated how far he'd progressed in his life, and how the *Cloverley* residents now viewed him.

As I left the Weekender, my eyes began to water, driven by my pride in Joe. I decided I'd find a convenient moment to tell him what I thought of him, just as he had taken a moment to tell me of his ill-founded pride in me. Our Lorraine's words from a few weeks ago, floated to the fore… she'd said that I'd forsaken the people to whom I could make a difference. Had I done this, and if I had, then why? Surely not for the love of money and prestige? I decided there and then, to make certain changes to my life, whatever it may involve.

*

The girls were collected from the garden, and we headed back along the lane towards the Doubleday's house. Time had just flown by and we hoped that Val would understand.

When we finally arrived, we found the atmosphere relaxed. The youngsters were sitting out in the garden, chatting to Val and her mum.

"Sorry we're late," said Joe. He bent over and kissed Val, then reached out and gave her mum a hug. "I didn't think you'd want to come, not after all the noise of yesterday, Jean," he added.

"Grandma likes noise, as long as it's our noise, Daddy," replied Daisy, who was seated on her grandma's knee.

"Of course she does; I'd forgotten that your noise is special," said Joe.

"Successful?" asked Val, looking over.

"So, so; it's become a bit complicated, but it'll all get sorted," replied Joe. "By the way, Mike says thanks for the invitation, but Janis is taking him out for lunch."

"Nice," said Val.

"Hi, Mum," said Lorraine. "I think it's wonderful what Dad's doing for you."

"It's for all of us, Lorraine. It'll do everyone the world of good to get away from the city every few weeks," I replied.

"Judging by the way you're acting, I'm surprised you don't think it wiser for our Angela to stay at home," said Lorraine.

"Why, what have the two of them been up to while I've been away?" I asked.

"Nothing… what's wrong with you, Mum? Val didn't have a problem leaving us; we're responsible, even Angela, but you always assume the worst," replied Lorraine.

"Val left you here… alone?" I said.

"Yes, she's a great mum. You may be a brain-box, but if I ever need someone to solve my problems, I'd stay well clear," replied Lorraine.

I remembered where we were, which was lucky for Madam, but her words nevertheless stung hard in some very sensitive places. I had just decided to change my life, and here I was, being given a knock back by none other than my own daughter.

477

Val approached as Lorraine left, "Dawn, I overheard most of that, and I'm not a great mum, despite what she thinks. Lorraine's just at that particular age when girls fall out with their mums. You two will be back on the same wavelength before too long," she said. She put her arm around my shoulder, and I felt the same bond as I had when we were little girls... that is before Joe had come between us.

I took her into my confidence and told her what I was thinking. "It was just our age, Dawn. We were barely awakening to life, and on the cusp of love," she replied.

"I'm sorry about Joe... coming between us," I mumbled.

"It's the present that counts, and as I look around me, I can't help thinking that we're doing a damned good job," she replied.

"Thanks, Val," I said.

James had been chatting with the youngsters, but I saw his eyes linger on me. I knew that my lovely man would be wondering if I was upset, so I gave him a wave, and floated across my best smile to relieve any such concerns. Val suddenly told me to have a word with Joe, who'd taken himself indoors... how understanding?

"Try the lounge, where you were yesterday, he sits there when he has things to work out," she told me. "This Brenda business sounds like one of those occasions. He always gets uptight and angry when he hears of anyone leaving their family."

Val then told me that she wanted a word with my James, and left to make her way over beside him. I sat for a moment a trifle confused, and then rose to do Val's bidding. She must have told James where I was going, for he didn't come after me, as he normally would.

Although the house was unfamiliar, I found my way to the room we'd been in yesterday. The door was ajar and I could see him seated in a chair overlooking the front garden. The light from the window shone on his hair and highlighted minute flecks of grey-white. I realised it was the contrast in Joe's hair colouring that emphasised it; James's light colouring concealed his flecks of ageing far better. Why was I thinking about hair?

Joe must have sensed my presence, because he suddenly turned my way... "Dawn," he said, with surprise in his voice.

"Val sent me to speak with you. She told me where to find you, so I've come," I replied.

He rose, met me halfway across the room, and enclosed his arms around me. We then walked hand-in-hand over to the couch.

"We can make this work," I began...

"I know we can," he replied. "We both love our families, and that's why we can make it work. Dawn, leave Angela and Brian to work out their future for themselves, whatever that may be. I want you back here owning the old Weekender or should I say, the new Weekender. I need to know where you are, at least some of the time, so I'd like you to assure James that everything will work out fine. We need to tie up the buying of the property first, and then, Mike and I will move it along, and sort out Brenda along the way. Val and I can always put you and James up here, when you come to visit as the build progresses."

"What's our Angela going to say when I tell her there's only an invitation for the two of us to stay?" I asked.

"She'll probably tell one of you that she'll take your place," he replied. "As I said, let them work it out for themselves, and we can look forward with interest to see what happens in the long run. Wedding bells will be ringing soon enough with Lorraine and Simon. They look like a couple to me, but there again... what do I know?"

We laughed, and made happy noises.

"I'm considering a move towards general practice; a calling, if you like, to serve my fellow man in a more practical, medical sort of way," I said.

"Who's going to look after your fellow women?" he asked.

We giggled.

"You might even find us living here full-time... we'll see what happens," I replied. "Joe, when I asked if you'd ever shown Brian the place where we sampled the waters of life, you said that you hadn't. Did you ever take Val... or anyone else, to our place?"

"No, Dawn, it has only ever been you," he replied. "I've almost... I've often wanted to, but just couldn't."

Our eyes met and fixed in a gaze that was both sad and happy. "Joe, the next time we come back here, will you take both our families to that certain lovely place you've miraculously just remembered existed?" I asked.

"If that's what you want?" he replied.

"It is," I answered...

*** THE END ***

Printed in Great Britain
by Amazon